THE HAI
SQUIRRELS

BRIAN LIVINGSTON

BE LIVING ENTERPRISES, LLC

Copyright © 2022 by Brian Livingston

All rights reserved.

No portion of this book may be reproduced in any form without written permission from the publisher or author, except as permitted by U.S. copyright law.

To Mom and Dad

You Built This

1

I was cradled in the adjustable warmth of my wife's passenger seat. Outside my window, the sun hung in an empty blue sky, but the passing forest lacked the activity and colors of warmth. The mountains looked cold, barren. During the drive the radio announcers had discussed spring and the start of baseball in between cheery oldies, but that had long since faded out; now if Claire turned the dial it would only give static. A pothole jangled my pack in the trunk.

"Only a little longer." Claire squinted at her odometer, throwing a glance at the printouts in my lap as we rounded a turn. We had spent the last thirty-five minutes winding up and down Mount Hampton to Grambling's Pass. "We're out here, Gabe. I mean, you're actually doing it." Claire overlooked another pothole.

"I know. It doesn't seem poss—"

"Are you excited to see Billy?"

I let out a sigh. "You know that's a long way off." Upon graduating law school, our dear Billy had shrugged off his small town roots in pursuit of wealth and partnerdom.

"But when you get to Pentland you're going to see him."

"That's the plan but Claire—"

"And when you do see Billy you're going to be?"

"Claire that's an *if*, and it won't be for months."

"Humor me."

"Like you said . . . I will be supportive, patient, and . . . something else."

"Loving."

"And loving, right."

"And you're not going to be?"

"A series of more negative adjectives more generally associated with me and my behavior."

"Thank you. That's all I ask."

"But, like I said, even under the best circumstances, that won't be for months."

"I know. But this, if nothing else, seems like a good opportunity for father and son to reconcile."

"You know if he hadn't left Bodette, I wouldn't have to walk three months to see him."

"That's merely a technical truth, Gabe."

My wife stopped the sedan in the gravel bulge that served as Grambling's Pass's parking lot. A bullseye of tall brown grass marked where cars had not driven in some time. I pressed my back against the seat warmer. She kept her hands gripped on the steering wheel, staring at the wooden sign for some time before speaking.

"Well, this is it. You're actually doing this?"

"So it would seem."

"Okay then, grab your bag and stand next to the sign so I can get a good picture to remember you by."

Ever since the Great Eastern Trail had appeared on my radar, Claire had verbally supported the idea, supplementing my research, accompanying me to various outfitters; but deep down I knew she had never viewed it as more than a passing fancy—a new car, a new ladder, a new toolset—which she figured to let run its course, choosing to stand aside and permit the scope of the task to discourage me rather than dirtying her own hands.

The ensuing battle of marital chicken would end with me sleeping out of doors and alone.

The trunks of Claire's vehicles had always provided an eccentric core sample of our lives: faded home improvement magazines; various merchandise from her store; worn clothes long ago marked for donation; sports equipment from our son's high school athletic career some ten years prior—layered top to bottom by date of discard. I lifted my pack from the clutter and made my way to the sign which appeared to be the lot's sole feature: a pocked wooden board with *GRAMBLING'S PASS Southern Terminus of The Great Eastern Trail* carved and painted long ago in flecked white letters. Behind the sign, the grey gravel winnowed into the brown dirt of the Great Eastern Trail. There were no other markings, nor any real warning that from this point flowed an immense trail of brown, hilly, rocky, mountain nonsense: a meandering pathway up the country's sciatic backbone.

"Did I tell you how Grambling's Pass got its name?"

"Several times, Gabe. I'm really trying not to think about it."

"Have I real—" I recalled our discussion over the previous night's hamburger casserole. John Grambling had been a successful Eastern businessman in the pioneer days who, seemingly on a whim, uprooted his family and set his wagons west in search of gold. According to legend, Grambling's Pass marked the point where his volatile whim struck again causing him to turn north, this time alone in search of beaver pelts, leaving his wife and family to about face and venture home. Mr. Grambling was never seen again. "Oh yea, sorry."

I was now experiencing a full body cold.

Claire, camera in hand, nodded me into place from just outside the driver's seat. The mountain gap served her well. Her skin had yet to lose its color; her body, through strenuous regimentation, retained its youthy tone. At fifty-seven she remained at full blossom. I rested my hands on the Trail side of the sign, just above the southernmost orange blaze, and put on a smile. After several in that pose, I shifted so that one hand remained on the sign while the other pointed down the Great Eastern Trail, contorting my face into a look of bewildered excitement. After several takes, Claire put away the camera, and came forward to grasp me in her strong arms. She locked her eyes on mine.

"Do you know what you're doing here, Gabe?" Her body wash mingled with the mountain air. She smelled like home.

"Yes. You helped me research."

She pursed her lips. The wind lifted the tips of her greying brown hair. "Gabe, once you take those steps, you'll have always taken those steps. And I don't think you're that Grambling jerk . . . I mean believe you'll come back at some point, and in some form, but it will only be because you felt the need to leave." She pulled my knit cap down over my ears which were beginning to feel pinched in the wind. "Just remember you don't have to do this. You can just hop right back in the car and go back home to the land of beds and wives. We can eat take-out and watch a hiking movie."

"You know that's not the same."

"We'll get you that TV you and Roger won't shut up about. The big screen. And a convertible for the weekends."

"I can't go home now. The whole town had a send-off party. The sign still says *Go Get 'em Gabe*."

"Please, please, please don't let that be the thing keeping you from home." She unclasped her hands and slid them down the ridged arms of my green down jacket, stopping to squeeze my fingers. She made a face and lifted them between us. "They're already freezing, look at your white little fingers. Where are your gloves?"

I turned around to show her my pack.

"Middle outside pocket. Just above the coffee mug."

She tugged and fussed about for some time, turning me on my feet.

"No . . . ." The tugging shifted to a different angle. "Here they are. Top pocket. Just above the hatchet." She came around and opened the wrist holes so I could slide my hands inside. When the gloves were on, she synched the fastener until the rope dug into my wrist. I felt like a kid getting dropped off at camp.

"And what makes you think you're going to need a hatchet?"

"Everything. Chopping wood for fires, clearing out paths, carving your name in trees with little hearts, self-defense, and, most importantly, shortening long sticks. It's probably the most useful thing I have."

"If you say so, but please don't ever take a hatchet to a bear fight. Just run or play dead."

"I'm a mountain man now, baby—no promises."

She sighed and tugged my jacket straight. "You're leaving me, Gabe."

"I'll be back before you know it."

She stared past me, down the Trail. "What's the name of the first town again?"

"Duncan. I wrote it on the pad by the phone. I'll call you from there in about a week."

"So I have to wait a whole week to hear your thoughts on sleeping in a tent?"

"You've heard my thoughts on the matter."

"Sorry, a tent that's not on the fescue by the azaleas."

"Correct. I will call you from Duncan in a week."

"So be it." She tugged my jacket collar close around my neck. "I love you."

"I love you too." My wife leaned in and kissed me.

The assorted clipped appendages chimed as I took my first northward steps: my first steps on the Great Eastern Trail. I had given this moment a great deal of thought: on the twelfth step, approximately the length of my living room, I would turn back slowly, give a dramatic wave, before carrying on heroically into the mountains—

"Gabe!" The mountains fostered the same echo as our stairwell. I snapped back, certain I had forgotten something, staggering as the weighty pack caused me to over-rotate.

My wife remained at the sign, now smirking. "Please go see Billy."

I gave a thumbs up and restarted my quest. The Great Eastern Trail crested a small rise then fell, putting Claire Jenkins out of sight.

I went to work on the gloves, trying to loosen the cords strangling my hands, but could not properly utilize the little nubby fastener with gloved hands. I had just removed one glove with my teeth when a disembodied hand ripped me down by my pack with a sharp pop. Less than twenty-five yards into the journey and I was on my back, something metallic clanged against a distant tree. I rolled over, locating the removed glove just north of me under a swaying branch. I slithered out of my pack and did an inventory check; a snapped band dangled where the coffee mug had been. I cursed the branch and looked out in the clanging's direction. An engine fired up in the lot.

I swooped my arms back through their straps and stood up. A pair of beady eyes stared down from the north—a squirrel, the Great Eastern Trail's first ambassador, stood garrisoned in the middle of the Trail, its front legs splayed in front of him, its back legs coiled, ready to launch. Its eyes boiled with assessing hate as it marked its target. I eased south.

"Hey there little fella. Don't mind me."

The squirrel remained at the ready.

"Seriously, I mean no harm. Just trying to pass by."

I took a step. The squirrel pounced on my boot with a tiny, full-throated roar, plunging his teeth into the leather. I whipped my foot back, losing my balance, again staggering to the ground.

The squirrel re-assumed his position. I observed him for a moment, feigned right, eliciting a defensive shuffle in that direction.

"Right then. Point taken." I initiated a full southerly retreat in time to hear my wife's engine fade out of the parking lot. "Dern it all."

I turned back around, inspected the squirrel, then stepped off Trail, arcing north through the brush. The squirrel remained homed in, emitting a malignant, cat-like growl as it tracked me like a jittery compass. I rejoined the Trail some yards north so that the squirrel now separated me and my wife, taking a moment to register its fuzzy little head and bushy tail.

"You know you'd almost be cute if you'd just calm down."

I backed up several paces before feeling safe enough to set my sights northward. There was nothing ahead of me. The Great Eastern Trail ranged straight through two rows of pines until dipping down and disappearing. I kept my feet moving, putting distance between me and the mean squirrel. I could feel Claire weaving down the other side of the mountain, towards our home, but away from me.

In our thirty-five years of marriage, Claire and I had never spent more than three nights apart. For three decades, my life had been clockwork: wake up; deliver the boy to school; deliver myself to work; deliver mail to neighbors; deliver myself home, go to bed. Each year, the Jenkins clan took one one-week vacation, always to the same beach near my parents. We had worked, raised a son, and retired without any major hiccups. While the schedule relaxed somewhat when Billy went to college, the only major alteration was an additional long weekend spent at a nearby lake.

Now I was to be away, alone, for up to six months. The clan was scattered.

Pentland, Billy's new, chosen home, was near the end of my intended route, perhaps five-sixths of the way up the Trail. I could picture his office, recalled from when Claire and I helped him move; Billy sitting in a swollen leather chair behind his oversized wooden desk; G. William Jenkins, III in staccato print on the smoked glass door. I had joked with Claire that Billy had stuffed the carpet so that his side of the desk was subtly higher.

Given the chance, the sun brought the southern Amicola Mountains to a more pleasant temperature. My goal for the day was quite modest: a gently sloped up and down jaunt from Grambling's Pass to Talon Shelter, the Great Eastern Trail's southernmost shelter. I strolled across the ridgeline, whistling and counting the orange blazes, placing a hand on each one to take in the smooth paint as framed by the pines' rough bark, tracking each set of ten blazes on extended fingers until that became untenable. The Great Eastern Trail was flat and soft beneath my feet, on either side the earth sloped down into the valley. I split the select pines blessed to have implanted themselves on the level ridge top from which they could look down on their off-kilter brethren. In my zipped, water-repellant pocket were assorted internet pages which I had printed to guide me at least until Jackson, the second town; they were of little use during the day when my sole goal was connecting orange blaze to orange blaze. Despite the loss of the coffee mug, my pack jingled with each step.

A few hours into my hike, about the time Claire would be returning to Bodette, I emerged from the close pines and onto a granite outcrop offering a sweeping western vista—a great place for my first snack. I located my peanut butter and tortillas, smeared and folded, then fumbled onto a boulder to count the rows of mountains fading into the horizon, each ridge a successively lighter shade of blue until the Amicolas became one with the sky. Clouds hid the sun, nothing stirred. I tried to remember the last time I had enjoyed such a view. Looking down on it all from above, I wondered if this was how the dark lords felt—if ever given the chance—upon completing their quest for world domination: entire civilizations wiped out to allow for some peace and quiet, an entire empty realm at their disposal. It was like existing in a painting. I formed my hands into the outline of my mail truck's slant-sided window and held them out in front of me, approximating distance and scale, to see what this world would've looked like from the offset front seat.

I checked my print-outs, confirming this was Bell's Knob, so named for a man who had lost his spectacles there some time ago. When it was time to leave, I slipped the print-outs into the water-repellant pocket, lumbered on my pack, and returned to the trees.

From the viewpoint, the Great Eastern Trail followed the ridgeline as it descended into the valley. The pine trees grew thicker, both larger and closer together, at the lower altitudes, boxing me in an endless grey hallway until the Great Eastern Trail flattened, spitting me out to slow down on the straightaway —I pictured my flexed feet spraying happy onlookers as my momentum sputtered through the final pool. Not too much longer, the old wooden sign marking Talon Shelter appeared. I patted it and followed the blue blazed side trail to the wooden structure, breathing easier, proud and relieved at having survived the first day.

Despite the squirrel, it had not been that bad.

According to the internet, the Great Eastern Trail's countless shelters were the nation's last true bastions of filth: three-sided log or board structures constructed by badge hungry scouts during the Trail's brief heyday. Over the years, scores of negligent hikers had discarded trash and food scraps so now the shelters were reportedly little more than drafty relics overrun with disease carrying vermin. Even alone, when I would not have to worry about snoring bedmates, and the cold kept the mice at bay, I had predetermined never to stay in one if there was any other option. Instead I would patronize the shelters' amenities, in Talon's case a water source and single picnic table, without actually booking an interior room.

I began preparing my first campsite, unclipping the various accoutrements from my pack, and removing interior items until I could access my tent. Using my foot, I swept a patch clear of sticks and small stones before laying out the tent's footprint, tugging each corner to fully open the rectangular strip of material which, as far as I could tell, served only to protect the tent's bottom, before staking the corners and laying down the much lighter tent fabric which drifted down like a deflated balloon. I then hooked the tent's corners to the stakes and clipped its spines to the poles.

Back home, Claire had laughed at my caution and care when, on several occasions, I practiced setting the tent up in our backyard. *It's a tent* she said, *it's literally made to be set up in the dirt. You don't have to be so dern dainty with it.* On one occasion she snapped a picture of me fumbling to crawl out of the tent, finding great mirth in how *ridiculous* my grey head looked poking out of the tiny opening. I liked the picture though; my naturally wiry frame and tan skin gave the impression I'd already spent considerable time outdoors. I looked adventurous, if one could ignore the playset and picket fence.

I furnished my portable house with pad and sleeping bag, filled my water bottles at the shelter's spring—shelters were almost exclusively situated near a water source—dropped a cleansing tablet in each, and grabbed my cooking supplies, humming as I settled in at the picnic table.

The sun rested behind the mountains, only a few valiant rays made it to valley floor. I measured water into the pot, snapped it onto the stove, and flicked on the flame, marveling at the blue flame's fierce resistance to falling night. My breath froze in the evening air, appearing for all intents and purposes like a smoker's smooth exhale—I had only very occasionally indulged in cigars over the years, but this was a sensation I'd always enjoyed. I leaned back and unleashed a great burst, watching it rise and dissipate above me, following it with another. I let out prolonged howl, cocking my ears as the trees absorbed the echo. Another one, this time with gusto, echoing off the shrouded mountains. Again and again I howled, each time straining my eyes and ears to capture every detail of my creations.

The pot gurgled, discharging a steady vapor with which I could not compete, bringing an end to my recreation. I added a measured portion of the minute rice, noting the diminished weight with reverence. As the rice cooked, I turned on my headlamp and went to examine the shelter.

According to the internet, the government had *opened* the Great Eastern Trail around the time of Billy's birth to a thunderous reception: would-be thru-hikers converged from around the world, boys' clubs hammered up shelters, and miniscule communities along the Trail enjoyed fleeting moments of relevance as hiker havens; for some time, the Great Eastern Trail reigned as a national attraction. But hiking can only hold the public's attention for so long; when the initial excitement wore off the Great Eastern Trail was left with an infrastructure undeserved for such an unutilized attraction.

One of the remnants of those glory years was that each shelter contained a logbook in which hikers signed their names and left notes as they passed through. According to several commenters, the logbooks were not only a great way of keeping up with those around you—they were often bursting at the seams with lively banter and delightful anecdotes. After some searching, I located the logbook in a green metal snap box and returned it to the table.

I focused my headlamp on the first page, unveiling a full sheet of posts from previous occupants. Each one used its own hiking pseudonym, another Great Eastern Trail tradition, to sign their entries. The first one read:

"Travellin' hard but lonely as a poor girl can be. Catch me if you can!" — Lowland Lady

"Not a bad night. The wind died down and let me get some sleep. I'm lonely too Lowland Lady but DAEMON'S PEAK BOUND!" — Onward

"Frodo in, Frodo out. What's one more cold night to a guy who's been in the woods for six months? Cruisin' to the finish line."

"No birds today" —Talon

"Oh the Joy to Walk these Woods,
And Leave the World of Material Goods
To Focus on these Times of Mine
In Search of Truth and Friends Devine" — Martin Tully

"It is fucking freezing" — Frothy G

"Those of you who suffer such an ailment might say it's cold. But I choose not to. Anyway, TIME TO BOUNCE. South in the mornin', north in the evenin', headed on up to the land I was born in. Homeward bound, bitches" — Jezebel

I continued reading as I ate.

The minute rice was more than just a financial decision; a local news station had run a segment on monasteries in which the monks live austere and silent lives, eating only plain rice, and exist in a state of constant self-reflection. The monks all looked so peaceful, striding behind the camera as if their simple lifestyle had granted them access to some deeper source of contentment.

My eating utensil was no ordinary piece of silverware but rather a space-tech camping spork crafted from the same material as the space shuttles which, when put to the task, effectively and efficiently shuttled each bite of warm, life-affirming rice from pot to belly. The cold air chilled the rice long before I'd finished, but it was a hard-earned meal after a day spent conquering mountains—I had no complaints.

I flipped the logbook's pages back and forth as I ate, reading and rereading the entries. The vast majority were loners; there was often a span of several days, sometimes weeks, between entries. When I had read each post, I lifted the book to return it to the green box—a folded piece of beige-brown paper slipped out onto the table. I checked the book for its source, wondering how I'd failed to detect it, then picked up the paper, noting its soft, almost leathery texture. It bore a simple poem:

> MONGREL COME, MONGREL GO
> LESS YOU NEED, LESS YOU TOW

The words were scrawled in all caps in a heavy, undisciplined hand. It was childlike, much worse even than Billy's earliest grade school scribblings, and suggested no hope of refinement. I read and reread the post. Mongrel had not taken the time to date it.

Darkness had taken a firm hold of the valley when I returned the logbook and made for bed. I had to flip-on my headlamp just to locate my toothbrush and toothpaste in my pack's top capsule. I brushed my teeth, stepped away from the tent to relieve myself, and nestled into my sleeping bag.

2

Breakfast marked the first red-wrappered *Juicerrman* bar of the Great Eastern Trail. *Juicerrman*, a relic from a now past fitness craze exalting bulging physiques in both men and women, boasted, and I quote, *enough calories to feed a village and a protein content found terminal in the smaller dog breeds.* For a huge portion of Billy's adolescence, they buttressed every grocer's shelf and inspired many lessor spin-offs. One of the perks of *Juicerrman*'s 'supercharged nougat' was its caffeine content: the equivalent of three cups of coffee, in addition to a 'scientifically-chiseled' protein/carb ration *designed for a sustained ass-kicking burst.* In one long running commercial a rather puny man consumed one then wrestled a bear to submission; there was a rumor this led to several exceedingly put-out widows filing suit. Unpackaged, the 'fortified-chocolate' ingots resembled an extravagantly large male member, earning them some unfortunate phallic-themed nicknames. Eventually, a hypersensitive public grew weary of enlarged hearts, hardening veins, and reportedly shrunken testicles. In fact, I would not have been surprised if I had bulk ordered the last remaining batch of *Juicerrmen*. Claire had agreed to utilize the esteemed government parcel delivery service to dispatch *Juicerrmen* to different points on the Trail.

The bar ignited my bloodstream. I broke camp, launching myself over Mount James, then Mount Allen. My heart pounded at such a pace that my legs raced just to keep up. My body went into overdrive; a kinetic ball of energy in my gut threatened to tear me apart if I didn't grant its release. It was an hour before I came down into the groggy sustained burst, legs pumping under a bleary brain as the Great Eastern Trail dipped into another valley. I shoveled in another *Juicerrman* at the base of the next ridgeline, which, according to my print-outs, featured Colton Mountain, noted as the Great Eastern Trail's first memorable mountain.

From the low point, the Great Eastern Trail began a long, steep ascent. I charged up the mountainside, excited for my first real test, ticking off orange blazes in bunches. My legs soon wearied, losing their chemical-induced spring such that I no longer thrusted myself up in great confident steps, but lamely heaved myself upwards. Two hours in, my legs went to rubber, trembling with each step, threatening, pleading, to give and topple. My face flushed despite the temperature; sweat poured out in swollen beads which stung against the dry winter air. I stopped to brace myself against a tree, catching my breath and turning back to examine my gains; the piney tunnel hid all signs of progress. I inhaled, exhaled, long and deep, trying to direct oxygen to my lower extremities. When my legs finally settled down, I pressed onwards. They were shaking anew in under a minute forcing an early lunch respite.

I propped myself against a particularly robust pine with my legs straight out in front of me—a sitting position championed by a long deceased youth soccer coach who insisted it recirculated blood all the way through our legs; one of those lessons that implanted itself early enough to engrain as gospel. The warm sweat cooled to a chilled condensation. I was shivering before I finished spreading the peanut butter. I ate quickly, pocketed a *Juicerrman*, and pressed on.

The break bought me some time but my legs re-rubberized before I could get too far. I rested, stepped, shook, then rested again, repeating this tedious stop-and-go for some time as the Great Eastern Trail ushered me into the guts of a cloud. The moisture collected on my clothes until it might as well have rained; my pants and jacket only served to weigh me down and keep the chill close. Every inhalation brought in a fresh bitter burst of humidity. Only my ears, warmed by my knit cap and escaping heat, remained comfortable. I trudged upwards, unable to perceive time or distance other than by the incrementally escalating convulsions in my legs.

At last my legs gave out all-together, bowing inwards despite urgent signals to the contrary. I managed to take a knee, preventing a full and fatal collapse, then allowed myself to fall forward, like a fool. My pack landed on top of me, forcing any and all remaining air out of my lungs. I rolled halfway over, still clipped to my pack, to inspect the very small rocks upon which I had recently tread. I wriggled out of my pack to sit up taking in deep, hoarse, mouth breaths, wondering to what extent I had underappreciated my mail truck which, despite its many idiosyncrasies, could be relied upon to carry the load from box to box. I went to reattach my pack but my legs shuddered under only one strap. I slipped out before it could drag me down, then considered my options: with carrying the pack off the table, I could push, pull, or roll it up the mountain, or leave the dern thing where it lay. After some thought, I settled on a method I'd used to get particularly heavy holiday season mailbags from loading dock to mail truck. Using a top handle I lifted the pack off the ground and, in that brief moment, kick pushed it forward so that it swung out in front of me. The steep slope limited its progress compared to a flat loading dock, but it worked. Step by step, kick by kick, I continued up the mountain, with frequent breaks, switching hands as needed.

Eventually the fog thinned, exposing gaps in the pines which expanded until the trees stopped all together. All at once, I stepped above the cloud bank and onto a small granite promontory rising out of an albino sea. I pushed my pack over and sat on it. Hills of pristine fluff blanketed the mountains—some rolling themselves into mounds of liquid cotton; others unfurling into luxurious linen valleys. I could hear the movement of clouds; the soft, surreal whir as they breathed past each other. Colton Mountain, the first milestone on the Great Eastern Trail, was mine. As the cool air stilled my legs, I again lifted my hands to give myself the mailman's perspective, searching my memory for the last time I had witnessed such splendor, or felt this rush of accomplishment—*it had no doubt been decades*. I unsheathed the cached *Juicerrman* as a victory treat, feeling a touch sinful for brandishing the lab room abomination in the company of such natural grandeur; but it was my moment to ruin, I had earned it, and I was hungry.

I felt good—free to move at my own pace rather than one dictated by traffic or mundane obligations. Gone were the shackles of the mail route with the constant stopping to cram junk mail into my neighbors' boxes. Since my retirement, television had dictated my schedule to an alarming extent. Meals, errands, walks, and other activities all had to fit into the gaps between sitcoms, sporting events, and news. Out here, I set my day, choosing how much time to a lot to each moment.

I could get used to this.

Just as the sun began to set I arrived at Dogwood Creek and its row of flat, quiet clearings dotted with old fire rings. I stopped to listen for some suggestion of life; the night was quiet and all the fires were out. I selected a clearing and set up my tent, bundling up as best I could before starting dinner, briefly considering making it a full day of *Juicerrmen*, but opting to preserve my supply.

I finished my rice and, without the entertainment of a shelter log, went to bed before the sun had fully set, feeling a slight twinge in my feet and knees as I crawled into my tent.

The temperature plummeted during the night, quickly enough that it brought me from sleep; what had been a mild day, deteriorated into a miserable night. The wind breathed through the darkness, toying with the loose tent fabric, displacing any warm air that may have otherwise accumulated. The cold infiltrated through both tent and sleeping bag. My ears burned. My body shook. Way down at the bottom of my sleeping bag, my toes began to ache as blood refused to make the expedition to the far extremities. I clenched and unclenched my feet into awkward foot fists forcing the blood into them, but it did little. The sleeping bag, which had been expensive and well-reviewed, was outmatched, serving only to occasionally pin pockets of frigid air against my body. My only comfortable bits were my hands and genitals, which formed a precious symbiotic trio deep in the bag's center.

The night dragged on; the constricting cold seeped deeper into my body as the trembling increased into nausea inducing spasms. The pain in my toes grew until I was certain they would fall off. I pressed my feet numbly against each other, still clenching and unclenching.

Outside the tent, branches creaked and swayed, pine straw whistled in the wind. Scraps of forest debris puttered through the campsite. Every creak rose the alarm. I lay awake for a long time, shivering and flinching at the sounds, waiting for one to evolve into the rhythmic footfall of an approaching beast. In the mountains I was a small pest, removable even by accident.

3

I resisted a full bladder until first light.

Morning seemed late in reaching the valley floor. The sunlight had neglected to pack its warmth. A frozen wall of air greeted me outside the tent. During my relief, my legs shook such that I kept no continuous stream, but rather scattered out a spray of golden blaster beams. I hastened my troll to its lair and dove back into the tent, which I now realized had been somewhat underappreciated during the night.

After a *Juicerrman*, I put my lawn practice to use, dressing and breaking camp at a frenetic pace. I shoved numb legs into reluctant pants, burrowed on extra layers, tied boots, and clawed through the flap to collapse my tent. Once actually set to task, my feet proved to be little more than swollen spongy bricks mortared to the end of my legs. Another complication arose as my gloves deprived my hands the digital dexterity required to undo the tent but, exposure to the paralyzing cold had the same effect—either way, my digits struggled to grasp eyelets and hooks, reducing me to pawing at them like a bear at a rubber honeycomb. After every attempt, I hobble-jogged around the picnic table blowing life into my hands until at last I had everything properly packed.

It was with a stilted, loping stride that I set off up the Trail for my third day.

As I walked, sensation eased back into my lower extremities —in the form of pain. My boots were not keeping their end of the bargain. The trees repeated themselves on an endless loop. I occupied my mind by keeping track of them, noting the differences: this tree has a branch about halfway up on the right; that tree doesn't have any branches until the canopy; this next one bares an imperfect blaze; until I lost track and became certain time was the thing repeating.

I wondered what my son would say about my journey so far. When Billy was six, the Bodette city council opened a community pool. Billy was so excited he made us buy him a calendar so he could count down the days. At each meal he asked Claire and me if he could eat or if it would give him cramps. He even wore a bathing suit to school the entire week before it opened. When Saturday finally came, we were there half an hour before the one-pieced lifeguard unlocked the gate. But once inside, all Billy did was weave around the perimeter, waggling his little floaties, and toeing the water from different spots, stepping back as crowds of children jumped in around him. At the end of the day, Claire asked him why he didn't get in and he said *because the water looked deep and he wasn't sure he could swim*. I'll never forget the brief look Claire threw at me over her sunglasses. In any event, Billy spent the night brooding then jumped right in upon returning the next day. That was the last time he'd ever shown any hesitation.

It took three additional *Juicerrmen* to make it through the day: one about three-quarters of the way up Mount Raymont when my knees started to stiffen; another when I stubbed my toe on a boulder at the peak and lost all feeling in my foot; and a final one after I'd cleared Mount Jarrett. The momentum of the third carried me to Hawkeye Shelter.

Coming down from the sustained burst, my body creaked under its own weight; the cold had frozen the irritation in my knees and calcified the sore spots on my feet. I did not know if the *Juicerrmen* temporarily solved my problems or only masked them—but they returned with a vengeance. I finished my initial prep work and hobbled over to the shelter to retrieve the logbook for some bedtime reading.

"The mountains sure are lovely . . . I'm told . . . Fog life." — Ragamuffin

"No views from the ridgeline. No views from Colton Mountain. No water on the ridgeline. No water on Colton Mountain. Plenty of water in the air. Sick of the mountains and sick of the fog. Ready for Duncan and a different day." — Onward

"No birds today.—Talon"

"Who goes into the woods without enough food? I do, dammit. Hungry and Duncan bound." — Jezebel

It was only somewhat satisfying to see others had shared my struggles. A folded slip of brown paper peeked from the logbook, bearing another simple poem written in a large childish hand:

> MONGREL COME, MONGREL GO
> TOWARDS THE END, I TEND TO SHOW

Just like the last time, I read and reread the line several times, giving it different cadences and rhythms. It seemed somehow insistent on sputtering out at its own pace.

4

My legs set overnight, fossilizing into kneed pillars. The morning *Juicerrman* helped, providing an electric burst and brief liquidity which carried me out of the tent and onto the Trail, but failed to do anything to aide my feet, on which blisters collected like fleshy barnacles as the swollen, misshapen masses turned in my frozen boots. Flames kissed my ankles as the flesh bruised, stretched, swelled, and tore. I changed my gait, walking mostly on the sides of my feet in short, slow steps, rolling the pressure to different body parts, so that when one area's pain grew too intense, I changed my stride or altered my foot strike: this time toes; this time heels; this time wide; this time normal. Soon everything hurt; but equally so.

The wind kept up a barrage of frozen daggers. It funneled at low points, striking with such concentrated strength that it threatened to either knock me over or freeze me upright. I tucked my chin low, fighting to retain sensation in my hands and feet.

Around mid-afternoon, the Great Eastern Trail dove between two massive boulders leaning over the Trail to create a protected and temperate interior passageway. I propped my pack against a boulder and stretched out my legs, working them over with my thumbs. It felt like massaging a bag of marbles. It had been long since I had put such a strain on my lower extremities; my legs resented my healing efforts, locking themselves entirely. Crannies and weathered nooks, some a knuckle deep, pocked the granite. I degloved and ran my hand over them, enjoying the texture. I tried to stand but rocked like a man on short stilts, cracking my head against the wall then sliding down the peculiar cheese grater granite.

I rolled over to my back and placed a gloved hand to my cheek; it came back positive for blood. The wind hissed above me. *What am I doing out here? In two days I felt like I'd aged three decades. I could be warm at home.*

I resolved to end my epic quest in Duncan. Claire would no doubt be relieved and all too happy to leave the shop and come get me. There was no telling what Billy would think; according to Claire, he thought she was playing a prank on him when she claimed his father *for real* intended to hike the Great Eastern Trail. I tottered for the rest of the day to Johnstone Shelter where I ate my rice and went to bed.

Nothing improved overnight. I went through the same routine that morning, alternating between blowing my hands and fondling the connections on my tent. My feet remained tender bricks. I wobbled through the day as the Great Eastern Trail drug me up and down a series of indistinct ridgeline bumps which may or may not have been considered peaks—although none were mentioned in my print-outs. I wondered what it took to qualify as a peak, or for a name, and if any of the lesser peaks resented Colton Mountain's bald head as the only one to qualify for bold font.

Back home, Claire frequently complained that there were not enough hours in the day—I found there to be too many. And too much derned distance between places. Bulworth Gap Shelter seemed an impossibility. One foot went out front to be replaced by the other, and the process repeated, each time achieving very little progress, and each time inciting screams of remarkably persuasive protest from my assorted bits. Eventually, the cold numbed my conscious mind, putting a distance between it and the pulsing painful rabble. I retreated to bleakness. Pain became my natural state.

I recalled a semi-fictional late-night movie in which a mob of starving peasants, after months of besieging the dictator in his compound, overcame his remaining guards and stormed the grounds only to find him alone in an empty room, reading a children's picture book aloud to the peeling wallpaper. At their intrusion, he'd looked up with sleepy, disconnected eyes, and the screen cut to black.

It was full dark when I reached Bulworth Gap Shelter. My bones were glass: my soft bits rotten fabric. Everything felt ready to shatter or tear. I let my pack fall to the dirt and sank onto the shelter floor. For several minutes, maybe hours, I lay there breathing, surrendering to the winter air. All day, the icy vultures had circled above me; now they swooped in to pick me apart.

The desire to stay down far outweighed any concern for hunger or nourishment. There was no impulse to set up a tent or prepare a meal. Thoughts of tomorrow drifted through my mind: Duncan was a town; towns had beds, warm showers, hot coffee, cheeseburgers, and phones. Feet permitting, Claire could be there by midday; we could be on the couch in time for the afternoon movies.

I cannot say how long I lay there, dimly wondering whether I was sufficiently dressed to survive the night, when the light whipped across the shelter walls. I raised my head in time to watch the beams work their way across the trees, accompanied by the growing drone of an engine—the road was near. I rumbled to my feet. I could be home tonight, at worst tucked in a bed. The internet had not advised the distance between Bulworth Gap Shelter and Duncan Ridge Road, but it had been very clear that Duncan proper lay less than two miles west of Bulworth

Gap. If the road was this close, I could be warm in under an hour.

I rolled into my pack and ran, feet be derned, turning left— which I figured to be west— following the road. In time all of daylight's ailments returned, slowing my pace and leaving me trussed by the guardrail. The asphalt was somehow even less forgiving than the frozen dirt. Several cars whirred by, catching me in their headlights, illuminating what I'm sure appeared to be a vagrant drunkard venturing down for a refill.

The internet had led me astray. Duncan was no town; it was a single stop sign lit by a pair of streetlights. The rest was darkness. From what I had read, Duncan boasted a diner and a motel but, standing at the crossroads, I could see the diner was closed, whether it be for the night or for all eternity, I could not tell. Boards covered every window of the neighboring gas station. My one hope was the Duncan Mountain Motel whose sign stood a short distance to my right, with a neon pink sign radiating the most beautiful word in the English language: *VACANCY*. I could get a place for the night, enjoy a shower, and make myself presentable when Claire came to rescue me in the morning.

A fine compromise.

A dingy office, separated from the world by smudged plate glass window, occupied the short leg of the L-shaped building. Its fluorescent light spilled out onto the sidewalk. I cupped my hands against the glass and scanned for signs of life. The analog clock on the inside wall read 10:07. There was no one manning the desk. I tried the door: it caught at the bolt. I tried again, this time harder, rattling the frame as the metal bounced against itself, but the door remained shut. I looked around; there were no payphones, no cameras, no sensors, no way for an innkeeper to tell if a wayward traveler had come seeking asylum. I returned to the door, shaking it anew, causing enough racket that even the most inattentive clerk, or patron, would have to acknowledge my peril.

No self-respecting motel turned away customers so early in the night, or left itself so unsupervised.

I pounded on the glass, then on the frame, shouting for aid until the clock displayed a passive 10:53. Leaning, panting, chin quivering, I collapsed to the ground and wrapped my hands around me knees.

There were no people, no lights, no cars.

There would be no shelter. All my hopes of warmth and food had been dashed. The wind picked up, pinning me against bricks.

Seeing no other option, I slunk around the back of the motel in search of a hidden or protected place to pitch my tent, or at least find respite from the wind. What I found was a vent coughing out hot air on the back wall, under which I laid my sleeping bag, curled up, resting my head on my pack.

I thought about my wife lying in our spacious and warm bed, my son under his designer sheets. Never before had a man leapt so willingly into homelessness.

The vent breathed hot and heavy on my face, and some hidden motor purred within the wall. I was lulled to sleep.

5

"You need to leave."

I started at the sound but, rendered immobile by my sleeping bag, mustered only a wormy spasm. It was the first voice I'd heard in almost a week. The owner stood over me, a dark silhouette framed by an unknown light.

"Is that clear, sir? Are you awake? Did you hear me? You need to get up, and you need to leave."

I blinked hard but couldn't free my hands to rub my eyes.

"Sir, did you hear me? You need to leave."

"I'm—" my jaw kept wagging but produced no sound. "I heard you."

"Good. Are you in need of assistance?"

I distinguished the blue of his uniform, that he was very young, and good looking, if a bit doughy. I also identified the light source as headlights from his patrol car.

"I've been better but no."

"Are you sober?"

"Of mind and body."

"That's good, sir. Now you need to get up, and you need to leave."

I fished my hands out of the sleeping bag, poking them out in submission. "I have a wife."

"That's good, sir. I'm sure she's very proud. You need to—"

"If you'll let me call her she will come get me. It won't be more than a couple of hours."

"I can't do that, sir. If someone sees you here, I'll have to take you in. You need to—"

"Can't I use your phone? I'll hide. No one will see me at all."

"Only phone is at the station, sir." He gestured away from the motel towards a building marked *Duncan Police Department*; I had all but slept in their parking lot. "If you are using it, it's because I've taken you in."

"Please. I'd very much like to call my wife." The young man shook his head. "She'd come get me. I'm a hiker. I'm not dangerous, just cold and misguided."

"I know what you are, sir. I don't recognize you which means you're not local, but not for one moment can I let you remain in Duncan. Laws and ordinances being what they are. You need to get up and you need to leave."

"Just one call."

"No, sir."

I weighed my options. "A second to collect my things?"

"Quickly, sir."

He watched me as I put together my pack, throwing several glances over his shoulder at the dormant police station. "I can give you a ride back to Trail if you'd like."

"Again if you'd just let me—"

"I cannot do that, sir. You need to get up and you need to leave. Quickly. This option expires."

I sighed and followed the young officer to his cruiser where he motioned me to the front seat. His patrol car was hot and warm air roared out of the dashboard vents. I put my hands up to them, flexing and unflexing until I could do so without tension. Flashing lights covered his dashboard. I counted three handheld radio transmitters. When we were out of the parking lot, he examined me with great interest, and lifted a sleeve of powdered mini-donuts.

"I got some snacks if you're—" I snatched them before I could catch myself. He watched as I battled the wrapper and shoved two in my mouth. "I'm sorry to do this to you, sir. I know you must be hungry, and frozen miserable up in the mountains. But we can't have folk spendin' their nights in the station parking lot. Laws and ordinances being what they are."

I finished the sleeve.

"Now maybe if you catch me in a year or two we can work something out, but right now, rookie that I am, I'm by the book." I stared out the window at the territory I had traversed in the dark the night before. "If them donuts dry you out, just check around your feet, one of those bottles should be sealed. If so, you're welcome to it." Them donuts had dried me out; I rooted through the sea of discarded plastic bottles at my feet, most of them full of a black residue, until I found an unopened bottle of blue sports drink. "There's the one. Have at it buddy. Hope you don't mind it being on the floor."

I twisted open the cap, not without some appreciation for my digital dexterity, and drained half the bottle in gulp. I redirected the air vents to my face.

"I slept in a parking lot."

"That's a fair point, sir. You know back in high school we used to spend a lot of time up on the Trail. Doing them things you can't be doing at nobody's folks' house." He looked over at me and smiled. "Met a lot of cool hikers passing through. Always dreamed of doing it myself. But now, times being what they are, being an adult and all, it just don't seem possible."

"I'm retired." I finished the blue drink. "Mailman."

"Congratulations, sir. I'm always happy to meet someone who's dedicated their career to the people." He stopped by the trailhead. I dropped the bottle amongst its peers. "Good luck to you." I nodded and exited. He whipped his cruiser around in that distinct law enforcement way, in stark contrast to the patient maneuvers of the parcel deliveryman, and disappeared back down the mountain.

I started on a *Juicerrman* and surveyed the slope in front of me.

"Dern it all."

Having failed at quitting, I determined to press on. For its part, the Great Eastern Trail held no grudge. All my friends: cold, hunger, fatigue, and pain, were there waiting for me, as if the Great Eastern Trail knew I didn't have it in me to leave it behind. Perhaps it was right; sometimes it's easier to remain in a direction rather than setting a new path. One of the benefits of the increasingly obvious over packing was that I had more than enough food to get me to Jackson.

One of the tenets of the Great Eastern Trail is that every road resides in a gap; hikers walk down into towns and climb their way out. Duncan was no exception. It took a great deal of climbing, and two precious *Juicerrmen*, to get back on the ridgeline. The blisters on my feet rubbed themselves open—I could feel their moisture in my socks. My knees threatened to shatter. I thought about Claire. I'd promised to call her from Duncan; thanks to diligent law enforcement, that was no longer an option. Even though I was ahead of schedule, it would have been nice to give at least status update, hear her voice, and beg her to come get me. She'd no doubt be worried and have to endure that worry for several days. I resolved to hurry to Jackson.

I started anew. A disembodied shadow crossed the Trail in front of me. I traced its source to a bird maneuvering through the trees. When it perched on a nearby pine's bare stalk I recognized it as a red-headed woodpecker, and a pretty good size one at that; the first non-uniformed lifeform I had seen since the squirrel. The woodpecker took a few probing pokes at its tree then turned to face the intruder in its woods, studying me with black eyes and a cocked head.

"No need to worry about me, birdy. No harm intended." I said it softly enough that a person at that distance wouldn't know I'd spoken. Claire and I had always loved birds, keeping a well-stocked bird-feeder outside our kitchen window which, over the years, had attracted all sorts of common and rare specimens, but never this variety of woodpecker. The woodpecker turned back to its tree, then thought better of it, and took off north along the Trail. I made a mental note to tell Claire.

My continued internment on the Great Eastern Trail did mean that I would get to experience Franklin's Spring, which the internet forums lauded as the *must try* water source on the Great Eastern Trail's southern half. It was one of the South's few high altitude springs; supposedly the water gushed forth from solid rock and spilled into a mineral rich pool. The print-outs advised to look for a small stream that crossed the Great Eastern Trail at a high pass, and that the thirsty hiker must only venture fifteen yards upstream to locate the spring. Some of my fondest memories were of drinking water. I had circled it as something not to be missed.

Once on the ridge, the Great Eastern Trail returned to its gentle up and downs, ticking off several minor peaks in the process. Eventually, the gurgle of water reached my ears, growing louder as I came around a small bend to find a swift stream crossing the Trail. The stream looked somewhat unnatural—there should not be water moving at this altitude. I turned left, following upstream about fifteen yards to a small pool, about the size of my neighbor's hot tub, surrounding the base of a boulder. As promised, the water spouted out from a crack about two-thirds up the rock face and cascaded into a pool. The print-outs had been dead on in their description—failing only to note the young red-headed woman soaking her feet in the chilly water.

She had her back to me, and appeared absorbed in thought, leaving me with the uncomfortable task of informing her that she was being approached by an aging woods-dwelling male. Being well versed in late night movies, I knew this dynamic all too well. Despite my best efforts, I would end up murdering this poor girl and go on the lam only to be dragged out of a gas station bathroom, clad only in dirty underwear, raving about the political right. As such, I searched for a way to make my presence known without frightening her, perhaps make it known that I would at least resist any violent impulses. I determined to just leave the girl be and pass Franklin Spring all together.

The girl turned around and smiled:

"Isn't this place great? You have to soak your feet. It makes them feel so much better. I know it's gross but I figure people can still get their water from the rock where my feet haven't ruined it." She turned her back to me, facing the pool. "That's a good spot over there. I sat there last time."

Suddenly, there was a lot being asked of me.

"I, um, If you don't mind sharing your water with an old man." It sounded anti-social, awkward. Even back in society it was rare that I had unsupervised conversations with young women. Even under the best circumstances, it was rare that my searches for wit bore palatable fruit.

"Well it's certainly not my water. The mountains are kind enough to share it with me." She was younger than Billy, with vibrant red hair, shocking after a week of dull colors, and freckles scattered under lightning green eyes.

I tested the water with a finger; it was frigid and mean. I did not want to subject my feet to it.

"You get used to the cold. The water extracts all the bad from your feet. They say it's the minerals, but I prefer to think it's something more interesting."

I gave her a sideways glance, frustrated this had become one of those cosmic masculine challenges which no man truly outgrows: if this young girl could sit here, smiling, with her feet plunged in this ice bath . . . I removed my footwear, rolled up my pants, and positioned myself on the bank opposite her, fighting a grimace as my feet slipped under. She laughed from across the pool.

"Give it a second. You'll thank me. What's your name?"

"Gabe."

"Just Gabe?"

"Gabe Jenkins."

"No trail name?" I thought for a second—the officer had called me sir.

"You're the first person I've met."

"It has gotten a little lonely out here. I'm Jezebel. I got named before I turned around. Dudes thought I was a Jezebel because of the red hair and I guess I'm a touch more intense than most of them would prefer." I was almost panting as the water brought my feet down to temp. Jezebel seemed an appropriate name.

"My wife Claire used to make me take cold showers to help my circulation. This is, um, much worse." It seemed time to mention my wife. "What do you mean *turned around*?"

"I started off going south from Daemon's. Now I'm hiking home to Lawson."

"Home? You're kidding. It's freezing out here. You should be celebrating in a warm bar."

"I'm not done yet. Still learning and still having too much fun. And the cold really just started last week. Most of it's been pretty nice." She removed her feet from the water and patted them dry with a camp towel.

"I really just started last week."

She looked up. "I love how that works. But it's just the time of year. It's gonna get far worse before it gets better. Everyone says this is the worst time to pass through the Donners."

The internet had highlighted the Donner Range as a dense collection of the highest peaks on the southern Great Eastern

Trail, known for its isolation, wildlife, and brutal climbs. Most hikers reached the Donners about two weeks after Duncan.

Jezebel slid back from the water, dabbed her feet dry, and pulled on her shoes. They were a brand, *Delmar*, I recognized from the outfitter. *Delmar* focused on ultra-light material in lieu of support.

I started to lift my feet out as well. "What do you think you're doing? You've got at least ten more minutes if you want to get anything out of this."

"My feet are fine. I really just wanted to wash them off." The cold throttled my bones.

"I can see your blisters from here. Don't be a wuss, give it a bit longer. I promise you will feel better." I lowered my feet, accustomed to the women in my life being right about such things. "Thank you. Did you stay in Duncan last night?"

I nodded.

"Me too. I didn't see you at the motel but you must've been there, that's the only place to stay. It's not my favorite. The sheets are so scratchy and my TV kept cutting in and out. And did you hear that jerk in the parking lot yelling and banging on the glass? I wonder what his problem was."

"The cold must've gotten to him."

"Amongst other things. Serious issues that one. Where are you headed tonight?"

"Tinsley Shelter. I need to get to Jackson and call my wife. I haven't spoken to her since Grambling's Pass."

"You won't make it. It's too late in the day, especially if it took this long for you to get here. Which, why didn't you call in Duncan?"

"My room didn't have a working phone." I shrugged. "Terd hole. Why can't I make it to Tinsley? Everything I've read on the internet says it's an easy hike from Duncan."

"You mean on those stupid forums? Those people are full of it. They go out with no packs, then a week later sit at their desks, drink hot coffee, and post details like they know what's going on."

"I can move pretty fast if I need to." This was baseless.

"You still won't make it to Tinsley Shelter. You should stop at Lightsey. That's where I'll be. You should make it well before dark and I'd love the company. It's just this weather, keeps people indoors. Everyone would rather rot inside than weather a little cold."

"Yep. Indoors. Warmth. Those idiots."

"Alright Mister Gabe I'll let you get out now. Any longer might actually be dangerous." I retrieved my feet from the depths and reached for my socks. "Now what're you doing? You can't put those back on wet feet. You'll be miserable. Use this." She wadded up a piece of fabric and threw it at me. I picked it up; it felt smooth and soft, not like any towel I'd ever seen.

"What is this?"

"It's a car shammy. At least it's a specific brand of car shammy. It's perfect for camping. Crazy light and super absorbent. We should be able to get you one in Jackson." One pass with the shammy and my feet were bone dry. "Just dip it in the water and wring it out if you don't mind. You seem nice but I don't want to carry your foot juice. In fact, you just keep it. How do they feel?"

"They're not feeling too much honestly."

"That has to be an improvement. The afternoon will tell us for certain. I'm going to head out now but please don't put that same pair of socks back on. Use a fresh pair if you have them. It will make your day go way better. I will see you at Lightsey."

She was gone before I could respond. I followed her instructions, putting on clean socks, and left several minutes later. It felt weird to have someone in front of me. For the better part of a week I had forged my own path. Now there was a young lady less than an hour in front of me. She had been right about my feet—the sharp, shooting pain allayed to a dull ache, permitting a more natural gait, which in turn benefitted my ankles and knees.

Despite Jezebel's words of caution, I still planned to make for Tinsley Shelter. According to the print-outs, it was no longer or more strenuous than my pre-Duncan days. I pressed hard, put down a couple *Juicerrmen*, and straggled into Lightsey Shelter after sunset.

The shelter area was laid out like a miniature outdoor amphitheater with the shelter serving as the covered stage. Jezebel was perched at the stage's edge, swinging her legs as she watched my arrival.

"Good evening Mister Gabe!" she hollered, "I'm so glad you stopped here. This is such a great shelter. Last time I was here it was clear and you could see a million stars."

I looked up at the dark sheet. "Not sure we'll be that lucky tonight."

I scanned the area hoping to ascertain the whereabouts of her tent site, and give it a respectable and socially appropriate birth, but could not locate it. "Are you staying in the shelter?"

"Just behind it actually. The wind comes in from that way." She pointed out towards the Trail. "And this way the shelter blocks it rather than my tent. I left plenty of room for you to join." I turned in the direction she pointed, noting the already brisk breeze. Her suggestion would be too close.

"I think I'll try up there." I gestured to a flat spot well in front of the shelter.

"But that's right in the wind. You'll be freezing."

"I have a method, and a dern good sleeping bag. I actually prefer the colder spots."

I set up my tent and returned to the shelter with my dinner set. Jezebel had her stove out: a little silver shiny contraption sitting on the table next to a soda bottle of clear liquid. I watched as she poured in a touch of the clear liquid and flicked her lighter, igniting a clear blue flame. She then placed a stand around the flame on which she set her pot of water.

"What type of stove is that?"

"Denatured alcohol. I made it out of an old soda can. It has some limitations compared to a canister stove, but it's way cheaper, and I've always dug the flame. You should see it when it gets real dark. It really glows."

"It's certainly different." Upon closer inspection, the contraption did resemble a halved soda can. It was also dented and well-worn, a rudimentary device not without a simple elegance.

I took out my equipment and began preparations for my own meal.

"Oh that rice is smart. People always want to bring in specialty foods that you won't be able to find in towns lacking real grocery stores. But rice, rice is everywhere. What are you putting in it?"

"What do you mean?"

"Sauce? Jerky? Cheese? Tuna? Sausage?"

"Just water and rice."

"Just rice!? Isn't that bland? Why are you doing that to yourself?"

"What's wrong with rice? It's cheap and easy. Cooks in a flash. I eat it all the time at home."

"No, Mister Gabe, I am well aware of the benefits of rice. But I bet you have it with something don't you. Chicken and rice. Rice and gravy. Pork chops and rice. And they make flavored rice packets and sides you know." Claire had made a similar point.

I took a deep breath, assessing my new companion.

"You know there are monks who take vows of silence and eat nothing but plain rice for years on end. And they lead simple happy lives."

"I very much doubt they are eating minute rice. And you're already out here hiking and leading the simple life. Your meals are supposed to be your indulgence."

"I like rice. Even on its own. All that flavored stuff is crap. Salty. Terrible. Crap." She put down her things and looked at me.

"Point taken. I'm sorry, but can I at least give you some sauce for your rice?"

"No you may not."

Our pots began to boil and we added our ingredients. Afterwards, her pot boiled over with smells, colors, and textures. Mine put out thin tufts of pale steam.

The rice was bland, tasting how Franklin's Spring had smelled, and just as cold before I finished it. When it was gone, I retrieved the logbook from the shelter.

"Are you following anybody yet? Sadly, I'm now confined to repeats. But I can recommend some great reads." I looked up, not sure how to respond to the question. "I always pick out a few and follow their stories as long as they last. You have to hedge your bets though because most folk, especially the wordy ones, don't make it too far."

"Oh yea. I guess I just read everybody's but I'm always looking for Mongrel."

"Mongrel's good. A safe one for sure, sort of the never ending story."

"What do you mean?"

"He's been hiking the Great Eastern Trail nonstop for ages. He just keeps going up and down, down and up, up and down. I actually followed him the whole way south about a week or so behind. But I don't know where he is now. He can be very, very fast and I have a sneaking suspicion he goes off-Trail."

"Is he some sort of hobo? Or a nomad?"

"He definitely keeps off the conventional radar. They say he has no ID, no birth certificate. There are many people who claim they spoke with him."

"What do they say about him?"

"Only that you have to experience him for yourself. Should I sign you up for the Wanderer's Disciples?"

"The Wanderer's who?"

"The Cult of the Disheveled. Parishioners of the Squirrel Lord. Divine Worshippers of the One True Mongrel. I'd get you a recruitment pamphlet but they don't have any. What they lack in formal literature they make up for in extensive disorganization."

"You mean beyond the limericks in the logbooks."

"I guess you're already familiar with the holy scripture of the unfettered."

I considered Mongrel's mythology as I located and removed the folded brown note from the logbook:

> MONGREL COME, MONGREL GO
> PICK UP FEET, DON'T STUB TOE

"Words to live by."

"No kidding. But I'm going to bed. If we get up early and make good miles I can get you to Jackson in three days. I would suggest you tag along. You'll have a hard time getting a hitch on your own."

"What makes you say that?" The internet had mentioned hitchhiking as a near necessity.

"Well, consider it from the driver's perspective. I'm either a defenseless young girl stranded on the roadside in desperate need of a knight in shining armor, or I'm an adventurous young lady purposefully unburdened by society's strict sexual constraints. Either way there is the perception that picking me up greatly increases a dude's chances of getting laid. You are just a skinny man trying to gain access to peoples' vehicles. Not quite old enough to not be threatening and not quite small enough to be pitiable."

"Been up pretty early every morning so far. Good night."

"Good night Mister Gabe. Stay warm up there."

It developed into a rambunctious night. An icy wind tore through the pass popping my rain flap like a towel in a boy's locker room, straining against its stakes, penetrating the tent walls, and taking the heat with it; I may as well have been naked laying on the bare ground. I thought of Jezebel, warm and protected in her cozy alcove, and cursed the societal conventions that had left me out in the open. I was up and waiting for her the next morning.

6

The next day's hike to Gallivant Shelter was only remarkable in displaying that Jezebel and I could start at the same time, at the same place, with the same distance in mind, and she would be resting comfortably at our destination long before I even considered finishing. She did not appear to put forth any extraordinary effort: each step took place at regular speed and covered an ordinary distance. She even joked and laughed at herself, but she was out of sight within a quarter of a mile and I was left huffing, puffing, and alone.

Just before sunset, I found Jezebel stretched out on the Gallivant Shelter picnic table.

"Mister Gabe! How was your day? I hope you stopped at Tinsley Shelter."

"How could I? You had me so worried about making it here. I barely stopped all day."

"And it still took you this long?"

"Apparently."

"Well Mongrel was particularly inspired," Jezebel struck an oratory pose, "MONGREL COME, MONGREL GO, DON'T YOU EAT THAT YELLER SNOW."

"I hope you didn't need Mongrel to tell you that."

"Chauncey Shelter tomorrow. With any luck we'll be in Jackson early the next day. Plenty of time to resupply, eat, and hang around."

"Resupply?"

"Yea, resupply. You know, purchase more food. More rice."

"Guess I can just eat and hang around. I'm not really out of anything."

"Not really out of anything?"

"The internet said I needed enough to make it to Jackson so I started out with enough to make it to Jackson. The internet also said I needed such and such an amount to make to Jackson, so I packed such and such an amount." I opened my food bag and showed it to her. She gasped and began going through my things.

"Mister Gabe the internet has failed you again. This is way too much weight. You'd save yourself so much trouble if you just went town to town." She sifted through the food pile. "Wait, is this a real *Juicerrman*?" She pulled out the red packaging. "My dad used to use these as hammers. Do you eat these?"

"Protein, caffeine, and calories. Everything a body could want."

"I thought *Juicerrmen* were illegal. How'd you even get them?"

"Internet."

"You are a confounding subject, Mister Gabe. More rice tonight?"

"But of course."

She sighed. "Of course. I set up my tent over there. It's not as good as last night but should be fairly well protected. Even with your *method* and sleeping bag, I'd recommend you do so as well."

"Thank you, but I think I'll try here by the shelter. Looks flat enough."

"If you say so Mister Gabe. Rest up. Big day tomorrow if we're gonna make Chauncey Shelter. And we have to do that if so we can get into Jackson in time for lunch."

Another sleepless, bone-chilling night ensued. Jezebel kicked at my tent before dawn.

"C'mon Mister Gabe. It's time."

"A whisper will suffice."

"The world doesn't turn for whisperers. Get moving. It's a long ways to Chauncey Shelter and you hike slow."

I staggered at my own pace as Jezebel disappeared into the morning darkness. My feet lit anew as the pre-noon hike undid the last of Franklin Spring's healing. It took three *Juicerrmen* to make it to lunch. Two more kept me moving until evening. At sunset, I picked up a sturdy stick, shifting the brunt of my weight to it rather than my crumbling feet, and so I trekked into the night.

It was after my dinner *Juicerrman* that a light appeared down Trail, bouncing through the darkness at head level, setting the red hair ablaze.

"Are you alright Mister Gabe? I was worried so I came back out."

"I seem to have a slight twinge." If Jezebel thought I was slow before, she would loathe my three-legged shuffle. "Are we close to the shelter?"

"Yea it's just around the corner. You're doing great." Even though I never officially stopped, she didn't have to move to carry on a conversation.

"Fantastic. Let's chat there."

Jezebel dropped in behind me. "Will you remain ascetic in Jackson or will you indulge in the mortal pleasures of town?"

"Reckon I could go for a burger."

"Reckon you could. But you have to liven it up a little bit."

"What do you mean?"

"This is town food, Mister Gabe. Town food is our reward for being out here. It's supposed to be the ultimate extravagance. You have to treat yourself. A burger is a good start, but for me it would have to be a bacon cheeseburger with a fried egg and a mound of chili fries, two sodas, and a milkshake—scratch that, two milkshakes and a soda. And that's just when we get in, for dinner I want pizza, extra-large extra-cheese with pepperoni, sausage, and pineapple, one for each of us. Served with beer, obviously. Now you go?"

"Go where?"

"Dress up your burger."

"Oh, um ketchup, maybe sliced onions, well definitely sliced onions. But not too many."

"You have to do better than that."

"What's wrong with my burger?"

"There's no cheese. And try not to end your extravagance with the phrase *not too many*."

"I'll just have what you have."

"C'mon, Mister Gabe. What do you think of if not food?"

"I guess I don't."

"That is increasingly unsurprising."

"Are we there yet?"

"I'm not gonna lie to you Mister Gabe—because I've already laid on some pretty heavy deception. I had to walk back a long ways just to find you. And at a much faster pace. I was worried you would quit if I told you the truth."

"I appreciate your concern. Are we close now?"

"We are closer now than we were when first we met."

We pulled into Chauncey Shelter at what must have been midnight. Jezebel cooked my rice on her stove while I set up my tent and crawled in. She read me Mongrel's post through the fabric as I ate:

MONGREL COME, MONGREL GO
GIVE THE ACT, THE OLD HEAVE-HO

7

Jezebel was already packed when I emerged.

"Good morning Mister Gabe. How'd you sleep?"

"Like a baby lamb."

"Glad to hear it. Do you want me to hike with you or are you okay?"

"Reckon I'm fine on my own. Thank you."

"I'll wait for you by the road. Remember, the faster you move, the faster we get mustard-onion burgers."

I limped along the ridgeline, still heavily reliant on my hiking stick, and well behind Jezebel who had made the astute point that there was no reason to stop for snacks with town food on the horizon; her talk of bacon cheeseburgers, milkshakes, and extra-cheese pizza infected my brain. I had been hungry going into Duncan, but her excitement, combined with Duncan's disappointment, had me in a near frenzy.

The quaint small town diner materialized as I walked: the checker board tile floor; glossy red booths; Formica counters and table tops; chrome trim everything, a homely middle-aged waitress freshening up my soda in between plates. Pie. Newspapers. Coffee. Heaven.

I found Jezebel slumbering by the road. She cracked an eye at my approach.

"What took you so long?"

"I thought I made good time. You just have another gear."

"How are your feet?"

"Never better."

"If you say so," Jezebel smiled, "hang back a second so I can get us a ride."

I retreated into the wood line as Jezebel stepped to the road, leaning forward almost into the lane, and stuck out her thumb. A few moments later the first car, a little beat-up coupe, passed by without so much as tapping the breaks. As did the next. The third, a gargantuan black pick-up truck, skidded to a stop on the gravel ten to fifteen feet past Jezebel. The driver, a husky anti-gentleman in a faded ball cap, rolled down the window.

"Oh goodness, thank you so much for stopping. I was worried I'd be stuck out here."

"My pleasure little lady. Where can I help you get to?"

I peeked from behind a tree until Jezebel waved me in. The man's face turned into a scowl.

"This your daddy?"

"Nope," Jezebel responded, "just a friend."

"Well sir," he said almost growling, "why don't you be a gentleman and let the lady take the cab."

I noted the tremendous hound prowling the cab's back row, hoisted up my pack, and delicately made my way into the bed, not wanting to violently perish because I'd scratched this man's rear panel. When all was settled, the truck roared out of the shoulder, sending up a spray of gravel, and flinging me against the tailgate. The frigid air swirled around the bed, slapping my face, and pulling tears from my eyes. I burrowed up against the back of the cab, hiding my face under my jacket, clinging to the liner's grooves as the truck rumbled over hills, around turns, frequently sending me airborne or smashing into the wheel wells. If I were a pettier man, I would have thought the fellow was attempting to eject me.

The truck slammed to a stop next to a motel and I scrambled out, much less concerned for the paint. The driver said good-bye to Jezebel, checked his rearview mirror, and sped off.

"How were things in the cab?" I asked.

"Seems he thought it was a pretty dirty trick, hiding you out in the woods like that. He and his wedding ring were definitely looking to rescue a young damsel."

We entered the office of the *Motel of the Pines* where Tucker, a sixtyish heavy set man, greeted us from his stool across the counter.

"Good afternoon friends. Room for the night?"

"Two actually. Two rooms, please."

"Two rooms. Yes, alright," he said, "we can certainly do that. Not too many hikers coming through yet, or anymore really. Y'all might be the first this year." He made the first notes on the blank paper in front of him then stopped and smiled at us over his glasses. "We get plenty of father-sons coming through but y'all are about the first father-daughter pair I've seen."

"Oh I'm not his daughter," Jezebel responded. I wished she hadn't—I was fine with old Tucker thinking I was her dad. His eyes narrowed at the correction.

"Well alright. Two rooms then," he shifted his weight on his stool, "he aint got ya kidnapped, has he?"

"No sir. Mister Gabe doesn't have the mustard to kidnap me."

The *Motel of the Pines* was not the sort of place where I'd normally lay my head—I certainly could never get Claire to stay there—but it was cheap, and Jackson's only lodgings. As it was, Jezebel and I agreed to shower in our respective rooms and meet for dinner in thirty minutes.

The room, though far from spotless, was vastly cleaner than its occupant and contained all of life's essentials: a TV, refrigerator, sit-down toilet, shower, and a full-size bed complete with a lifeless comforter and thin pillows—a halfway house for people reintegrating from the wild. I dropped my pack, sat down on the floor, and picked up the phone. I dialed, then hung up before it rang, suddenly aware of my problem: what was I to say? A long delay in calling. A female companion. Even under regular circumstances there's no casual way to tell your wife you're having dinner alone with a younger woman.

The mental image of Claire huddled by the phone, wondering if I had perished in the mountains, put finger to button.

"Hello dear," my wife's voice sent chills down my spine.

"Hello sweetheart."

"Where are you?"

"Jackson, at the, um, *Motel of the Pines*. Sorry I'm late calling. I hope you weren't too worried about me."

"No more than usual. I told you that your expected pace was ambitious so I built in a couple days before I started to worry. Although I do believe you promised to call from Duncan."

"I know, I'm sorry. I couldn't call from Duncan. There was some . . . unpleasantness."

"Unpleasantness?"

"A run-in of sorts."

"Explain."

"Well I walked in late and the motel was closed. So I figured if I couldn't stay inside the motel I would just stay outside the motel. Get some of that residual heat. And when I woke up, there was an officer over me, so I . . . well I guess I got arrested."

"He took you in for vagrancy!? Gabe it's been less than a week. Why didn't you call me from jail?"

"He didn't take me to jail. He said I had to leave and made me get in his cruiser and drove me back to the Trail."

"So he didn't take you back to the station or write you a ticket or anything?"

"Not that I'm aware of."

"Then why did you tell me you got arrested?"

"Well, circumstances being what they were, I thought that counted."

"That's not really getting arrested Gabe. Sounds like he just gave you the bum's rush."

"Well that's good. I guess I've never pondered that distinction before."

"I'm so glad you were finally able to clear that up. Beyond getting mistaken for a vagrant what's—actually wait—sounds like you were correctly identified as a vagrant. Tell me again, you were sleeping outside the motel?"

"Yes, but not by choice."

"That's true for most vagrants. Just stay put and I'll come get you . . . What was it the Pine Motel? Doesn't matter, there can't be that many in Jack—"

"Claire, don't."

"You don't want to come home? It sounds like you're miserable."

"For parts of it yea, but I also made it to the top of a really amazing mountain. And there were these outstanding clouds everywhere, and the cold has just been brutal and I was all alone until a few days ago I . . . Claire."

"Gabe."

"I've got to tell you something."

"Why you're out hiking in the middle of winter instead of home enjoying your retirement with your charming wife?"

"No. I'm working on that though. I need to tell you that I'm having dinner tonight with a hiker."

"Oh my. Is she a cute hiker?"

"How'd you know it's a she?"

"Why else would you tell me about it?"

"Right. Well yes, a little bit. But I pro—"

"Enjoy your dinner, Gabe."

"You're not concerned?"

"No dear I am not. Not about that at least. I've known you for a while now. Beyond trusting you completely, I bet you're so caught up with not appearing like you want her that you make it very uncomfortable for her. Like you did with all of Billy's college friends. Or any female server ever. So just enjoy your dinner and try to let her as well. If you must insist on staying out there, you have my blessing to eat in good company."

"Thanks. But if you'll excuse me I still have to shower. It's been like, a week. I will call you later?"

"Go shower Gabe. I can smell you over the phone. So by all means go shower before you eat with this poor girl."

"Thanks. I love you."

"I love you too." I started to put down the phone when I heard Claire's voice echo off the bedside table. "Wait Gabe!"

"Yes, dear."

"Please call Billy."

I hung up the phone, thought for a second, checked the time, and called Billy at home. When it got to voicemail I disrobed for a shower, coming to a full stop when I caught the mirror. The man looking back at me was already much thinner than the man that had left Grambling's Pass. My cheeks had pulled in, tightening across my face, and were covered in a peppery fuzz that melded into my grey hair. The hair itself, usually neatly combed over, stood straight up in alternating patches making me look like some sort of mad man.

The pressure was wanting. Water spilled out of the head in a single, thick stream. But it was a hot stream. I turned my face up to the nozzle, letting it pour onto my forehead and roll down my body. I gave each troubled body part its own individual session, letting the water warm and soothe. Torrents of brown streamed from my feet to the drain, darkening each time lather reached virgin territory. I remained in the shower a long time, scrubbing and rescrubbing until the complimentary bar of soap was little more than a grimy sliver. Only then, when my fingers were good and pruned, did I dry off, put on my cleaner pair of underwear, rain pants, and my least funky shirt.

I had no sooner fell onto the bed when there was a pounding on the door.

I found Jezebel similarly clad in clunky pink rubber shoes, rain pants, and a lime green rain jacket. Her hair took on an even brighter hue when degreased.

"Mister Gabe, I know the best place."

Jezebel led me down Main Street, past several nice mom and pop establishments, and then turned left off it, heading in that direction until the buildings began to thin. I did my best to pretend my feet didn't hurt. At last, she stopped and pointed at a gas station.

"A gas station? I thought we were supposed to dream big."

"No not a gas station. A restaurant attached to a gas station."

She gestured to a small red and yellow sign next to the door: *Pete's Dank Chicken*.

"Jezebel, I don't think this is the place for me. We passed several fine looking restaurants."

"What do you mean? It's perfect."

"I mean I very much do not want to eat at this gas station."

"Mister Gabe this place is amazing. Just give it a try—if you don't like it we can go somewhere else. Have I ever led you astray?"

"Few strangers have."

Jezebel threaded through the aisles of greasy, salty, and sweet treats to a back counter under a ceiling mounted menu and a few unpadded booths. Emblazoned on the menu in garish red-framed yellow letters was the slogan "EXPERIENCE THE SAUCE." The interior walls may have once been white but years of accumulating hot grease had intermingled with the paint, leaving them an oozy yellow unflattered by the fluorescent lights. The smell was intoxicating; a mix of spice and grease that reminded me of the family reunions of my youth. The menu's only variety was in quantity and whether they mashed or fried the potatoes. Jezebel ordered an eight-piece bucket, all dark, with the fried potatoes, and, after some deliberation, an additional side of mashed potatoes with gravy. I limited myself to a three piece with fries.

We took our numbers and Jezebel selected the booth nearest the gas station's refrigerated beverages. Jezebel plucked two napkins out of the dispenser and handed one to me.

"Here; put this in your lap."

"I don't think it will be much help. Judging by the walls."

"It's important that we display our civility when we find ourselves in such a dignified establishment."

She laid the napkin across her lap, making a show of smoothing and resmoothing it until it had surely torn. I placed mine just above my knee where it caught the ventilation and see-sawed to the floor.

The attendant approached, arms laden with two grease-splotched buckets, which she set in front of Jezebel then left, returning with a tray supporting two Styrofoam bowls: one filled past the brim with mashed potatoes, the other with fries. On her third trip, the attendant brought my single plate of fried chicken and fries. I inspected a drumstick: no rat feet or visible roach bits. It did seem quite thoroughly fried. I was all set for an exploratory nibble when Jezebel exclaimed—"Wait!" all but slapping the chicken out of my hand. She dashed over to the fountain drinks, returning with an opaque plastic squeeze bottle marked *Dank Sauce* in something resembling Mongrel's handwriting.

"How could I forget the *Sauce*?" She doused her buckets, clearing an inch of the bottle, then slid it over to me. I picked it up, inspected it, and squirted a puddle on a spare napkin: black and red flakes suspended in orange goo. It appeared to have a mayonnaise base and be exactly the kind of thing one should never eat when encountered unrefrigerated in a gas station.

"I will have to pass on the Dank Sauce experience."

"Do we have to do this song and dance with everything? Just eat it Mister Gabe. If you get sick, then I'll get sick and we can be sick together." She finished her first piece and snatched the bottle from me to more thoroughly douse the second. I dipped the prongs of my plastic non-space spork in the goo and gave it a taste. Finding it agreeable, I put a thin line of it on my drumstick.

Pete's Chicken was a masterpiece—a salty, peppery, crunchy, juicy, happiness explosion glorified by the mild sweetness and bold spice of the Dank Sauce. The first bite opened the floodgates to a rampant hunger as hot grease paraded through my veins like a liberating army, bringing with it rations and sweet, sweet freedom, spurring jubilant crowds in regions the minute rice couldn't muster a handshake. The pent up frustration of over a week spent in the freezing cold subsisting on rice and expired exercise bars flamed as I charged through my ill-fated order, gathering speed as I went. Jezebel cheered through a mouthful of chicken when I ordered another batch, this time a bucket, smothering the surface of each piece in life affirming Dank Sauce. Then even the new chicken was gone, leaving me out of breath, pinching at the final crumbs between gulps of fountain root beer.

"I'm sorry I doubted Mr. Pete. I am a believer."

"The more stubborn the convert, the sweeter the sauce. You haven't even fully gotten the hunger yet. It'll come." Jezebel was speaking. "All this hiking, all the calories burned, converts you into a walking trash compactor. It's pretty epic, especially when you get the chance to let your horses gallop."

With great effort I lumbered towards the door, an overburdened mosquito fighting for altitude after stealing too much blood. Jezebel pranced to the register toting a pint of ice cream and a twelve pack of beer.

"It's gonna be hard to go back to plain minute rice after experiencing the sauce."

"You won't have to." She pointed at a bin chock full of precious orange nectar packets.

Back at the motel, I put on sports television and laid down on the floor, elevating my feet on the bed. The miracle at Franklin's Spring was now a distant memory—I was in pain. The well-dressed turdballs on the television argued about sports. I was set to fall into a lengthy slumber when there was a knock at the door. I used my hands to boot scoot my torso so I could just rotate the knob. Jezebel entered with the twelve pack.

"Mind if I join?"

"Do I have to get up?"

"By all means, stay down. That looks quite comfortable." She opened two cans, setting one by my ear. "What are we going to do about your feet?"

"We?" I poured some beer into my mouth.

"Yea we. Do you want to start hiking alone again?"

"No, but I do have to wonder what my wife would say about *us* becoming a *we*."

"You know what I mean. What are we going to do about your feet?"

"Go to the hardware store, get a saw, or maybe an axe and cut them off. You can choose the instrument because you'll probably have to perform the surgery."

"What would your wife say about that?"

"That it'd keep me from wandering off again."

"There's a good outfitter in Hunker Down. They can get you set up with some more appropriate shoes. That way you don't have to hike the Donner Range in work boots. It will probably require taking a day off though."

"That'll work for me. But I certainly don't want to slow you down."

"I'm in no rush. I hurried South, this is my victory lap. Now it's time for me to just *be*." "Be what?"

"Just be. Make sure I'm pointed in the right direction before I cast off."

"This is fun. Cast off on what?"

"Life. I have one year left in school. And from this angle it looks like after that you just lump on the conveyor belt: work, marriage, kids, retire, and wait to die."

"Let's see: I've had a career, marriage, kid. I'm retired. Am I just waiting to die?"

"That's up to you, man." She finished her first beer and pulled out another. She even drank fast. "How old is your kid?"

"Billy is thirty."

"I see. Are you and Billy close?"

"Used to be. He moved to Pentland."

"Deadbeat artist?"

"Far from it. He's a lawyer."

"Oh I do see. Is he single?"

"I wouldn't know."

"Billy doesn't talk to his father much?"

"No, Billy doesn't talk to his father much. But I'm told that cuts both ways."

"That's so sad. Was there a falling out?"

"Only when he moved to Pentland."

"Pentland isn't too far from the Trail. You could go see him."

"That is actually the plan. It may well be the only thing Claire likes about this endeavor."

"Claire your wife?"

"Claire my wife."

"I bet he comes around. The Great Eastern Trail is wonderful like that. It always puts things into perspective. Helps you find the right words to say to a person."

"Person? I told you he's a lawyer."

We laid in silence for a long time. The baseboard by my head clanked and kicked; warm air breezed across my torso. I imagined Jezebel racking her brain looking for a new, more suitable topic for conversation. Two and a half beers provided the courage to ask my question.

"Have you seen any squirrels since you've been out here?"

"Yea, plenty. They're everywhere, especially when it's wa—"

"No, I guess, have you had any . . . encounters with squirrels on the Trail?"

"I'm not quite sure what a squirrel encounter is but, no. Why?"

"No reason."

"Oh man, Mister Gabe, you have to tell me."

"Well, right outside Grambling's Pass, I mean maybe twenty-five steps in, a branch snagged on my coffee mug; it whipped me down on my back and launched the mug into the woods never to be seen again."

"That's actually something we need to talk about."

"When I regained my senses there was a squirrel staring at me from the north, all crouched down as if preparing to pounce. I tried to step by and, it . . . it lunged at me, tried to bite me through my boot."

"Was it rabid?"

"No, it appeared very much aware of what it was doing."

"What did you do?"

"I tried to talk to it, calm it down, you know be the adult, and when that didn't take, I turned to head back to Grambling's Pass. Just in time to hear my wife's car leave the parking lot."

"YOU TRIED TO QUIT OVER A SQUIRREL?!?!"

"Yea, but, it was a very mean squirrel."

"What are we going to do with you Mister Gabe?"

"That's actually not the only time either."

"That's not the only squirrel encounter?"

"Not the only failed quit. You remember that fellow rattling the door and making a scene at the Duncan motel?"

"Oh man."

"That was me trying to quit. I ended up sleeping behind the motel and getting driven back to the Trail by a deputy. Didn't even get a chance to call Claire to come pick me up."

Jezebel opened maybe her fifth beer. "I hope you've gotten this out of your system. Because it's pretty clear the Great Eastern Trail isn't going to let you off that easy."

"Well it needs to warm up and flatten out. I'm generally more of a *path of least resistance* kind of guy."

"Don't worry, Mister Gabe. I happen to have it on good authority that the Great Eastern Trail has taken a very special interest in you."

"Has it now?"

"Oh yes. You have a very special hike ahead of you if you just pay attention and mind the squirrels, but first, we need to discuss your pack."

"What's wrong with my pack?"

"There's too much shit in it. And shit on it. You're carrying too much shit, Mister Gabe."

"How do you figure?"

"You sound like a jar of loose change rolling down the Trail. I could hear you like two minutes before you got to Franklin's Spring. I thought a circus had gone for a hike."

"Everything I need I have, and I need everything I have."

"You're almost half right." Jezebel stood up, turned off the television then lifted my pack to thunk it on the breakfast table. "Tell me, what this is?" She lifted a thick plastic cartridge clipped to the outside of my pack.

"It's an electric GPS compass. So I know which way to go and don't get lost."

"Have you found the orange blazes in any way lacking?"

"Well, no."

"Have you turned it on since you've been out here?"

"Well, no."

Jezebel unclipped the compass and tossed it in the trash.

"Hey! That was expensive." She opened my pack. "What makes you think you can go through my pack? You can't go through my pack." I tried to stand up but failed. "Young lady, I forbid you to go through my pack."

"You're carrying too much. It's going to wear you out. And you rattle so much that if and when we ever come across any animals, they'll be long gone by the time we'd get the chance to see them. And, more simply, it's really annoying."

"I've seen a squirrel and a woodpecker."

"Yea, and confused the life out of them. Let's do it this way— I'm going to show you an item: if you can name it, say what it does, and convince me that what it does has import relative to its weight, I'll let you keep it."

"I decline your proposition."

She slid a skinny metal cylinder off the outside of my pack. "What is this?"

"It's my extra flash—" She tossed it in the trash with a *ka-chunk*. "You didn't let me explain."

"You said extra. Extra is an automatic disqualifier. We don't have the luxury of carrying extra. Now, what is this?"

"Snake bite kit. You put the cup over the wound and pull the draw—" *Ka-chunk.* "Great. What if I get bit by a venomous snake?"

"Then you'll die wondering whether that bullshit could've saved you rather than knowing it could not. What is this?"

"That's my hatchet. It's like an axe but smaller and more portable."

"But equally as useless." She made to throw it away—

"Challenge!"

"Challenge?"

"Yes, challenge. I, I challenge the call on the field."

"Acknowledged." Jezebel lifted hatchet for closer inspection. *Ka-chunk.* "The call stands."

Jezebel went on, putting down two more beers as she filled the trashcan with my belongings, laying the few survivors on the table.

"Okay what's this?"

"That's my space-spork. It's very light and I use it to eat."

"This can stay. And what are these?"

"Really? Those are socks, two pair, including the pair on my feet I have three. I suppose that's two too many."

"Goodness no. A hiker can never have too many socks. Welp that looks like everything." She fingered around the side pockets pulling out a notecard sized piece of paper, turning it around to reveal photo of Claire, Billy, and me in front of our house. "Holy shit, Gabe. Is this your wife?"

"Yea, I had no idea that was in there. Claire must've—"

"She's beautiful." She handed me the photo. "Very well done."

I studied it, recalling Claire calling Roger over specifically to take it before Billy set off to Pentland. *When had Claire slipped this into my pack*?

"Are you going to throw this away as well?"

"Quite the opposite. We need to protect this, give it more prominent placement." She removed the *Local Recommendations* binder from a drawer and tore out a segment of lamination, carefully folding it around the photograph before placing it in my pack's zipped topped capsule. "So they'll always be on your mind. Is there anything else?"

My pack looked naked. "Wouldn't tell you if there was."

Jezebel gestured at the overflowing trash can. "Mister Gabe, all that shit in there was full blown unnecessary. It was slowing you down and making your trek harder, and less fun. You'll thank me when you set out tomorrow. That is, if you're not planning on quitting."

"I told Claire not to pick me up today. Reckon that's a good sign."

8

The knocking woke me.

My body possessed all the aches and pains a man my age deserves for a night spent on the floor. I wanted more sleep, bed sleep, but the knocking forced the issue. I stood up and cracked the curtains: Jezebel.

"Come on Mister Gabe I'm hungry!" She pushed in, accompanied by an arctic burst.

"Did you ever consider just getting that tattooed? Save yourself the trouble of repeating it."

"Collect your dirty clothes and we can do laundry and resupply before we head out. Tucker said he can give us a ride back to the Trail at eleven. After that we'd have to hitch or walk."

"I was kind of hoping to take it easy. Maybe watch a movie."

"We're taking it easy in Hunker Down. We can't slow down here too."

"Who cares? I thought this was your victory lap."

"Yes, *my* victory lap. For you, the Great Eastern Trail is still a momentum game. And since you seem to have all the personal momentum of chilled molasses, each time you slow down you risk stalling out forever."

"You mean the kind of stall after which I go home?"

"The same. Get your things."

We dropped our things off at the laundromat, set the machines, and headed to the Smilin' Pig Grocers, Jackson's only grocery store. A giant red pig face floated over the entrance, beckoning shoppers to hoof on in for *squealin' good deals*.

The store wreaked of vinegar. Burned out fluorescent lights created intermittent patches of yellowed dimness. Jezebel snatched up a basket and bee lined towards the candy aisle. *Don't dilly dally* she had told me *in and out*. I had enough rice to last until Hunker Down and only needed tortillas and peanut butter which I located easily enough, selecting the store brands from the plethora of options. The pig flashed a white toothy smile from the side of the jar. I stopped by the frozen food aisle to pick a couple breakfast burritos before locating Jezebel.

After the pig, we switched the laundry and headed to the post office for the most important stop in town: *Juicerrm*en. The post office was part of a commercial duplex visible from the laundromat. Jackson, although much more significant than Duncan, was not large enough for anything to be real far away.

A frail and ancient woman greeted us from across the counter.

"Mornin' y'all want stamps?"

"Midge," Jezebel whispered into my ear on our approach. "No, scratch that, Delia. Or Eudora."

I checked the woman's iron-on patch: *Fran*.

"No stamps, thank you. But I should have a package here for me."

"We got lots of packages."

"That's good. I just need the one."

I gave Fran my name and information, sending her creaking into the backroom, from which she returned emptyhanded.

"You'll have to get your package. I can't do the liftin'."

"Ma'am I actually used to deliver mail. It's a federal issue if I come past this desk."

"I can't do the liftin'. I'll watch, make sure there's no foolin'." She raised a crooked finger at the backroom, "It's yonder in the corner. Don't do no foolin'." I picked up a package of about the right size intended for a Robert Zimmerman.

"That ain't it! Yonder corner."

I recognized Claire's clear, decisive handwriting on the package next to it. It was alarmingly heavy—I dreaded adding it to my pack. I also wondered how many uncertified people Fran had given access to the town's mail on account of her weak arms.

We returned to the laundromat and microwaved our burritos, munching as we waited on our machine. With breakfast burritos, and indeed most microwaveable goods, I always found it safe practice to test each portion with a nibble prior to fully committing. Jezebel dove right in, and though she did not complain, I could tell she paid for it on several occasions.

Tucker, up from his stool, leaned against a white panel van in the parking lot. After a final check of the rooms, we tossed in our packs and hopped in. Tucker had the van off and moving before we buckled. He yelled at us over his shoulder as he drove.

"Y'all won't believe some of the folk that come down out of them mountains. I picked up a fella one time that had fallen on a stick and had it go right through his arm." He took his hands off the wheel and pointed at either side of his fleshy bicep. "Still had it in him when I when I got him in the van. There he was, just a-waitin' real patient by the side of the road. If it hadn't been for the damn broomstick through his arm, you wouldnta known nothin' was wrong with him. Had another girl, she tried to put a spell on me . . . ."

Jezebel yelled back at him, emoting in all the rights places as the pungent wreak of old sweat inundated the van. I had not noticed it in the woods, or even in town, but, even clean, Jezebel and I saturated the cramped van's airspace like a pair of two-legged smokestacks, producing in me an urgent nausea that threatened to significantly increase my motel bill. I stuffed my nose into my clean jacket but the wreak snuck through and in, as if it was coming out of me. If Tucker noticed, he did not let on.

Tucker dropped us off in the same spot at which Jezebel had tricked yesterday's truck driver, spinning out with a wave amidst a cloud of gravel dust. With great gasps, I took in the cool air. The ridiculousness of my decision making set in—I was leaving a perfectly good and warm bed to wander in the wintry mountains. Jezebel turned to look back at me from the wood line.

"You coming?"

"Yea. One second. Getting my breath back. Did you not notice the smell?"

"What smell?"

"It was horrible in that van."

"Was it? I did not notice that. It's nice out here." With that she turned and disappeared into the pines.

When my system cleared, I began the steep climb out of town, starting on a *Juicerrman* as I prowled up the mountain. Whatever cocaine-poison ingredients the *Juicerrman* scientists had used, it made for an effective energy bar. I launched myself up with great enthusiastic strides, admiring my abilities. Just when the sustained burst began to taper off, the Great Eastern Trail leveled out and I was back riding the ridgeline. Only at the top did I remember Jezebel's purging of my pack.

After lunch, black clouds drifted in from the west, bringing with them a sinister chill and the foreboding smell of moisture. I increased my pace, and took another *Juicerrman* boost, but it appeared destiny that the two of us, storm clouds and Gabe, would meet. I had not yet experienced a storm on the Great Eastern Trail, but had been alive long enough to fear one catching me out of doors.

Tentacles of clouds swarmed the mountains until all was grey. A smattering of preliminary droplets, then rain became my world. Shoes, socks, clothes, all drowned in the deluge. The Great Eastern Trail slickened, and I took a mighty fall, crashing shoulder first into the mud, sloshing as I tried to regain my feet. Once upright, the Trail clung to my shoes in great muddy clumps. I fought for each step, tilting, lifting, and sliding each boot until the muck relented with a begrudging *FUP WOP*, only for me to lose the foot again a very short distance north. I was fighting quicksand—lifting one leg, put a strain on the other, pressing it further down into the increasingly soft mud. I toiled through the day, wondering why I hadn't simply quit as planned. Eventually, I reverted to a trick oft utilized on the particularly long, hot, rainy, dull, monotonous, or otherwise unendurable mail truck days—I directed the entirety of my focus solely on the next mailbox. I did not have to make it through the whole route, only past the next driveway. Likewise, I did not have to make it to Daemon's Peak, nor did I have to make it to Paulson Lean-to, where Jezebel no doubt waited dry and warm; I only had to take the next step, only when that had been accomplished would I focus on the next. Eventually, one of those steps would mark my desired arrival.

I kept my head down, repeating my progression until a whole new set of muscles in the front of my legs, muscles which I had never before been utilized, screamed their displeasure at lugging my weighted feet out of the mud. The mud got softer and softer, chewing up more and more of my calves; I pushed harder, digging myself into and out of deeper and deeper holes, until finally I put forth the exertions necessary to clear a foot only to have it pop free, sending me face first into the mud. The water saturated my eyelashes.

Rolling over, I found my right sole had remained in the mud rather than lifting up with the rest of the shoe, and was now gone; the Great Eastern Trail had swallowed it whole, leaving no trace of even a footprint. I dug around, excavating mud by the scoopful where my sole should have been. I panted by my sole's impromptu grave, wiping the accumulating slog from the bottom of my right shoe. Water was already working its way upwards through the exposed fabric.

"Dern it all. I mean, just, gosh dern it all." I slung a handful of Trail at nearby pine. "I could be at home."

On a dry day a tall individual could sit in Paulson Lean-to with their feet on the Trail. I was not that individual, and this was not that day. Jezebel was deep in the shelter, bone dry, perusing the logbook. She had set up her small tent in the shelter.

I plunked down in the shelter with a wet slap.

"I guess I made it just in time."

"A part of me that worried you'd moved on to the next shelter."

"In this storm? No way, I saw this coming and bailed. I hate hiking in the rain. Plus without me you're just an old man alone in the woods eating plain rice. And that's like the saddest sentence ever." She had gotten very casual in referring to me as old man, one of many downsides to our growing report. "You need to get out of those wet clothes ASAP. Once you stop hiking you lose all that warmth and it gets real, real quick."

"I have to set up my tent."

"Couple things: one, just change in the shelter; and two, just stay in the shelter. Your tent is less than useless in this kind of rain."

"I fear that would be inappropriate."

"I'll close my eyes." I gave her a look. "Mister Gabe I assure you I have zero interest in what you have to offer."

When she'd turn her back and covered her eyes, I started peeling off the wet, brown clothes. The Great Eastern Trail had only permitted them a couple hours of laundered freshness.

"Why would I set up my tent in the shelter?"

"It's a pretty simple trick. The shelter saves your tent from taking a beating. The tent keeps in some extra heat. Once again I saved you a spot."

"I'll be okay once I'm in my raingear. After that I'm pretty confident in my tent."

"Mister Gabe, please, you saw those clouds. We're about to get smoked. There's no reason to do that to yourself. It's actually pretty dangerous."

I set up my tent on a small flat spot in front of the shelter so that it rested partially under the overhang and I could get in and out without exposing myself to the rain.

"See, I'll be fine."

I crawled back into the shelter to cook my dinner, squeezing in two packets of Dank Sauce, pressing through each packet like a tube of toothpaste, making sure to free every last viscous drop. The Dank Sauce transformed my white rice into a hearty, honey-hot stew. Enticing strands of Dank Sauce trailed my space spork each time it lifted off from the pot. Just like in the restaurant, it coated my mouth in both warmth and heat, thawing my frozen body from the inside. The densified rice even kept its heat longer, permitting the pleasure of a warm final bite. When all was done, I scraped the sides on the pot in search of missed morsels, sucking on the space spork like a little kid on a lollipop.

Jezebel began reading aloud from the logbook, giving dramatic readings of each entry. I only half paid attention until she got to Mongrel for which she took on a deep, gorilla tone, beating her chest in a thumping rhythm:

> MONGREL COME, MONGREL GO
> TRAIL HIT ME, ROCHEAUMBEAU

I repeated the words, stamping the floor, dropping my voice deeper and raspier than her frame permitted.

9

The storm erupted in the night, pummeling the mountains with a swirling rain. Water poured off the shelter's overhang onto my fabric roof. I watched in dim terror as the ceiling sank under its own weight until it had no choice but to share its burden with me. Soon my sleeping bag hung limp and heavy around my shivering form.

By morning the ceiling almost touched my nose; the walls bowed inward. My joints jerked in involuntary spasms. I wiggled my way out the close quarters like an aluminum worm, pushing out the rainfly, releasing a slushy chunk which slid down my back. Jezebel, safe in her sheltered shelter, was yet to stir. The world floated around me. My hips quaked and I could not reach full height. My limbs swayed in dull response to commands. The stillness moved faster than I could respond. With a numb elbow I swooshed ice from my tent, losing my balance with the follow-thru. Then, the world pulled away from me.

I awoke in a warm, dry place. My tent had taken on a new hue, bright orange rather than forest green. Unnaturally warm globs weighed down my feet and chest. The orange shield peeled in half—Jezebel entered my sanctuary.

"Thank God you're awake. How do you feel? Are you warm enough?"

"Um yea? Why . . . Am I naked?"

"I left you the dignity of your briefs. I figured you'd rather freeze to death than lose them in front of me." She walked me through the events of the past hour. She'd woken up to a crash and found me 'lumped' in the snow. "Circumstances have forced us to an unwanted intimacy Mister Gabe. And I do not like it. I wouldn't normally recommend eating these but I've heated a *Juicerrman* for you. I tried to melt it into rice but, whatever the ingredients are, they don't acknowledge temperature changes. I think the caffeine and whatever may actually be helpful, considering the circumstances."

She handed me a warm bottle. "Put this down the sleeping bag and retrieve the other ones for me. I've had enough old man body for one day. How do you feel? Can you move your fingers?" I clinched my hands, and curled my toes, everything moved as instructed.

"They seem to be in working order."

"Good. You've chosen a real shit place to do this. You stay put for now but we have to move at some point or we're going to get blasted again tonight. There are already clouds on the horizon. The next shelter is significantly lower and should do us better. You suck on that *Juicerrman* while I make some tea."

I remained in Jezebel's tent all morning while she fed me warmth and broke down my soggy tent. When I could play a game of *rock, paper, scissors,* and produce the motions in real time, Jezebel said it was time to go. It was early afternoon.

"This is actually pretty dangerous, Mister Gabe, both the weather and what you've done to yourself. Let's stick together today so I can keep an eye on you."

Jezebel had done what she could to dry out my belongings, but there was little to be done without a fire. As it was I donned my one dry shirt and crammed myself into one of Jezebel's jackets. There was little to be done about my legs; I slithered into my half-dry rain pants. I had had the presence of mind to keep my boots in the shelter so they weren't dampened by the rain. Unfortunately, they were frozen solid; I had to force my tender feet in, working over the laces with my fingers before they permitted themselves to be tied.

The extended downpour had flooded the Trail, turning it to muck, on top of which the snow had fallen and frozen. Each step landed on the ice, then cracked down two or three inches. It was a short day but the entirety of it was spent going downhill; Jezebel had been right about the next shelter being at lower altitude. My entire body paid dearly for the return to sea level; my right foot took the worst of it. Without the support of its sole, the shoe did little to dampen the impacts. The pain progressed from soft tissue into structural as the bones flattened under their load. Once again I attempted to accommodate it with my stride, utilizing a long left step, short right step, resulting in an exaggerated limp. I worked from orange blaze to orange blaze, Jezebel the fire burning my behind. There was nothing to do but press on.

"How long has your shoe been like that?"

"Just since yesterday, the Trail swallowed the sole."

"I didn't know they were that bad otherwise we would've gotten you new ones in Jackson, somehow. You're just going to have to suck it up until we get to Hunker Down."

"It was fine until that damned mud." I hobbled on for a ways. "Jezebel, if you and Claire ever cross paths, or communicate in any fashion, would you mind not mentioning the part in which I nearly froze to death and you undressed me?"

"I thought you said that Miss Claire was understanding."

"We all have our limits. Is Hunker Down as cozy and adorable as its name suggests?"

"It's fine, probably the best town you've been through. It pretty much needs to be since it's the last one before the

Donners."

"Thank you for warming me and probably saving my life."

"My pleasure Mister Gabe. You're my patient."

"Great. Don't tell Claire."

My boots were the first things to go when we reached Douglas Fir Shelter. The boots themselves came off easy enough. The socks were less forgiving; the fabric had fused to my sloughing foot skin, forcing me to peel them off inch by inch, taking great swaths of translucent flesh with them—a living mummy gently freeing himself from his bindings.

"Mister Gabe look!" I looked to where Jezebel pointed in the shelter's corner. "Someone's left a stack of dry wood. We can actually have a fire tonight."

Jezebel arranged the wood in the fire ring and had it lit well before I finished setting up my tent-this time in the shelter. I hovered closed to the fire, switching my feet from right to left to prevent a burn. She read from the logbook as we ate, acting out the posts in the deep, salty baritone of a seafaring explorer.

"Douglas Fur Shelter Log: The Expedition's Eleventh Day; Captain Barclay reporting. An unforgiving chapter in our northern expedition. The snow fell thick and slowed our progress. Although our food stores, having been recently supplemented in Jackson, are quite sufficient and should comfortably last us to Hunker Down. North until tomorrow. North until the End.

Morale Report: Fair"

Next she read Mongrel's, again taking on her gorilla persona:

MONGREL COME, MONGREL GO
SNOW COMES DOWN, SUN DON'T SHOW

We turned in before the sun had even fully set.

Life was better under the shelter. The wind did not strike as hard and, when it did start raining, I was double protected from it. Only my feet continued to struggle, sinking into a deep, familiar throb. I shifted them around each other, wiggling and stretching, clenching and unclenching, but the pain continued to grow, setting up headquarters in the ball of my right foot. Jezebel's voice, disembodied by the tents, came through the night.

"Mister Gabe?"

"Miss Jezebel."

"Don't do that again."

"I do not intend to."

"Whatever hang ups you've brought with you out here, you need to get rid of those too. I'm worried about the Donner Range."

"What are you afraid of? I'm the one that almost died."

"I know. That's what I'm worried about."

We were up early the next day, stomping over the crunchy earth.

The Great Eastern Trail charges for its lessons: to hike the Great Eastern Trail is to make a thousand mistakes and pay dearly for each one. The first night out of Jackson, I failed to listen to my sage companion and nearly froze to death. Before I'd even started, I'd stubbornly chosen my trusty yard boots as my footwear and each step was a pulsing reminder of that mistake. By the time we reached Elem Still Shelter, a march which witnessed the end of a great many brave *Juicerrmen*, I could hardly put weight on my right foot.

It snowed again that night, giving way to a frightfully cold morning. The layers of frozen snow thickened the Trail's protective ice sheet such that it no longer gave way under every step but rather collapsed only in terrifying sporadic episodes. Each time my world shook as the ice tilted and shattered; the cracks and screams echoed across the mountains. My crippled right foot overshadowed all other concerns. Jezebel, weighing far less and toting a lighter pack, took far fewer trips through the ice.

That night at Pelham Shelter, I lay awake in my cold, stinky tent, my head swimming with thoughts of beds, warm showers, cheeseburger platters, and intact shoes. I could already feel the thin, worn motel sheets embracing me as I watched a B movie and gorged on microwaved goods. I was tired, beaten down, and injured, but there was hope for the day. First light found me already disassembling my tent. Jezebel stirred, popping her head out of her tent, looking like a sleepy red-headed mole, saying she would catch up with me later.

On the backs of three *Juicerrmen*, I plowed through the slush. Nothing could stop my stuttered gait; barring death, I would be warm and well fed by nightfall, burrowed under layers of dry sheets watching whatever cable had to offer. Pain grew, boiled at unbearable, and simmered to numbness. My body pared down to its essential functions. But still I moved.

Jezebel caught me much earlier than my pride would have preferred, and stayed with me the rest of the way, ensuring that I did not go down for good.

Hunker Down was one of the few towns which the Great Eastern Trail cut directly through, briefly coexisting with Hunker Down's main thoroughfare. My feet threatened to pop like water balloons against the asphalt. We stumbled through two empty blocks to the Hunker Down Mountain Inn, a white washed structure with a peeling red roof. The door to the office had a knob which, under normal circumstances, would have presented no challenge, but my fingers could not feel to grip, barely registering its existence against the cold. I rubbed the brass several times, swishing off its rounded form at odd angles, then slumped against the door frame with a moan. Jezebel stepped up and vanquished the wooden door. Together we poured into the office's tepid warmth.

A skinny teenager, very pale and clad in dark jeans and a black t-shirt, seemed to be the only person working. His desk sat inches to the left of the door. He even had a window looking out at the front stoop and must have watched as I pried and cried at the door. The teenager looked at us with a level of sincere disinterest that I had forgotten actually existed in this world after Billy's teenage years.

"Two rooms, please."

"We require an extra deposit for hikers. Because of the filth."

"That's fine. Just two rooms please." I had to brace myself against his desk.

"Deposit up front. And I need both your names. For the rooms."

"Gabe Jenkins."

"Charlotte Hamilton." I glanced over at Jezebel. She kept her eyes on the desk. The teen's thin fingers plucked up two keys and tossed them on the desk. Hunker Down Mountain Inn only had one row of about ten rooms so we found our rooms without direction.

The room was altogether drab; light filtered in through the curtained window, falling on the formless comforter; everything, carpet, curtains and wallpaper, was maroon. Claire could wait until I was warm; she would certainly detect the distress and pain in my voice as is. The shower, God bless it, had both pressure and heat. My right foot had ballooned up to almost double the size of its mate, and was spotted with tufts of sloughing skin. Both feet protested their continued use. Against all my hygienic impulses, I sat down bare bottom on the faux porcelain, soaking until the water lost its warmth. Back on the carpet, I stopped in front of the mirror and inspected my reflection—my transformation was almost complete. My chest, already unspectacular, was almost concave; my ribs protruded out through the skin. My beard had come in full, outpacing my hair, which was unprecedentedly unkempt. I detected hints of a blossoming wildness which the meek caterpillar would not have recognized in the butterfly. I assumed my position next to the baseboard, and fell asleep.

10

The light from the cracked door spotlighted a figure towering over me. I yelped and attempted to stand, managing only to briefly arch my back before flopping back to the floor with a thump.

"Your daughter insisted that I check on you." The teenager's thin shoulders were stooped with apathy. He exited before I could respond, unmoved by the shirtless middle-aged man writhing on the carpet. Jezebel entered, scanning the room before locating me at her feet.

"On the floor again Mister Gabe." I made a move to cover my chest with a pillow. "Oh yes, please do cover up."

I lifted myself to me feet. "What condition do you think I would've had to be in to get that fellow to show some concern?"

"This is a concerning scene."

"It's the only warm spot."

"Well leave it. It's time to eat. I've got a real treat for you."

"Another gas station?"

"No, but it's definitely one of the greatest restaurants in the world, and you barely have to walk."

I wiped the floor grit off my back and put on my rain jacket. "Is it a warm restaurant?"

"Just follow me."

My long-suffering feet responded poorly to the fresh onslaught of cold air. The hot shower and opportunity to dry out for the first time in days had done a great deal to alleviate the more superficial pains, but the deeper demons held strong. I panted as Jezebel led me across the street. Her *place* was the Hunker Down Buffet, a generic looking restaurant clinging to life in a dying and darkly shingled strip mall. After another clinic in unbridled overconsumption, we returned to the hotel where I informed Jezebel that my old, over-stuffed behind was taking a nap. Once in my room, I retired to the bed, belly brick intact, and turned on the television. When the nausea subsided, I called Claire and filled her in on the frozen time since Jackson, leaving out the bit about my collapse and unconscious intimacy with Jezebel. Once again, I considered the time and called Billy, getting his voicemail.

I took my time the next morning, permitting myself to get involved in a soap opera—a wayward daughter's return home is marred by a terrible secret. The clock's glowing green digits read half past ten when Jezebel knocked on my door—even I was getting hungry.

"The motel clerk said she would take us to the outfitter this afternoon."

"The little tike is abandoning his post?"

"No. It must be the tike's day off. *Her* name is Cassie. She's much nicer. But now we must eat breakfast."

Jezebel led the way to a small diner, ordering her standard, a healthy portion run through an exponential multiplier. I added an extra side of hashbrowns to a 'scrambler.'

"You're moving much better today."

"Behold the healing indoors."

"It's always important to tend to your wounds in town."

"As if you've had any. I don't think I've seen you so much as grimace."

"The Great Eastern Trail dealt me my share of beatings. It finds everyone's weaknesses and pushes. Though I'm proud to say I've held up."

"Are the Donners really that bad? Claire and I have stayed there at the lodge in the past. Seems like they're just more mountains."

"They can be. But the Great Eastern Trail goes out of its way to hit all the tallest peaks, Fulcrum Mountain, Mount Crawford, Mount Benjamin, not to mention Mount Herring—the highest point south of the Kingstons, it was hard in decent weather, steep climbs and descents; the Trail just never runs flat. If the weather is nice we can make good time, but the Donners tend to get a little stormy at winter's end."

Cassie overflowed out of the front seat of her mismatched coupe; one hock rested out the window. I took the back seat and Jezebel hopped in the front where the vinyl seat hid her from view. Cassie got to chattin'.

"Just don't know how y'all do it. All that walkin'. Don't y'all get tired?"

"I do. Mister Gabe though, he's a machine."

"This one time my man Randall and I decided we were gonna hike up Francine Falls. They say it's short but there's these stairs up and down so you can see the falls at different spots and Randy he took me all the way to the bottom so we could get the best view. And I swear it was 100 degrees and I was just sweatin' and cussin' and making him stop at every bench to sit. By the time we got back to the car I told him I woulda left his ass if we didn't have them kids. And another time . . . ."

Cassie dove into another story highlighting her distaste for outdoors, exercise, and Randall. After a brief highway stint, she pulled into the outfitter, a stand-alone structure made to look like a log cabin standing unaccompanied in the front corner of an otherwise modern strip mall. Cassie kept the heat running while Jezebel and I entered—the interior décor stayed true to the log cabin theme. Travis, a clean cut young man in a flannel shirt and red down vest, greeted us at the counter.

"Howdy! What can I do for y'all?"

"My friend here needs new hiking shoes. His current pair tore up his feet, then fell apart."

"It's always good when feet outlast their shoes," Travis shot me a smile.

I pondered the practicality of Travis's vest; it always struck me as odd the times at which people chose to wear vests. Today, for example, was much too cold outside for a vest to suffice and the store's interior was much too warm, almost stuffy, to necessitate layers.

"Alright buddy. What shoe size are you?"

It took me moment to register that this question could only be answered by me. "Eleven."

"Okay and what type of shoe are you looking for?"

"Well I have been hiking a lot." I recalled how brutal it had been for teenage Billy to be caught out in public with his father. Claire had long ago stopped shopping with me altogether. Travis returned with a box labeled *Prado PeakSeekers*.

"Alright my man, strap these on and give me a couple steps." I removed my camp shoes, unleashing an unholy hell, and hurried on the PeakSeekers. Jezebel stepped back. Travis stood firm. Once the PeakSeekers were on I looked at Travis and counted out two steps. Travis gave me a look.

"Up and down the aisle, my man."

"You want a little runway action?"

"If it suits you."

I took off down the aisle, swaying my hips between the freeze dried meals. "Well there's problem number one. Those things are flopping which means that you ain't no eleven. Let's try a ten and a half."

I turned back to Travis. "I've been wearing eleven for forty years."

"Shoe sizes differ brand to brand and style to style, my man. Just give these a shot."

"I know my size."

"Mister Gabe, I'd think he would know."

"No, I would know. I have elevens that are older than you."

"And how are your feet doing?"

Travis disappeared into the back.

A tall slender poster on a nearby pillar caught my eye. It showed the eastern seaboard in minimal detail. A blue line zigzagged at odd angles, cutting through vast tracts of wilderness, managing to miss each and every major city and point of interest, as if by design. Someone had marked a red dot low on the Great Eastern Trail and written *Hunker Down*.

"Hey Jezebel come look at this." She put down a pair of shoes and stepped over. I held my hand up to the poster. "All I've been through and I've only gained about three inches."

"If that."

"I mean look how much more I have to do."

"Look how much more you get to do. It'll be fun, for the most part. You'll get through it."

"Really felt like I've done more than that."

"Maybe you'll feel better if you lean in closer."

I bent at the hips. "Now the rest of it looks insurmountable. I can't even see the top."

"Then walk over and look at it from the far side of the room."

"Then I wouldn't be able to read it."

"How 'bout I walk you through it. Pull back the curtain. This big green area is the aforementioned Donner Range. After that it's Tyree—a town I missed coming south. Couple days after Tyree it's the Plains of Caroline. The Plains are long and flat; you'll like that. There's also an old homestead there. Some folk says it's haunted. There's some cool balds after that—"

"Balds?"

"They're like these giant mound things the size of mountains that don't have any trees on them. There's a parking lot and always a bunch of people there, but it's pretty epic nonetheless." She worked her finger up the map as explained. "Hatfield's fine, I guess. Kilgore has a movie theatre. Mountains. Mountains. More Mountains. Mountains. Oh, Qannaseh, that's like the unofficial halfway point. Mountains. Mounta—"

"Unofficial?"

"Well, yea. No one's actually measured it all out but you know. It's here." She thumbed it. "Which appears to be about midway."

"I feel like I should be writing this down."

"Mountains. Sacred Place, boo. Skip, skip, mountains, skip. Oh Tawnamac River and Campground is cool. You'll get to canoe across the river. Mountains . . . moving on . . . . Let's see, West Boelein, that's like a suburb of Pentland and the best spot to get a train into Billy town."

"Noted."

"Boelin. Copper Swamp. That's pretty neat, in a strange flat scary swampy way. Whitton, pretty dead. Bowleg Park, that's fine. From there you follow the Bowman River for a while. Oh, then Farragut which will be your last town, last night actually, before the Kingstons."

"Like Hunker Down for the Donners."

"Sure. Except the Kingstons are a whole 'nother level."

"That hard?"

"That hard and that gorgeous. Big granite mountains and shimmery lakes. They're like something out of a fantasy novel." She stepped back, squinting at the poster, as if disappointed. "Unless you get caught in a storm; then it can be a harrowing rescue story. Mt. Charles is the highlight: highest point on the east coast."

Travis, who had reappeared with a fresh box, looked on over my shoulder.

"The Kingstons take you down into Butonken, nothing to see there." She lifted on her tiptoes to reach the most northerly points. "After Butonken you're pretty much there. Just a morning stroll to the base of Daemon's. By that point you'll be a hiking machine. It shouldn't be a problem at all."

"Especially when you're cruising up it in your new size ten-and-a-half *Prado Peakseekers*."

On the way back to the motel Cassie provided an extended version of her and Randall's trip to the local water park during which she had contracted her current rash.

11

The next morning a translucent waxy crust coated my feet—two nights of sockless open-air sleeping had permitted the blisters to dry and harden. Jezebel and I met in the parking lot to tackle the necessities of breakfast and resupply. We needed to be both well-equipped and light; we would reach the Donner Range the following day.

On the way out of town, Jezebel stopped and pointed at a building. After a moment, I saw what had caught her eye: Pete's Dank Fried Chicken.

"I told you these places were everywhere. How's your supply?"

"Low. Unfortunately, it's too early for fried chicken."

"Okay, first of all, it is never too early for fried chicken. Second, just go in and snag some packets."

"You mean just walk in and take something without paying? That is my definition of stealing."

"Then your definition of stealing needs a clarifier on that something being for sale or not offered to the public. The store doesn't make you pay for the packets. They are complimentary. Therefore, it's not stealing."

"Complimentary with a completed purchase."

"Look at it this way—if they don't have a value on the item, and don't intend for you to pay for them, then they can't call it stealing. It's the same as going in there and using the bathroom or enjoying the air conditioning."

"We are pretty far apart on this."

"Come on, you want to be eating plain white rice through the Donners?"

"Fair point." I set down my pack, formulating my plan: it was to be a tactical strike. I would stroll in unnoticed, discretely slip the packets in my pockets, and be back in the woods before the clerk knew what'd hit him—no one would know I was there. I pulled my knit cap down low and did what I could with my collar.

The door jingled. "Hi! Welcome to Stop'n'Go. How are you doing today?"

I gave the clerk a bewildered nod.

It was a similar set up to the last Pete's, faded aisles and the sign in back, but I still required a full loop to locate the packets —inexplicably by the drink machines. I scooped up as many as my two hands could hold and walked towards the door.

"Have a nice day."

I exited to an empty parking lot. Jezebel waved at me from two blocks down.

"What're you doing all the way down here?" I said when I reached her.

"They got super mad at me last time."

"Last time?!"

"I'm too recognizable." She tugged on her red hair. "That's why it had to be you. No offense but you're very forgettable."

Cars passed by in surprising numbers as we walked down the road. It dawned on me that it was 10:45 in the morning and these people were going about their daily routines; life went on for the rest of the world as Jezebel and I wandered through the woods.

Once more we trekked upwards out of civilization's cradle. It hadn't been warm while we were in Hunker Down, but sunny and comfortably above freezing. Two nice days had dried the ground allowing us to tread on firm dirt as the good Lord intended. My legs felt springy and strong. I galloped up the incline in great buoyant steps, keeping up with Jezebel for quite some time.

That night we camped at Tugaloo Creek; I had learned to let Jezebel make the decisions on where we should camp and how far we should hike in a day—I had also forgotten to print out new print-outs and didn't have much information to offer. In any event, it seemed entirely plausible that I could simply follow her up the Trail. We set up our tents on the banks and, with no logbook, turned in early.

We entered the Donner Range with momentum, breezing by the sign marking the entrance to Donner National Park, and firing up the extended southern slope of Fulcrum Mountain, climbing all morning and into mid-afternoon, until we sat on Fulcrum's peak, watching the sun drift west across the sky. I studied the crests of Fulcrum Mountain's northern associates, and the deep gaps between them.

A light snow fell as we set up camp in Fulcrum Shelter. Jezebel collected sticks and debris for a fire—we huddled near. The snow was invisible in the darkness, only coming into view when it ventured into the fire light; the bigger flakes disappeared with a sizzle. The snow smothered the fire before we finished eating.

"You think it will stay cold? You know, keep the snow frozen."

"I would think so. Why?"

"I mean I'll take snow over slush. Don't you think?"

"I think each element presents its own set of problems."

MONGREL COME, MONGREL GO
WELCOME TO, MY FIASCO

By morning the snow blanketed the mountainside, smoothing out the nooks and crannies, bringing everything into white uniformity. I used a gloved finger to wipe a miniature snow wall which had accumulated on a low-hanging branch. It rarely snowed in Bodette; I relished the soft crunch of the powder compacting under my new shoes. The mountains were subdued, quiet, and beautiful.

The Great Eastern Trail bottomed out then began climbing up Mount Crawford. After a long hike, we found the peak shrouded in clouds.

"Such a shame. This was such a pretty spot the last time I was here."

"Would've been nice to see the world wrapped in white."

"I think we'll still get our chance Mister Gabe. This snow's not going anywhere."

"How ominous. At least this means we're close to the shelter. My feet are freezing. The *Peakseekers* let the melting snow seep through. At least the boots were impermeable to water."

"Until they fell apart."

The snow started anew as we moved down the mountain.

Cow Hide was the smallest shelter yet, perhaps only intended to sleep six sleeping bagged hikers, or alternatively, two slightly overlapping tents. If it had been constructed facing any other direction, the interior would have been filled before our arrival. As it was, it took only a few swift foot swipes to clear the floor.

The snow fall increased as we set up camp; the temperature fell with it. We set our stoves up just outside our tents, poking our arms through slightly unzipped flaps to perform the necessary cooking motions. I listened to Jezebel perform her nightly readings through the wall.

MONGREL COME, MONGREL GO
WET THE BOAT, LEARN TO ROW

12

By morning the snow had piled almost level with the shelter floor; a frozen crust had formed which required significant rigor to crack. Jezebel and I decided to stick together, me walking in lead. I used a *Juicerrman* to chip away at the ice sheet, working from orange blaze to orange blaze, resting a gloved hand against each one as I scanned the whiteness for the next, connecting the dots through the falling snow. When there were no blazes, I stuck to the narrow clearing between the trees in hopes it remained the Great Eastern Trail. Bloated snowflakes collected on my hat, sleeves, pant legs, even the tops of my shoes, stinging my face, and melting through my clothes to stifle my body heat; the Great Eastern Trail used my own machinations against me. The temperature drop had not been quite as drastic at lower altitudes; even though the snow was deeper, it had a less rigid crust through which I could simply plow using only my forward momentum. I ate the *Juicerrman* and started Mount Benjamin.

Mount Benjamin's peak was not a friendly one. The wind seared through the trees which I noticed were no longer grey pines but hardwoods, cedars and elms, in shades of golden brown and red. I degloved and ran my hand over the nearest one, admiring the hardy southern pioneers. Jezebel shuffled off to the side off the Trail:

"Mister Gabe, try this!" She jumped into the wind with arms outstretched, letting it blow her back on path.

"I'm old. I don't jump anymore."

"Come on just pretend you're young."

"It will shatter my legs."

"Give it a try. You're made of sturdier stuff than you think."

I gave an elderly hop, just enough for the wind to tossle me a few inches. When I survived, I hopped again, this time accelerating off bended knees, clearing an eastern yard. Jezebel smiled. "Great now watch this!" She turned into the wind, a plane preparing for take-off, took two hard steps then launched herself, moving forward until the wind caught her and roughly returned her to her launch point. "Can't do that in good weather."

We made camp in Sally's Shelter only a couple hundred yards from Mount Crawford's peak.

"Next is Mount Herring." Jezebel's voice drifted through the tent wall. "The Wizard. It was my favorite mountain last time, the peak was the best view I've had since way up north. You get up above tree line and its one big panoramic view. You can spin circles and all you see is mountains and trees. It must be even more gorgeous with all this snow."

MONGREL COME, MONGREL GO
LET ME STRIKE MY THINKING POSE

The tent in which I awoke was much smaller than the one in which I'd gone to sleep. I worked an arm free and tapped the fabric near my forehead—it held firm. I pressed against the tent flap until the barrier gave with a crack, then shimmied out to have a look. The winds had shifted, ushering the falling snow into the shelter and covering our tents in significant powder, converting them into prefab igloos. Jezebel's tent was a smooth mound next to mine. Prior to my sophomoric fumbling, we must have been the fairest set of bosoms in all the land.

It was just a white varnish now, maybe two inches, but the snow kept coming. I watched as the cap of a water bottle was drowned out from the world.

"Jezebel . . . Jezebel!" I had to yell to be heard over the wind. "Jezebel! Get up. It's important."

"It's still dark, let me sleep."

"It's not dark; it's snow. Lots of it. It's still coming."

Jezebel rustled in her tent for a second before her capped head popped out. "Oh shit."

"Exactly. Do you think we should stay put? Hunker Down as they say."

"No, unless the winds change again this shelter's done for. We need to move."

"Turn back and head to Hunker Down?"

"Back over the peak? No, Mister Gabe, we move north. If we can make the next shelter we should be okay."

"That doesn't seem ideal."

"If we had a choice sure; if we stay here they're going to pull us out looking like freezer burned meat."

"What if we get stuck out on the mountainside?"

"Well that would be a terrible tragedy."

We walked close, cracking through the ice sheet, and maneuvering around the higher drifts. We lived blaze to blaze, zigzagging down the mountain, expending great effort to achieve indiscernible gains. The Great Eastern Trail straightened and steepened, necessitating shorter steps and a backwards lean. Even then we fell frequently; we took turns swiping the snow off each other. The swirling flurries hid the trees around us, rendering the world small. Movement meant warmth; I wondered how long it would take to die if I stopped.

The avalanche started below me, a great wet crescendoing swoosh—Jezebel disappeared into the abyss. It was still rumbling when I called her name.

"Jezebel . . . Jezebel?"

I scrambled down the Trail, whipping my head left and right.

"Jezebel?!"

"Mister Gabe!" The voice sounded distant.

"JEZEBEL?!"

"I'm right here dummie." I turned to see a freckled face smiling at me; everything below her neck, even her pack, was drowned by the snow. She was just a head protruding from the whiteness.

"What the heck happened?"

"I couldn't tell you. I was just walking, minding my own, then all of a sudden the world ended. You think you could get me out?"

"Are you okay?"

"I think so. But it is starting to melt into my clothes. So please get me out."

Jezebel wriggled her arms above sea level. I grabbed her sleeves and leveraged my weight to pull her free, falling back on the snow in the process. She flopped down on her stomach next to me. I noticed a great red splotch on her face, a white bullseye marked where she had collided with something during the fall. I could see where snow had infiltrated her layers. When we pressed on, it was at a much quicker pace.

Spuchaymun Shelter sat about a quarter up Mount Herring; we reached it well after sunset. Cold and miserable, we set up our tents, cooked our food, and went to bed. I zipped up my sleeping bag to the crash of distant lightning and approaching thunder, keeping watch of the tent walls to make sure they didn't sink or darken.

13

My tent maintained its volume through the night although the storm continued to batter the roof. In the morning, I exited to find the shelter now possessed a fourth wall, a white wall, thicker and more sloped that its brothers, bricked and mortared by a night's worth of windy accumulation. Except for the dull, grey light slipping in between the snow and roof, all was darkness. I approached the wall and peeked through the slot—the wind bent the trees at their bases, whistling through the branches and whipping debris across the clearing. It was a bunker's view of a battlefield.

Jezebel popped her head from her tent. "Is it time to go?"

"You know I really don't think it is. Come have a look." Jezebel went to her tiptoes against the wall and came down.

"We shouldn't be out here."

She retrieved her stove and went about preparing her breakfast.

"What are we going to do?"

"We're going to wait it out. I'm going to make some hot tea."

"Wait it out? In here? It's freezing. I can actually feel it getting colder."

"I know. That's why I'm making tea."

"We can't make a run for it? Try and get somewhere?"

"Which gigantic mountain would you like to climb? We are at the mercy of the Great Eastern Trail."

I returned to my tent, listening to the wind scream as I read from the shelter log. Apparently Mount Herring was a cunning and fiery wizard—we were not the first to be ensnared by its tricks.

"Stormed in alone. But at least it's free and I'm here with my favorite person" – Ironfoot

"Long day in the shelter. The rain won't stop falling. The wind won't stop blowing. The tree's won't stop breaking." – Onward

"Stuck." – Belly Dancer

"No birds today." – Talon

It did not appear to bother Mongrel.

MONGREL COME, MONGREL GO
TROUBLES COME, DO NOT SLOW

After a few minutes Jezebel unzipped a sliver of my flap and pushed through a mug of tea. "Stay warm, Mister Gabe. This is going to suck." I listened as she zipped herself into her tent and nestled into her sleeping bag.

"This is not how I envisioned my time on the Great Eastern Trail."

"Snowed in on a mountain with a shockingly gorgeous young woman?"

"Especially that last part."

"What did you picture?"

"Didn't honestly think I'd make it this far. Beyond that, I thought it would be men swapping tales around campfires, you know, drinking whiskey and smoking cigars."

"Did you think the Great Eastern Trail was going to take you through the wild west?"

"It does seem misguided."

"Do you even drink whiskey? Or smoke cigars?"

"I used to smoke cigars."

"Why used to?"

"I lost my source when Billy moved out. I would steal the cigars he thought were hidden under his mattress."

"Is that so?"

"Oh yea. I honestly don't know where, or when, he bought them. They certainly weren't offered in Bodette, or any of the neighboring towns. Every cigar I've ever purchased was just awful. But his were wonderful. I stole his whiskey too."

"You stole booze from your son?"

"He kept it in a velvet pouch under the closet floorboards. One time he actually caught me lifting them. Claire wanted an old fashioned and he caught me, bottle in hand."

"What'd you do?"

"I covered. Acted like I happened across it and was angry with him for keeping it in the house. Told him how stupid and disrespectful he was to conceal contraband in the home we provided for him."

"Did you make him pour it out?"

"Nope, sent him away for two weekends with his grandparents."

"So you and Missus Gabe could drink it undisturbed."

"So me and Missus Gabe could drink it undisturbed."

"Unbelievable. You know my dad caught me drinking one time."

"Reckon it's a rite of passage."

"Not this. This was mostly sad. It was just me and one friend, Tiffany Desoto, we were maybe sixteen and had gotten a hold of a bottle of bourbon, *Yeoman's Pride*. We didn't go anywhere, we didn't even do anything. We just sat on either side of the ottoman passing it back and forth. My dad came down about halfway through, smelled it, and found the bottle under the couch."

"Did he let you have it?"

"Nope. He made us sit there while he checked every closet in the house, under every bed, every nook and cranny . . . looking for the boys that had been there with us."

"You're kidding."

"He even called the neighbors to ask if they'd seen any suspicious cars hightailing it out of the neighborhood. Because daddy didn't think that two young girls could put that much of a hurtin' on a bottle of *Yeoman's Pride*."

"Not the last time a man underestimated you."

"I will say that Daddy thought he hid that bottle. But I after he went to bed, I found it, and drank every last drop."

"Stubborn has a new name."

"When I set my mind to something. All it cost me was a trip to the hospital and every remaining weekend of my junior year."

It was almost afternoon when the pitter patter of rain softened and disappeared. Jezebel leapt into action.

"This is our chance. If we move fast we should be okay."

"Move fast to where? Like you said *mountains on either side*. And it's still very dark."

"It's fine, the wind is gone which means the storm's clearing up. I mean, why else would it be getting quiet?"

"Because it's pulling back for the knockout punch."

Jezebel kept packing. "You can stay here but I'm making a break for it. I've had about enough of Spuhchaymon Shelter."

"I thought we were having a nice moment." I started packing too; I was not staying up there alone. When our packs were settled, we began scooping down the wall.

I heard the rumble first. "Jezebel wait."

"What now Mi—"

"Listen!" I put my hand on her shoulder.

The rumble grew into impending destruction—not one sound but innumerable sharp, soulless collisions. Through the widened slot we watched a barrage of chicken nugget size ice balls batter the picnic table. We did what we could to rebuild our barrier, reconstructed our tents, and settled back in.

The cold accompanied me into my sleeping bag; I had unpacked any warmth my tent may have offered. My legs constricted up through my sleeping bag; my hands yanked down to meet them. I lay on my side, fetal against the world, watching the light dim through my tent walls.

I removed the family photograph from pack and leaned it against the tent wall so I could examine it without exposing my hands to the cold. I remembered the day it was taken, how proud Claire and I had been of our boy. I remembered telling Billy it was important to go out and see the world, if only to confirm that Bodette was the best place in it.

"Jezebel."

"Yea."

"I've been thinking about what food I want when we get to town."

"What's that?"

"Steak."

"That's a sta—"

"Not one of those pack of cards regular steaks, one of the big bone-in ones that hangs off the plate."

"How thick?"

"Inch, two inches, whatever restaurant thick is. As thick as they'll cut it. Cooked just past rare."

"Sides?"

"Mashed potatoes. The really fancy kind with the little green flakes, and that special melted butter, and gravy, definitely gravy. I want the steak to be so big, and the mashed potatoes so plentiful, that they each get their own dish. I want them to take up so much room that no one can sit next to me at the table, only across."

"Beverage?"

"You know, I'm not normally one for wine. But I'm picturing a place Billy took us in Dullamore Canyon. You know that place out west? It was our last trip as a family, Billy's third year of law school. Billy insisted that we go to this one steakhouse, by far the most expensive restaurant I've ever been too. And we, well Billy, ordered us these special steaks with a name I couldn't pronounce. But Billy knew. He always knew that kind of crap. I gave him hell for it. Especially when he took his time ordering the wine, *pairing the wine*, he kept saying. I never admitted it, but the whole experience really was amazing. I couldn't finish my steak then which obviously felt like a shame. But I'd like to think I could now."

"Why was this your last family trip?"

"Billy finally admitted he wasn't coming back to Bodette, had already taken a job in Pentland, and there was some . . . unpleasantness. We exchanged words—something along the lines of him being an ungrateful, snot-nosed social climber, and me being a lethargic nobody who had wasted his life ferrying messages."

"Was this at dinner?"

"Just after. We behaved at dinner. But he'd kind of dominated the trip and, when he told us that, I just sort of cracked. It was just a very sudden and overt way to realize my son had surpassed me."

"Sounds like a fun trip."

Something heavy crashed against the shelter walls.

"Mister Gabe, why are you out here? The more I learn about you the more this seems . . . out of character."

"I don't rightly know."

"There must be a reason."

"Not any good ones."

"Tell me a bad one."

"Well, Claire, my wife, owns a hardware store and runs commercials on the local station. One night she got the itch to go back through our old cassettes and rewatch one in which eight year-old Billy was digging in the backyard with a red shovel. I forget the premise but that part was admittedly cute."

"Adorable actually."

"So we were perusing through the cassettes and, naturally, she got distracted and I ended up watching this old news clip of a young couple about to embark on the Great Eastern Trail. *Journey of a lifetime,* the news anchor called it. And they ran a couple screens with a whole bunch of facts about the Great Eastern Trail—its length, the number of mountains, how long it takes to hike, and what not. I thought it looked fun. Even went so far as to comment *I think I could hike that Trail.* At which point Claire laughed. I asked what she was laughing about. She said the thought of me hiking, camping, embarking on an adventure. I told her well maybe I just would hike that there Trail." I paused to tuck my hands deeper into my groin. "Ordinarily this would have been the end of it, except our dear Billy called at that precise moment and Claire just had to tell him how his father was bound and determined to hike the Great Eastern Trail. Billy told his friend Len who still lived in Bodette. Len told his dad. His dad told his bullhorn of a wife. And soon the Bodette Rec Center sign boasted that Bodette's very own Gabe Jenkins was embarking on a grand journey up the eastern seaboard."

"So that's it?"

"Our church put my name in the bulletin. Asked parishioners to pray for me on my pilgrimage."

"You never even made the actual decision to hike the Trail? You just let yourself be pressed into it?"

"Never been one to stir the pot."

"Damn your consistency, Mister Gabe."

"It's good that you're out here, doing this now. Taking life by the horns. Because there's some truth to what you said about life being a conveyor belt. Within three years of graduating college I was married with a child on the way. What was once a fun and steady government job became necessary income and insurance. For maybe three decades there I was just a squirrel, hoarding acorns and tending my nest. There was always something to be patched up before the next day could happen. My path was set for me before I'd even taken an informed step."

I ran my thumb across the picture then returned it to its pocket. "And I know it's particularly hard for you to picture this, but retirement is a whopper. You spend so long climbing life mountain, raising a family, building a career or whatever, then all of a sudden you're at the top, and the next thing on the horizon is the end. Even if you somehow manage to wrap your head around that, you still end up turning around and seeing all the paths you could have taken, all the other places you could have ended up."

"Based on that picture it seems like you chose a pretty beautiful path."

"I suppose I shouldn't complain. It's just that I never really developed a skill. I just wish I had taken a moment when I was young to consider where I wanted to go, put my foot in the ground, and mustered a charge at greatness."

14

A glorious and well-defined beam sliced the morning gloom, evincing a hard wince after thirty plus hours of darkness. I watched particles drift in and out of its path, briefly dancing in the illumination before drifting back into obscurity. The storm had subsided— I could almost hear the trumpets harkening a new day.

Snow still blanketed the ground in rolling drifts but the air carried hints of warmth. The sky glowed an energetic blue. I was stiff, but well-rested, hungry, but carrying little, and in a few minutes we were at full gallop, bounding upwards to Mount Herring's peak. I emitted my usual huffing, puffing, grunting and groaning while Jezebel glided along with her usual lackadaisical resolve.

The peak of Mount Herring stood alone, well above tree line, gazing down upon its Donner brethren. The peak showed the world to be a very big place; but we had no equal. I sat down on a rock to catch my breath.

"So this is what it's all about, almost a week of drudgery for one pretty view."

"Would you rather no view? Because the drudgery is guaranteed. Anyways, it's not just one view, it's a million."

"If you say so." I shaped my hands into a lop-sided box.

"What're you doing?"

"Just checking what this would've looked like from my mail truck."

"Did your route ever take you past views like this?"

"Well, no. But the new high school is a sight to behold."

She pulled down my arms. "Your dum-dum mail truck is blocking the view. You've earned the right to be up here. Don't spoil it with something stupid." Jezebel started twirling in long, graceful circles. "Every way you turn, that's all part of it. Try it."

"You're asking me to twirl?"

"The world gets to turn, why can't we?"

I pivoted, more soldier that ballerina—to the South, Benjamin, Crawford and Fulcrum, submitted beneath us, cloaked in white, kneeling at the feet of their conquerors. I had seen their worst and I had conquered. To the West the mountains rolled out into the distance, the near ones white with snow, the far ones a familiar distant blue. A different realm lay to the North. The low-lying landscape was not quite springtime green, but close, a barrel of static energy waiting to explode.

I had envisioned the hike down Mount Herring's northern slope being steep and wet. I found it pleasant and bone dry, as if the storms of the last few days had been completely contained to the interior Donners. The *PeakSeakers* squished out their remaining water. I removed my cap to permit the soft breezes and warm sunshine to soothe my tormented scalp.

Maybe out of habit, or maybe just in case, we set up our tents inside Butch Shelter. I watched as Jezebel constructed a fire in the ring, setting sticks one on top of another in a series of vertical squares until it resembled a roofless log cabin. When that was adequately sized, she set tinder inside and set it ablaze. The tinder put up a small fragile flame that peeked through the cracks, strengthening its hold on existence until it engulfed the walls in clean sheets of flame. When the flames were almost as tall as her, Jezebel sat down and started her own dinner.

"You're not gonna keep feeding it?"

"I started it, I nurtured it. Now it's on its own."

The flames kept me and my Dank rice warm through dinner. Jezebel brought out the shelter log.

"Oh wow a double feature!" Jezebel displayed a brown slip in each hand. "Looks like Mongrel's posted again after turning around."

"Everything's comin' up Gabe."

> MONGREL COME, MONGREL GO
> NIGHTINGALES SING ROOSTERS CROW

And for an encore:

> MONGREL COME, MONGREL GO
> RICH STAY RICH, PO' STAY PO'

"A touch more political than his regular postings."

"I guess everyone starts thinking their opinions are worth something."

When my pot was empty, I took it upon myself to collect more wood. Jezebel watched as I tried to match her delicate placement.

"Do you think ol' Mongrel gets lonely?"

"Reckon so. Unless he's found a cure."

"A cure for loneliness? Mister Gabe that's too much wood, and too close. You're smothering it."

The fire shrank to red embers.

"It'll catch . . . hopefully." Bits of fire snarled through gaps in the wood. "Anyways, it sounds like Mongrel needs a father."

"Well Mister Gabe, you held me in check longer than most; you just might be the man to crack him."

"Mongrel come, Mongrel Go, Meet Ol' Gabe, Then Go Home."

Jezebel stood up and adjusted the fire, blowing on the embers until it roared to its pre-Gabe glory. I lounged across the picnic table bench, propping my feet on my food bag.

"You see, Jezebel, this is more what I had in mind when I came out here. This is pretty dern nice."

"Seems like you need to stop expecting stuff Mister Gabe. You're pretty terrible at it."

We stayed up late, cooking the rest of our food and trading stories. Tomorrow was a town day, and a short hike at that. I was just getting to sleep when Jezebel's voice came through the fabric.

"I want to thank you Mister Gabe. These last few weeks have been the most fun of my hike. I'd never hiked with someone more than a couple nights. It was nice to have steady company."

"I've enjoyed it too. I always wondered what it would be like to have a child that wasn't ashamed of me."

"That's sweet, I guess, but mostly sad. Also, I think I was the adult in this relationship."

"You're probably right. Thanks for raising me."

15

The next day's story was the fall of Mount Herring, the Donners' last and greatest warrior—the Great Eastern Trail rode the mountain's northern slope down to something approaching sea level, putting an end to the great bloodline.

Jezebel stood by the road for almost an hour without a car passing. At last she sat down next to me on the embankment and joined in stretching her legs. It was late morning and the sun put out a soft light. The unburdened air flowed with the breeze, caressed my face. I could see mountains continuing uninterrupted into the horizon through the notch carved by the road.

I awoke to a quick series of accelerating taps on the tree above me. Opening my eyes, I located the source about halfway the trunk where a small black body supported a red blur. It was the only sound in the valley and the first non-Jezebel sign of life I had observed on the Trail since Franklin's Spring. The woodpecker gave a probing burst before flitting to another spot a couple feet higher. I lay still, watching it hop up, down and around the tree, out and back on branches, speed tapping in search of grub, before flying away just as the rumble of rolling gravel and screeching brakes snapped me out of my trance. A car whipped around the corner and through the gap, passing by without noticing us.

Jezebel leapt from sleep to feet in a manner old men can only dream of. "Alright we are in business."

"That guy isn't picking us up."

"Yes but, Trail secret, cars almost always travel in packs."

Within five minutes I was seated in an SUV driven by a small man who seemed less perturbed by my presence.

"Y'all planning on staying at the motel?"

"If they'll have us. I hear there's not too many places in Tyree that will."

"Craig will take you if you'll pay."

"We'll pay. Have you seen any other hikers? We haven't."

"There ain't many but y'all ain't alone. I work on the other side of the mountain so I come through often. Give hikers a ride when I see 'em. Just dropped off some young fellas this morning. Wild bunch, looked like they'd been in the woods a bit too long."

After fifteen winding minutes the mountain road straightened out into the starched grids of Tyree. Tyree was larger and cleaner than the other Trail towns but at some cost. We drove through block after block of stately two-story homes with nice green lawns sealed off by picket fences displaying the diversity of white. Families, dressed and arranged as if posing for catalogues, lined the lawns and sidewalks, grilling, socializing, and exercising their well-groomed dogs.

"What's the industry here?"

"Ain't none. Tyree's a mistress town. All these fat cats live and earn their money elsewhere then come spend it here. It's slammed most holidays and weekends, but it's a ghost town during business hours."

I leaned over and whispered to Jezebel, "seems very unTrail." But she remained staring out the window.

Several minutes into Tyree the driver pulled off the road and down into a parking lot tucked in a gully behind, and under, a shopping center, stopping in front of a dingy row of white doors. The building's roof reached the level of the grocery's dumpsters. There were no other cars in the lot. I wondered what percentage of its business this fellow drove in. We thanked the driver, booked our rooms, and separated for our obligatory showers, naps, and phone calls.

Jezebel had skipped this town going south so, when we ventured out for dinner, we did so without a plan. Ornate brass lamps dotted the streets, embering to life to cast each corner in a romantic glow. We walked through Main Street's two parallel strips of brick buildings, each store front professionally refurbished in approximation of quaint and wholesome. Parents ushered their kids to the other side of the street at the sight of us. Young couples pressed themselves against the bricks as if our poorly clad condition was contagious. We passed a steak house with a vested maître d, a barbecue restaurant with a piano player, and a *Modern Cuisine Joint* whose cheapest entree was more than our room. Jezebel barely said a word.

On the far side, when the shops and restaurants starting dissipating, we came across *The Pickled Onion* which displayed no overt signs that they wouldn't at least take us in and feed us at a reasonable price. Not wanting to walk any further, I stepped in without asking Jezebel.

A stern young man, blonde and rail thin, intercepted us at the host stand, taking a moment to inspect our clothes.

"May I help you?"

"Table for two please."

"You're hoping to eat here?"

"Quite a bit actually." He looked around, I presumed for an adult; finding none, the young man sighed and marked the paper in front of him.

"Okay, right this way." He led us through the restaurant to a table in a deep corner tucked behind a decorative armoire. "Your server will be with you shortly." He turned and left. The light from the overheads only just reached us. Even the music was quieter. A small bouquet and a pair of upturned glasses rested on the white tablecloth. I flipped both glasses and ran my hand across the tablecloth, tugging at the corner.

"Been a long time since I ate somewhere like this. Even longer since I've done it with someone that wasn't Claire." Jezebel didn't respond; her fingers twisted at the loose ends of the tablecloth as she stared at the base of the bouquet. Our waitress approached, clad in all black with long brown hair except for the left side, which she had shaven almost clean.

"Good evening. My name is Sara and I'll be your server tonight. Can I get you some drinks to start?"

"Just water for now. We may need a second. It's probably going to be a long order."

"Okay great. I'll come back with some bread." She stepped away, paused, and stepped back. "Are y'all hiking the Great Eastern Trail?"

I smiled and nodded.

"Oh my God that's great! We never get hikers in here."

"We haven't exactly been embraced."

"I know it's stupid right? Like, the Great Eastern Trail is right there. The snobs in city council think y'all look homeless and frighten the constituency. But I've always thought y'all would add some charm to this stuffy town. Let me get y'all something to drink. We have great wine."

"I'm sure you do but it might be wasted on us. We might save our money for food."

"Okay," she leaned in close, "well a bunch of these ass-holes don't finish their bottles. I think it's a power move to show they don't care about wasting money. I usually pour them out in the alley," she winked, "but tonight I'll bring them to you. I've been saving a third of a bottle of our house cab sauv that is truly divine."

"That will be lovely. Thank you."

She straightened up. "And I'll bring out some of our signature homemade bread as well."

"Did you hear that? Free wine! And free bread."

"I heard."

"Since when do you not get excited about food? I know it's not a gas station but you may yet like it." Jezebel pulled her head up and looked at me, tears filled her eyes. "My God, Jezebel. What's wrong?"

"Mister Gabe . . ."

"Yes."

"You know how you're leaving Tyree tomorrow on foot and hiking north."

"I'm aware."

"I won't be."

The words stuck in the air, silencing the room.

"What . . . what do you mean?"

"I mean I've finished. I'm done."

Sara returned with our wine and bread. "Here y'all go." She poured out two glasses. "I'll let you know what else turns up." I thanked Sara and returned to Jezebel who fiddled with her napkin in her lap, doing a marvelous job pretending she wasn't weeping.

"Are, are you not having fun anymore? We just went through so much. I mean, are you sure?"

"I'm sure. Hiking with you has been the most fulfilling time I've had on Trail but, but that's part of the reason."

"So that's it? What about the rest of your hike? You're just quitting."

"It's not quitting." She caught my eye. "There is no rest of my hike. You remember, in that outfitter, all those parts of the Trail I skipped over?"

"I recall."

"Those are days and weeks of my life I don't want or need to do again."

"But you'd be with me this time. It'll be different."

"That's the bigger problem, Mister Gabe. The Great Eastern Trail is supposed to be about self-assessment, and breaking habits. I'm, I'm where I need to be but if I stay on, you're just going to keep following me, do as I do. It'll defeat your purpose. There are things out here you need to encounter on your own."

Tears continued streaking down her cheeks. I checked around the restaurant to make sure no one noticed the old man sitting with the weeping young woman, now grateful for the dim corner.

What would life be like hiking without Jezebel?

"I do feel like I'm abandoning you, but this, this has to happen. Are you mad at me?"

"Of course not," I paused trying to think of something that wasn't a mindless platitude. "If it's time it's time. I'm a grown man. I made it before you and I reckon I can make it now too."

"You were an old man eating rice alone in the woods. You were an old man who tried to quit because it got cold and he saw a squirrel. I wouldn't call that making it."

"I'm still here aren't I? I'll be fine. Slower, but fine."

The tears stopped and I raised my glass. "To a completed hike." Jezebel tapped her glass against mine; we both took a long sip.

"Is this good wine?"

"It's the right color."

Sara came back for our orders and offered a quarter bottle of *'exquisite'* pinot grigio and a single glass of *'admittedly mediocre'* merlot.

"Both please," Jezebel responded. I hoped the dim lighting hid the redness in her eyes. Sara departed as Jezebel lumped butter onto a piece of the bread and took a bite. Her eyes widened and she covered her mouth.

"Oh Mister Gabe this is spectacular. This is like the best bread I've ever had." I remembered my own hunger and buttered up a piece of my own. We devoured the rest and sent Sara back for more when she brought our new wines. Two baskets later Sara presented the first course: thin cuts of delicious meats, cheeses, and crackers, plated with ill-advised aesthetic care; any precision or concern that had been put into the food was wasted on us, like paint on firewood. The courses kept coming, culminating in two heaping piles of pasta. For the first time I kept up with Jezebel; we were both still hungry after the entrees. The restaurant was almost empty when Sara came out with two bubbling tins of chocolate.

"Okay guys I've got something extra special for you now." She pulled a bottle of champagne, still corked, from behind her back. "But this one will cost you. I want stories." We nodded and she moved a chair and a glass from another table, providing everyone with a generous pour.

"What kind of stories?"

"I don't know. Tell me what it's like to hike the Great Eastern Trail?"

"Cold. Almost exclusively. But Jezebel here would know better. She's actually hiked the whole thing going south."

Sara turned to Jezebel. "Wow the whole thing? And as a girl too. Did you do it alone?"

"For the most part. Hiking through the winter sort of guarantees not too many folk will be out there. I'd definitely been alone for a long time before I met Mister Gabe."

"You might be the first girl ever to meet a man in the woods and come out with a happy story."

"Ol' Gabe's about as harmless as they come."

"What about you Gabe? Any good stories?"

"I," I burped on my wine, "saw a squirrel."

"Yea and he tried to turn around and quit."

"It was a very mean squirrel."

"Oh wow. What're you gonna do when the rabbits come out?" Jezebel spewed champagne back into her glass.

I washed down chocolate with champagne, then followed that with more chocolate.

"So squirrels aside, what is it like?"

Jezebel set down her glass. "It is an indescribably big experience. So many cool places, so many cool people, and every day you get to wake up in the middle of the woods and hike to a new place. Every day you have this great feeling of independence and freedom."

"Then why are you stopping right in the middle?" I felt the chocolate dribble down my chin when I opened my mouth.

"So you can have that experience. Also, there's a difference between quitting and finishing. You have to feel when you're done. I could go back out tomorrow and start walking but that doesn't mean I would be going anywhere."

"How am I supposed to know when I'm done?"

"Do like I did: hike until you're sure." Jezebel leaned across the table with a napkin and wiped my chin. "It's time to fly on your own little birdie. I'm not helping you if I give you every answer."

We regaled Sara with stories until the last of the champagne. She listened, smiling, nodding, cringing, and laughing as we went along. It felt good to have someone else take interest in our trials, and I could tell that Jezebel enjoyed it. Around midnight Sara gave in.

"Ok Gabe—Mister Gabe, Jezebel. It's been fun but it's time for me to get home. I appreciate y'all filling me in on the grand trials of the Great Eastern Trail."

Sara asked if we needed a ride and we agreed; I watched through the rear window as the empty streets passed by. "The Tyreeians turn in early."

"I think they prefer Ty-rex's."

"I thought it was Ty-rannosaurs."

"Ty-recians."

"Ty-rants."

"Nailed it."

The wine and food settled in my belly in sleepy ecstasy. Upon return to the motel, I laid down on the bed and fell asleep with my shoes on.

The wine woke me in the night. The many-colored combination precipitating a groggy and distant sensation; I had to consider my thoughts before I could think them. Nature was calling; I crept to the bathroom, gripping the coarse carpet with my toes. Once back in bed, a reproachful headache kept sleep away; I lay awake, sweating out the wine and staring at the popcorn ceiling, listening to the rattle of the radiator. The next day I would leave Tyree and return to the wilderness alone. I would hike alone. At night, I would simply arrive at a destination, eat, and go to sleep.

It seemed unbearably lonely.

16

In her seemingly infinite kindness, Sara had offered to drive Jezebel to the bus station a town over where my companion could catch a bus to a larger city, re-crossing the Great Eastern Trail somewhere near Qannaseh, and then ride a northbound train to Lawson. Jezebel was hoping to surprise her family if not that evening then early the next morning.

After breakfast, Jezebel and I stopped by the post office for *Juicerrmen*, before returning to the motel so the clerk could drive me back to Trail. I assembled my pack, checking and rechecking the floor, bathroom, and underneath the bed, lest I lose something else in Tyree. When I was certain that all my belongings were safely in my pack, I made my calls.

I found Jezebel sniffling anew in the parking lot.

"Thank you, Mister Gabe," she wrapped her arms around me. I patted her back, wondering what I possibly could have done for her.

"Thank you, Jezebel. I'd be dead without you, or worse, off-Trail."

She pulled back. "Sorry to leave you a lonely old man again."

"It's not so bad. You've taught me to put things in the rice. I'll write when I get the chance. Let you know that I'm doing okay, and still on."

"Good. Just don't quit Mister Gabe. This is very important."

"Of course not."

I loaded into the van. Jezebel slid the door shut and stepped back, waving as the van drove out of the gulley and onto the street. The clerk dropped me off at the parking lot, leaving me to climb out of yet another gap.

Birds flitted from tree to tree with quick, fretful squawks, sending their shadows flickering across the Trail. Squirrels chittered in mass, crawling up, down, and around the trees in pursuit of nothing, pausing to haunch up and set their beady eyes on me. Brilliant orange newts, maybe skinks or geckos, only a toothpick in length, decorated the Trail, flattening themselves against the Trail as I tip-toed around them.

The day moved slowly. Jezebel had replaced the mailboxes in my motivational trick, breaking up the long days into more manageable portions. In my struggle to stay on and survive, it had not crossed my mind that there may be a significant purpose to hiking the Great Eastern Trail, something to be gained. Jezebel had insisted the Great Eastern Trail whispered a truth that went well beyond its metes and bounds, a truth she had finally obtained; a truth that would present itself to me if I stayed the course and opened myself up to mountains.

I was just proud of myself for not trying to quit. *I am Gabriel William Jenkins, Jr.* I worked the longest, most populous mail route in Bodette for forty years with only the occasional mishap. I do not need anyone to tell me what to do or show me the way.

I took the afternoon in one big session, passing the Tinker Town Shelter well before dark, and pressing on, determined to let the setting sun select my campsite. Soon after the shelter, the Great Eastern Trail broke out on a long-exposed ridgeline. The green mountains rolled out on all sides like a sheet of crumpled velvet. The sun sank below the western peaks, gilding the sky with a spectrum of pinks and oranges. I set up my tent on the ridgeline; it was a risk to camp so exposed but I figured it may well have been Jezebel's departing wish that I camp at such an interesting spot. I perched myself on the western side of the Trail to cook dinner and enjoy the sunset. My tent stood alone on the promontory, accompanied by neither tree nor stone. Jezebel already seemed a world away. Claire and Billy seemed even farther. I thought back to my lonely days before Duncan. And all the lonely, circular days making the mail route. I ate my Dank Rice in darkness and settled into my sleeping bag.

The morning light shined cool and green through my tent walls. I crawled out, *Juicerrman* in hand, to watch the sun burst over the horizon. When I could see the full orb, I started north. The Great Eastern Trail continued uncovered, naked before God, riding the ridgeline's narrow edge. Jezebel had warned that the sense of seclusion on the Great Eastern Trail was often a trick, that someone could be fifty yards behind me for days and I'd be none the wiser; but, here on the ridgeline I could see for miles in either direction— I was certain that I was alone. To the North lay a great flat grassland Jezebel had referred to as the Plains of Caroline. According to Jezebel, the Plains had supported a farming community which had withered out generations ago; the Great Eastern Trail wove through the ruins of barns and homesteads. Jezebel had warned that ghosts haunted the ruins.

The Great Eastern Trail began its descent after lunch, dropping down into the tree line—down remained the worst direction. Even on dry ground in temperate weather with lightened load and good shoes, the juiced gravity lit fires in my knees and ankles. I passed the day in silence, stopping at Flatbottom Shelter to examine the log.

"Captain Barclay reporting: Expedition Day 18. Our weary expeditionary force found no quarter in Tyree. Indeed, we were all but chased out of a local establishment which we hoped only to patronize. I suppose we are truly becoming one with the wild woodland creatures and have no place in this "civilized" world. As it goes, we are prepared and ready to cross the Plains of

Caroline, and perhaps encounter its less-than-natural inhabitants. Good tidings fair travelers.

Morale: Low"

"Just passin' thru. Going to cowboy camp further on so I can clear the Plains of Caroline during daylight, hopefully. Not trying to get involved in all that." – Onward

"No birds today." – Talon

Mongrel's familiar brown sheet slipped from the back pages.

MONGREL COME, MONGREL GO
PLAINS GROW DARK, SPECTERS GLOW

I checked for further references in the log; it was more of the same: "Gonna hurry through;" "Not spending the dark hours there;" and the like. I recalled a weekend Claire and I had spent in a 'haunted' bed and breakfast; I forewent a great deal of sleep, snapping to attention every time the house settled or the wind blew, flicking on the lights and checking the closets to ensure our safety. In the end, it was a frustrated flesh-and-blood wife that forced our early check-out.

I stood up to leave, move lower down the ridge, and cross the Plains in daylight; however, when I reached for my headlamp, I found that, despite my redoubled efforts, I had left it in Tyree along with Jezebel.

17

I resolved to spend my night at the homestead, if only so I could write to Jezebel that I had faced my squirrels. The ridgeline disappeared at noon, sloping into the mammoth, grassy, mountain-rimmed bowl that was the Plains of Caroline. Thick, tangled groves of brush, clustered around pine and oak backbones, dotted the fields. I wove around the clusters as the Great Eastern Trail shifted from the dark forest dirt to the sunbaked clay of the unshaded meadow. Golden stalks of wheaty grass swayed at hip level, often leaning far enough over the Trail to brush tips with its brothers on the other side. Brightly colored birds hustled from grove to grove, chirping through beaks full of twine. A crunch under my left Peakseeker alerted me to the presence of insects; I swatted an itch on my bicep, lifting my hand to find I had dispatched my first Great Eastern Trail mosquito.

I found the homestead at sunset: a square of crumbling stone walls long overgrown with grass and weed. I dropped my pack near an old fire ring and stamped down a patch of high grass to set up my tent. When my new home was built, I explored the ruins, locating the bases of several other structures, including a large one which must have served as the barn. I tried to picture families living there amongst the grain and livestock as the lively sounds of daytime petered out with the light, leaving only the ascending wind.

The night grew cold. I gathered wood for a fire, following Jezebel's instructions, giving my cabin four walls and carpeting it with a handful of thatch but, when I set my lighter to the thatch it embered out without so much as charring the walls. Another attempt yielded the same result. I straightened up, surveying my surroundings before flicking on my camp stove and holding it to the thatch. The smaller stuff lit easily, and I fed the fragile flame twigs and branches until it could hold its own. I turned off the gas and started feeding on the larger sticks and logs. The more substantial pieces retained a great deal of winter's moisture, sizzling for some time before finally succumbing to the heat with great smoky exhalations. I stacked them one level at a time, steering clear of the shifting plume streaming over the ruins. I inspected my work—it was more random and disorganized than the tidy sheets of a true Jezebel campfire, not to mention its bastard source, but it was mine and I had lit it.

I rolled a log near the fire and sat down to set my stove up proper, pouring the water by firelight. When the rice was tender, I reached into my food bag in search of Dank Sauce packets, and stopped—

The woman stood motionless, staring at me from next to her ruined home.

The smoke outlined her like a linen sheet, parting and passing through her figure. Scraps of spectral fabric popped in and out of existence behind her as the smoke gave body to the ends of her dress. I could feel her eyes searching me in the darkness. Any and all oxygen fled my lungs. My heart wrestled against its constraints, trying to free itself from the doomed and dumbfounded body. My brain sent no signals. I didn't move. For a long moment, nothing happened.

"I . . . I can—" The fire burst as the cabin collapsed inwards. I recoiled, toppling backwards. When I regained my senses, she was gone, or at least not where she was. The smoke drifted unimpeded into the plains.

I remembered to breathe, panting as I scanned the ruined house. The wind howled over the stones. The image of her formless body watching from the doorstep carved itself into my brain. Mindless, I retreated to my tent, abandoning my meal to chill in the valley air—I was the idiot coed seeking refuge in the closet, or under the sheets, rather than running out the unmanned front door. I knew this, but was helpless to change course. I could have been packed up and moving down the Trail in three minutes; but to open the tent flap was to risk coming face to face with the featureless Caroline. Whatever happened outside the tent would happen despite me. I huddled in my fabric womb, scrutinizing my fire light dancing on the walls, taunting my cowardice. I waited for the woman to reappear, this time within the confines of my tent, and finish the job. I cursed Jezebel. I missed Jezebel. I missed my wife and longed for the photograph she had snuck into my pack—inaccessible outside the fabric. If Claire was here, that mean old ghost would have some explaining to do for interfering with her evening. I imagined Caroline's final assault screaming to a full stop before Claire's crossed arms and icy gaze, her shadowy posture wilting under my wife's sharp tongue. Long after the fire burnt out, I lay awake waiting for death or daylight, twitching at each fresh burst of wind.

18

I leapt out at morning's first light, scrambling around the campsite, collecting my belongings, eyes set firmly on the dirt. There was still rice in my pot when I shoved it into my pack. My mind replayed the previous night's events—the fire, the smoke, the woman standing eternal watch over her home. A very loud part of me advocated that I file it all away as a dream. But it felt real; the thought of it brought tears to my eyes, set my hairs on end. It was over an hour before I remembered my morning *Juicerrman*.

By midday it was very hot—the bowled landscape seemed to focus the sun's heat on the Plains. My short bottoms moistened as the Trail s-curved across the flat ground, sometimes dodging groves or the occasional rock formation, but mostly on its own accord. I wondered if the Great Eastern Trail had a minimum mileage, like a word count on a school paper, and saw this as an opportunity for verbosity, or if it normally ran straight but Caroline had curled it up to retain her grasp on me. I cut the curves close, leaning out from over my legs to shave off precious seconds, moving as quickly as I could without breaking into a run. The northern mountains grew bigger throughout the day.

I skittered to a stop inches away from the steel-postured young man sitting cross-legged in the middle of the Trail.

"Hey, oh dern, sorry I didn't see you there." He did not acknowledge my presence, leading me to worry he was a daytime specter. "What, what are you doing down there?"

Still nothing.

"Are you okay? Do you need help?"

A horrible rattle sounded from just up the Trail. I looked up at the source: a thick, brown serpent sat coiled and at the ready not four feet from me; its eyes set squarely on my new friend—its tail a loud, blurry warning.

"I would ask that you be quiet," he still did not move, "and consider taking a step back."

I took several big steps back, doing my best to keep my heart in my chest, having never before experienced the enormous rattle live and in person.

"Did, did he already get you? Bite you, I mean. Let me get a stick. Or a rock." I thought about dragging this dying boy back through Caroline's homestead.

"He means no harm."

The young man leaned back and pushed himself south, away from the snake. When he was at a safer distance, he stood up, unfurling to an enormous height. He was clad in mesh shorts, a cotton t-shirt, and a straw hat, all spotlessly clean. Despite the heat, and the snake, he showed no signs of perspiration. When he finally looked down at me I saw that he was actually very young, perhaps still in his teens.

"I was learning about snakes." The voice was much deeper than his slender frame suggested; it seemed to require a great deal of thought and energy to produce. I considered touching him to make sure he wasn't another apparition, but decided apparition or not, he likely wouldn't respond well. I leaned around him to check on the snake which remained focused on us.

The boy wore an impossibly small pack that couldn't hold much more than a water bottle and a granola bar. He kneeled back down to face the snake, extending a long finger to his right,

"Go." The snake, if anything, responded by coiling tighter, pumping extra venom into its rattle. My new friend stood up and looked down at me. "Much to learn."

He knifed into the grass, banana-ing around the rattlesnake and rejoining the Great Eastern Trail a few yards down. I followed, running to catch up after giving the snake a much wider berth on much shorter legs. He moved in great purposeful strides, like a slow motion gallop, which made him immensely difficult to keep up with—although I intended to do just that. Despite his oddities, he was a welcome living comfort.

"What do you mean learn about snakes? What exactly are you trying to learn by doing that? How fast you die if you get bit? I mean, did you ever consider a book?"

"If I thought books would suffice, I wouldn't need to come out here would I?"

"I'd say there is a pretty substantial middle ground between books and having a staring contest with a rattlesnake. And far away from a hospital no less."

"Not if you're trying to learn what I'm trying to learn."

"Right . . . Where are you planning on camping tonight? I had sort of a long night last night and I'd rather not do it alone again."

"There are others. I will stop when I find them."

"Others that didn't stop for the snake?"

"No, they hike fast and miss many things."

"I would've been okay missing that too. You never said your name."

He planted a foot and turned, meeting my eye with a startling intensity, extending a hand. "They call me Cass."

"Nice to meet you Cass." I shook his hand. "They call me Mister Gabe." Cass narrowed his eyes.

"Mr. Gabe?"

"The mister is more colloquial rather than a, um, formal salutation."

"The Trail gave you this name?"

"Well a girl on the Trail. The first part at least. I've been Gabe for a while now."

Cass turned around, resuming his pace. I settled into silence, walk-jogging behind him as we crossed the remaining Plains of Caroline and returned to the woods, climbing a gentle rise out of the valley. For long hours Cass did not stop, not even for a drink. I choked back my list of questions, most of them parental, for fear of annoying my new companion. Cass did not seem like one for conversation, and I was at his mercy. He stopped suddenly again, and again I almost bumped into him.

"What happened to you, Gabe the Unnamed, that makes you such persistent company."

I struggled with the facts of the previous evening, trying to arrange them in such a way that didn't make me look crazy.

"Last night I camped at the homestead ruins—" He turned fully around to face me.

"You have witnessed the smoky woman?" I nodded. "I did not have the pleasure."

"It wasn't a pleasure. It was terrifying. I was alone at the ruins, enjoying my fire and about to enjoy my dinner, when I get this feeling that I'm being watched. I look up and there's a figure staring at me from the smoke. Dern near gave me a heart attack." My stomach growled at the mention of dinner. It had now been sometime since I'd had a full meal.

"Was she beautiful?"

"No, just terrifying."

"You should be honored. Ms. Caroline does not reveal herself to everyone who passes by. You have been chosen."

Cass resumed his long striding.

"How far ahead did you say your friends are? I don't usually hike in the dark."

"They stop when they find a suitable place—or when distraction takes them."

Night set in around us. My legs, which had grown more than capable for my shorter outings, at a more favorable pace, began to ache and slow. Cass pulled farther and farther ahead, disappearing for stretches as I wound down. At last, snatches of shouting and laughter echoed down the Trail. An orange glow appeared on the horizon, growing until I came upon a great bonfire with violent flames rising to double my height, bending, whipping, and roaring through the still evening air, licking the branches above them. Around the fire danced a muscular young man, shirtless and hairy, with a thick beard and a tangle of shoulder length brown hair. Another less intimidating youth, sat potbellied and pale in the grass. Homemade cigarettes dangled from both their lips.

"Gentlemen this is my new acquaintance Gabe the Unnamed."

They stopped and stared at me echoing, "Gabe the Unnamed," in staccato unison.

"Gabe, this seated and scrappy fellow is Speck." Speck gave a fervent wave from his seat by the fire. "And that unhinged fur ball is Bear." At his introduction, Bear picked up his pace and provided us with three laps around the fire.

"Evening gentleman."

"Gabe has seen the smoky woman."

"Good on you Nameless Gabe. How was she?"

"Oh, great. Really lovely lady." I noted the smoke drifting into the trees.

Cass removed a small packet from his pack and cast it on the ground where it unraveled into a silver first responder's blanket. He sat down cross-legged, selected a little baggie from his pack, and started rolling cigarettes. Two other silver blankets glimmered from the far side of the fire.

I set up my tent across the clearing near the wood line, putting a safe distance between myself and the bonfire. I had hiked well past my preferred bedtime and covered by far my longest distance in a day. I cooked my dinner, ate by my tent, and settled in without returning to the fire. I made a point of retrieving the family photo from my pack to spend the night with me in the tent. I held up the photograph, catching glimpses of it in the fire's ample light. It had been taken just before Billy left for law school— to that point the farthest he had ever ventured from home. I kept my thumb over his face to better focus on my wife, wondering what she was doing, what she had eaten for dinner, whether she had gone to bed, and what she would think about my present situation. *What am I doing out here? What's keeping me out here? How can I miss home this much but still not feel the need to return?* The lads stayed up late chatting, laughing, and rustling around. I fell asleep, alone, but comforted by the sounds of the living.

19

I stoked the still glowing coals, coaxing out a small flame to keep me company while I broke fast on a *Juicerrman*. Three shiny, unnatural boulders dotted the clearing, giving off a metallic crinkle every time an occupant shifted in his sleep. Beyond that, all was quiet and calm.

The Great Eastern Trail picked up where it had left off, steadily climbing without ever becoming steep. I passed a shelter, went up and over the wooded mountain then started back down emerging onto a treeless earthy swell. A sea of brown grass waved in the wind. All around me the layers of faded blue mountains stretched to the horizon.

A gravel road split the valley ahead of me, meeting the Great Eastern Trail in a parking lot between my swell and the next. I spotted a small structure, perhaps a bathroom, which stood at the end of the lot neighbored by a covered kiosk. Several cars were parked in the lot; people scurried up the hills like fleas on a turtle. Some kind souls had erected chest high fence posts marked with orange blazes to guide hikers in. I maneuvered from post to post, stopping at each one to marvel at the slightly adjusted views.

The structure was indeed a bathroom complete with running water. I set up camp at the sink, splashing my face and shoving my hair under the faucet, rinsing both with palm fulls of hand soap, lathering far up my arms as my sleeves would allow; if the door had offered a lock, I would have indulged in a full shower. As it was, the mirror revealed a good looking, if at most semi-clean, retiree. The sunshine and warmth had colored my features. My grey hair curled down over my ears. My beard had progressed into a thick salt and pepper mat. I looked all together tanned, capable, and adventurous.

The kiosk itself was just a board displaying several maps and park announcements. A large map of the balds, as it referred to the area, named the Windy Place collectively, and Little Hill, Big Hill, and Roundtop Mountain, individually, occupied the majority of the real estate. I was happy to find that there was a third bald and that this new formation would require a good portion of my day.

Next to the bald map was a vertical map of the Great Eastern Trail with a red dot marking the balds advising *You Are Here*. I lifted my hand to the map—I had added another finger since the outfitter but could still thumb to forefinger the area separating Little Hill from Grambling's Pass. Many northward hands remained.

I judged my pace against the day hikers who, out for a lark, ambled up the slope, stopping for pictures each time they lost their breath. Burdened with a purpose, I moved with precision and efficiency, always conscious not to waste a step, tracking down a family of four which had been over halfway up the bald when I had left the kiosk. Upon seeing me, the young mother jerked the near child aside and shouted to her husband who did the same with his ward, retreating so deep into the grass the littles one almost disappeared. I gave the dad a wave and friendly *excuse me*, receiving in return a belated nod and a look that said *holy shoot you can talk*.

At the top, I selected a clear spot comfortably away from the respectable folk to lounge and enjoy a peanut butter wrap and a

Juicerrman. I had long ago learned to eat the peanut butter wrap first as *Juicerrmen* ruined my stomach for lesser food. I looked back over Little Hill to the south and Roundtop Mountain to the north, verifying that Big Hill, despite being a *hill,* was the largest of the balds. It seemed a big get for hills to have one of their own ascend markedly higher than a nearby mountain.

The gravel road wound through the countryside like a meandering stream reaching its final pool in the parking lot. I scanned the horizon in vain for the more vital artery from which it stemmed. People came and went through the parking lot; regular folk coming out to dip their toes in the mountains and still be home for supper. They gathered near cars, spent long minutes inspecting the map, and gestured emphatically at different portions of the surrounding landscape.

Two dark figures broke over the crest of Little Hill, trampling down the slopes like a pair of roving barbarians; their pace and laser beam focus starkly opposed the idling public below them. An elderly couple populated their war path, creeping up the hill, their meeting inevitable. Closer and closer they sped, the barbarians moving three lengths for every one of the couple's, until, at close range, the couple caught sight of them and, much like my family of four, buried themselves in the grass. The barbarians blew past them, down through the parking lot, leaving herds of shocked tourists in their wake, until they were marching their way up the southern slopes of Big Hill to where I now picnicked.

"Good morning, Nameless Gabe."

"Good morning Speck, Bear. Fair number of people out here. Didn't realize this was a destination."

"A good chance to scare the normies."

Bear stood back, stamping at the ground and surveying my picnic site. His shirt had once been someone named JoJo's work uniform. The iron-on label on the right breast read *West Dot Foundry.* I presumed it was Bear who'd torn off the sleeves.

Bear's eyes widened when he saw the *Juicerrman* lying next to me. He looked at me, grunted, then nodded at it.

"You're familiar with *Juicerrman*, Bear?"

Another nod.

"Would you like one? I have plenty."

He nodded again, inching closer.

I took out a bar and handed it over. "Be careful. They're a real kick if you haven't had one in a while. I've developed something of a tolerance."

Bear ripped off the wrapper and lifted the bar to his mouth horizontally like a chocolate harmonica, wolfing it down from there, finishing with a beard full of super nougat. He snorted, twitched his eyes, and raised his arms in triumph. I feared that perhaps the rush of caffeine, sugar, and artificial adrenaline would be too much for a boy of Bear's excitable temperament. I offered another to Speck, who declined.

"Where's Cass?"

"He walks slow. He's always stoppin' and lookin', lookin' and stoppin'. Doesn't catch up until nighttime." Bear bent over and stroked his beard in mock inspection of a blade of grass.

I thought about walking up on Cass conversing with the snake.

"I guess I saw that. Where y'all headed tonight?"

"Bear stops when he's done. I'm just along for the ride."

"I fear I may have just lengthened your day."

I pointed to where Bear had started off—Speck gave an underhand wave as he took off in pursuit. They rumbled down the Big Hill's northern slope, startling fresh communities of domesticated *normies* as they went. I waited for a little bit to see if Cass would appear. When he failed to, I packed up to follow Bear and Speck down Big Hill and over Roundtop Mountain.

A cluster of clean folk huddled at Roundtop Mountain's northern wood line. It was as if this marked the delineated end of their kingdom; they milled about, staring at the trees, before retreating to safety, casting tense glances over their shoulders as they went. As a recovering *normie*, I considered myself an ambassador of the Great Eastern Trail and took it upon myself to be as polite and unintimidating to passersby as possible, but they showed little interest in conversation or proximity. I left the nice smelling crowds and re-entered the woods.

Bear and Speck did not hike long; it was only mid-afternoon when I smelled their fire and caught them lounging around Boss Bottom Shelter. Bear had removed his torn shirt and lay on his back in slapping a rhythm on his hairy belly. Every movement set off an impressive display of sinew and muscle. Speck lay next to him with his closed, still shirted, whistling softly around a cigarette. I greeted them and sat down on a log. I did not remove my pack.

"This it for the day?"

"Unless the mood strikes."

"It's early yet, think I'm gonna press on."

"Camp alone?" Bear broke off his rhythm and set his eyes on me.

"You're welcome to camp with us Nameless Gabe. We'd be happy to name you."

"It's okay. Us old folk gotta get in the miles while we can. Don't know what I'll feel like tomorrow."

"If that's your journey, Nameless Gabe. Enjoy your night."

I stood up and turned to leave.

"GABE!" Bear's voice was a hoarse bark. He was no longer looking at me.

"Yes, uh, Bear."

"Bar?"

"Oh, sure." I fished a *Juicerrman* out of my pocket and tossed it next to him.

I once again brought the family photograph into the tent that night, but it was too dark to discern.

20

Cass must have woken up early, and restrained himself from stopping to stare down animals, because I never caught wind of him, and the first pastels of sunset were working their way up from the horizon when I stumbled across him sitting cross-legged and erect on the rock face, contemplating the western sky.

"Another snake?"

"Good evening Nameless Gabe. How was your adventure today?" He did not look at me.

"Uneventful. Just enjoying the nice weather."

"I would not grow too attached my friend. The birds speak of rain."

"The . . . birds?"

He raised an arm in the direction of a flying v of birds. The rear right bird had drifted outside the line, giving the v a sloppy cursive tail. "They have seen storms in the west. There shall be no sun tomorrow."

"The birds?" There were no clouds on the horizon.

"Do you doubt their travels?"

"No, not so much their travels."

"I would ask you to withhold judgment until the morning."

I left Cass at the rock and walked past the next shelter, where I assumed the lads would stop, pitching my tent in a small clearing.

***

I awoke to the soft patter of precipitation. By mid-morning fat pellets filled the air, saturating all, and turning the Great Eastern Trail into a slop line. Not long ago this would have been a weird sensation, to not seek cover, or at least send up an umbrella, when confronted with inclement weather; I found it to not be wholly disagreeable. Indeed the rain's most immediate effect was to make me wet, a condition which did not threaten my progress. The callouses on my feet acted as a layer of impermeable wax, though I still made a point of maneuvering around the edges of puddles. My pre-lunch *Juicerrman* stood strong, beading water like a waxed convertible. The real disappointment was the very expensive rain jacket which only repelled water for about half an hour before relenting, growing heavy with moisture, and dragging across my armpits.

I passed a shelter sign around noon and turned down the side trail to eat lunch out of the weather. A small pond spread across the shelter's entrance, collecting water even as I approached. I skirted its left bank to where it came closest to the shelter corner, which was still about a three foot separation, removed my pack, and heaved it into the covered area before bracing my feet. Unburdened, I bent the knee and launched myself over the water, belly flopping on the wood with the rickety splat, army crawling forward to secure my position. I bunkered down in the back corner, opening the shelter log to read as I prepared my wrap. Mongrel had not been here, or had at least not written. Others detailed the nice weather and pleasant evenings they had spent in these confines.

Bear tramped into the clearing as I finished my lunch, plowing through the growing reservoir without breaking stride, leaving a beige *v* of foaming wake. With a grunt, he propped himself up on the edge, only inches from the watery sheet pouring off the roof. Not once did he turn towards the back where I sat in silence, unsure whether he was aware of my presence. I held Bear in the same esteem as wild animals in terms of general unpredictability and dangerousness—I certainly did not want to startle him. Bear swung his legs like a toddler as he pulled his pack from his lap and began to eat.

Pretty soon Cass came down the Trail, followed by Speck. They were deep in conversation, projecting to be heard over the roar. They split around the puddle and hopped in at their respective corners; both with much greater grace than I'd exhibited.

"Good afternoon, Bear. How is your adventure?"

"Fine. Gabe the Unnamed is here." He cocked his head in my direction. "He's back there bein' weird."

I waved. "Howdy, lads."

Cass patted Bear on the shoulder as the arriving pair settled on either side; all three lit up a fresh cigarette, forming a rather striking illustration of adolescence.

I packed up my belongings and prepared to reenter the rain.

"Cass it would appear your birds were right."

"Nature has no reason to deceive."

"Right. Of course. I'll see y'all down the road." I hesitated at shelter's edge unsure of how to safely, and gracefully, maneuver back into the rain.

"Gabe!"

"Yea."

"Bar."

Bear shredded the red wrapper as I gave up, clamoring off the platform into mid-calf water, which really didn't change the conditions within my shoes beyond contributing a fresh layer of filth.

I hit the Great Eastern Trail and turned north. The cold rain displaced any water my body worked so hard to warm during lunch. Bear caught me first, his wet stomps detectable and distinct over the downpour. I stepped aside when he got close; he grunted and passed. Cass and Speck caught me about an hour later, sneaking up on me until Speck was close enough to grab me and yell "NAMELESS GABE!" before disappearing around a soppy turn.

When I found the first shelter empty, I set up my tent.

> MONGREL COME, MONGREL GO
> IN THE TUNNEL, DEPTHS UNTOLD

21

Morning confronted me with the unpleasant task of slithering into wet clothes. I pushed into heavy pants, and snaked flat hands through a soggy, two-dimensional shirt. A pair of dry socks constituted my one luxury, although they too were marked for imminent ruination.

I passed the lads' lopsided disco balls less than a mile into my hike. The rising mist of yesterday's rains blessed the sunlight with body such that it beamed through the canopy, fostering a holy atmosphere on the mountain. The rocks and dirt glistened in the morning light. Clusters of light green buds and dark green leaves filled the undergrowth. The Trail spent the day's early parts going down.

I was about to stop for lunch when I encountered the perfectly round semi-circle, about as high as my Bodette chimney, bored into the granite cliff face. I leaned in to assess the darkness. The light ended about ten feet in—after that it could not have been painted a more convincing black. There was no sign of the other side. I retreated to the sunlight. An orange blaze marked at doorbell height extinguished any hope that the Great Eastern Trail did not pass through. I sat down on a log, embarked on a *Juicerrman*, and considered the situation as a butterfly rested on my shoelace. Above ground, it had developed into a nice day with a pleasant temperature. Naturally, the Great Eastern Trail had other plans.

"Okay what would Jezebel do? She'd go in the dark scary tunnel. Jezebel *did* go in the dark scary tunnel. And if Jezebel went in and came out then if Gabe goes in he should . . . ."

I wasn't going to retreat, I needed to march. I stood up and leaned into the tunnel. It was still dark. Too dark. I straightened up to breath the light air. I reached for my headlamp, then remembered its demise. Even without it, the first steps were easy. The sunlight graced my back, a comforting hand through a new trial. But the light dimmed and departed. I encountered a long pool of water, only an inch deep, spreading across the tunnel floor. The splashes of my footsteps echoed into the darkness. I shifted to the side, keeping a hand on the wall. The mountain's colossal weight pressed down on my shoulders. I tried to count my steps but was sucked into distraction by the lingering reverberations of my footfall. Time stalled as the darkness grew heavy, pressing against me. My legs softened, their passive resistance against further excursion into the blackness. I stopped and listened.

Could I be the source of all that sound?

Something else occupied the tunnel.

I could hear it shuffling between the reverberating splashes. I stopped, waiting for my echoes to fade. Silence. *You're okay, Gabe. Mister Gabe. You survived the Donners. You will survive this.* But there was no place for life in the blackness. Panic set in. I turned back at the entrance, I thought, but found no light. I turned around, then back, then lost track. The cool wall behind me was my only anchor. I breathed in resolve and turned what I thought was north, tip-toeing along the water's edge, pressing myself against the wall until I could go no more, sliding down the stone in miserable, shaking defeat. I unhooked my pack, pawing for the zipper to the top capsule.

Again the sound of footfall. Something was headed towards me, from in front of me, rising up from the bowels of the mountain. It stamped swiftly through the water, at home in the darkness. The beast's wet footfall and heavy breathing caromed off the walls, filling the tunnel. I wrapped my hands around my legs, keeping still in hopes it would simply pass by. I closed my eyes, listening to the stamping grow louder and close.

It stopped next to me. A fearsome paw grasped my shoulder.

"Gabe?" I cracked an eye. There was a soft click and a finger of light hovered in the darkness, illuminating the left side of Bear's face.

"I . . . I fell."

He squatted and looked me up and down then turned to examine the darkness.

"Injured?"

"No, I'm fine."

"Sleeping here?"

"No . . . no, no. Just, um, I fell."

"Then, please, come with Bear."

"I'm fine. There's no reason to—" He pulled me up by my armpits and set me in the opposite direction from the one I'd been tiptoeing.

"Isn't, isn't this the wrong way?"

"No, Gabe. This is north. Never stop in the darkness." He tapped the light against his temple. "Plays tricks. Here." Bear pressed the light source into my hand. Lifting it closer, I found it to be a light-up sword toy that at some point had accompanied a kid's meal. He stepped behind me, put a hand on my shoulder; we started walking, now right down the center. I held the diminutive light up in front of me where it failed to reach the walls. Bear hummed behind me, linking snippets of several melodies which he seemed to think were one. His heavy splashing squashed any other sound.

Soon I was blinking in the light of a new day. Bear smiled, wiping his brow in mock relief.

When my eyes adjusted I inspected my surroundings to make sure Bear hadn't led back to the tunnel's southern end; I did not want to relive that adventure. I looked back at the tunnel—*Dorchester Railroad Co.* was carved in neat letters in the granite above the gaping hole.

"Long tunnel, Nameless Gabe. Very dark."

"No, kidding Bear. I think the Dorchesters lost some money on this one."

Bear looked up at the sign and shrugged. He tapped his pockets. "Nothing to spend, nothing to lose."

The day remained nice on the other side and Bear accompanied me for the duration. The Great Eastern Trail was deep brown and soft to the step, a far cry from the lifeless grey cement of my early days. Insects ruled the low areas of the forests. We stopped frequently to inspect their movements through both land and air, amazed that life could pull itself out of the dirt in such numbers. I took an aching knee to inspect a line of black ants marching from pine to oak. A winged something performed endless loops through the branches of a budding green bush. The squirrels were out as well; their scurrying kept me on my toes.

The Trail trended downwards for most of the morning, bouncing upwards around noon to return me to grey trees and silence, winters final stronghold. I decided to take my lunch on the slopes of the ensuing descent and informed Bear. The boy grunted and prowled past me, eyes locked on the ground, not watching his feet but scanning around the Trail's edges, kicking up the leaf litter then bending at the hips to inspect what he'd uncovered.

"How ya doing there Bear?"

"Bear is good. Bear is hungry, but Bear is good." He had the same look of focused distraction Billy so often wore when I tried to talk to him during his homework.

"Right. What you're doing?"

"Hunting." He stopped, planted a hand on a tree to survey the clearing, then crept over to a thick oak log he must've thought he'd previously overlooked.

"GABE! Look." He'd already plucked something from the earth by the time I joined him, holding the flesh toned, dirt flecked mass between his thumb and pointer finger, gaping at it with the open-mouthed wonder of a prospector at his gold.

"What have you got there?"

Bear closed his eyes for a second, furrowing his brow. "Settler's Fowl." A nod emphasized each syllable.

"Maybe you should put that down. We really don't know if it's pois—"

He unhinged his mouth to a frightening breadth and popped in the nugget, dirt and all, cheeks dimpling in a satisfied smile as he worked it down. He turned behind him and returned with a smaller, dirtier specimen, holding it out to me.

"Oh, I couldn't. They, uh, they do seem rare."

"There are many." Bear shifted to side so I could see his bounty—he had indeed hit the motherlode. He extended his hand anew; his look suggested there was a lot riding on my acceptance.

"What, um, does it taste like?"

Bear closed his eyes as he considered this question. "Squirrel!" The word shot out before his eyes opened. "But . . . easier to shoot." Two dirty hands closed the fungus in mine. I rolled the mushroom over, inspecting its cratered, swirled, almost brainy texture, fingernailing out the larger grains. After one final glance at the boy who'd saved me from the darkness, I took a bite.

It was understandably gritty, with sour dirt undertones, but the mushroom itself was smooth and salty with hints of beefs. On the whole it wasn't too far from a nice burger—apparently I'd wasted a lot of money eating red meat rather than squirrel.

"Good?"

"Good, Bear. Actually pretty dern good."

"Good. We pick them all."

Bear set to picking, giving each cap a careful twist and lift, eating most, piling the survivors between his left hand and his chest. When he was done he cradled his bounty like a pebble baby, losing several as he stood up, and several more in pursuit of the fallen. I dug through my pack and removed a grocery bag from my last resupply, handing it to Bear.

"Smart Gabe." He pointed into his mouth with his free hand. "Dinner. Better than bar."

When the bag was full Bear put his hand down in the bare patch and looked up at me. "Leaves. Slant. Oak."

"Leaves. Slant. Oak. Got it. Thanks, Bear."

"All the way to Daemon's. Not every time. But many."

I followed Bear for the rest of the day as he strutted through the woods with his bulging grocery bag swinging at his side. Twice we stopped to binge on fresh batches of Settler's Fowl.

Cass and Speck found us at sunset, reclining around the outskirts of Ensfield Shelter. I set up my tent nearby and sat down at the table to prepare dinner. Bear plopped down next to me, devouring Settlers by the household in between draws from his cigarette. When my water boiled I poured in the rice and replaced the top, opening it up several minutes later to add the Dank Sauce.

Bear tapped my shoulder after the first bite. I turned to find him shaking a meaty mushroom, gesturing first at me, then at my rice. I raised my hand to decline but he only pulled back his arm and produced a no doubt dangerously-stored unsheathed knife, and cut off a series of clean, even slices. I nodded my thanks, propped the slices between space spork and thumb to dump them into my pot, doing my best to mix them. I lifted a sporkful for an exploratory bite; the Settlers' Fowl's tender meatiness melded perfectly with the Dank Rice while also inching me closer to covering all the food groups—two if you counted dirt. I inhaled the whole bowl, skimming my space spork across the bottom when no significant morsels remained. Another step removed from plain white rice.

"Thank you. I really enjoyed that."

He nodded and exhaled a line of smoke. I removed Mongrel's note from the shelter log.

MONGREL COME, MONGREL GO
COST OF LIVING, TOO MUCH TO OWE

I read it a couple of times, rubbing my hands against the parchment.

"Cost of living too much to owe." Bear rested a hand on my shoulder as he read the passage aloud. "Mongrel is weird Gabe the Nameless Unnamed. Mongrel is very weird."

Before I could respond, he hopped out of the shelter and started his fire.

It was just one full day and then, hopefully, the town of Kilgore the following morning. I was stiff, sore, and tired, but felt sure that a nourishing night of beds, movies, and town food could bring me back up to full speed.

I had one foot on the Trail when the crinkling aluminum turned me around to where Bear's head poked out of the closest mound.

"Gabe leaving?" He did not attempt a whisper.

"Just headed north. Thank you for your help yesterday. I don't know what I would've done without you."

"Good, Gabe. I'll catch you soon." The mangled hair disappeared under the foil. I turned to leave—

"Gabe!" I turned back. "Bar."

It was Speck that caught me at lunch. Together we ambled through the afternoon, stopping frequently to inspect spring's wonders. Salamanders were studied and flowers sniffed. Butterflies had their paths charted. Deep in the afternoon, long after Bear had blown by, we stopped in a clearing for a snack.

"How'd you fall in with the lads?"

"Cass and Bear were at Talon Shelter my first night. Smoking and dancing. Doing their thing. It looked like fun so I bummed a cigarette and joined their journey."

"That simple?"

"Not much point in playing hard to get."

"Did they ever say anything about their past?"

"I never ask and they never tell. That's the best part of being out here—a whole new you."

"You're barely old enough to know the first you. Why do you need a new one?"

"I'm nineteen years old with a mechanical engineering degree. Do you know that means?"

"The old you is a genius."

"That the old me was placed on a track when he was five because he solved every question in one of his parent's old calculus books. Since that time he's been placed in advanced mathematics classes, college classes, and forced to spend his summers interning at engineering firms watching old men count steel girders."

"I'm guessing you got tired of math problems."

"No, don't get me wrong, I love math to the nth degree. I just . . . I read an article once about a guy who traveled the world for four years, working, staying in hostels, going on adventures. Then one day he came across a jungle hut next to a volcanic beach. He found out it was a popular breeding area for some rare sea turtle and the people who lived in the hut had dedicated their lives to defending the baby turtles from poachers, crabs, and raccoons. He fell in love and never left. In the article he said he never would have found his purpose had he not journeyed out."

"So you're making sure you don't miss out on your turtles."

"Sure, you could put it that way. Maybe it's just a good excuse to see the world."

"What do your parents think about this?"

"If I'm being honest . . . they're scared shitless. I was a somewhat docile and willing student, and clearly I'm an indoor kid," he jiggled his belly, "so this came as quite a shock. They've definitely put on a brave face and tried to be supportive but it's pretty obvious they're terrified their golden boy wandered off into the woods rather than do something in furtherance of his career."

I thought about Billy leaving for Pentland. " That's very decent of them. Do you have any idea how hard it is for parents to watch their sons move on?"

"Do you have any recollection how hard it is for a son to stay put?"

My thoughts turned back to the pensioned mailman. "A whole new me . . . . I don't think my wife would love that. What about Cass thinking he can talk to animals? Is that part of him being a whole new him?" I directed this question at a herd of electric orange newts. The newts cocked their heads in unison, maintaining eye contact as I leaned in closer.

"The Trail does seem to endow some of its travelers with . . . abilities, or at least increase the probability of coincidences."

"What are you saying? What abilities?"

"Well, just pay attention to Bear. He is invincible. I've seen him take some truly awful falls and pop right back up. And you saw a ghost or whatever. So strange shit happens out here."

"So you do think Cass can talk to animals?"

"Nothing has torn him to bits yet. But I also wouldn't plan my weekend around his forecasts."

"What is your ability?"

"Just pay attention, Gabe McNameless."

That night the four of us camped at Pilgrims Shelter.

MONGREL COME, MONGREL GO
DAMN FINE CHICKEN, PETE N' CO

22

I was the first one to make the Kilgore road the next morning. A layer of leaves covered the road, which was silent, and appeared to have always been. A soft breeze blew through the clearing. It seemed unthinkable that a sputtering, groaning motorized vehicle had ever or could ever be permitted to break this serenity. I decided to lay down for a nap and wait for the lads.

It was not the lads that woke me but less invasive woodland creatures: deer, two does and two fawns. They were big eyed, peaceful, and less than ten yards away from where I lay. Their thin, knobby legs supported bulky block torsos. As of yet they were unaware or unconcerned with my presence. I watched one of the fawns wobble, as splay-legged as a dog on ice, across the asphalt to nestle in the grass near me. Its sibling soon followed. Their fragile ribs bellowed in and out with each breath. The one nearest me chased a wandering beetle with its nose, jumping when the beetle took flight.

All at once the adults' heads shot to attention. They peered intently over my shoulder. I had always been fascinated by the instinct that compelled deer to verify something was a threat before running away—as if something had ever sprung from cover to bid them good health. In this instance I could not observe what concerned them, but it must've failed the test because the adults streaked off the roadway, followed closely by the children who had to scramble up to their feet to keep up with their guardians.

Several moments later the lads sauntered from the woods behind me, laughing, yelling and smoking.

"We were getting worried Nameless. None of us wagered that you could make it to road before us."

"Didn't see any reason to stop with town so close."

"A wise man."

"Might as well press on though. I've seen more deer than cars."

They exchanged smiles. "Not to worry," said Cass, "we have ourselves what some might refer to as a ringer—Speck here's got the gift. He's been touched."

"Touched?"

"You flatter me," Speck disengaged from his pack and strutted across the road, making a show of setting his feet, rolling and squaring his shoulders, then digging in like he was batting cleanup. When his stance was set, he kissed his thumb and shot out his hand, an energetic smile plastered on his face. The silence returned. He looked like a child, dressed by his mother and sent out to wait for the bus—there came the sudden roar of an engine. A big red pick-up truck whipped around the bend, jolting to a stop at Speck's feet. The driver, a massive bearded man in a blue baseball hat, slapped the side of his door, keeping his eyes on the road. I stood wide-eyed and astonished as the three lads piled into the bed.

Three heads turned to me from the bed.

"Quickly you nameless goose. The train is now departing!" I took a cautious step toward the truck, handing my pack to Speck and hopping over the tailgate.

The truck accelerated out of the parking lot, slinging itself around the curves, dips and bumps of the mountain road, all the while threatening to eject its cargo. I braced myself in the back corner wondering if these were the only drivers that picked up hitchhikers. Bear thrust his head over the side allowing the wind to whip his mane into a brown plume. Cass and Speck did what they could to shield their cigarettes.

"How do y'all know this guy?" I yelled over the wind.

"If we knew him, we wouldn't have to hitch." The truck punctuated this comment by going airborne off a bump in the road, landing with a rattling thump, jerking left to regain the road. Bear cracked his head against the rear window and came up smiling, letting out a howl as he returned his face to the wind.

"But that's the bit right? I mean what are the odds that guy shows up just as Speck does his dance?"

"Significantly higher than you'd imagine."

"Seriously what's the trick?"

"The Great Eastern Trail."

"The Trail called someone to give you a ride?"

"There's more to this Trail than meets the eye, Gabe of No Appellation. It's not intended for serious people."

The truck roared to a stop in a parking lot on the outskirts of Kilgore. The driver gave his side panel two more pats, waiting just long enough for us to tumble out of the bed before rumbling back to life. I watched it drive off, half waiting for it to vanish in a puff of smoke, but it drove down the road like a fully manifested vehicle, and only turned out of sight.

A four lane interstate roared to our left, burdening Kilgore with all the trappings of an exit town: gas stations, chain restaurants and cheap motels; all slammed into one half mile strip. Signs crowded each side of the road, shouldering against each other to more visibly announce the availability of burgers, fries, milk shakes, petroleum, and premium cable. Kilgore looked like the place other towns came to shop for their generic establishments—a buffet of buffets. A hungry hiker's paradise.

"Where to?" I asked when we reached the corner.

"Lunch," replied Cass, "the basics must come first."

Cars rushed down the road, weaving around each other as the occupants struggled to fill tanks and bellies before rejoining the interstate. People crammed into parking lots, scurrying in and out of store fronts and cars, arms laden with drinks, snacks, and children. It was far and away the most activity I had seen since starting the Great Eastern Trail. First we passed Fran's Smokehouse, a massive family eatery with a line out the door, then Bill's Pump'n'Pay, which offered us little. We crossed a side street into the parking lot of another gas station, this one almost empty; we were almost through the lot when a familiar emblem caught my eye, glowing up and to the right of the door: Pete's Dank Chicken.

"Hey fellas," they all turned around and looked at me, "let's eat at this gas station."

"It good?" asked Bear.

"It's great. I—" Bear shrugged his shoulders and passed me towards the door. Cass and Speck followed.

The Kilgore Pete's was just as inauspicious and poorly lit as its Hunker Down and Jackson sisters. Grease flavored the air, coating my nostrils like a perfume. The smell of chicken brought a change over the lads; they mumbled in low tones, stony eyed and serious. They slinked around the aisles to the back counter, wolves closing in on a kill. Bear ordered first, pointing and grunting until the clerk properly announced his order—an inferno hot twelve-piece super family meal-deal bucket, all dark, with three orders of mashed potatoes. The inferno option was either a new addition or store specific. The grimy picture above the twelve piece showed a healthy and vested family of five smiling white-toothed over an immense bucket. After a moment of consideration, I waved at the cashier from behind the lads and pointed at myself, signaling that I would cover the tab, then let the other lads proceed with their orders before putting in for my eight-piece with double mashed potatoes, and fries.

I grabbed a half gallon of root beer to pair with the chicken, scooped up two handfuls of Pete's Dank sauce for the table and slid into the booth across from Bear who had already picked up his fork and knife, holding them in the ready position, focusing on the exposed table in front of him like a batter waiting for a pitch. I feared for the unfortunate chicken that drew that slot. Cass and Speck joined us, followed quickly by the food.

The wolves pounced. Jezebel had no doubt devoured vast quantities, but she had still retained her human dignities—the lads consumed, fed, and feasted on the fried flesh. The bolted down table shifted and squeaked as the lads ripped, tore, and swallowed. All three finished before I had even picked up my fourth piece. None had touched the Pete's Dank Sauce. None had thought to select a drink. When the bones lay bare, they slouched back, breathing heavily as they waited for me to finish. Sweat matted Bear's hair to his forehead. I shuddered to think what happened to the bones that should have occupied his tray.

"What'd y'all think?" I asked, the first words since Bear had claimed the booth. They grunted positive responses.

When I had finished I pocketed a big batch of Dank Sauce packets and we roamed the gas station, doing our bare bones shopping for the next leg. I checked out and found the lads waiting on me in the parking lot, smoking cigarettes.

We turned left out of the gas station lot, back towards the road that had brought us in. Several blocks down there was a sign for the Traveler's Motel, which was on our side of the street and advertised rates comparable to the motels of towns past.

"What about the Traveler's Motel?" I asked, pointing towards the sign. All three stopped and looked at me.

"No motels Nameless Gabe. City living distracts from our purpose," said Cass.

"I'd hardly call this a city."

"We have our own place."

"Your own place?"

"Bear found it. It is close enough."

"Does it have beds? Showers?" But Cass had already started walking.

"I wouldn't expect it," Speck said as he passed by.

Bear strode back down the original road turning off into the brush to weave through a couple rows of stunted pines. The lads' place was a spare cinderblock structure with cement floors and a tin roof. What it lacked in door, it also lacked in ventilation and windows. No beds. No showers. No television. No phone.

"So you'll ride in cars and eat at restaurants but you won't sleep in heated rooms with comfortable beds?"

"Who are you to criticize where we draw our lines?"

"I'm the guy that has to suffer by them."

"This is not a forced march, Nameless Gabe. You're free to go."

This thought had not occurred to me, and I weighed the idea of going into town and getting a room. Bear put a hand on my shoulder.

"You'll rest well, Gabe. This is good place. Special place."

"Reckon I'll see where the night takes me."

Bear's special place served much the same purpose as a child's treehouse, only these children already spent the entirety of their days amongst the trees. Bear and Speck stalked each other around the structure, peeking out from around corners, finger pistols drawn, emitting emphatic *PEW PEW PEWS* as their bullets ricocheted off the walls. Cass perched himself in the crook of nearby oak, blowing his smoke into the branches.

I reclined against the oak's base to watch Bear and Speck at their game—Bear would hightail it into the woods at full sprint, screaming *GET THE HELL OUTTA THERE* as Speck peppered his retreat. Then Bear would be down in the dirt, army crawling through the tall grass, making hand signals to invisible allies to ambush his target and retake the shed, only to pop his head up above the grass like an overgrown Meer cat, alerting Speck to his presence and reigniting the hostilities. I recalled playing a similar amusement in which Billy prowled the backyard attempting to dethrone his father by storming his playset castle. I found sleep on the battlefield.

My eyes opened to the sun setting on successful peace negotiations; the combatants were seated around a roaring communal fire, flames higher than the cabin. I watched Bear attempt to light his cigarette in the flame, losing some hair in the process. My body had burned off the excesses of lunch. I was hungry anew. I decided to make a solo run into town, get some food, and see if I could get my hands on a phone to call my girl back home.

I tiptoed through the high grass and turned left at the road. By the time I had reached the main strip, I had long since decided on pizza, and now was left with the generally arbitrary decision of selecting one pizza restaurant from the four in sight. I'd weathered many a family road trip, and well understood the difficulties of selecting a restaurant in a town like Kilgore—tourists will always provide steady business to even the worst of places, meanwhile neglecting better restaurants for the fault of having a dimmer sign or being an extra thirty yards removed from the interstate. My experience allowed me to develop a tried and true system—I located the establishment with the brightest, gaudiest sign, eliminated it, and went with the next closest one: Alfredo's Pizza Experience.

The restaurant was empty. The manager, a full-bodied domestic, filled a plastic lawn chair behind a checked red and white Formica counter. I estimated how much pizza it would take to feed the lads, doubled it, then ordered and displayed the cash on the counter, plunging a generous amount in the tip jar before asking to use his phone. After some deliberation, he assented and I assumed the plastic throne. Claire did not pick up so I left a message explaining why the missed call was from a rural pizzeria. After the call, I remained in the chair, shifting to watch the man and a teenager go about pulling my order from the freezer. The phone rang and I picked up.

"Alfredo's Pizza . . . ," I glanced at the sign, "Experience. How may I direct your call?"

"Hi, my name is Claire Jenkins. This is crazy but I think my husband just called from your restaurant."

The manager rushed towards me from the kitchen, I covered the mouthpiece and whispered *it's my wife* and he calmed down to just a confused and disapproving look.

"Well that's very interesting madam. There are several men here. Could you tell me how handsome your husband is so I can select him for you and perhaps suggest the proper pizza with which to pair him."

"Handsome's not really the word . . . He's the one that looks like a mailman got lost in the woods—but, if handsome is an option . . . ."

"Hello Claire."

"Hello Gabe."

"How did you like my phone presence? Pretty convincing right?"

"Oh yes. You really made me want to order pizza."

"Would you like me to take down your order? We do deliver, I think."

"I'm all set thanks."

"You'll be happy to hear I escaped the snow . . . which is a pleasant change, but Jezebel got off the Trail in Tyree."

"I thought she was doing a whole 'nother hike."

"Changed her mind. Said she felt like she was done and couldn't imagine doing the whole Great Eastern Trail again. So off she went."

"So you ran her off? Can't say that I'm terribly disappointed that you're no longer hiking with a young lady whom you clearly adored."

"Adored? I wouldn't say adored. Besides Claire you know it wasn't like that . . . She found my aging body revolting."

"Good taste. Are you still planning to go see Billy?"

"If I must. Reckon I'm having too much fun out here, have to balance it out."

"Gabe."

"Sorry. But you know what I mean."

"Are you still calling him?"

"I mean, you know, when I get the chance."

"You need to call him Gabe. He wants to talk to you."

"I'm calling him."

I heard a sigh. "So are you hiking alone now?"

"I was alone for a bit but I met up with some young fellas. Cass, Bear and Speck. Walked up on Cass having a sit down conversation with a rattlesnake."

"A conversation with a rattlesnake?"

I recounted my initial meeting with Cass.

"Had he been bit? Was he delirious?"

"Delirious might be the word for all three of 'em."

"Who knew that Gabe Jenkins, who almost never leaves his house after 6PM, would become lord of the wayward youths? Did you get my package?"

"I will before we head out tomorrow. Those *Juicerrmen* are irrefutable. If you could send the next box to the post office in Casas that would be great. I go through them pretty quick now since I have to share them with Bear. How are things at the store?"

"Your *Juicerrmans* are boxed and by the door. The store is good. Very busy. I'll let you know all about it when you're done."

"Why not now?"

"You're either here or you're not *Mister* Gabe. Right now, you're not." This struck home, sending an empty feeling through my stomach. I measured my response to gage her true level of displeasure.

"Do I still have a rumpus room?"

"There is still a room there." *Not too deeply angry.*

"I am excited to see you in couple weeks. Qannasseh is like the unofficial halfway point of the Great Eastern Trail. It's sort of a big deal to get there. You'll be like my prize."

"How honored I must be. I'm excited to see you too. Or to meet Mister Gabe rather, get a taste of this strange entity that's snatched my husband's body." The manager tapped me on the shoulder, plunked four large boxes on the desk, and crossed his arms.

"It's actually Gabe the Unnamed, or Nameless Gabe now, Claire, but my food is here so I've gotta go. I'll talk to you in the next town. I love you."

"I love you, too. Please be safe."

After I placed additional cash in the jar, the manager assented to letting me make another call. I looked out the window—it was a weekend and the sun had now fully set. I rolled the dice and called Billy's work number, leaving a message on his paralegal's machine.

With that I picked up the pizzas, thanked the manager, and returned to the club house.

The lads were laughing when I returned, having somehow conjured some libations: a case of light beer and a plastic bottle of *Cattleman's Whiskey*, already a quarter empty, warmed by the fire. Bear jolted when I put the pizzas down next to him, whipping around to check the tree at which I'd napped.

"Where'd you get pizza? Magic?"

"I paid for it. I don't want to know how y'all got booze. And did y'all really not notice I left? It was at least an hour."

"Are we the keepers of the Nameless?" yawned Cass.

"I think the words y'all are looking for are *thank you*. But here's pizza. Bought and paid for pretty much like every other pizza ever."

Each manchild snatched a box and retreated to the fire. With limited options, I rested my pizza on my lap, hurrying to eat it before it scorched my loins; the lads rushed to eat it because that was their way. When their pizza was gone, they returned to their booze and cigarettes. Cass rested back on his elbows, staring at me through streams of smoke. I thinned my lips and nodded at him, twice, before setting my eyes on the fire. Finally he spoke:

"So tell us Nameless Gabe. Give us the benefit of your aged wisdom. What are we to do with ourselves?"

"What do you mean?"

"What purpose have you found? What should we do with our time here on this planet?" He patted the ground. "What mistakes have you made that we should avoid? What productive steps should we replicate?"

"What makes you think I've taken any productive steps?"

"You're not dead."

"That's true. I have succeeded in not dying." The three lads gazed at me, faces glowing in the firelight. I worked back over my work and family life in search of an anecdote. "Don't . . . uh, be over ambitious." I looked around, nodding. "But . . . also, definitely don't settle."

"As you say Nameless Gabe. What of death?"

"Delay it."

"Presumably you're closer to the final wall than the rest of us. You've at least spent more time approaching it. What information, if any, have you gathered about the other side?"

"That's certainly a grim way of calling me old. I really haven't given it too much thought."

"Then what do you think about?"

I thought for a second. "I don't know. Maybe . . . the steps I haven't taken."

For a long time no one spoke. The lads stared into the fire, each mouth slightly askew, working their cigarettes.

"I want a big death." This was Bear. The alcohol smoothed his cadence. "Like the movies. I stagger out of the flames with a pretty girl over my shoulder, carrying her to safety. With my dying breaths I lay her down as she professes her love to me."

"Yes!" Speck jumped in. "And you have to be wearing bad ass sunglasses, the really big dark kind even though its dark out, and one of those awesome leather jackets."

"Obviously I will be wearing my leather jacket."

"And the girls just a-weepin' because she's realizing now that it's too late that she's been wasting her time with that accountant jabronie—it's you she loves."

"Obviously it's me she loves. I saved her life while wearing that bad ass jacket." Bear took a long pull—the first reported case of booze improving a man's diction. "And as I die, she cradles my head." He acted out the female's part in the scene, cradling an invisible head in his arms. "I take off my glasses and look up into her eyes . . . and whisper something . . . awesome to her like '*never give up Mildred, never . . . give . . . up . . . .*'" Bear, forgetting his part, lolled his head to the side.

"That's it, man. Nailed it."

"I hope you boys get your chance. But I'm going to bed." I staggered up to my feet. "Enjoy your health, lads."

Even through the pad and sleeping bag, the structure's cement floor was markedly less forgiving than frozen dirt of some of my prior evenings and further still from the lumpy softness of the motel mattress I so desired. That being said, it was cool and quiet; the bare cinder block walls provided that ineffable sense of being held captive that had evaded me up until that point.

23

Rain pinged off the tin roof; but it was the smell that woke me. The rain had forced the lads, and their gear, inside such that all four of us were laid out next to each other, parallel and close; I awoke pinned against the far wall. The stench was palpable, and emitted its own heat, as if the lads' wretched particulates were decomposing around me. My back was a column of fire from having slept so close to the cement; I could already feel the bruise on my hip where it had slipped from the pad during the night.

Speck's timid snores marked the time, somewhere between a sigh and a gasp, as if he was nibbling the foul air. I rolled over and pigged my nose against the wall, doing my best to breathe only cinder block. And so I stayed, focusing on a batch of scribbles, marked no doubt by a prior passerby, in the near corner. I closed my eyes and recounted Billy's youth baseball and soccer seasons, which I knew by heart: a time honored trick I'd often used to find sleep in dark places. Billy had just doubled in the third game of his age-fourteen baseball season when the light grew strong enough to discern the scribbles:

Mongrel. Mongrel. Mongrel. Mongrel. Mongrel.

Each inscription featured a different degree of wear and had been carved with a different tool. There was no accompanying limerick, but the myth had been here on several occasions, lifting the proverbial leg with each visit. Looking towards the corner, I found *BEAR* carved in much deeper letters.

The rain stopped. In the dim light I attained my feet and tiptoed around the lads, trekking back into Kilgore where I found an all-night diner complete with brilliant chrome trim and big plate glass windows.

The lads were up when I returned, but not moving. While Jezebel moved along the Great Eastern Trail with purpose, like a guest in someone's home taking a straight-line journey to the bathroom, the lads lounged, making themselves comfortable at every opportunity. Three nods acknowledged my presence.

The walk into town, and endless coffee, had loosened my back somewhat, but it still ached; I found a knotty tree to rub against, doing what I could to work out the tension. I was anxious to get moving and stay loose. After several idle cigarettes and odd bits of pizza the lads began to stir, swiping their belongings into their meager packs and drifting out towards the road. Once there, Speck went through the same routine he'd put on the day before —setting his feet, digging in, rolling and squaring his shoulders. I studied his movements as if the truck was hidden up his sleeve. The engine flared behind me, this time a small coup, roaring out of Kilgore to return us to the Trail. Speck flashed a puppy smile and hopped in.

Back at the Great Eastern Trail, the lads embarked on a cigarette while I pressed on, sensing an opportunity to get left behind given the day's constraints. I made good time up the Trail's steady incline, chugging along, nibbling on a *Juicerrman* as I made it over the initial climb and started down into the ensuing gap. A rustling commotion at my feet sent me reeling backwards. I fell on my pack, kicking my legs against the dirt to continue in that direction as the rustling developed into a sustained rattle. I regained my feet and located the source—a black mass of muscle coiled just to the right of the Trail. I also noted the rattle lacked the same heart-stopping ferocity of Cass's acquaintance; tracing the snake to its tail, I found the rattle to be the result of flesh and scales being battered against the dried leaves.

"That's quite the little scam you've got going there. You scared me half to death. Guess I didn't need all that coffee." His slitted eyes tracked my approach. "No need to worry. I may not believe you but I mean you no harm."

I paused, thinking about Cass and the rattlesnake, the birds and the rain, Speck's ever ready drivers; I glanced south down the Trail. "Well, maybe it wouldn't hurt to check if you have something to say."

I sat down facing the snake, making sure to stay out of its non-lethal striking distance. In addition to being rattleless, my friend was sleeker too, shiny rather than a brooding matte. The face on his narrow head betrayed a please-believe-me earnestness much more endearing than the rattlesnake's unbridled malice.

"It's okay buddy. I'm not going to hurt you. I'm just trying to see what you're about. Now, let's just be quiet for a second."

I caught the snake's eyes and tried to clear my mind. For some time we sat like that, facing each other in the dirt.

The rattling never faltered.

"You can cut that out, little fella. Like I said, no harm intended. I just want to talk—"

"Snakes can't talk, Gabe."

I lurched forward, away from the voice, sending the snake slithering into the underbrush. Bear, in a rare display of stealth, had crept up behind me.

"I know. I just, you know, Cass just predicted the rain so I just —"

"Cass always predicts rain. Sometimes it rains anyway."

Bear shook his head and disappeared down the Trail. I stood up and started to follow him, turning to the vacated spot before I left.

"I'm sorry I bothered you little buddy," I said, now only to the brush, "although next time you should be yourself."

I walked alone for some time, trying to discern what had possessed me to attempt conversation with a snake. I was also embarrassed to have been caught, even by Bear, whom I found standing on northern slope of the next mountain, examining a tree, hands clasped behind his back.

"Bear, you alright?"

"Nameless Gabe, what is this here?" He kicked the debris on the ground.

"I don't know Bear. Leaves?"

"And this ground, is it flat?"

"No it's . . . slanted."

"And this tree, is it pine?"

"No it's . . . Settler's Fowl!" I set down my pack and lifted the compacted layer of leaves revealing a fresh bounty of mushrooms.

Bear grinned and removed the grocery bag.

24

Four sunshiny mountain days followed. Bear continued his lessons in mushroom foraging beating his chest in excitement when, on the third day, I located my own stash without assistance.

The fifth day provided a new opportunity for Speck to showcase his gift and transport us into Casas. My aged back demanded a bed; there could be no repeat of the Kilgore disappointment. I was hurting and needed to sleep on a mattress under a roof. Given what the lads had told me, it had probably been a long time since Bear and Cass had slept in real beds. Speck went through his routine, summoning up a silver sedan which dropped us off on Church Street. The driver did not speak.

"A proposition, lads. I'm old, my back hurts, and I'm dirty. I miss chairs and television something fierce. How about I get us a pair of rooms here in town, my treat?"

"Towns for food only." Bear scanned the empty streets.

"We do not do towns, he-who-has-not-been-named. You know this truth."

"This will be my adventure. And I said I would pay."

"Money is not the issue."

I spotted a movie theatre down the road, displaying its current offerings in black letters against an oranging backlight. *The*

Raiders (*actually T_e R_ide_s*), a schlocky looking action movie whose trailers I'd derided before setting off, was playing tonight at 7. "Right, never mind that for now. How about this, there's a movie theatre just down there playing a war movie." Bear jolted around in the direction in which I was pointing. "I'll thrown in movie tickets."

"Movie?" Bear said.

". . . And a large tub of popcorn. For each of y'all."

"Popcorn!?" Speck's eyes widened.

"Buttered popcorn. Think about it, comfy seats, laps full of popcorn and candy. And fizzy soda."

"Moovvieee."

"Maybe one night in town wouldn't hurt."

Cass narrowed his eyes. "It is the pinprick that undoes the balloon."

"We won't undo, Cass, promise. It would be, um, a celebration of how far we've come out here, physically and spiritually, or whatever. Especially when we don't enjoy it."

"What say you Bear?"

"Movie." Bear gaped at the glowing sign.

Cass turned to look down on me. "If it be the will of the group." Speck pumped his fist behind him. Based on my calculations, the entire endeavor would cost me less than one night out with Claire.

For accommodations, we split into pairs—Bear and Speck in one room, then me and Cass, the clear frontrunner, somehow, for least stinky lad, in the next.

I showered first, exiting to find Cass sitting on his bed, legs crossed as he rolled cigarettes. His hands were a blur of motion: pinching, placing, cinching, squeezing, rolling, and licking; his eyes never left the television. A battalion of tightly wrapped, uniform creations lay in formation around him. After days in the woods he should have been filthy beyond repair, and certainly more cognizant of befouling a good bed; but, here he was relaxing, eerily clean, and unperturbed on his sheets, pumping out regiments of hand-rolled unfiltereds.

I shoved my dirty clothes as far in the corner as I could, making a mental note to do a laundry run at some point, and dressed in my rain gear. I laid down and watched a few minutes of the game show on the screen. A big-haired lady in a floral dress spun a giant wheel, coming up one rung short of the life-changing grand prize.

Cass remained settled on his bed when I awoke, still rolling cigarettes but watching a new game show; this one featuring a slight young man screaming out the answers to riddles as a glass box closed in around him.

"What is your plan?" he asked. He never looked at me. The non-descript floral wallpaper backdrop, combined with the game show and the old wood-paneled television, lent to Cass's mystic air, giving the impression of something independent of time and place.

"We could always eat. If the others are ready."

Cass lifted his big hand from his cigarettes and pounded the wall behind him.

"Is Bear hungry?" The wall roared back. Cass unloaded his ingredients from his lap, pocketing more than a few for the road.

Despite his responsive howl, Bear remained shirtless on the floor, smoking and staring at the television. He had located, or created, some scrap of cloth which he'd fashioned into a bandana; he laughed maniacally at a forgotten sitcom.

I had been wise enough to book two smoking rooms and even wiser to pay cash. Smoke clouded the room but I could not smell it over the rotten stench of sweat and moisture. Everything felt close and hot. It was like some swampy barracks over which Bear reigned supreme. Speck was in here too, of that I was certain, but I could not detect him at present.

"Bear, would you like to go eat before the movie? Maybe a shower? Or two?" He did not respond; in fact, he had done nothing to acknowledge our presence in the room. Bear roared as a fat man tumbled through a coffee table.

How long had it been since he'd watched television? And would a full-blown big budget action movie overload his circuits?

Cass waited for a commercial then walked over and flipped off the television. Bear was on his feet in a second, hissing through clenched teeth.

"Movie. Bear. Remember we are going to a movie."

"Movie?"

"Movie, my friend, and Nameless Gabe is providing town dinner."

Bear wolfed down his food, all but lifting the bottoms of everyone's beers to help them keep pace. The food was unremarkable, just a chain designed to imitate a local establishment, but it deserved better than this. Once seated, Bear's popcorn vibrated in his lap as if it was still popping. It was a prime time showing, and apparently a Saturday, but the tiny theatre was almost vacant. I estimated that it would be out of business by the time I reached Daemon's Peak.

A burger, two beers, a padded chair in a still, lukewarm room —I was asleep before the coming attractions.

A loud noise jolted me to consciousness. *Had it been an explosion or a snore?* I glanced at the lads; their eyes, even Cass's, were locked on the screen. The backs of their seats could have gone up in flame and it wouldn't have singed their shirts. All three were hunched forward, arms planted on the seats in front of them, gaping at the screen as what I assumed was the last soldier, brawny and bare-chested, stalked a horrible looking creature through the jungle. He caught the creature in an opening, and just as the creature was about to turn the tables, apparently through the utilization of some gruesome wrist-based technology, a spear flew in from the woods, sticking the creature in the side. Two seats down, Bear gasped. Another spear caught the creature in the throat as he spun frantically discharging a blue laser into the jungle. A fleet of spears descended at once, sending the creature to his knees. Bear cheered as an aged man, I assumed the chieftain, strolled out of the jungle, whispered *this is not your world*, and finished it with an intricately engraved dagger which he subsequently held up to his cheering people. The credits rolled over our goodly hero kissing a local maiden and boating off into the sunset.

Bear danced around us the whole way back to the motel. Reenacting scenes, stumbling over the local's accent. Speck launched invisible spears at passing cars. Even Cass joined in, miming his reenactment of ending the beast with the dagger. When we returned to the motel, the lads convened in the room next door, while I went to my room, turned my TV on, then off, and listened to the lads giggle through the wall.

It had felt good to play dad again. Billy and I had gone to the movies with some regularity, even during his college years, and had spent endless hours criticizing and critiquing. He no doubt would've found many fatal flaws in tonight's feature.

25

The early sun lit the room despite the thin curtains. Cass must've fallen asleep in the other room, because there was no trace of him. Even all the cigarettes were gone. I pressed my ear against the wall—nothing stirred; I curled up in bed and turned on the television. I called Claire and, after confirming the day, Billy at work.

I became captivated by a recap of the previous day's sports. For the first time in a long time the baseball season had started without my rapt attention; I consumed the condensed highlights in one big non-contextual lump. The hour long segment had played through twice when Cass shuffled through the door, bent at the hips with his head parallel to the floor, leaving the door half open, and folding into his bed.

I dressed and slipped out the door en route to breakfast and *Juicerrmen*.

Cass was smoking a cigarette when I returned.

"Good morning."

"It is time for the day's adventure."

"Okay then. Wake up your friends, especially our ride conjurer, and let's do it."

Cass banged on the wall behind him, yelling for the occupants to get ready. When no response came, we put together our packs and went over to meet them. The room was a fire hazard: alcohol soaked the air; empty beer cans, crushed and whole, littered the floor; both beds boasted shredded pizza boxes. Only one boasted a boy—Bear had not made it into bed, instead somehow finding sleep with his shaggy head on the bathroom tile and his big splayed feet out in the hall.

The television was still turned on to a premium channel, now displaying a regrettable romantic comedy, but I had no doubt that last night the lads had indulged in something approaching soft-core.

"Rouse them. It is past time."

"My days of waking up grouchy youths are long gone. You shouldn't have stayed up so late. Doing whatever ever y'all did." Bear's right foot scratched against the closet door. "Tell you what, I'll take Speck. You can deal with that."

Speck had shoved his head under two beds' worth of pillows, dampening his mousey snores. I found a soft shoulder and shook.

"Speck . . . Speck."

Speck's bewildered face erupted out of the scratchy linens, sending pillows flopping to the floor. He groped about blindly, until locating the trash bin and relieving himself.

Despite their pitiable conditions, the lads were quick in their preparation, raiding a gas station for their breakfast, each emerging with a fistful of pre-packaged cinnamon rolls which Bear scarfed down as he walked. Speck only nibbled. I took the opportunity to enjoy another bottle of root beer.

We turned the corner onto the road that had brought us into Casas and went some ways down before Speck stopped us.

He licked his finger and held it up to the wind. "Okay fellas, this is our spot." Speck stepped out to the road, collecting himself into the stance, kissing and extending his thumb, but without the crispness and enthusiasm of his prior performances. Still, like clockwork, a ragged minivan rattled around the corner.

I didn't understand the mechanics of it, but I was learning to accept the lads' mischief.

The trash bag covering the back passenger window shrieked until the van dumped us off at the Trail, stopping for the exact amount of time it took for us to unload, before accelerating around a turn and back into the ether. This time the lads took off up the slope and were soon hidden by the blossoming trees. I labored after them, struggling against a bellyful of hashbrowns and root beer. It seemed a miracle that the lads could smoke as they did and retain the lung capacity for their carefree scamper. It also seemed a miracle that the lads could drink as they did and retain any strength at all. But the powers of youth can only be dulled by time.

I recalled how angry I had been when Billy had taken up cigarettes in high school—on one occasion borrowing my car and neglecting to remove a half empty pack of a high-brow brand from the center console. When confronted he had tried to say they were Claire's, before promising to quit. However, he '*stealthily*' kept up this habit, sneaking out to smoke on the back porch under Claire and my window, until he met a forward minded, and very pretty, young woman at college who thought the habit repulsive, at which point he declared smoking the dark evil of our age. The real disappointment was that the cigarettes, which I had no taste for, replaced his cigars under the mattress.

I caught up with the lads that evening, finding Cass reclining near a roaring fire. He had perhaps forty cigarettes resting on his chest.

"Evenin' Cass, hope you weren't too worried abo—" a creature leapt out from behind the nearest tree brandishing a crooked stick:

"WELCOME TO EARTH MOTHER FUCKER!!!"

I stumbled back, managing two desperate, uneven steps before finally falling. A series of irretrievably pathetic moans escaped my mouth. I put up my hands to fend off the attacker.

Bear, shirtless and smeared with dirt, stood over me. The hot blood swelled in my neck and cheeks—I could feel my face glowing red.

"Nice to see you Bear."

He smiled down at me, revealing two rows of inexplicably white teeth, and offered me a hand. I waved it off, choosing instead to remain stewing on the ground.

"It's from the movie, Nameless Gabe. The movie you took us to."

"I must've slept through the part where they terrified the poor old man." My buttocks hurt from where I'd thumped down.

"I didn't think you'd fall." On a more human face, his expression would have resembled shame.

"It's fine Bear. Just a little warning next time you get the acting bug."

He once again lifted me to my feet by my armpits like he was picking up a doll, taking a moment to brush the dirt off my backside. I followed him to the fire, waddling, not really knowing what to do with myself. Cass and Speck studied us through their smoke.

Bear was quiet for the rest of the night. I went away to set up my tent and returned with my food bag and the shelter log to read with dinner, flipping through the tattered pages until Mongrel's soft brown note fell into my lap. I unfolded tonight's musing:

> MONGREL COME, MONGREL GO
> MAKE DIVERSE, YOUR PORTFOLIO

After dinner, I stayed up for a while as the lads re-reenacted their favorite scenes, going to bed when they began storyboarding the sequel.

26

We spent the next five, maybe six, days immersed in the wilderness, climbing mountains and picking Settler's Fowl. The day before I would meet my wife in Qannasseh, or rather the day in which I intended to get into Qannasseh to clean thoroughly in preparation for my wife, the lads stopped short at Rabbit Pond Shelter.

"Gabe. Wife tomorrow?"

I nodded the affirmative.

"Good. Follow."

Bear led us down a short side path, little more than a game trail, which opened up on a great pool of still water.

"Welcome to Squirrel Lake!"

The lake's surface was smooth and still, but somewhere nearby water rushed over rocks. A couple of the lake's namesakes scurried off the beach as Bear, already disrobed past my point of preference, mauled into the water.

I pulled down to my skivvies alongside Cass and Speck and strode into the cool water, pausing at its initial lap of my gentler regions. The pond was clear despite the recent rains, and never got over chest deep. Speck and Bear wrestled in the shallows. The pond's name was well-earned—grey bodies stood erect on most every branch, beady black eyes monitored our movements.

One squirrel had poked out from a hole in a tree, crooking his furry arm like a conductor leaning from his train.

From the center I discovered the source of the rushing water—a waterfall, maybe eight to ten feet, cascading into a nearby alcove. I waded over, stepped under, and looked up; it had been a long time since I'd showered, no doubt too long, longer than any other period of my life. The icy water released me from the sticky film which had incased me for several days, thickened by the rain. I was happy that I would see Claire at least somewhat clean—most store bought body washes advertised a mountain stream fragrance anyway. I kneaded my dirty clothes under the waterfall; if I were a more attractive man, the scene would have resembled a laundry commercial.

That night we camped amongst the squirrels. Bear built a fire, painting the water in a shimmering orange sheet. Just outside the firelight, the rustling was constant; emboldened squirrels ventured close enough that the fire often caught their eyes like a pair of thieving marbles. I sat back from the smoke, and went to bed early, determined to walk slow and get to town early.

Once in my bag, I lay awake trying to picture Claire out here hiking, cavorting with suspect youths, and swimming in mountain lakes. It seemed impossible that she could join me out here; not because she was physically incapable, but because I had changed by walking to this point, having overcome rain, snow, mountains, pain, and cold—even taken on a new name. Now I could not be sure what she would see when she saw me, or I her.

We awoke to the screams—first a jumble of confusion, then genuine pain and alarm. I vacated my tent to find Bear and Speck standing on their blankets, peering into the darkness. Cass's blanket was an empty aluminum wrapper glinting in the firelight. Bear picked up a burning log from the fire and marched off in the scream's direction. Speck and I followed. The screams continued until we found Cass huddled on a log, clutching his hand. The boy toughened when he saw us, and perceived the concern in his peers' eyes, straightening his back and stifling his whimpers as best he could. Bear lowered the log towards his friend revealing a dark stain streaming through his fingers, spreading down his shorts.

"Cass are you okay? What happened?"

Eyes reflected from all levels behind him.

"I am fine. It is nothing."

"You were screaming and I can see blood."

"I am fine."

We all stepped closer to Cass; Bear going so far as to place a hand on his back. My fatherly instincts took hold.

"You're going to have to show me your hand."

"I . . . don't want to let go." His breath came in deep, anti-rhythmic snorts.

"Cass, there's not much I can do for you if you don't let me see it."

"I am fine. It is—"

"Dog dern it Cass. We need to see what's going on."

Cass separated his hands and Bear lowered the log revealing a batch of shredded meat fit for tacos. Something had torn him from wrist to forefinger. Blood oozed out concealing the wound.

"What the hell happened?"

"I, I was communing."

"With a wolf? A coyote? Did a bear bite you?"

Cass took a deep breath and leaned in close to me. Speck and Bear bent over behind him, eyes wide.

"A squirrel."

"A squirrel!? A squirrel did this to you?"

"He did not wish to commune."

"You don't say."

Bear handed his torch to Speck then took Cass's squirreled hand between his paws and pressed, looking down and then up at Cass. Cass caught his eye.

"Ow."

Speck put a hand on Bear's shoulder and shook his head.

"We need to get you to a hospital."

"I, I am fine. It is nothing."

"It's a wild animal bite, a rodent bite, exactly the type of thing that gets infected and causes problems."

"I am fine. It is nothing."

"No." I stood up, surprised by the firmness in my voice. "We need to get you to a hospital. At minimum you need stitches and, more than likely, a whole batch of shots. Otherwise who knows what just got ripped into you."

"If it is so willed."

"Cass I will show you what is so willed; you'll wish the damned snake had bit you." Bear and Speck now looked only at me.

"I am fine. It is nothing. See." Cass lifted his injured hand in a display of good health—a sizable shred of hand did not make the journey, choosing instead to remain in his lap. Cass noticed it to, as did Bear and Speck. For a gory moment we all stared at Cass's lost flesh.

We did our best to wrap and secure the remainder of Cass's hand, burrito bandaging the shredded meat in Jezebel's towel. Bear offered to carry him, an offer Cass declined, and so we made our slow trek the rest of the way to the Qannasseh road in tight formation, keeping Cass between Bear and myself; Cass muttering his occasional protests although he walked without further urging until we reached the road.

Qannasseh was another town in which the Great Eastern Trail joined Main Street, but it was after an extended road walk and, given Cass's condition, we decided Speck should use his gift. A sedan pulled around the corner and we ushered Cass into the backseat, trying to conceal the extent of his bleeding. It was alarming how much blood Jezebel's towel could retain; I had the brief morbid thought that maybe we could wring it back into him. Prior to Grambling's Pass, this all would have seemed very strange.

The driver dropped us off in front of the hospital. Cass had done well to suffer his injuries near a town with such an establishment. We piled out under the emergency room awning, and Bear and I assisted Cass out of his seat.

The lads huddled together in the waiting room, clearing a family from a row of padded chairs, while I got the check-in clipboard from the front desk. I sat down across from Cass to take his information, feeling like a census surveyor contacting an aboriginal tribe. Bear sat next to him; the fluorescent lights laid bare each and every speck of dirt and accentuated each greasy smear.

"Okay Cass, they're gonna need your actual name."

"My name is Cass." He kept his chin tucked into his chest.

"Allow me to rephrase. They are going to need a name that's going to show up when they plug it into their system—generally these names consist of three parts."

Cass lifted his head and scanned the room, as if anybody in there gave a dern what his name was, then leaned in as best he could and whispered, "Stanley Herbert Kinsell."

"Stanley Herbert Kinsell?" I projected. Cass pursed his lips and nodded. "Good. Thanks *Herb*. And where were you born?"

I sifted the information out of Cass, waiting out his adolescent refusals during each round. His obvious pain played in my favor. When the form was completed, the veil had been lifted from the twenty year old mid-westerner seated across from me. I turned in the form and ventured down to the payphone bank by the bathrooms.

After some doing, and several coins, I managed to get the hotel in Qannasseh and leave a message for Claire to meet me at the hospital. From there I went into the bathroom and vigorously rubbed my body down with the brief squirts of water emitted by the push button sinks, stinging my armpits with copious hand sanitizer before changing into my 'cleaner' set of clothes. I didn't blame the squirrel for what it'd done to Cass, but it was very inconvenient.

I returned to Cass and Bear arguing with an orderly who was attempting to take Cass back to treatment.

"Cass, Bear, what's the problem here?"

"Won't let me back. Family only. Says I'm not family."

The slight orderly flinched each time Bear gesticulated. I figured it had something to do with Bear's status as a walking biohazard. His nipple poked through one of the *o's* in *JoJo*. She looked up at me. "Hospital policy. Are you this boy's father?"

"Um yea. As a matter of fact I am."

The orderly looked from me to Cass, scanning over several obvious differences, but apparently decided not to make a thing of it. "Okay then. Come on back." She pointed at Bear. "Get him to stay out here."

I nodded at Bear and ushered Cass through the door.

The orderly guided to a closed white room with instructions to wait. Cass positioned himself in the operating chair, sitting slouched, limp, and pitiful. His good hand kept reaching to his pocket for the cigarettes he'd left with Bear and Speck. Jezebel's ultra-absorbent towel was swollen with blood. Massive red splotches covered his shirt and shorts, and even the occasional splatter on his socks.

"You're gonna be okay, Cass. This kind of stuff is sort of a right of passage."

"…"

"And I think we're good to remove your bandages. I imagine the doctor will have something a little more sanitary."

Cass kept his injured hand cradled in his lap, and kept his eyes locked on the ceiling.

"It's gonna be fine Cass. You're young and heal quickly. We're just lucky this didn't happen to me. I'd be down and out."

"Why?" He looked up me, revealing the tears streaking down his cheeks. "Why would it do this to me?" Cass writhed his long body, double foot stomping at the bottom of the chair. His hand bobbed against his chest in what must have been an excruciating rhythm.

"It was a squirrel. It probably thought you wanted to eat it or steal its acorns."

Cass looked up and nodded. "I just wanted to commune."

"Squirrels aren't in on your cosmic shenanigans."

He slumped back into the examination chair. "Everything. Everything on the Great Eastern Trail is in on it."

"You really think that you can just sit down and chit chat with wild animals and nothing bad will ever happen?"

"If all is one, then there is no conflict."

"I'll grant that this Great Eastern Trail is a pretty strange place full of ghosts and super hitch-hikers, but I would need a little more proof about what it all means before I started cornering wild animals."

"The snake didn't bite. And the birds told of rain."

"But the squirrel tore the devil out of you."

"So you think it's all . . . all bull shit?"

"I don't know. I genuinely have no explanation why Speck can summon a ride at every turn simply by wagging his thumb, or why Bear seems to be fully invincible, or the ghost I saw, but just because all this is possible, doesn't mean anything is possible. There have to be limits. And I'm pretty sure we just found one."

The doctor knocked and entered. "Ok, Mr. . . . Kinsell, it says here you had a run in with . . . a squirrel." He looked at Cass over his chart.

"It was a very mean squirrel." I don't know if that helped Cass.

"Right. It shows here that you are up to date on your tetanus?"

"Yes. Maybe two months ago."

"You stopped to get a tetanus booster on the Trail?"

"No. My parents insisted. Before I started."

"You've only been on Trail for two months?"

Cass groaned.

"Sir, please."

I tried to calculate the brief amount of time he'd been on the Great Eastern Trail before I'd found him sitting face to face with a rattlesnake.

I stayed with Cass throughout the doctor's examination, acting as interpreter when I could tell the patient could not understand the question—or the doctor the answer—and holding Cass's good hand as they provided the many necessary injections when a person is savaged by a wild rodent. Cass locked his eyes on the ceiling as they approached with a long series of needles, whimpering with each prick, grinding my knuckles together. After they—somehow—stitched his hand back together, I helped a nurse load a groggy Cass into a wheelchair and escort him back out into the waiting room.

Red hues of sunset glowed through the blinds. A third person had taken my seat, the back of her grey-haired head hovered above the padded chair, facing Speck and Bear. The lads sprang up at the sight of their friend. My wife turned around.

I had made sure she would be there but was nevertheless stunned to see her. She rose to her feet. The light seemed to follow.

"Claire . . ."

"I figured these two must be with you."

My feet took me to her, where I hesitated to hug her, painfully aware of my present condition. She did not. We kissed before she leaned back and studied my face, tugging on my cheek beard.

Claire was impossibly clean; a bright and unwrinkled light pink shirt, spotless white shorts and her short hair perfectly combed and set.

Claire turned her attention to the boy slouched in the wheelchair.

"This is Cass. He's usually a little, um, more lively. A squirrel bit his hand and a nurse gave him a great many injections."

Claire drove us all back to the hotel where, much to the chagrin of the diminutive and mustached owner, we booked an extra room for the lads, who, for once, did not have to be bribed to sleep indoors.

27

We helped tuck Cass in then Claire led me up the staircase to our room. Each and every feature: armoire, bed frame, nightstands and desk, was stained hardwood, ripped from the forest and darkened to some ancient landlord's preference; each and every piece of fabric was floral maroon.

I showered hard, tasked with removing both the salty, savory mountain scents and the hospital grade hand sanitizer; I wore out the thin sliver of fragrant soap, finishing with several doses of shampoo. When I stepped out of the bathroom, Claire had the windows open and was sitting on the balcony overlooking Main Street. She looked out of place in this segment of my life; she had only ever existed under different circumstances in a different place.

I started to slip into my rain gear when Claire called out from the balcony.

"I have some of your old, you know, Bodette clothes. You'll be much more comfortable in those. Look better too."

The regular clothes were folded neatly on the bed—khakis, collars, tired boat shoes, thin blue socks, and a belt my father had given me upon graduating college.

Carefully, I applied the clean clothes, doing my best not to taint them with my touch. When it was done, I checked my new old self in the mirror—the clothes wore like a temporary uniform. I had lost enough weight and volume, an inch here, a fraction there, that my shirt hung low over my shoulders and billowed out around my waist. My pants parachuted out below my knees. Underneath the clothes I found that Claire had also brought me a new, nicer, headlamp per my request.

Claire laughed at the sight of me, covering her mouth with her hand, and setting down her drink.

"What do you think?"

"If I hadn't pulled the clothes from your drawer myself, I would say they're someone else's. That's more or less your face, but they don't seem to go together anymore. Although I'm really just glad you won't be eating dinner in a rain jacket." She stood up, lifted my mustache with her finger, and gave me a kiss. "Now, are we going to try to clean the Trail clothes or burn them?"

I put the clothes and quarters in the machine, set it to its most cleaningest cycle, and rejoined Claire outside. We strolled hand-in-hand through Main Street's caramel nighttime glaze, landing at the bar at *Blaze Café*. Claire ordered a glass of red wine while I got a chocolate infused beer.

"How was the ride up here? I hope Highway 81 didn't give you too much trouble."

"It was easy Gabe. I was in a car going seventy miles an hour with air conditioning and talk radio. It only took about eight hours." She tilted her head and looked at me over her wine. "You walked here."

"Almost two months." I took a goodly swig of beer, thumping it down with a cough. "The Great Eastern Trail is not a path for getting places. I'm not even sure that miles and minutes are the proper units of measurement for it."

"Then what is the proper unit?"

"I really have no idea."

"Come on, tell me about this grand journey that's taken you away from me."

"What do you want to hear?"

"Tell me about Jezebel."

I took a hesitant sip. "I forget what I've told you, but she was amazing. I met her when it was still cold, walked up on her soaking her feet in an icy spring, casual and smiling like she had her toes dipped in the neighborhood pool. It was like she was impervious to cold, or emanated some undue warmth. We helped each other get through the Donners."

"And you sent her packing?"

"Something like that. She, um, just said she was done. Felt like she had completed whatever she'd come out here to do."

"And what about these boys you're hiking with now?"

"The lads . . . they're a little more, um, wilder. I told you I met Cass trying to converse with rattlesnake."

"So he's crazy?"

"Well maybe. No real excusing the squirrel. But he really believes it, that he can talk to animals. Or can learn to, I guess. You know that snake didn't bite him. Cass's real name is Stanley Kinsell if you want to bother him. And Bear is just a wild man. He charges through the woods fueled by homemade cigarettes and foraged mushrooms. I think he's invincible. Speck's more on our level. He's just along for the ride. His thing is that he can hitch a ride whenever he wants."

"His thing? He can just make a car appear out of nowhere."

"Driver included. It's the derndest thing I ever saw. All he does is go up to the road, do a little routine, put his thumb out and the next thing you know a car comes out of nowhere, just a-rumblin' around the corner."

Claire looked at me with raised eyebrows. "Quite a crew you've assembled, Mister Gabe. Although it was touching to see you playing father to Cass. Even if he is a snake talker. Speck and Bear told me about you taking them to the movies. Reminds me of when you used to pay attention to your own family."

"I told you I'm Nameless Gabe now. The lads say I haven't earned a name and Mister Gabe's too simple to count."

"Well as long as a part of you is still Gabe."

"I guess I need to stay out here until I get a new one."

She put her soft hand in mine. "No Gabe, Mister Gabe, Nameless Gabe, husband of mine. You need to get this out of your system and come home."

After a few drinks we switched from the bar to the dining area —a chance to show off the excesses of a hiking appetite. Claire sipped her wine and picked around the cheese in a salad, as I put down two appetizers, an entrée and a dessert meant for two.

"I hope this appetite doesn't last after you're finished. I'll have to open another store just to feed you."

"I wouldn't worry about that. Once we're back on the Trail you'll see it's actually pretty cheap to feed me."

"Oh goodie."

"Speaking of . . . are you excited for tomorrow?"

"Nervous is the word I'd use. I don't think I've been camping since college."

"No, remember that spring just before you got pregnant we went camping at Slay Djinn Falls with Roger and Martha? And Roger got drunk and almost fell into the fire, and when I saved him he got mad at me for grabbing him and stormed away to pass out by the river."

"And then the next morning he was covered in mosquito bites."

"So yea that was the last time. It's only been like . . . thirty years."

"Sure. Except for that time I was camping next to my car with dear friends and my husband. Three decades ago. This time I'm going into the woods with a stranger and, if I'm really lucky, three feral boys."

"Well, when you put it that way."

28

I woke up well before Claire, spending the interim floating in the gentle, fragrant embrace of a real hotel's mattress and linens. The embroidered curtains glowed with sunlight. Next to me, Claire resembled a sleeping queen. Before embarking on the Great Eastern Trail, I had never noticed the subtle colors through which the sun displayed its genius, the way a ray of light could blossom on my wife's cheek. I recalled standing with Jezebel on the peak of Mount Herring and the experiences reserved exclusively for those who'd earned them.

I kissed Claire to wake her up. She smiled and rolled over to talk to me.

"Is it going to be this comfortable in the woods?"

"Of course. Your sleeping pad inflates to a queen and your sleeping bag is two-thousand thread count. There's even little woodland elves to bring you breakfast pastries and tea."

"No there's not."

"No, but there are man-eating squirrels."

For breakfast the Main Street Inn offered bite size scones and other pastries paired with fruit, coffee, and tea; all made available on dainty silver platters lined on a wooden dinner table. None of the thru-hiker's essential food groups: meat, salt, eggs, starches, or mammal fat, were present in sufficient quantity. There was no sign of the lads.

Claire, a novice, selected three morsels from three separate trays and poured a small cup of steaming green tea. I considered taking a whole tray from the serving station, and likely would have in more sympathetic company, but settled for two plates loaded with flaky pyramids of delicately crafted pastries.

I set the plates down on the table, popping two pastries into my mouth before taking my seat. Claire used her thumb and forefinger to elevate a pasty, nibbled a portion off the edge, and closed her eyes, covering her mouth with a straight-fingered hand the way she did when really savoring food.

"Gabe have you tried one of these yet? They are divine."

"It's possible. Which one were they?"

She opened her eyes to the empty plates in front of me.

"Never mind." She selected another pastry, setting the half finished one back on her plate. "You know some people take the time to taste their food."

"Those people aren't actually hungry."

We paid the breakfast bill and went to coordinate our departure with the lads. When she'd called to reserve the room, the innkeeper had agreed to keep Claire's real world car and luggage until she returned from our hike in three or four days; Claire didn't love that I couldn't give an exact day, or method, of return. The plan was for us to hike into Sacred Place where we would wrangle her a ride back to Qannasseh.

The lads did not answer our knocks. Nor could I smell them through the door.

We exited the hotel to check down Main Street. A bedraggled young man, dirtier even than Bear, with a sloping poof of greasy brown curls, slept on the bench near the entrance. I stationed myself between him and Claire as we scanned down the sidewalks.

"I guess we can find them on the Trail."

"Your lads aren't here." The young man did not open his eyes. Claire and I glanced each other, then moved to walk down the street and distance ourselves from the vagrant's ramblings. He spoke again. "They've relocated to the park at the end of Edgefield Avenue. They'd very much like to see you again." He kept his head propped against the metal armrest, eyes closed against the sunlight.

"Are you talking to us?"

"If you will listen. Go see the lads."

"Okay which way to Edgewood."

The young man raised his finger, pointing past his head.

I took Claire's hand; we followed his instructions for a few paces before stopping. "And since when do we listen to cryptic hobos?"

"I've sorta been doing it for a while now. Plus, why would he lie?"

The lads had started a fire and lay around it on picnic tables. The well-trimmed grass was scored where one of them, presumably Bear, had dragged the tables into circled wagon formation.

"NNNNAAAAMMMMEEEELLLLLEEEEEEEESSSSSS GGGAAAABBBBEEEEEE!" Bear fog-horned our approach, raising a beer. Each lad had his own bench, and each bench had its own twelve-pack of beer. It was nine in the morning.

"Annnnd guest," Speck chirped.

Cass remained supine on the bench, his injured arm raised on the tabletop.

"Y'all don't look like you're going anywhere."

"Cass needs to heal."

"I remember. Just didn't think that would slow you down. Unfortunately we are about to head out."

"One more beer? One more beer with Bear?" His face displayed his surprise with this turn of phrase.

"Come on Nameless Gabe. You'll probably never see us again. You can drink fast."

I looked at Claire, who nodded. "Alright just one. Then we have to bolt."

Bear reached into the case; one by one, he tossed me two light blue cans of lukewarm refreshment, then pounced up to sit on the top level of his picnic table, patting the spot next to him. Claire shifted to the other side of me and sat down on the far end of the bench.

"I'd like to thank y'all for taking care of my husband, even if he has turned into this grizzly morning-drinking, all-consuming beast."

"He was like this when we found him, ma'am." Speck couldn't stifle his smile. "We were actually all going to stop hiking and get desk jobs before your husband convinced us to stay."

"The Unnamed is a very bad influence."

"Is that so? What else are you hiding from me?"

"He fell in the tunnel, remember Nameless?"

"A tunnel? Why didn't you tell me about that?"

"I had a minor breakdown in the middle of a very dark and inordinately scary tunnel. It's not one of the highlights."

"Speaking of—Cass how long did the doctor say before you can hike?"

"Yea Cass when can we leave? You didn't mention."

"He didn't."

"What do you mean he didn't? Do you have to have a check-up?"

"I mean the hospital called my parents. They told me to stay here. I'm getting picked up in two days."

"Your parents are coming to pick you up?"

"You're not going to finish the Trail?"

"It is as you say. Apparently there're several rounds of required shots after you get bit by a squirrel. You are free to go on without me."

Speck looked at Bear who spoke. "No, we stay together. See you off."

I pictured Cass, the boy who'd stared down a rattlesnake, riding home in the back of his parent's station wagon. I reached the bottom of my can, which meant it was time to go.

"I'm sorry to hear that Cass. I hope your hand heals well and you can start on your next adventure soon but Claire and I really must be off. We have a ways to go and I'm not sure how fast Claire will be able to go." Claire and I stood up to leave. Bear leapt up and wrapped me in his arms.

"Goodbye Mister Nameless Gabe. It was weird hiking with you." His hug lifted me off the ground.

"It was weird hiking with you too, Bear." Claire stepped back and extended a delicate hand. Bear took it in both of his.

"You take care of him Missus Gabe. He needs help."

"Don't I know it."

"I must say I'm proud of you staying with Cass, making sure he gets out okay. Didn't know y'all could sit still for two days."

Bear shrugged his shoulders. "Mongrel say 'tend your wounded.'"

"Mongrel? In one of his posts?"

"No, Mongrel on bench. Mongrel see Cass. Mongrel say *tend your wounded*." Bear wagged a finger.

"Mongrel's here!?" I looked at Claire. "The cryptic hobo! Did he tell you anything else? Did he talk in rhymes?"

"Hello. Tend your wounded. Goodbye. No rhymes."

"Did you hear that Claire?! Mongrel is here, in Qannasseh. We actually met him."

I hustled back towards Main Street, turning well before Claire had cleared the last block. But the bench was empty. I sat down where my hero's head had lain.

Claire sat down at his feet.

"You certainly made an impression on those boys, Mister Nameless Gabe."

I ran my hand across the armrest. "The lads have, *had*, a good system."

"Is that what you'd call it?"

"Sure, I mean, all they want is to learn and be happy. And I mean to have the courage at their age to leave home and do something like this. Jezebel too. It's really remarkable. I didn't get that until, well, until now."

"And would you say they're doing well out here?"

"For the most part they've managed to have a good time."

"Until this."

"Well yea. But Cass should've known not to mess with squirrels."

29

We collected Claire's bags, and our packs, before visiting the front desk where the mustachioed man seemed to be on eternal duty.

"You're the pair that's hiking the Trail to Sacred Place?"

"And beyond."

"You'll just follow on that way." He gestured to the right. "Great Eastern Trail kicks left off Main Street about three-quarters of a mile down then shares the Azalea Turnpike, which is really just a bike path running by the creek. Somebody decided to give it a funny name. After a couple miles the Trail splits and heads up Schools Mountain. If you want to save yourself some trouble, and really take in the scenery, you can skip that turn and stay right on Azalea. It stays flat and keeps with the creek, wraps round the mountain and meets up with the Trail on the other side. Never leave the shade. Don't have to climb a foot. It gets you there faster and makes for a much nicer day."

"Duly noted. Thanks. We will give you a call when we get to Sacred Place. Should be about four or five days."

We exited the hotel and headed north down Main Street. Claire's first orange blaze took us left off the asphalt onto the flat gravel of the Azalea Turnpike. As promised, the Trail followed the bike path for a couple miles as it paralleled a mountain stream populated by fly fisherman and, presumably, fish.

"Well this isn't so bad. I don't see what all the fuss is."

"I wouldn't get used to it. This is a pretty singular stretch."

"It can last as long as it likes."

Two orange blazes signaled the end of our warm up. The Great Eastern Trail rifled straight up the mountain.

"What are you doing? The trail continues flat in front of us."

"No, the Trail goes up. That's just the bike path now. These two blazes mean we have to turn."

"But why? What about the Azalea Turnpike? If it's all the same to you, I'd like to opt for the faster and nice day."

"It's not all the same to me. We're hiking on *the Trail*, the Great Eastern Trail, not the Azalea Turnpike."

"I came up here to hike *a* trail with you. Doesn't have to be *the* Trail. What's wrong with taking the easier route if it gets us to the same place?"

"It's not about getting places. It's just about the getting. I don't want any asterisks next to my hike."

"Next to your hike where? Gabe, I really think you're be—"

"No!" Claire's eyes widened. She took a step back. "I set out to hike the Great Eastern Trail. And I intend to hike every damned step of it. If you want to stay on Azalea Street then just wait for me there."

Claire considered me for a second, then nodded and stepped up the unkempt embankment. I followed. Together we climbed the mountain, talking sporadically but mostly walking in silence.

At the top, I sat down and pulled out a *Juicerrman* and my water bottle. Claire, red faced but composed, sat down next to me. Thin rims of sweat lined her collar and the seam of her Bodette Bucks hat. She studied the orange blaze leading down the mountain, then giggled to herself.

"What's so funny?"

"It's just that, you've basically just traded mailboxes for strips of paint."

"No I haven't."

"Think about it, you've essentially just straightened out your mail route."

I set my mind to coming up with a more palatable metaphor. "I really don't like the way you've put that."

"But this is what you've been doing every day?"

"Minus the flat part, sprinkle in some rain or snow. I guess, the heat's a relatively new obstacle. *Juicerrman*?"

"I can't believe you bought those. Remember when they just disappeared from stores? Someone paid a lot of money to make sure we never found out what they do to us."

"Probably. But they make me hike like a fiend. Would you at least like the last bite?"

"I'll pass."

We finished our respective water bottles and pressed on, marching through the afternoon heat. It was a very still day, muggy even at altitude. It felt surreal to have Claire out here though I couldn't pinpoint the words to describe it. She was from a starkly different portion of my life, a distant realm which I had once occupied, and had now she had breached some vortex or risked a black hole to accompany me. I loved her and appreciated her presence; but, there was no catching her up— there had been too much activity and too many unusual experiences since I had left her at Grambling's Pass.

The Great Eastern Trail lilted increasingly to the right, coming to a point at a treeless rocky promontory permitting Claire's first unobstructed view. Each successive ridgeline and peak caught the waning rays at their own particular angle, reflecting a unique shade of glossy green. The sky above glowed a vibrant pink. Claire stopped behind me, placing her hands on her hips as she took in her surroundings.

"Okay. I can see why you might do this."

"Every now and then the Great Eastern Trail comes through for you; although it does make you earn it."

"You can see Qanasseh over there." She pointed to the right. I looked and saw the red bricks poking between the trees.

"It looks so quaint. I wonder which one was our little hotel."

"One in the middle I guess. We've come so far. Even in just a day."

"Hard to believe isn't it. The Great Eastern Trail keeps you down or hidden for so long that it feels like you're going nowhere—then, all of a sudden, it lets you break out and see what you've accomplished."

"It's a shame you can't see all the way back to that place I left you off."

"Grambling's Pass? You'd need some keen eyes."

"Well you can see ghosts. Cass can talk to animals. Speck can hitch. Why draw the line at seeing long distance?"

"You forgot Bear the invincible. And recent evidence weighs in favor of Cass *not* being able to talk to animals."

We removed our packs and sat down on a well-placed boulder overlooking the valley. She rested her sweaty head on my sweaty shoulder. We watched the sun set deep into the evening before resuming our hike in the twilight.

"You might have been right about leaving the Turnpike."

The Great Eastern Trail wound down the ridgeline towards sea level. We re-crossed the Azalea Turnpike just after sunset. I was just about to start looking for suitable trailside spots when the sign for Bobby Fricks Shelter appeared out of the darkness. A short side trail led us to a decrepit three-sided structure with a small stream running at its rear. I found a flat spot and set up the tent as Claire refreshed herself in the stream. Once she finished, she inspected the shelter as I laid out the pad and sleeping bags.

"Do people actually sleep in these things? There just has to be mice."

"Some do. They're life savers in the rain. I end up doing it more than I'd like. And one of us might be tonight. I forgot to account for the lack of space inside the tent. It's going to be a little bit tight."

"Well then we just get to snuggle. Or you can let me have the tent to myself."

"Snuggle it is. Let me show you how I make dinner." Food bag in hand, I led Claire over to the picnic table and laid everything out.

"Gabe I watched you practice this at home. Remember you singed the cabinets?"

"Yea but it's cooler out here. And there aren't any cabinets. First you light the stove." I opened the gas canister, flicking the spark which caught and created the blue flame. "Then you add the water to the pot, put it on the stand and wait for it to boil. While that's happening you take out the rice, Dank Sauce."

"Right. And what is Dank Sauce?"

"Reckon I don't know for sure. Jezebel took me to this gas station fried chicken joint and they had this glorious fried chicken, I mean just outrageously good, and it comes with Dank Sauce."

"Gas station fried chicken you say."

"But it's so good. And there are a bunch of them. I guess I just never looked for them before but they are everywhere."

"So you're meal, our meal, is minute rice and gas station fried chicken sauce?" I nodded. "Oh lucky me."

"You're the one that was concerned my pension wouldn't cover our retirement."

"Okay. Let's see what it's about."

I built a fire to look at during dinner—collecting wood, building Jezebel's cabin, and lighting the interior tender. It lit unaided by my stove.

"I remember when you used to have Roger come over to start the grill."

"I'm a man now baby. Mister Gabe. Master of Flame."

I took my place next to her at the picnic table to eat and watch my fire consume the wood. My eyes strayed from the fire as Claire took her first bite.

"Okay . . . okay. You might be on to something," she nodded.

"I didn't believe it either. But it's great isn't it. Just like Jezebel told me and I told you."

"I mean I wouldn't want it for a real dinner but it's good. For out here. And where's the, uh, the logbook. The one with the Mongrel doodles or whatever."

"Right." I jumped into the shelter. "It should be . . . here it is. And *here* is Mongrel's note." I lifted the brown parchment.

> MONGREL COME, MONGREL GO
> DO NOT TRUST, THAT CLEAN HALO

"What does that mean?"

"I don't know. They're always sort of like that. I like them. They just sort of rattle around your head while you're hiking."

In the tent, I had to sleep on my side to accommodate Claire and, at first, it made for some epic wilderness spooning, but soon my left arm fell asleep, tingling up to the shoulder. It required quite a rustling production to roll over and relieve it. Once accomplished, my right arm began to tingle almost immediately, and soon I found myself returning to my left. After three such turns, Claire snapped at me, leading to the discovery I could brace my backside against the tent wall like a vertical hammock, and achieve just enough comfort to permit sleep.

30

In the morning I slugged my body out of the tent until my legs cleared and I could leverage a nearby sapling to lift me upright. I paced around the campsite, almost dragging one leg, swinging and flexing my right arm. When the numbness subsided, I sat down at the picnic table for a *Juicerrman*. The first fingers of sunlight cleared the mountains, setting the woods in a soft tone, revealing everything's location without the sharp detail of afternoon. Birds chirped bright songs from the branches. Claire emerged some time later, crossing her arms against the morning chill.

"I thought I sent you off with a mug and instant coffee."

"They didn't make the cut. Didn't you notice how trimmed down and quiet my pack is."

"What happened?"

"Jezebel happened. My feet happened. My back happened. It was too much of a burden to carry every convenience. So she made me get rid of them."

"Jezebel . . . she's kind of starting to sound like your Trail wife."

"She'd prefer Trail mother. But if I hadn't listened to Jezebel we'd probably be having this conversation at home."

"Mmm. We do have good coffee at home."

I offered the last bite of my *Juicerrman*, which was refused, then let Claire collect herself at a leisurely pace, knowing she would be slow to rise and quick to boil without her morning brew. When she seemed ready, we set off for our daily dose of north. From the shelter, the Great Eastern Trail started up a long, lazy ascent. About halfway up, we came across a gnarled oak tree whose fallen leaves carpeted the angled ground. Almost instinctually, I walked over to the base and commenced kicking through the decomposing leaf litter.

"I'm scared to ask, Gabe."

"Just give me a second." I took a step to the right, then dropped my pack and got down on all fours.

"If you get up now we can pretend this part of the trip didn't happen."

"Claire look!" I gave the round cap a soft twist, turning to display my prize. "Settler's Fowl. You want it?"

"Want it?"

"Yea. They're delicious. Bear says they taste like squirrel, which I do have to take his word for, but they'd certainly be easier to shoot."

"Gabe that's just a mushroom."

"No it's not. It's Sett—"

"A mushroom that you picked, from under rotting leaves."

"I mean technically, yea."

"And you're going to eat it."

"I was thinking we could eat them together. Looks like we found a good haul—Bear would be jealous. He showed me how to find and pick them."

"Bear being the hairy, monosyllabic invincible one?"

"He is pretty hairy, isn't he."

"Oh Gabe, I'm really trying here."

"Here let me eat a couple first and you can see how I don't die." I started to pop a couple in my mouth.

"It's fine. Just give me a piece." She took a pinch and, after some scrutiny, placed it on her tongue—her face stretched and contorted.

"Goodness."

"Pretty amazing, right."

"That is a pungent flavor. Are you sure you're supposed to be eating these whole?"

"That's how Bear does it and look at him." I started tossing Settlers into my grocery bag.

"Remember when you used to be a mailman?"

The afternoon sun brought out large, black flies which patrolled the air en masse, buzzing around our heads, putting an end to the morning tranquility. All of a sudden something sharp hit the back of my neck, I slapped at it and felt a vile crunch against my spine. The dark gooey remnants of an enormous fly, along with a tablespoon of my own blood, oozed down my palm. Claire cursed behind me, signaling that she had been bit as well. Two more hit each of my arms before I could turn round, retreating to safety during my indecision as to which arm to clear first. Claire sprinted past me, slapping at her neck; several blood trails ran down her back. I followed, waving my arms against the onslaught.

The droning intensified as the Great Eastern Trail edged lower until finally bursting forth from the trees onto an isthmus squeezed between two stagnant, weed-eaten ponds—the epicenter of the fly invasion. The air vibrated with beating wings. I could feel the hell flies landing and slipping off my face, usually unable to grip because of the sweat—still some intrepid and determined individuals pilfered their share of the feast. My lungs burned—it was the farthest I'd run since high school but to stop was to be eaten. The infested isthmus dragged on for some fifty yards, offering us up like legged buffet nuggets. I pictured one of us tripping and being cleanly erased from history. Not far from the pond's northern banks, the land began to rise. The droning lessened. We maintained our frantic sprint until it was gone altogether, and then some—at which point Claire threw herself down on the ground. Her chest bounced against itself in search of breath. Bleeding welts covered her arms; one little turdball had even taken a chunk out of her lovely cheek. I collapsed next to her.

"What the hell was that Gabe? You forgot to mention the mile long swarms of flesh eating flies."

"That was my first encounter."

"Mean little bastards. I mean, where have you brought me? I honestly didn't know we had domestic swarms of man eating flies. Is this what you left Bodette for? Is this more enjoyable than spending your nights at home with me?"

"If I'd known there'd be weaponized flies on this portion of the Trail I would have asked you to join me somewhere else."

"Where, Gabe, near the beginning with the freezing snow or the middle part with the snakes and teenage vagabonds?"

"I don't know. Maybe there's a nice bit further north."

Claire poured water on her wounds, dabbing them with a handkerchief. I reached into my pocket for a mid-morning *Juicerrman*. When we found our breath, we stood up and continued to higher altitude. The Great Eastern Trail rose at a light slope, away from the horrid flies, and onwards to safety. We did not encounter the flies again that day.

Claire and I camped for the night under a grove of massive hardwoods. I made an easy fire out of discarded limbs; we sprawled out next to it with our backs against a downed oak. The fire danced against the ancient trees, giving the space an otherworldly feel, like we were two travelers in a fantasy land, enjoying a quiet evening after some great peril.

"I'm sorry I snapped at you earlier, after the flies."

"Those were stressful times."

"I do not enjoy being eaten."

"You reckon any of the repellants in your store would've helped?"

"I can't say that I'd recommend any of them against actual carnivores, maybe the Holman's."

"Orange can?"

"Orange can."

"That's the good stuff."

We ate our dinners, this time with Settler's Fowl, watching the darkness settle in amongst the trees.

31

The Great Eastern Trail returned us to low altitude early the next afternoon; the distant hum foretold of another onslaught. This time we were prepared. Claire donned my rain jacket, zipping it up, cinching the hood low and tight around her face; sunglasses shielded her eyes. I equipped my cold weather gear and wrapped an extra shirt around my head, leaving a small breathing hole. We advanced, waiting for the moment when the droning grew all-encompassing. At my mark, we took off, tucking our chins and swinging our armored limbs against the attackers. The flies ricocheted off us like so many pellets. We were making it unscathed when I opened my mouth for a whoop and felt two hot poison darts lance the back of my throat. The filthy sour sweetness of insect filled my mouth. I cacked and heaved to spit up the blood and bodies as I stumbled through the masses. I was still spitting when the Great Eastern Trail lifted us up out of the fray.

"Well that went much better," Claire said unwrapping her coverings.

I could not speak. The back of my throat seared and swelled, leaving my voice a painful, hoarse whisper.

"What happened to you?"

I opened my mouth wide and pointed in.

"Oh Gabe . . . It looks like a snake bit the back of your throat." I held up two fingers. "Yea, two bites I can see that. How much does it hurt?"

I held my hand over my head.

"Well what should we do? Let me see if I have something in my pack."

"Nuh." I gestured North. "Waahlluck." I cursed the hiking gods for setting an injury here when I should've been leading my wife.

The swollen lumps were two burning flails bouncing in the back of my throat, hanging low enough to slap my tongue. The taste of pus and disease was beyond compare. After an hour, we came to a small spring pouring out of the rock like a spigot and running across the Trail. I held my mouth under the spurt, letting the cold water collect in the back of my throat. The water cooled and numbed. When I spit, it came out streaked with an awful yellow which drifted in clumps down the Trail and into oblivion. I repeated the process for several minutes until the spit came out clear and the acrid insect taste was diminished. The pain subsided enough for me to attempt eating a *Juicerrman*; but the way remained shut. The searing pain returned as soon as we stepped away from the spring, throbbing in duplicate with each movement. Deprived of its charged-nougat nutrition, my body began to slog; a violent headache swirled against my skull.

By the time we arrived at Nomrah Nah Shelter, it was all I could do to keep my eyes open. We turned onto the sidetrail and found two tents occupying the clearing. The first was a little beige tunnel with orange seams that rounded off on one end. The other was a canvas teepee. A mottled white dog with a brown spot rimming his right eye loped up the trail to greet us. I had the brief mailman instinct to flee, but Claire knelt down to pet it, which it briefly permitted before popping around to lead us down the path, throwing frequent glances over its shoulder.

Twangs of bluegrass music floated through the air as we drew near; two figures conversed at the picnic table.

"Greetings, newcomers. Will you two be staying with us tonight?"

I grunted a reply, impatient for day's end.

"Yes. I'm afraid we've had about all we can handle today," Claire responded.

"Oh excellent, excellent. And would you like ocean or garden view?" he pointed at different spots as if they actually offered different vistas. The newcomers were old, sporting scroungy heads of grey hair paired with matching silver beards. The differences were a matter of degree; one beard was significantly longer and one set of clothes almost reduced to rags. The other man's gray head had all the markings of what had recently been an expensive haircut; even in its current state it remained proportional and the overall look was pleasing, like a well-manicured yard only temporarily gone to seed.

"Whatever's furthest from the elevator, please," Claire answered, "and please have someone take our bags the rest of the way." The man smiled and drank from his flask.

"If that was an option, I'd have someone doing it myself. My name's Music Man and this loquacious type is Hopper. How long are you two out?" Hopper did not look up.

"I'm only out until Sacred Place. But Gabe here has been walking since Grambling's Pass. He's aiming to go all the way through." Claire rubbed my back as she spoke.

"Ah! Allons my dear Gabe. We are brothers in pilgrimage. I picked up Hopper in Casas. He's a relic from a past life." The dog nuzzled his master's hand off his knee. Music Man obliged with a pat. "Hope Monroe didn't give you two any trouble."

"No trouble at all. Just guided us in. I'm Claire." I identified the source of the bluegrass music as an ancient wood-paneled handheld radio resting by Music Man's hip. It reminded me of one I had cherished in my youth with a faux wood finish and a plastic handle. I wondered how he was getting it to play all the way out here. I thought of Jezebel and her warmth: Speck and his ever-ready drivers.

"I'd be surprised to hear otherwise. Folks call me Music Man on account of the radio. Did you two encounter the flies?" I noticed his arms and legs were no better than ours.

Claire nodded. "Two times. Gabe had a couple get at the back of his throat."

"Try and return the favor did ya? Ill-advised, my friend. But I've got just the medicine if you're so inclined." Music Man reached behind him, retrieved a mason jar three-quarters full of a clear liquid, and slid it across the table. I lifted it; it had all the markings of water—clear, non-viscous, but demonstrated a menacing lightness of movement. When I twisted open the lid for an inquisitive sniff a harsh sterile sweetness assaulted my nose; as far as I could tell, the mason jar contained pure, undiluted malice.

"Gabe honey maybe you should ask what it is fi—"

I took a sip. A stringent nasal punch set me in a coughing fit which yanked at my wounds. Claire put a hand on my back.

"Not much of a drinker are you Gabe. Well, the first cut is the deepest; give it another try, only this time don't breathe until afterwards. Hold your nose if you need to, like one of those kids in the old medicine ads." He pinched his nose in demonstration, taking another pull from his flask.

I tried again. The medicine stung something awful as it sterilized the bites; however, rather than just irritating the wounds, the moonshine seemed to collect the pain and carry it down into my stomach, where it fired up an electric warmth.

"Not bad, Gabe. And now one more for good measure."

"Maybe that's enough Gabe."

I pointed at my throat. "Mehduhsihn."

This time I took a much larger pull, handing the jar off to Claire who used an extended arm to return it to Music Man.

Everything in my body relaxed; I felt both heavy and light. My mind floated in detached observation. I croaked a thank you to Music Man which felt like it should have been very painful; but nothing registered. It was like monitoring a street riot from the top floor of a skyscraper.

Claire and I sat down as Music Man took another liberal pull and handed it on to Hopper who pushed it away with the back of his hand.

"I do not intend to drink after you."

"You really think anything bad can survive in that jar. It's the perfect beverage—self-sterilizing and generously intoxicating."

Hopper instead took a long pull from a metal water bottle.

Music Man offered up another round and I partook before beginning my dinner preparations. The world loosened around me, or I became unstuck in it, watching myself from a distance. My movements were big, slow and exaggerated, manifesting long after my brain sent the command. I looked up smiling after each completed task, nodding my head to the thumping bass of Music Man's radio. Claire and Music Man conversed around me but I leaned over my pot, focused on my mission. I found myself having trouble balancing upright and attempted to disguise it by swaying in rhythm to the music. I resented Claire's watchful gaze as I portioned out the rice, sauce, and Settler's Fowl into the pot.

Across the table, Hopper propped a rolled plastic bundle on the table and swept it open, revealing his shiny metallic camp stove, cooking utensils, and food. From left to right he removed each item and adjusted it into place. Once his stove was set, he watched me, mumbling to himself as I pushed my spork through the Settler's Fowl, reducing it to haphazard chunks.

"What do you have there?"

"Mish Mash. Rice, Settler's Fowl, Dank Sauce." It still hurt to speak.

"A mish mash . . . ."

"And you?"

"Let's see." He pulled out a shiny aluminum package about the size of a lunch box and held it up to his face. "Tonight it's a pork manicotti with a parmesan mozzarella blend." He placed it on the table, nudging the corner parallel to his stove.

"No Dank Sauce?" I wagged a packet at him.

"I have my own herbs and spices, thank you. A special blend I've assembled over the years." He lifted and straightened a little plastic baggie. "If you'd care to split from Dank Sauce." Hopper slid the baggie over to me. "Be easy with it. It's quite strong and rather irreplaceable out here."

I opened up the bag and gave a sniff—a sharp and sobering sourness cut the haze. I flinched and pulled away; it smelled like weapons grade potpourri. Claire leaned in to take a sniff. "Not too much Gabe."

"Never mind the smell. In the right proportion, it becomes a rather subtle complement to any dish."

I took a pinch of it between my thumb and forefinger, rubbing them over the pot to distribute the seasoning into the Dank rice, stirring it in with my space spork. I allowed Claire the first bite; she scrunched her nose in a grimace.

"It's mostly just bitter. I'm not sure that I care for it. Sorry."

She handed over the space spork and I took a bite. Gone was the embracing warmth of gas station and forest, sapped by the sickly sweetness; even the meatiness of the Settler's Fowl seemed diminished, replaced by a thin, cold taste that undermined the accumulated flavors. The rice felt dry and grainy against my tongue.

I slid the pouch across the table, shaking my head.

"It is rather an acquired taste." Hopper's water boiled and he poured it directly into the silver bag, resealing it and shaking it before letting it rest on the table.

Claire and I pushed through the rest of the pot, trading off the space spork after each bite, occasionally coming across a precious scoop untainted by Hopper's special blend. Hopper ate his manicotti in silence. When he was done, he dismantled his stove, wiping down and replacing every part just as it was before dinner, before rolling up his plastic contraption. Music Man shared a bag of chips with Monroe and sang along with his music. I tapped the rhythm on the table.

We continued drinking; the more I drank, the more I drifted out of reality. I tongued my throat wounds and felt nothing; I tongued my teeth and felt nothing. Indeed my tongue was a puffy mass of numbness. The music danced through me, lifting me upwards. Each sip of Music Man's mason jar tasted increasingly like water.

"You are going to ruin your hike tomorrow." Claire's voice, wise as always. Her hand was on my bent elbow.

I looked at the mason jar in my hand. "We only have to get to Sacred Place. I'm good." I tapped my chest. "I'm good hiker."

"It's no mere meander down the hillside into Sacred Place." It took a second to locate Hopper at the end of the table. "You have to get over Mount Ward, the highest peak before Mt. Charles, and covered in rock in stone to boot. It will be hell on a drunkard."

With that Hopper removed a jar of hazelnut spread and two slices of flattened bread from his pack and disappeared into his tent.

"Is he eating that in his tent?"

"Every night. He says it helps him sleep."

"Seems . . . dangerous."

"It's not advisable. However, he is right about it being time for bed." Music Man, who had gone pull for pull with me in addition to extensive solo work with his flask, stood up and shook his pack, setting off a cacophony of clinking glass. "Don't worry my friend. There'll be more tomorrow night." His voice had softened, mellowed, and played nicely with the music.

Monroe, laying at his master's feet, lifted his head at the noise, then stood up.

"Is that whole pack filled with booze?"

"There's some dog food in it."

"Remind me not to smoke next to you."

I went to escort my bride to our marital tent and realized that I had not thought to set it up. With great effort and concentration, I removed the poles and fabrics from their bags and laid them on the ground, closing an eye as I attempted to connect two poles.

"Goodness, Gabe." Claire took the poles from me and began working on her own.

"You don't know how."

"It's color coordinated."

She had the tent set up by the time I rolled out the pads and sleeping bags.

32

My insides dissolved into a liquid during the night. By morning that liquid had expanded beyond its container. I wriggled out of the tent, darting as deep into the woods as the need permitted. Claire was seated at the table when I returned.

"Sounds like we're lucky you made it out in time." The morning sun cast an unsympathetic glare. "That *medicine* probably killed everything in your stomach. It's basically hand sanitizer."

"I do feel a touch cleaned out."

"How about your wounds?"

I tongued around my mouth. "All gone. I guess I'll weather some, uh, digestive interference if it means I can speak." I removed two *Juicerrmen*, handing one to Claire. "You're going to have to give me minute to get going." Together we nibbled our breakfast, interrupted by one more scamper to privacy. When I felt steady enough, we moved on.

Hopper's tent was long gone but Music Man's teepee still stood by the side trail. Monroe nuzzled his spotted head out of the flap and rushed out for some good-bye pets.

The sun was up and blistering. I was sweating before we turned onto the Great Eastern Trail, and exhausted within half an hour. We caught an early glimpse of our daily opponent, Ward

Mountain, through a break in the trees. The Great Eastern Trail took its sweet time winding down to its base. Claire and I wrapped ourselves in our protective layers as we approached the bottom but encountered few flies, crushing the outliers with brutal swats.

"You think it's because there's no water on this side?"

"Probably. Or maybe it's because I'm filled to the brim with insecticide."

We worked our way through the valley and up Ward Mountain's southern base. The trees gave way to large stretches of smooth, steep, exposed granite. We searched for cracks and grooves to prevent a high-stakes slide down the mountain. The heat reflected off the stone, baking my feet through my shoes, taking advantage of its second opportunity to scorch our virgin flesh—burnt offerings to a fiery god.

We crested without a pause, scurrying back towards to the northern trees. The sun reignited the lightning in my belly; it boiled up my throat, making several surging attempts at escape. The world wavered in front of me. My stomach lurched. Darkness tugged my consciousness, urging me down into a pleasant release. My booze burdened mind buckled under the scrutiny. I took a knee and lost my breakfast, crawling sideways into a boulder's scant midday shade.

Claire took several steps before she noticed. "How you doing, Gabe?"

"Oh not too bad. Just a little dizzy."

She came back to me and undid my straps. "Did someone have too much fun last night?"

"Just looked like a good spot for a break." Claire's figure, blurry and opaque, towered over me, shielding my eyes from the heinous sun. No amount of blinking could bring her into focus.

"This ought to help." I felt water drip across my forehead. Claire pressed her plastic bottle into my hand. I took a sip and slipped out of my pack so I could lay on my back.

"How has Music Man been hiking so long drinking that angry substance?"

"You'll notice he was still in his tent when we left. Do you want another *Juicerrman*?"

"Water first. But yes I do." The name alone ignited a body wide yearning, something separate from hunger.

"Okay well drink some more water and stay out of the sun for a minute. Then I'll get you one."

I remained laying on back with my eyes closed. Claire squeezed water onto my forehead at intervals. When it was time, and I could count her fingers, she asked me where the *Juicerrmen* were.

"Main compartment. Black bag. Third from the top."

I kept my eyes closed as she handed me one the unmistakable bricks. I took small bites, kneading them in my mouth, hesitant to swallow lest I see it again. The chemical goodness pushed through on its own, unaided by my digestive track, displacing Music Man's poison as it went, replacing it with its own invigorating blend. By the time I was three quarters through, the hazy storm had dissipated and clarity had returned. I finished Claire's water and sat up.

"Feeling better?"

I nodded, extending my thinned arms and flexing.

"I'm sorry you have to do this. I thought this would all go differently."

"Don't apologize. I get to tend one of my boys. And when you're done with the Trail we're going to have a talk about your addiction."

It was still a long time before we came to the road into Sacred Place. When we did, the *Juicerrman* had worn off; I plopped down in the darkest area of shade.

"Now how do we get into town?"

"I do not know. It's been a while since I've had to worry about it."

"So what do we do?"

I slouched down so that my head rested on my pack. "Sleep. Generally things just work themselves out. We can walk if need be."

Claire checked the ground. "You say people hitchhike out here?"

"The young folk do. Jezebel and Speck, but it's harder for old men."

"What about me? You don't think I can get some lonely gentleman to pull over?"

"I never said that. I just—" Claire had already returned to the roadside and, pack still on, presented her thumb.

Two cars passed in quick succession, not so much as tapping the brakes. The third discarded a beer can.

"There's more to it Claire. Speck has this whole elaborate routine. Even Jezebel poses and smiles. You've really got to sell that you don't mean harm."

Claire dropped her pack and unleashed her hair from its bun.

The next car, a small green coupe which hadn't been moving with much gusto in the first place, rolled to a stop. A diminutive old lady manned the wheel. Claire waved and opened the trunk for our packs but found it full of cookies and pastries. The lady cranked down the window.

"I'm comin' home from a bake sale. Your school bags will be just fine in the backseat." The glass had only made it halfway down when she reversed course and started elbowing it back up.

Claire took the front seat. I crowded into the back next to Claire's pack, and underneath mine. The old car eased into motion, letting gravity propel it down the mountain, from what I could tell unaided by the little old lady's right foot. A blue SUV skidded to a weaving crawl behind us.

"Thanks for picking us up. I know we can't smell good."

"Oh it's no problem. My pleasure really. I love seeing a woman out here, not one of those young frilly girls, but a real woman." The car veered as the old lady flexed her arm.

"Well thank you. I've really just done the last few days. Gabe here has actually—"

"And an older woman too." She leaned her grey head forward as if she was yelling at someone on the other side of the windshield. The tiny car bounced from white line to yellow line, always staying in the correct lane, but only just. I swayed with it in the back, considering the persistence of nausea. "No offense, obviously. You know I used to walk. Two miles a day, every day, with my friend Delia. Ballard Street to Royal Street. Royal to Calhoun. Then back to Ballard. She's dead now, Delia, so she doesn't walk anymore and Royal Street is no longer fit for walkin'."

"I'm sorry to hear about Delia."

"Eh?"

"I'm sorry to hear about Delia." Claire matched her volume.

"Don't be. Royal Street was the real loss. Walt wasn't one for activities, except for baseball. He's gone now too, and it's just me and the church. Worked the line from the war until the day he died, Walt did. Where are you two headed?"

"The Dowery. It should be on, um, is there a Fern Street."

"Fehn Street, yes. That won't do. I will not be taking anybody there. That place is no good." She turned around to direct this to me. Her car crossed the yellow line.

"It's okay we've actually already booked a room. It's only one night."

"Well you'll just have to cancel. I will not drop a nice lady like you at such a place."

"What about me?" I leaned between the seats. "Can you drop me off there?"

"You'll be staying with me and that will be the end of it. I have an extra bedroom for you."

"It's really okay we have no problem—"

"That will be the end of it."

"We really don't want to put—"

"That will be the end of it."

Sacred Place had been a mill town. We passed row upon row of identical white houses laid out in an even grid. Some of the houses remained pristine on their square lots, others had browned or fallen in, corrupting their block's neat lines with leaning fences and reeds of tall grass. Gladys's was not one of these houses—rather it was quite possibly the neatest on the street. The white paint popped against the blue shutters; no leaf dared blemish the charcoal gray roof. Every blade of grass stood tight and even in ramrod straight rows.

A pair of hikers had never been so out of place as Claire and I were inside Gladys's domestic museum. We tread slowly, clutching our packs against our stomachs as we maneuvered the narrow gaps between old wooden pieces of furniture bearing countless glass, crystal, and familial trinkets. The house featured an unfathomable number of framed photographs, no pair containing the same people, and none portraying anyone resembling Gladys. Gladys led us down a green hallway, stopping by the stairs.

"You two married?"

"For thirty years now."

"Then you can stay upstairs in Doug's room. First room on the left. I don't get up there much anymore. But it should be decent. I'm just right here." She pointed at a door down the main hall. "If you can get clean, we can have dinner."

If it had been long since the room was cleaned, it did not show. A pristine white quilted comforter hung off the bed, running parallel to the floor from bed post to bed post. A dustless wooden desk stood at the bed's foot. Pictures and books adorned the shelves in every corner.

Claire showered first, then me. The water pressure, which had apparently been reduced to accommodate the diminished resilience of an old lady, rendered the shower a delicate affair.

The virgin soap bar had been carved into an intricate blossoming flower that refused to lather. I rubbed it, scraped it, and pulled on it without earning the first bubble. When I stepped out, I discovered Gladys's plethora of white towels.

"How did you get clean? I couldn't get any water or soap." I asked Claire upon returning to our room.

"Women have our methods. You didn't use the flower soap, did you?"

"I tried to. Although it didn't do me any good."

"That was ornamental. That flower had probably been sitting there for twenty years."

"That would explain why it's so hard. Petrified soap."

"Yes. It's not meant to be used."

"Then don't put it in the shower."

Claire and I took to examining the different pictures, drifting clockwise around the room like museum patrons, watching an infant progress through childhood to adolescence and graduation. Like most boys, he started as a baby in a blue onesy with *Douglas* embroidered across the chest, then a light haired toddler in overalls with a plastic gun, then on to sports, school, and church pictures until he left home and became unavailable for further photography.

"I wonder where he is now."

"Probably off living his life. Approaching retirement. He can't be too much younger than us, based on those outfits."

"I wish my parents had kept my room intact."

"You wish everyone had kept everything intact."

The kitchen was small with a linoleum floor and Formica countertops. Light filtered in through pulled blue curtains. Gladys put out a cheese plate for us, a precursor to dinner, which only amounted to about four pieces of cheese, with an extra cracker and thin cut of salami per person.

"Miss Gladys, are we staying in your son's old room?"

"You are. Doug's. It's just like it was when he left too. Never saw any reason to change it."

"Where is he now?"

"He's just a few towns over in Chesterton with his family. He owns a hardware store there."

"Oh really, I actually own a hardware store as well." Gladys shot my wife a disapproving look. "Do you still see him?"

"Never as much as I'd like."

"Well that's nice. Our son lives in Pentland. He's an attorney." Claire looked at me over her empty plate. "He doesn't come home as much we'd like."

"They never do. Doug don't come see me but once a week."

I put down my shot of tea, trying to catch Claire's eye. "What's for dinner?"

"Dinner? We just ate."

"Ate?" I scanned the empty saucers which had contained the scant offerings. "I just, uh, it's just that hiking makes a man powerful hungry. I was hoping to maybe get a burger and see a little more of what Sacred Place has to offer. Is there someone where we can walk?"

"I'm afraid that is not an option. I don't like my door being opened and closed at nighttime. Let's the bad air in. I won't have it. And I won't have you wondering unfamiliar streets in the dark. It won't do."

I noted the sturdy beam of sunlight dissecting the curtains. My stomach, and hangover, made me press. "We can get something to-go and be back before dark. I would really do better with a bit more food."

"If you're unsatisfied, sir, you're welcome to go, but you will not be welcome back in this house. I won't have it." Claire pressed my foot under the table.

"The meal was fantastic and filling. Is there anything we can do to help you clean up?"

"I will handle my own plates thank you. You may retire to bed now. I ask that you keep noise to a minimum. Good night."

"Good night, Gladys."

"Good night."

We left Gladys washing dishes and made our way upstairs to Doug's bedroom. I opened the window and, finding it without screen, judged the distance to the lawn below.

"I'm gonna make a break for it. Grab a burger and a milkshake, maybe two. You want me to bring you something back? We can knot the bedsheets. I don't care if I have to sleep on the sidewalk."

Claire came to the window and looked out. "Gabe, don't end your hike on Gladys's lawn."

"I think I can make it. I'm certainly hungry enough to try."

"You don't even know if there's anything around. The town looked dead."

"There's always a gas station Claire. *Always*. A man can do pretty well for himself at a gas station."

"Don't you have *Juicerrman* bars in your pack?"

"Yea but I want town food. Things get weird if you put down too many *Juicerrmen*."

"Then there's nothing left to do but go to bed."

"It's not even dark out. We went to bed later than this on the Trail. Didn't this kid have a television, or board games, or even a deck of cards. A stash of potato chips. Or booze."

"Maybe, Gabe. Why don't you check under the floorboards?"

Claire left the room to brush her teeth. I went after she returned. The upstairs carpet felt worn and thin under my feet. The entire structure groaned with each step; I could imagine Gladys berating the ceiling for violating the noise ordinance. I found Claire in bed, with the white blanket pulled up to her neck and the sheets still tucked in underneath every edge of the mattress.

"Gabe, why doesn't this seem weirder?"

"That we've been taken captive by a crazy old lady who refuses to feed us and makes us go to bed in the early afternoon?"

"Yes, that. This should seem very strange to me but, for whatever reason, it just doesn't."

"Welcome to the Great Eastern Trail. Everything's so weird out here that it's hard for anything to stick out. You're just getting used to it to the lifestyle." I rolled over and inspected a picture of Doug with his brothers. "How about Doug the champion. I mean, can you imagine seeing Billy once a week?"

"I know. That would be so nice."

"Would it? A weekly opportunity for him to criticize our cooking then pressure you to redecorate?"

"He can be a bit much."

"He can be a nightmare."

"Gabe, don't do that."

"Do what?"

"Try to turn me against him."

"I just want you to admit that he can, on occasion, be a nightmare."

"I'm not going to. And you're not going to say anything like that when you see him. Now, have you considered at all what y'all are going to do together?"

"I have very much tried not to."

"Have you at least been calling him?"

"Yes, dear. Each and every town."

"Gabe . . . ."

"Each and every town. I promise."

"Which number?"

"His number."

"His home or at the office?"

"Why? What is he telling you?"

"He's telling me that, while he has many missed calls, y'all haven't actually spoken."

"Bad luck I suppose."

"Which number Gabe?"

"…"

"Damn it, Gabe. I mean, God damn it. He says he calls back when he gets home and it just rings and rings; or worse, some shop owner or clerk picks up. One time he thought you'd picked up a hooker."

"I've called him at work too."

"Yea he mentioned that. He came in on Monday morning and had poor Diane return a call to a pizza place."

"It was actually the pizza place I called you from. Alfred's I think."

"God. Damnit. Gabe."

"What!? I'm happy out here. I'm out here doing something for me. Trying to figure something out. Can't this trip be about me?"

"It is all about you. Only about you. For a month and a half now it's been nothing but the Gabe Show featuring Mister Gabe, Nameless Gabe, and the Merry Band of Societal Misfits." My wife hissed at me from her pillow, somehow managing to inject her whisper with a full dose of venom. "But in the end it's no different than the weight set in the garage, next to the deconstructed sports car in the garage, next to the yellowing stack of two hundred pages on the history of government subsidized home-to-home parcel delivery which is also in the garage."

"I thought you supported those? I thought you supported this?"

"I did for those. It was somewhat charming to bring you dinner and a beer as you cranked away in the garage or you'd wash your hands and join your family at the table. But now you're just gone. Did you ever consider that? I'm home alone and you're just gone. I mean how long were you retired before you decided to do this?"

"I didn't decide to do this. Len's wi—"

"Bullshit Gabriel. Don't feed me something I don't eat. It was two months. You spent two months at home before you decided you couldn't stand me and started plotting your escape."

"Claire it wasn't like that."

"Oh it wasn't like that. You were fine being with me? Then why didn't you ask me to join."

My mouth wagged, starting several words but finishing none.

"Exactly, Gabe. You didn't even think about that did you. Just wanted to go on your own little perfect adventure starting where that Grambling shit abandoned his family. Never even crossed your mind to include that miserable battle-axe you call a wife."

"You would've said no."

"Of course I would've. I have a business and friends and happen to be quite content with what we've spent three decades building in Bodette. But you just left like you didn't give a shit about any of it. I had to slip in a family photo just to make sure you wouldn't forget us."

"Claire pl—"

"And if it's not about reconnecting with your son I don't know what else could be important enough to take you away. It's just selfish."

"He left you too."

"He's our child. That's what children do when they grow up. That's what each and every one of the young hooligans out here has done. What Billy wanted, what he needed, Bodette couldn't offer. So he manned up and went somewhere that did. You can't begrudge your son for trying to make something of himself. Y'all weren't always like this."

I wanted to argue more, plant my feet in the ground and refuse to see the boy. I settled for rolling over to watch the shadows cross the ceiling.

33

I awoke to the greasy rattle of a small engine—a nudge of the window curtain revealed a stout middle-aged man mowing the lawn. The rattle waxed and waned as he paced back and forth across the lawn. I slipped out of bed, happy to put some distance between me and my wife.

Morning's shadows stretched across the house's interior, connecting walls and table legs. I snuck down the stairs, doing my best to minimize creaking; if Gladys was up, she was not making any noise. I made it to the sunroom and sat down on the couch, flipping open the top coffee table book *The Rural World*. I was skimming pictures of farmers standing next to their tractors when the front door opened—someone wiped their feet on the mat.

The yardman passed the sunroom, stopped, and returned.

"Who the fuck are you?"

"No one. A guest of Gladys's."

"Mom doesn't have guests. Who are you?"

"A hiker. Great Eastern Trail. Gladys gave me and my wife a ride into town last night and then invited, well, demanded that we stay." I pointed to the ceiling. The man remained standing in the doorway.

"You're telling me that little old lady in there took in two strangers out of the woods."

"This little old lady, um, Gladys, took a liking to my wife. We were planning to stay at the Dowery, had a room booked and everything, but, the lady, Gladys, refused to drop us off there. She does not think highly of that establishment."

"And you're a hiker?"

"I am. On the Great Eastern Trail."

"And you were going to stay at the Dowery?"

I nodded.

He pointed a thick finger at me. "Stay." The man disappeared from the doorway—a door opened and closed somewhere down the hall. "Okay, be very clear: why are you sitting in my mother's sunroom?"

"Again, my name is Mist—, um, Gabe. My wife, Claire, and I are hiking on the Great Eastern Trail. Miss Gladys picked us up driving back from a church thing but refused to drop us at the Dowery, instead bringing us to stay with her. You know, here. She made us dinner, sort of, and my wife's still sleeping upstairs. I was sleeping but I woke up to you mowing the lawn and came down here to get away from the noise."

He scanned the room then gave me a long stare. "Okay," he said at last, "my name is Doug. Sorry to drill you but it's pretty concerning to find a dirty old man sitting in your mother's sunroom." His shoulders relaxed. "She took in two strangers, you say?"

"In her defense Claire really is quite charming."

"Right. Well mother will eat me alive if I sit here dirty as I am, but if you come outside we can talk."

I closed the tractor book and followed him through the front door where he parked in a plastic banded lawn chair. I sat down in the one next to him. If possible, the yard was even neater than it had been when we arrived.

"So you're hiking the Great Eastern Trail?"

"I am."

"The whole thing?"

"It is starting to look that way."

He reached into a faded red cooler in between the chairs and pulled out a pair of tall black cans, shaking one at me, rattling something in the can. I accepted it with a smile.

"And the wife's doing it with you?"

"Only the last couple of days, since Qannasseh. Yesterday was actually her last day."

"Much more practical."

"She's always been the smart one." I took my first sip. The beer was smooth, but thick and filling; it quelled the hungry rebellion in my stomach.

"What sparked it?"

"Excuse me?"

"What sparked you embarking on the Trail? We're about the same age. I assume you've worked up until now. What jolted you out of your job and into action?"

I considered my usual story and revised. "I was a mailman. For thirty-five years. I have paid off my house, raised my son, and triggered my pension. One day I woke up and it just seemed like a tremendous waste to spend any more driving around in circles."

"You know, some may have taken that as an opportunity to spend more time with their loved ones."

"Claire's mentioned that. I've spent a lot of time in Bodette. I needed drastic action."

"Right. Just the one kid?"

"Just the one. But he's educated, grown, and gone. He pretty well out-paced his old man; he's a lawyer at a firm in Pentland. I 've been instructed to see him." I rested the can on the chair's plastic arm. "This is good beer."

We sat and admired the small town morning. The air was cool but with undercurrents of heat. I finished one beer; Doug provided another unprompted.

"This is good what you do here. Coming by, mowing the lawn, visiting, seeing, your mother."

"It's easy enough. I'm only a couple of towns over, so I come by every Saturday morning and trim things up, even if they don't need trimmin', eat breakfast with her, usually out of here by noon. She appreciates it and it's a good chance to get some time to myself. Plus I like to make sure that she hasn't opened her home to riff raff."

"Smart. Claire and I have to mow our own lawn."

"I was wayward once. Thought myself a cowboy and wanted to be a rancher. I spent six years out west." He gave me a sly look.

"But you came home."

"It's not enough to have everything you want, got to make sure there's not something better out there too. Turns out it's just about the same everywhere."

The door opened behind us and Claire stepped out of the house.

"There you are."

"The mower woke me up. Claire, this is Doug. Doug is Gladys's son."

"I thought you'd left me again." Her smile was only directed at Doug. "Nice to meet you. We certainly noticed that the lawn is in fine order."

Doug stood up and brushed his hand against his jeans before offering it to Claire. "Thank you." When he sat down he lifted another beer out of the cooler and shook it at Claire. "I think we can sneak one more in before mother finishes breakfast."

"Thanks but it's a little early for me."

Doug handed the beer to me; it was half empty before I set it down.

Gladys rapped on the back window shortly thereafter, signaling that breakfast was ready. We relocated to the kitchen table where Gladys set out a pan of muffins and a plate of bacon then removed herself to her room to '*make herself decent.*' I had a sturdy buzz going from the beers on the empty stomach and grinned each time a crisp piece of bacon snapped into two, emitting a spray of mouth-watering shrapnel.

"Nothing says home quite like burned bacon and dry muffins," Doug said.

"We'll take what we can get."

"I suppose you can't be too picky out there."

I tried on several occasions to meet Claire's eyes but she kept them on a tight track between her meal and her host. Doug evidently had developed quite the hunger from his yardwork; all three of us were chasing biscuit crumbs through the bacon grease when Gladys returned, dressed and made up for the day.

"I see you enjoyed my breakfast. Where are you going today? I'm having the church ladies over for tea at two."

"Well I need to get back to Qanasseh for my car. I was planning on just calling a taxi."

"Nonsense. I'd be happy to drive," said Doug.

"I couldn't make you go all that way."

"It's only twenty minutes, and there's a parts store I like over that way."

"Twenty minutes." Claire locked her eyes on me. "It took Gabe and me almost four days."

"And what about you?" Now Gladys too turned her crooked gaze on me. "Where are *you* off to?"

"Well I was hoping to make it to the grocery. Beyond that, I'm mostly just trying to get out of town."

"I think I can handle that too. If you two don't mind leaving soon."

The buzz slipped into weariness as Claire and I packed in silence, bringing on an acute awareness that I had not received my prescribed dose of town food. My stomach grumbled as we loaded into Doug's truck.

"Any chance you could just drop me off at the Dowery? I'd like to get something greasy and spend a day off my feet. If it's no trouble for you."

"You sure? It really is a shithole."

"That's about what I deserve. I promise not to tell your mom."

Some plucky soul had attempted to fill the potholes in the Dowery's parking lot with gravel but succeeded only in applying a layer of fine grey dust to the cratered asphalt. The building itself was a dull beige, ornamented by brown moisture stains streaking down from the roof. I booked a room and returned to the truck. Claire stood by the tailgate.

"Gabe, come here." Claire retrieved her pack and dumped its contents until she was able to remove a tied grocery bag; through the thin plastic gleamed the familiar red wrapper of my favorite super fuel. She dropped the bag at my feet. "So you don't have to budget through your next leg."

"You, you carried these this whole time?"

She nodded. "I'm not going to ask you to come home and I'm not going to ask you to quit this stupid endeavor but you will go see your son. You've built this thing up to be way more than it is and you will patch things up before it gets out of hand."

"Of course, I'll go see him."

"And when you're done out here, assuming you come home, I don't ever want to see one of these things again, but for now these should keep you moving north, towards Billy."

"Of course, I'm coming home."

"That's . . . very good to hear."

"I love you."

She nodded before she spoke. "I love you too. So does Billy. Please remember that."

I clutched the bars as Claire climbed in the passenger's seat. Her head shook in the window as Doug jolted over the potholes, taking my wife to her car, so she could drive back to our home in Bodette—a journey she would likely complete by nightfall.

34

A hot slab of air oozed out when I opened the door. I secured my belongings and locked the door to go find a diner. I was prepared to have a very quiet day when a voice called my name; two familiar faces poked out the neighboring door: Hopper and Music Man—Monroe, a third, panted his doggie smile from Music Man's side.

"Where are you off to all by your lonesome?" Music Man said through his mustache, "and where's your purty wife?"

"The good lady has deserted me."

"Sorry to hear that."

"I figure to fill the void with a burger and a milkshake at the diner."

"Oh don't go there. That place is terrible and doesn't allow dogs. We know a much better establishment unfettered by any antiquated notions of canine prejudice." The three of them started walking out the other side of the parking lot.

"We didn't see you two around last night."

"Claire made friends with the old lady that gave us a ride into town. She ended up taking us in for the night."

"Sleeping in a stranger's house. I can't say that I've checked that box."

"Did she feed you well?" Hopper's first words.

"She fed us like we were two old ladies over for morning tea. That is to say—no. Although her son gave me some beer."

Their restaurant was a pizza shop about half a mile down the road. Hopper and Music Man had stayed at the Dowery the night before, teaming up for a pizza dinner and a drive-in movie—they had enjoyed it so much that they decided to do the whole thing over again. Music Man pulled cheese scraps off a small pizza he had ordered specifically for Monroe, placing them on a plate on the ground where the dog gulped them down. I explained in greater detail the food situation at Gladys's as well as the forced wake up time and that I felt entitled to an actual town day. I did not mention my marital spat. On the way out, I ordered a meatball sub to pair with a television movie. After a quick resupply, the afternoon was mine to waste.

Once in bed, the black phone stared at me from the nightstand, thwarting my efforts to become engrossed in an old detective drama. It was Sunday; there was a strong possibility that Billy would pick up if I called his home number. I scooted away from the phone, such that the TV stand's faux wood sides blocked the near portion of the final car chase; I could only make out the last names of the credits as they rolled down. A caption announced that an apocalyptic action movie, old enough that Claire and I had seen it together during our courtship, would be starting up next. I picked up the phone.

"William Jenkins."

"Hey Billy. It's Dad."

"Da . . . Hey Dad. How are you? Where are you calling from?"

"Sacred Place."

"Sacred Place? Is . . . is that a church?"

"It's a town."

"Let me get my . . . Okay I see it now."

"Yea, not too far from you really. I'm planning to come see you in a couple weeks. Just calling to make sure that's okay."

"Of course it's okay. It's great, Dad. Mom actually told me. Just, um, any idea when that will be?"

"Two, maybe three weeks. Depends how long it takes me to hike."

"Dad you're going to have to give me more detail than that. Are you at least aiming to get here on a weekend?"

"I don't know. I can't really control it."

"It seems like you would have full control."

"It's hard to explain. I'll do what I can but I'll just have to call you when I'm closer."

"Okay. Please do. Don't get me wrong I'm very excited to see you but I'm very busy right now. We have a lot of deals setting to finish up and the schedule has been pretty unforgiving. I want to be able to set aside some time for you but that takes planning."

"I'll certainly try to fit your schedule."

"Okay . . . but I'm about to step out so I have to go. Thanks for calling. I'm excited to hear about your hike. Bye, Dad."

"Bye, Billy."

I set down the phone and stared at the screen. I was asleep before the old world ended.

***

A wet nose prodded me awake; once again, there was a man standing over me.

"You should really lock your door."

"You should knock."

"That's what I have the dog for. Come join me in the parking lot."

"The parking lot? Why?"

"We have chairs and booze. You look like you want a drink." Music Man's shorts, not much more than underwear, emphasized his long skinny legs.

I considered my situation; I did not want to be alone with my thoughts. "What do you have to offer?"

He grinned, tapping his nose as he disappeared through the door. I shuffled after him, finding him cradling a glass bottle of brown liquor. "This. This is what I have to offer and this is my plan for the evening." He presented it as a server would a bottle of wine. "Would you like me to add one to the reservation?"

I sighed. "I was hoping to do some hiking tomorrow, but I think I can clear my schedule."

"You'll be hiking just fine. I will grab some glasses." He set the bottle next to my feet and retrieved a paper cup and his radio, still playing bluegrass.

"None for Monroe?"

"He doesn't handle it too well. But he's happy just to be here." On cue, Monroe lifted his leg against the front tire of the inexplicable luxury car parked three spots to our right, trotting back to his owner when he was done. Music Man poured a cup, handed it to me, and raised his own glass. "Come, Gabe. Let us get drunk and mean."

"Aye aye. What do you reckon is the story there?" I asked pointing at the sedan. "Staying at the Dowery, when you can afford a car like that?"

"I'm here. And I used to have two."

"Two!"

"Two luxury sedans for Mr. Van Durgess. To go along with my convertible and a motorcycle." Music Man gave himself a three second pour and took a sip from the bottle.

"You know you can only drive one at a time."

"Thought I wanted them."

"And now you're walking."

"And now I'm walking."

"I guess I used to have two cars. One minivan that we just never got rid of after Billy left. One white rolling cube with the driver's seat on the wrong side."

"Never got me one of those."

"You're not missing out." I took a sip; it was light, but left a residual, percolating heat. "Much more palatable than that hellfire you gave me on the mountain."

"Do not worry, my friend. That's on the menu as well."

"Oh good," I said taking a more confident sip. "How long have you been out here?"

"You watched me sit down."

"I mean hiking, you know, on the Great Eastern Trail."

"Don't think I started too long before you. But I actually started on the other Great Trails before that."

"There are other Great Trails?"

"Indeed. Western, Central, Southern. And, if you're really about something—Northern."

"How long did those take you?"

"Still on my first dog."

"Did that thing make those trips as well?" I gestured at the radio.

"Brightening every step."

"And it just constantly plays no matter where you are? Doesn't need signal or a cord or nothing?"

Music Man studied me for a second. "Sure."

The shadows crawled across the parking lot until it was full dark. The Dowery's floodlights kicked on behind us, basking us in a cheap orange spotlight, sending our shadows stretching down the concrete corridor. Music Man swayed anew.

"Should we get Hopper out here before it gets too late. Maybe get some dinner. I'm not sure how long I'll make it swilling bourbon on an empty stomach."

"Damn fine idea. Damn fine. Let us wake his fat ass up." He pushed himself out of his chair and tottered over to the door facing the luxury car. Monroe remained on the ground, eyes locked on his master. Music Man got to the door, glanced at me, then unleashed hell.

"Hopper! Hopper! Get your old ass out here and get what's coming to you." After his initial barrage, he stepped away and waited with his arms crossed. "Old bastard better be making himself decent." He resumed his assault with vigor. "Hopper you fat sack of bastard I know you're in there. Get your ass out here and have a goddam drink so Gabe can get his dinner."

The door cracked—a wide-eyed young woman, maybe twenty-five, poked her face under the chain.

"C-can I help you?"

"Holy shit. Way to go Hopper."

A man's voice, decidedly not Hopper's, bellowed from inside the room. "What the hell are you doing? Close the fucking door." The door shut.

Music Man turned to me, pointing at the door.

"Did you see that shit?" The next door flung open—Hopper sprang out shirtless and pot-bellied, brandishing an eye mask.

"What in the hell is going on out here? Can't a man get some damned sleep at this motel?"

Music Man's gaze switched from door to door. "Evenin' Hopper. If you put some pants on, we may have a story for you."

When Hopper was clothed, we filled him in. At the conclusion, he sat quiet for a moment before grumbling, "Those horny shits ruined my nap."

"I wonder who he is. Driving his fancy car to sleazy motels to enjoy that pretty young lady."

"I guess we are close enough to Pentland now, could be some hotshot businessman from there."

"Or a hotshot attorney."

"We attorneys have no need for fleabag motels. We simply enjoy our support staff in our offices. This is a man that's trying to hide his face. Fifty-fifty we recognize him when he comes out."

"Hopefully he doesn't leave while we're at dinner."

"Dinner? Who could possibly think of dinner at a time like this. This is now officially a stake-out. No way am I leaving this spot. I'd rather starve. That sumbitch is going to come out some time soon and I'm going to put my eyes on him."

"Why? Can't we just go eat? I mean, how do you even know he will come out soon?"

"Because it's past dark and nobody worth a shit actually sleeps with their mistress. At least not at places like this."

After some discussion Music Man recalled that the pizza place delivered—I put in the order. The pizza came and went; we had almost finished the bottle of bourbon when the door to the luxury car's room cracked and out strolled a middle-aged man in a pristine suit with a crisp buttoned shirt and tie pulled up the neck. The Dowery floodlight spotlighted him as he twirled his car keys around his finger, whistling an upbeat oldie. Monroe, bless him, snarled, the first noise he'd made all evening, evincing a jump from the man and sending his keys skittering down the pavement. He squinted in our direction as he bent to pick them up.

"Gentlemen."

"Nice looking lady." The key scraped against the paint.

"Can I help you?"

"And your wife. I imagine the judge will find her situation very sympathetic."

"Fuck you, old man."

"I am your future, my friend. All your decisions lead here." The door slammed. The engine roared to life and the car whipped out of the parking lot, bottoming out over several potholes.

"He wasn't much interested in conversation."

"Guess he made his point in his room."

35

Despite the bourbon, I was outside in my chair in time to watch the natural light reclaim the parking lot. For breakfast I finished off the remnants of last night's pizza, capping it with a *Juicerrman* and several cups of thin lobby coffee.

The girl emerged during my second cup. She was clad in grey sweatpants and a faded pink hoodie, keeping her head down as she slipped backward out the door; she maintained her twist on the knob until the bolt aligned with the frame. She saw me, shuddered, then scurried to a rusty coupe parked by the lobby.

Music Man and Hopper emerged soon after to lock their rooms and return their keys before setting off walking out of the parking lot.

"Aren't we going to get a ride back to the Trail?"

They stopped; Monroe cocked his head. "How many cars you seen this morning?"

I thought about the girl. "Not many; but Claire and I were able to get a ride in."

"No. Claire was able to get a ride in because *she's* a shapely woman. We're just three scraggly old men. Hobos to the untrained eye."

"So we're walking all the way back?"

"If you were still a respectable God-fearin' mailman, would you let us in your car?"

"I was hoping one of y'all had a plan."

We climbed the same slope that had permitted Gladys to neglect her gas pedal. Cars passed intermittently and close; the passengers did double-takes at the trio of haggard old men trudging up the roadside. Monroe, in his perfection, knew well enough to keep on Music Man's right, away from the road, only straying out to avoid a particularly thick bramble. The sun rose high, heating the road. We stopped for a minute at the trailhead, gathering ourselves with sighs and sips of water.

"Well shit gentleman," said Music Man, pouring water into his hand for Monroe before taking some himself—as far as I could remember this was the first non-alcoholic beverage I had seen him consume. "Nothing like a strong warm-up."

Hopper, red faced and wet, grunted a reply. I told them to go on without me while I took a moment for another *Juicerrman*. They complied, leaving poor Monroe standing at the trailhead, switching his worried eyes back and forth between me and his departing master; his true loyalty prevailed and he loped away.

The Great Eastern Trail continued the road's upward march but, being capable of much tighter turns, weaved upwards at a gentler slope, pinging me back and forth across the hillside in shaded comfort. The forest was now exclusively hardwoods. Sturdy red trunks filled the air with an authoritative, institutional fragrance; it was like walking through God's office, and quite conducive to tranquil thinking.

Without Claire I was free to set my own pace. It was clear my wife had missed the point of the Great Eastern Trail. The freedom it permitted. I woke up when I wanted, hiked when I wanted, ate what I wanted. There was no job to consume my days, leaving me only scraps.

Why should my son continue to weigh me down?

I thought about my call with Billy, dissecting his tone and word choice to determine whether he actually wanted to receive me, or had been well-coached by his mother. It was now less than two weeks before I would be forced to meet with him. Would he meet me in his fancy office, or perhaps some trendy overpriced Pentland restaurant? Despite Claire's sympathy, I still felt compelled to berate him but struggled to piece together exactly what for.

Opportunities for discipline had always been rare with him. Throughout his childhood, Billy had kept himself on track: good grades, sports, student government; he had even been a self-motivated dresser. He was far too competitive to have any of his measurables slip behind those of his peers. From a young age, Billy was always cognizant of the next step, and only took it when he was good and ready—but he always took it. I rarely even got to offer advice.

Music Man had a fire going when I arrived. The campsite was nowhere specific, just a spot on the mountainside; it wasn't even flat. Monroe trotted out to greet me, extracting the toll for safe passage then wagging his tail as he escorted me into camp. Hopper had spread out a blanket and lay on his back, hands resting on his belly. Music Man looked up and waved.

"Did somebody trip?"

"What do you mean?"

"I mean is somebody hurt? Why did you stop here?"

"It's got good vibes."

"Good vibes? It's crooked. How are we going to sleep?"

"Good vibes are important. Help me sleep easy, hike better. Monroe thinks so too."

"It's where the damn dog laid down," Hopper said without raising his head.

"You'll be fine. Just make sure you pitch your tent so that your head's up, you know, above your feet. Otherwise, unless you're some kind of weirdo, you won't be able to sleep."

I found a suitable spot where the grade was somewhat lessened, and set up my tent, kneeling like a golfer on the green to examine my lie. Hopper and Music Man were deep in conversation when I returned.

"One more deal. For old time's sake."

"What old times? I only ever worked with your father."

"That's not true—remember the electric shirts?"

"That was at the request of your father."

"So? You still worked with me."

"And it fell through because you didn't read the reports. It's actually the one blemish on my professional record."

"You can't just stay out here hiking forever."

"Why the hell not? I'm not hurting anyone."

"Because you've got a marketable skill, a trade, something to offer. You spent a lifetime negotiating contracts, mergers, deals that nobody else could have made happen. You should be making a fortune. You should be making a fortune on *this* deal."

"Whatever you need or want me for, I'm not going to be a part of it."

"Why not? Don't tell me your ego won't let you. And don't tell me you've lost the desire. And don't even try to tell me you don't want to face going back to the firm because I promise if you walked in the office tomorrow the goddam founder would rise from the grave to greet you with a case file and a cup of coffee."

Music Man leaned back and pulled Monroe across lap. Monroe rolled over and gratefully accepted a pensive belly rub.

"I'm not going to be a part of it. I've spent enough time trimming figures and shifting ampersands."

"I don't think what you're doing out here is any better. If you're going to be miserable, you might as well turn a profit. We could make a fortune on this deal."

"I'm not miserable. I've just had enough."

"Your skills aren't the kind that lose their edge with age. And this mystical bullshit has somehow only increased your brand."

"Hopper, just be quiet and look at the stars."

"I'm only trying to get you to do what you were born to do."

"And I'm only trying to get you to shut up. We're in a nice place here. The breeze is cool and the fire is warm. Just relax for a second and quit with that shit."

"This won't be like the shirts. I've done my research. We are going to make a fortune. It's impossible that we don't. I just need you to figure out the details, assuage the more hesitant minds and, you know, stroke the egos."

Music Man turned to me. "What do you think Gabe? Should I forsake my woodland lifestyle and return to the city?"

"Oh I'd rather not—"

"It will put an end to this."

"It kinda seems like the thing that drove you out here in the first place."

"Couldn't have said it better myself."

"Yep. Down from on high. The mailman speaketh." Hopper removed a jar of fancy hazelnut spread, two slices of bread, and crawled into his tent.

36

The next few days passed without much excitement as the Trail went for a jaunt in the foothills. This did not mean less climbing, only that it was broken up into smaller, more repetitive chunks; instead of gearing up for one or two big, marginally stimulating mountains, each day was spent scrambling up and down oversized mounds permitting no sense of grandeur or accomplishment. If the Amicolas were the deep end, we occupied the kiddie pool.

At night we huddled around Music Man's fires, listening to his unstoppable radio, legs aching as we prepared for another day. Music Man and I traded pulls of medicine; Hopper gorged on his hazelnut spread. We went in and out of Pelfrey, spending another night in a motel, and patronizing a frigid, punk-themed diner. On the fourth night out of Pelfrey, and the last before we were to make the road to Paukin, Music Man set up camp near a stream between two hills. I found him tending the fire; Hopper had assumed his base position: flat on his back, hands on his belly. Monroe escorted me to my seat.

"No views, no waterfalls, no peaks. Just up and down, up and down all damn day. Nothing to show for it but this damned heat." Hopper, having failed in his attempts to persuade Music

Man to return to the corporate world, settled for a constant verbal assault of his new one.

Music Man looked up from his fire. "The past few days have been less than exciting. I will grant you that."

"Less than exciting?" said Hopper, "they were pointless. Wear my ass out day after day with nothing to show for it. Like hiking a treadmill."

"Think of it as a chance to cover some distance. We have been making some big miles since Sacred Place. What else could you want?"

"Want? I want a cool breeze and a nice backdrop to my lunch. Sweeping vistas and grand landscapes. A photo for my desk to discuss with clients."

"You endured a hot day, unaided by cool breezes or views, and came out further north."

"To what end though? It's just more hiking tomorrow."

"There is no end, Hop. Out here the means are the end. You need to relax and just enjoy the experience."

"I liked you better when you were an attorney."

"You're probably the first person to say that."

"Seems pretty clear that he's out here to distance himself from that." I don't know what compelled me to speak.

"No. Don't buy this shit. He's trying to camouflage the fact that he's alienated everyone in his life by coming out here where everyone's alone and nobody has friends, families, or visitors. Back in the real world, when there's no deal to be made, nobody has any use for him. He's a goddam leper. He's made sure of that. But out here, he fits right in."

I glanced at Music Man who didn't take his eyes off the fire. "Maybe we all just need to get to Paukin tomorrow and put our feet up for a night."

"Put your feet up in Paukin? Where in the hell do you expect to do that?"

"I haven't picked the spot exactly but every town so far has had some sort of accommodations. Don't see why Paukin should be any different."

"Because Paukin isn't a town. It's just a shithole stretch of highway that happens to have a name."

"Hopper's right, Gabe. Paukin is actually where I came to get on the Trail when I worked in Pentland. When we get down to Highway 168, the only structure for forty miles is going to be the Paukin Gas Station. I don't even know where the attendant lives."

I started early the next day, breaking my fast on a *Juicerrman* before setting off as the hills continued their ad nauseum sprawl. I hated to admit it; Hopper's frustrations were warranted. It was the hiking equivalent of treading water: a good bit of up, a dash of down to keep equilibrium, and repeat. Each and every day a great deal of effort was expended to remain at waterline. I counted eight mounds before lunch.

I reached the bottom and put my toes on the edge of the pavement, glancing from side to side; the highway was a ribbon tied around the base of the hill, wrapping out of sight on either side. There was no sign of the gas station. Highway 168 represented the first landmark in the better part of a week, and it marked nothing. If Music Man's gas station did exist, I had no way of knowing which way would take me there and I'd be derned before I wasted steps in this region.

Heat is a venom that seeps through parched skin, sapping strength, and damaging organs. My legs were tired; my feet hurt; sweat stung my eyes. My *Juicerrman* tasted of sweetened ash. I let the first bite fall from my mouth and drank the remnants of my water; it dissipated like it was being sprinkled on desert sand. I slumped under a tree, readying myself for a roadside nap.

Monroe's implausibly wet kisses beckoned me from the darkness. His master stood over me as well but withheld his affection.

"How you doin' there partner?"

"I'm not in bed with a root beer. Where's Hopper?"

"Hop's draggin' ass back there somewhere. He's been pretty sour all day, especially with no town in sight. Figure to give him a little space. These hills are doing him real bad."

"Your friend's not exactly a charmer."

"I thought you'd at least be on your fifth roller dog by now."

"I do not know the way."

Music Man put his hands on his hips and shook his head. "Afraid I can't help you there pal, but your tree seems pretty sure."

I sat up and turned around: there on the trunk, not five feet above where I had been laying someone had carved *PAUKIN GAS STATION* in thick block letters with a westward arrow. Clear as day.

"Can't say I ever would've noticed that."

"One must always look to the trees for guidance, Gabe."

We decided to wait on Hopper before heeding the tree's advice. In his agitated state, Hopper was liable to miss the road altogether and thus exceedingly unlikely to notice the tree's instructions. Music Man laid down next me with his head on his pack while Monroe curled up between us, resting his head on my leg, giving me a dose of the doe-eyes until I gave in and scratched his ears.

Since we had met up the night before Sacred Place, Hopper had been, simply, a drag— constantly grouchy, constantly whining, incessantly caught off guard by even the most foreseeable aspects of hiking. I loathed his distended belly and moist heaving breaths which could be heard well before he came into view, increasing in viscosity when he laid down on his back. This trip was my grand once-in-a-lifetime adventure, my chance to find peace with the world, and he was dragging it down with his paunchy short-sightedness.

By the time Hopper came off the mountain, I was red with hunger. I whipped on my pack and was fifty yards ahead of them before Music Man had even explained the tree carving. I could hear Music Man calling my name as I marched down the highway. The blood pooled and boiled in my cheeks, my hate expanding to include both Hopper and Music Man; the two companions with whom I had been burdened and who seemed dedicated to desecrating my hike. The Paukin Gas Station was less than half mile off trail, visible immediately upon taking the curve; I cursed each step, knowing full well that each one meant another in the opposite direction, and neither brought me closer to Daemon's.

The gas station was an ancient structure of warped flaky wooden slats which some long dead soul had seen fit to paint a deep blue. The outside made clear it did not contain a deli. I set my pack down on a cracked stone picnic table, checking to see if there was anyone around to steal it, before splitting the pair of dilapidated pumps in pursuit of sustenance and blood sugar. The offerings were scant; most of the wire racks, both refrigerated and non, were bare. I settled on the last two sticks of *Bug Meat Jerky*, a jar of off-brand peanut butter, four pouches of *Insta-Soup*, and some questionable trail mix. Barring a cache of Settler's Fowl, it would be another *Juicerrman* heavy segment. For right now food, I selected three bags of chips and two microwave burritos; the ancient cashier directed me to a splotched and gooey microwave hidden behind the tobacco products. In normal life, the red-brown spattering on the microwave would've raised some prohibitive health concerns, but I convinced myself that nothing bad could survive in a microwave. I loaded the burritos, fired it up for two minutes, and was outside eating by the time Hopper and Music Man made the store.

"How's the spread, Gabe?"

I raised my burrito. "Lacking."

Hopper just stood behind him, looking disdainfully at the food. The chips, were off-brand and pickle flavored, selected over *Lime Madness*. The burrito cheese had the consistency of dried plastic; the beef turned to powder in my mouth.

They rejoined me outside momentarily to munch with displeasure. When I had scraped all the stubborn chunks of dried cheese product off my paper plate, I stood up and left. A warm full belly would have made the sun brighter and the air more pleasant. As it was, I seemed heavier and sweatier.

It happened all at once—my stomach swelled and turned to stone. I was just able to dart off Trail and avoid ruining my shorts. The second incident soon followed, with the third hot on its heels. That was not the end of it. The exhaustion of perpetual pooping brought me down quick. I collapsed against a tree barely an hour from Highway 168, sweaty in the shade. My skin constricted into goose pimples as waves of nausea crested like a dismal tide. The groans sent the squirrels scurrying to watch from the higher branches. I closed my eyes and breathed, trying hard to let this pass.

For the second time that day I awoke to Monroe's kisses. Each warm wet lick eliciting waves of tingling relief. He nuzzled under my hand.

"Not now boy. I think I'm dying." Monroe gave me a look that said death was no excuse then rolled over to scratch his back in the grass. His master followed several minutes later, looking up at the sun still high in the sky.

"I was hoping to go a little farther than this."

"Bad burritos. Very bad gas station burr—." A colorful emission followed the words. Music Man took a step back.

"Although this spot is not without merit. I'll gather some wood."

The illness submitted its own reply. My face flushed and fell, flushed and fell; each flush left my body incrementally hotter. My internal alarms blared; all remaining troops were called to duty. My stomach swished and churned. I attempted a sip of water, fighting my arm up to my mouth, just a drop to quell the flames—my throat muscles seized in yet another oral emission, destined to be repeated. Monroe stayed with me through the worst of it, hopping back at each heave to watch with concern.

Reality fogged and swirled. I laid back and closed my eyes.

My pack was gone when I woke up. Monroe remained laid out against my left leg. The volcanic pulsing had subsided into a steady internal sway. The setting sun pitched the canopy in a golden glow. I called out for Music Man. He responded from behind me.

"Just a minute, sir. Hopper's got this shit too. Apparently the Great Eastern Trail wants me to play nurse today."

"Where's my pack?"

"Over yonder. I went ahead and set up your tent. Figured you wouldn't be up to it. You really shouldn't carry so many of those red bars. Might as well be made of bronze."

Says the man carrying a rickhouse. "How far am I from the fire?"

"It's about ten yards behind you."

"I'm coming."

"Easy does it."

I propped myself against the tree and worked my way to my feet. Monroe pushed up to his haunches, cocking his head as he watched. The forest breathed around me, rocking the ground with it. Up on my feet, I found the air to be lighter and cooler; a breeze snuck between the trees. The fire was close—several deliberate, heavy steps got me there. My tent was a blurry green lump on the other side, out of reach for now: when the time came, it was only one more set of deliberate steps away. To my left, Hopper lay on his side muttering his ailments. Music Man was behind him, setting up Hopper's familiar orange shaded tent.

"How you doin' Hop?" The muttering punctuated into a sharp, hard grunt. "Yea, me too."

"Gabe, can I get you anything? Food, water?"

"No thanks. Sort of a one way street."

"Okay well you just let me know if that changes."

Monroe rejoined me; this time sleeping against my right leg. I gazed into the fire, letting its heat roll over me. Sweat balled on my forehead, cheeks and arms, accumulating until gravity dragged the beads to the dirt. Darkness took me.

I opened my eyes to Music Man eating by the fire. Monroe remained nestled against my leg, now damp with perspiration. There was no sign of Hopper.

"How's your other patient?"

"Relieved to have something significant about which to complain. How are you?"

"Ready for real sleep."

"This is the time when a real doctor would tell you to drink some fluids and be referring to water and electrolytes and, while I don't disagree with that, I generally prescribe to a different method." Music Man removed a jar and set it next to me. "My thinking is that there is something alive in your gut that shouldn't be and what's in that jar will not abide anything being alive in your gut. So my prescription is to drink this and kill it."

"Like anti-biotics?"

"Yes. Of a very literal variety."

"Let's see if I can keep it down."

Music Man's medicine was merciless, flaming down my throat like drain cleaner through a clogged pipe. I gave it a second to fully blossom before following it with a swig of water which went down like rain on charcoal. I took the opportunity to go to bed, thanking Music Man as I departed.

***

The pain pulled me from sleep; not anywhere in particular, but everywhere with particularity. My joints protested movement;

my skin protested contact; my muscles protested their existence. I was no longer nauseous but my stomach still gurgled, hitting the rinse cycle when I snuck down a few sips of water. It was dark, the deep dark of night, and I saw no sense in moving. Chills came and went. A headache grew out as an ice pick pressed out through my sinuses. I thought about Claire warm and healthy in our bed; Billy warm and healthy in his. I could be with her, Claire, with a roof over my head, a bowl of hot soup, and a cabinet full of medicine, having dodged this devilry by eating her more than adequate cooking rather than tainted burritos. But I had chosen this. Billy, if and when I saw him, would surely think this whole endeavor insane—a step outside the forward progress to which he had dedicated his life. I imagined trying to explain it to him.

Music Man began rustling not long after first light, humming along to his music box as he fed Monroe. The sounds of rustling sticks and crackling suggested a fire. I crawled out of my tent, sleeping pad in hand, to lay down and absorb the warmth.

"Morning Gabe. How you feeling today?"

"Diminished."

"Aren't we all. Your friend Hopper was up all night, throwing up the food he hasn't eaten yet."

"Probably the most useful thing to come out of his mouth. But I'm sure he's being very stoic about it."

"Yep. That's the word I've been looking for. Have you eaten anything?"

"Haven't felt the inclination."

"You should consider it. You've spent months ramping up and fueling your metabolism only to abruptly choke it off. It will save you some significant trouble if you do. Probably a good time for one of those horrible steroid bars."

"If you got any more of that moonshine, I'd sure like to make sure the enemy is obliterated. I'm not inclined to harbor any prisoners."

"My kind of patient." Music Man handed me the jar.

My descaled stomach launched its minions on the bar like a swarm of ants. Various support systems kicked back into motion as a dormant factory surged back to life. Music Man suggested we stay put for the day to let Hopper and me recover. A series of short naps framed my morning. Music Man kept the fire burning throughout, collecting sticks from an ever-widening perimeter and stashing them in an ever-dwindling pile, always humming, tapping, and often dancing along to his eternal music. In between naps, I watched Music Man place the branches in the fire at odd and deliberate angles, sometimes setting wood aside when the timing wasn't right for its girth or shape, no doubt losing his knuckle hair in the process. The result was a neat and complex knot of flame. I traced the threads from the coil at the bottom to their release at the top.

37

The march recommenced the next day. Music Man and Monroe trailed with Hopper, ensuring he did not fall behind—or quit all together. I passed the day alone, stopping for the evening in a clearing amidst a grove of elms and sycamores. It was a more than suitable spot, after a more than suitable distance, and I did not want to push my luck. I had already eaten dinner, rice flavored with soup mix, and was wrapped in my sleeping bag when Monroe jingled up the Trail, followed by the heavy trudging of two old men.

"Over here!!" I flashed my headlamp.

"Yea we see you, you oaf. Come out and say good night to Monroe before he puts his paw through your tent."

I unzipped to find Monroe shaking and whinnying—if I had unzipped any further he would have jumped in the tent with me. He quieted down when I scratched his ears then rejoined his master.

"Hopper, how you doing?"

"Not too well," Music Man answered, "he made it though." Hopper took his position on his back as Music Man set up his tent for him. "Quite the achievement, to hike all day, make it this far, when you feel like he does." Hopper groaned again.

"I can empathize. Y'all need any help?"

"I think we got it. You just get on to bed. Make sure we don't have two sick oafs tomorrow."

I bid them good night, listening as Music Man ushered Hopper to bed then built himself a fire.

Two more days to Billy.

The next morning my first act was to stretch my arms far above my head, twisting my stomach this way and that. I hopped out of my tent, kicking my feet in broken rhythm, relishing the good and unbridled feelings after two days of illness. Hopper too looked much improved; Music Man still spent the whole day hanging back with him, leaving me to hike ahead at my own pace. Music Man's only instruction was that we had to make it past the Tawnamac River if we wanted to reach West Boelein in two days. From West Boelein I could catch the train into Pentland and my son.

Although the Great Eastern Trail remained shaded and smooth, a heavy humidity induced an unwarranted degree of sweatiness. I marched through the day, sights set on crossing the Tawnamac River. After so long in the woods, and a nearly infinite number of steps, there was a growing sense of resentment towards each additional obstacle as simply tacked on opportunities for misfortune and injury: rivers, heat, Billy; unnecessary speed bumps between me and Daemon's. I'd proven myself, my dedication, countless times since setting out from Grambling's Pass. *Did I really need to be crossing a river at this point in my trek?* I found myself tip-toeing around rocks and roots. Music Man had mentioned nothing about how I was to actually cross the river.

I walked quickly, vaguely worried that if I did not complete the miles now, some emergency would arise and pull me from the Trail, or make them impossible, but the Tawnamac did not appear and the day's hike was fast becoming one of my longest. I worried about Hopper, Music Man, and Monroe behind me. They were no doubt moving at a crawl. I recalled from my schooling that the Tawnamac did enjoy some historical significance as the early settlers in the area had constructed what was believed to be the first bridge on the continent connecting its shores, but that bridge had come and gone long before the city's skyscrapers lined its southern banks. By noon, the looming confrontation with Billy pressed out all other thoughts.

The sun was beginning to set when I first heard the whiny buzz of engines. The trees parted shortly thereafter, opening up on the vast expanse of the Tawnamac. The river was wide and slow enough to be confused for a lake. Anchored boats and pontoons crowded against each other, orbited by brightly colored inflatable moons and bobbing heads, emitting a chorus of loud cheers and bolts of laughter. I could have crossed the river from boat to boat without wetting my shoes.

A collection of faded canoes, strewn as if by storm, guarded the shore. A large wooden sign read:

> CANOES ARE CHEAP AND NOT WORTH STEALING
> THEY ARE FOR DAY USE ONLY
> PLEASE LEAVE CANOE AND PADDLE ON FAR SHORE
> SINCERELY
> FRIENDS OF THE TAWNAMAC
> CANOES ARE CHEAP AND NOT WORTH STEALING

I selected a red canoe that creaked and bowed when I lifted it, slid it into the water, and pushed off, marveling at the ease with which the canoe glided through the river. The red hull weaved amongst the boats and floaters who took no notice of the hobo paddling amongst them.

Different portions of the river played different styles of music: the boaters on the near shore played an unfamiliar fast paced music which transitioned into the familiar music of my youth, now termed 'oldies' as I neared the nicer boats in the center; then twangy country as I approached the far shore. Ten minutes later, I lugged the canoe and paddle onto piles of their friends.

Dozens of campsites, composing the Tawnamac River Campground, occupied the river's northern shore. I crept through family barbecues, company outings, and guys weekends. The campground rang with the crisp, carbonated release of opening beer cans; hordes of people experiencing the great outdoors seated next to coolers, within spitting distance of their cars; a community of voluntarily displaced city folk capping off their day of boating and lounging with hot dogs, burgers, pulled pork sandwiches paired with fries, chips, various mayonnaise based salads, and countless other salted snacks. I came to an unoccupied site on the outskirts, breathing in the greasy, salty aromas of my neighbors' unearned feasts as I set up my tent, staring down the barrel of a dankless pot of warmed soup rice.

"Excuse me, uh, sir." I turned around, recognizing the patriarch of one of the shoreline families. He had receding brown hair and was perhaps in his late thirties with the soft build of a man who sat both for work and recreation. "Are you a thru-hiker?"

"Not yet."

He gave a confused look.

"I'm hiking but I'm not done yet."

"Great. Amazing actually. I didn't know people still did that. Would you mind coming to talk to my kids? They noticed the Great Eastern Trail and would love to meet a real live thru-hiker."

"Sorry. I've had a real long day. Not much in the mood for—"

"We have hot dogs, burgers too. And more beer than we know what to do with."

"Where's your site?"

The man led me back through the campground; this time as an insider with access to their delicious wares. He paused behind an SUV before we entered a site with two blonde toddlers running laps around a fire while a blonde woman clutching a glass of red wine attempted to read a book.

"What's your name?"

"Gabe."

"Sorry I meant your trail name. You are actually a thru-hiker right?"

"Mister Gabe then. Mister Gabe I guess would be my trail name."

"Okay, Mister Gabe then; if you're just a regular homeless man I can't let you around my kids." He smiled and turned the corner. "Sam, Jenny this is Mister Gabe. He is one of the thru-hikers I was telling you about."

The kids stopped in their tracks, staring at me, jaws gaping like fish; the boy gripped a stick capped by a flaming marshmallow. I felt like a zoo animal on display. "Hi kids." The man handed me two hot dogs laden with cheese and chili. His wife pulled a beer from a red and white cooler. *Zoo animals do get handfed.*

"Come on. Ask him all of the questions you were asking me earlier."

The boy spoke first. "Mister Gabe, how long have you been hiking?"

"Um, must be about two months now."

"But where do you go potty?" Both kids giggled and stepped forward. I looked at the parents, who shrugged.

"Well I guess I try to hold it until I make it to a bathroom, but every now and then, when I just can't make it, I have to go in the woods."

"Have you ever gone poopy in the woods?"

"More times than I care to mention."

Both kids let out an extended *eeeewwwwww* before the sister chimed in. "But how do you flush? Mommy says you always have to flush."

"There's no flushing in the woods."

"But what do you do with it?"

"Kids why don't you ask Mister Gabe how far he walks in a day, or where he sleeps?" I took the opportunity to shotgun a hot dog.

"Yea Mister Gabe where do you sleep?"

"In a tent with a sleeping bag. I just set it up whenever I'm done hiking. It's pretty nice actually. Like a sleepover."

"Do you have friends with you?"

"Most nights. But they sleep in their own tents."

"That sounds fun."

"It actually is usually pretty fun. When I'm not cold, sick, or injured."

Sam and Jenny peppered me with questions for the next half hour, giving me a chance to recount my journey—mom and dad kept me supplied with fresh hot dogs and beer. I answered the kids' questions in between bites, gulps, and fits of indigestion.

"I wish I could eat as much as you Mister Gabe." The boy said after what must've been the sixth cheese dog, or the third burger.

"I'm not like this at home. It's all the walking."

"I wish I could walk all day. Then I could eat whatever I want."

"It's definitely a perk."

"Is your family hiking the Trail with you?"

"No, they're back at their homes."

"Don't you miss them?"

"Well of course I do."

"Then why don't you go spend time with them rather than pooping in the woods?"

"Well I . . ." I pondered the implications of this question then noticed Music Man and Hopper pass under the streetlight, heads hanging low. "Sorry kids, if you'll excuse me, that's actually my Trail family over there and I have to make sure they find their way home tonight. It's been a real pleasure talking to you and I hope you both grow up to be thru-hikers."

I bounced off with a belly full of hot dogs, beer in hand; I was about to call out when a thought struck that brought me back to the family's campsite.

"Excuse me, uh, sir, would you happen to have any extra hot dogs and beer for my friends?"

The hungry hikers finished their hotdogs before I'd shown them the spot; Music Man donated one to an all-too-grateful Monroe. The father had seen fit to gift us the rest of his beer in the cooler. Hopper and Music Man each drank as they set up their tents and I, for a change, kindled the beginnings of a fire, trying in vain to conjure up Music Man's ordered chaos of flame but had to settle for a wild Bear fire. Music Man maneuvered around his mobile abode, humming to himself, finger drumming on the taut fabric. Hopper remained insistent on being dour, punctuating each step with a grunt, never placing something on the ground when it could be dropped or thrown. Music Man and I stayed up late, drinking beer, then medicine, and listening to his radio while he corrected the fire.

"He's not any better. He moves faster. But he's not any better. He bitched and moaned all day. I mean literal fucking moans. *Uuurrrggggggggghhhhh aaaagggghhhhhhhh.* I don't know what the hell to do with him."

"I'm not sure why you asked him out here. Doesn't seem that he's ever been pleasant company. Even under ideal circumstances."

"He's a former client. More accurately, the son of a former client. Not much more than a miserable fuck up with the right last name. Whatever deal he is trying to work out, I imagine no one will touch it; he thinks adding my name to it will change that. I'm taking the opportunity to show him a simpler life."

"I appreciate you involving me in that."

A burst of Hopper's snores cut through his tent. "He continues to be out here. So I guess there's still hope."

Our conversation shifted to the remaining portions of the Great Eastern Trail—only a short, eventful stretch separated us from Daemon's Peak.

"The Kingston Mountains, Mister Gabe, are by far the best part of the Great Eastern Trail. I used to summer there as a teenager. You've never used the words *sweeping* or *breathtaking* so accurately. That's when you really get to feel like you've gotten out of it all; when you look down over the craggy, hardwood forests dotted with lakes, ponds and rivers. Dangerous for sure, day after day of rocky, exposed ridgelines and majestic views. The Kingstons can be . . . temperamental. A calm sunny day can turn into stormy nightmare in a heartbeat. The rain makes the rocks wet and slippery. The wind unsteadies your steps. It can mean death if you get caught out on that ridgeline in a mountain gale. It's just as big an experience as you can imagine. But if the weather cooperates and you play your cards right, Peggy Bardin will let you get familiar behind the landscaper's shack."

38

According to Music Man, only two miles of flat Trail separated the Dullston Shelter from the town of West Boelein and its train station. Unfortunately, it was a commuter train the last of which departed well before dark. As such, the plan was to stay at Dullston and leave early the next morning to catch the first train into Pentland.

It was yet another soupy mid-summer day. Sweat flowed down my back; my shirt slapped and stuck with each step. I tried to count back to my last shower. Had it been with Claire? There had been no shower in Paukin. Pelfrey? Maybe. The new sweat breathed life into the old sweat; the stench split the clean air, acting as a funky wedge as I moved north. Tomorrow would be an important turning point, a historic pivot for the entire Jenkins family line. Perhaps for the better. About mid-day I uncovered a patch of Settler's Fowl, my first since Claire, and filled my grocery bag.

I turned left onto the shelter trail. A small stream paralleled the side trail, emanating from a piped spring under which the water pooled to a depth of maybe four feet. I dumped my pack, trimmed down to my undies, and dipped a toe—it was cold, colder than it had any right to be in the company of such heat, sending an invigorating jolt through my body. I thought of my meeting with Jezebel at Franklin Spring so long ago—this time there was no young woman no invoke my modesty. I crept in on bended knee, legs trembling. I forced my head under the pipe, feeling the icy blades knife down my spine, finger combing the water through my hair and beard. When my body felt as clean as possible I collected my clothes to hold them under the pipe, soaking and wringing until the wastewater came out clear. I then exited the water to wipe down my pack, and anything else which threatened to emit an unpleasant scent. My trusty *Peakseekers* were last and longest.

I remained there, reading from the shelter log for a long time.

"Bear came right up to the shelter to help me with my dinner. Let me scratch his head while he licked a spoon of peanut butter. Sweet little thing." – Ironfoot

"A bear paid me a visit last night. Sure wish you dickweeds would stop feeding them." – Tonsilitus

"Made a new friend last night. I think someone's been breaking the rules." – Chimney Fat

Mongrel's note slipped from the pages:

MONGREL COME, MONGREL GO
IN ALL SERIOUSNESS DON'T FEED THE GODDAM BEARS

My feet had shrank by the time Music Man and Hopper appeared on the side trail. Hopper looked grim and Music Man bored, or frustrated, or bored with being frustrated. Hopper disrobed to collapse on his back in the shelter. I removed my feet and went to set up my tent, shirtless over my rain pants, lifting my arms to let the breeze clear my pits. I made sure to sit upwind of Music Man's fire. Hopper soon snored from the shelter.

The Settler's Fowl had been a necessary find as time had deflated my food bag. I poured in the last of my rice and soup mix and cut up the mushrooms. Beyond that, I was down to one *Juicerrman*. With any luck, Billy would not have thrown out the box Claire shipped to his apartment.

After dinner, Music Man and I conversed in hushed tones, not wanting to bother the sleeping Hopper; this was not so much out of politeness as it was to keep him asleep and silent. Music Man was '*tired of his shit.*' For once Monroe did not stare at me as I ate, remaining by his master, disinterested in a pot of soup flavored rice and mushrooms. Music Man motioned the jar in my direction.

"No thanks. Trying to stay sharp for tomorrow."

"Strange. If anything, tomorrow sounds like a good reason to drink more."

"I don't suppose you have any interest in coming into the city."

"Do not suppose that I do. I've spent more than enough time there and it's less than dog friendly. We'll pass the day in West Boelein, probably bunker down at another cheap motel and spend the day off our feet, eating chips and drinking beer. How long will you be in the city?"

"It depends on Billy's hospitality. And if he wants to see his old man."

"I'm getting the impression that you're the one that's being slow to come around."

"It'd be nice if you came with me. Y'all might actually have something in common, with the lawyerin' and all."

"You deal with your own shit, Gabe. Besides, you don't want advice from me. I'm not out here as a reward for a well-tended marriage."

"What do you reckon *he's* going to do?" I motioned to the shelter.

"Keep walking I suppose. Although, I'm afraid the next nudge will be enough."

"Maybe that would be best. He, um, does not seem to like it out here."

"He doesn't like anything. He's no better in the city. I only agreed to listen to his pitch to get him out here and hopefully clear his head. Hopper's done nothing but squander and get himself in trouble. He needs to clear it all and start over."

"Those burritos did the only clearing I've seen."

Music Man tightened his fire. "What are you going to say to young William?"

"Reckon I have no idea."

"Well, from what I can gather he's moved up to Pentland to pursue his career and you're butt hurt because you feel like he's left you behind."

"I wouldn't say butt hurt."

"Or is it that at a very young age he has already verifiably outpaced his mailman father?"

"I'd rather not get into it. I'll just figure it out."

"You're going into a very important negotiation Mister Gabe. It's vital that you have what you want and have delineated a route to getting there. Otherwise you'll get eviscerated."

"You think he'll eviscerate me?"

"Like a prince in waiting."

"I guess I'd like to have something to offer him. I've always been somewhat . . . complacent. And he and Claire are on the other end of the spectrum. Legs always moving, always making decisions, eyes on the prize. That kind of stuff. Meanwhile, I wasted a lot of time driving in circles. Never really developed any skills, or got great at anything, to make myself useful to him. I mean, at least Hopper's dad gave him something to squander. The foundation Billy's built for his life is already higher than anything I could bequeath."

Music Man took an extended sip, watching me over the jar.

"It's just a tough thing to put your finger on. You know they're doing away with government subsidized parcel delivery all together? I am the last of the career mailmen. My job was of so little value they didn't even replace me."

"I am not surprised. It is an ill-advised and antiquated system given our current digital infrastructure. But look at *me*, Gabe, you could've done a whole lot better, and a *whole lot* worse."

39

A series of high-pitched shrieks pierced the darkness. I snatched my headlamp, kicking out of my sleeping bag as the shrieking sharpened, accompanied by a growl and the sound of tearing fabric. I poked my head out of the tent, directing my light at shelter: a bear—an enormous bear—had its front feet propped on the floor and was leaning in. Its shoulders heaved as it thrashed at something within. The bear took no notice of my light, keeping its head buried in the shelter; its hulking black body glistened against the night. The source of the screaming remained hidden as I ran my hand through my pack, eyes set on the bear, groping for a suitable weapon until my hand grasped something sturdy and hard—so armed, I threw myself into the fray.

My headlamp revealed a frantic scene—the bear had Hopper pinned in the back corner as it ripped at the foot of his sleeping bag. It pulled back at my approach, sliding its top half out of the shelter and turning to assess its challenger. The bear stood up, rising as if it was growing out the ground. At its apex, it opened its mouth and let loose an indignant roar, slamming back down on its front paws, shaking the mountains. I presented my weapon in all its red wrapped glory. I saw my doom in the shining ghost blue eyes.

"Oh dern."

I stepped back keeping the *Juicerrman* extended in front of me; my last line of defense. The bear stalked towards me, taking in great angry snorts of air, lowering its head to the bar.

The bear stopped.

The ferocity left its breathing, replaced by quicker, searching sniffs. It lifted its giant snout to the wrapper, sniffed, and recoiled, pulling its neck back into its shoulders like a frightened turtle. The bear studied the overpriced candy bar and the imbecile wielding it. Sensing my moment, I thrust the bar—it recoiled again; this time stumbling backwards over its hind legs. I was about to repeat the process when a horrible snarl, fouler even than the bear's, came from behind me, a white missile blew by my feet chasing the bear, now in full retreat, into the night.

The snarling grew distant and disappeared.

Pulse racing, I stared into the darkness for a second then turned my light into the shelter, trying to catch my breath. Hopper remained painted against the back wall, clutching the remnants of his sleeping bag to his chin. The bag's foot end had been ripped to shreds; only the main seams remained to suggest the bag's intended shape. Spurts of down filler carpeted the floor.

"Did you see that Hopper!? Did you see that! I looked that bear right in its bear face." I flicked my wrist, fencing the bar through the air. "Sent him back into the darkness." Hopper did not move, trembling in the far corner. "Hopper, you alright?" I didn't see any blood.

"Al-alright?! No I'm not alright. No I'm not alright. I just got mauled by a bear." He took a breath. "And you ask if I'm alright?! Obviously I'm not alright." The woods rustled in the departed bear's direction. "Oh fuck."

I turned my headlamp, readying my *Juicerrman*; Monroe trotted out of the darkness, tongue lolling almost to the ground, to sit on my socked foot.

Music Man emerged, rubbing his eyes and shouting for Monroe.

"What the hell have you gotten into? Damn dog ripped a hole trying to get out."

"Monroe and I just chased off a damn bear."

"He did what?" Music Man bolted to his companion, rolling him over, and rubbing his hands across his stomach, sides, and back.

"You're checking on the dog? I got fucking mauled by a fucking bear. Biggest bear I've ever seen was up here in the shelter trying to tear me to pieces. And you're checking the dog."

Music Man looked at me.

"That is pretty much what I saw: bear was propped up in the shelter tearing at something then I popped out and scared it."

"Me. The fucker was tearing at *me*."

"Well damn Hopper. I'm sorry. You seem okay. Where did he get you?"

"My sleeping bag. I woke up because I heard licking, thought Monroe was getting into my hazelnut spread so I went to push him away and put my hand on this big ass head. Then the son of a bitch went ballistic trying to eat me alive."

I scanned the floor, locating the dented jar of Hopper's against the far wall.

"Hopper why would Monroe have been able to get into your hazelnut spread?"

"I woke up a little bit ago and was hungry on account of not eating dinner so I decided to have some spread and bread. Must've fallen back asleep without replacing the lid."

"You slept next to an open jar of hazelnut spread?"

"No I was eating it when I fell asleep."

"So yes."

"No. No, you don't get to do that. Don't even try to make this shit my fault. That fucking bear tried to kill me."

"That bear didn't give a shit about you. It was only here because you lured it in with your delicious hazelnut spread. What'd you expect it to do? You're just lucky it didn't actually get a hold of you."

Hopper pushed his socked feet through the hole in the bottom of his sleeping bag. "Yea, lucky is just the word I was looking for."

I parried invisible blows from invisible foes. Music Man's gaze fell on my *Juicerrman*.

"You eating in bed too? You in there covering yourself in peanut butter and bacon grease?"

"Not since Claire left. I heard Hopper scream and in the darkness, with all the commotion, this was all I could find. It frightened the bear something terrible though. He was coming at me until he caught a whiff of it. Then Monroe sent him packing."

"The bear was scared of your candy bar?" Music Man snatched the *Juicerrman* from me and inspected it. "What kind of chemical nonsense are you?"

"A weapon's only as good as its wielder. But if they'd put *too extreme for bears* in their advertisements they'd probably still be in business. I'm never sleeping without one again. Although I'm not sure I'll be able to eat any more."

Music Man let Hopper and his useless sleeping bag share the warmth of his mobile abode, opening the space by sending Monroe to spend the night with me. Monroe went without a fight, strutting through the flap and laying down as if he'd slept there every night of his life. I zipped up and squeezed around him, placing the *Juicerrman* behind me so there'd be bear repellent on both sides. Monroe let out a long sigh and was soon in the rhythmic breathing of sleep. I was too excited to sleep, instead replaying the events over and over in my head—Monroe, *Juicerrman*, and I had chased off a dern bear and he'd be a fool to come back.

This was a tent of heroes.

40

I woke up early the next morning, relishing Monroe's and my final moments as a heroic duo, giving his belly a worthy rub. The dog remained a shadow on my tent wall as I eased through every preparatory step, trying hard to keep my heartrate low and my skin dry. I started to unwrap the savior *Juicerrman* but then pictured the bear's confused face, and instead sheathed it in an exterior pocket. Glimmers of sun had just appeared through the trees when I snapped the final straps.

"Goodbye Monroe. I have to go play dad for a while. Hopefully I'll see you on the other side." The dog trotted next to me down the side trail until I turned on the Great Eastern Trail. There he stopped, sat, and watched me continue north, having undone all yesterday's efforts to rid myself of smell—I wreaked of dog.

After about an hour, the Trail edged near the sleeping town of West Boelein; a short side trail took me in. West Boelein's outskirts were picturesque: a host of old wooden homes centered around a bricked main strip with a mountain backdrop. The hardware stores and breakfast cafes flipped their signs as I passed. A patchwork of green signs led me to the train station.

The station was the epicenter of a different town: chain restaurants, coffee shops, and department stores occupied the bottom floors of sharp-edged, pastel colored apartment complexes from which people flooded the streets, bustling about in well-fitting suits, sporting leather briefcases, and barking into their phones, taking no notice of the peppercorn in their saltshaker.

I found a manned kiosk and asked about getting to Free Market Square, the finance and media hub in which Billy's tower was located. The kiosk lady glanced up from her magazine and assured me that I couldn't miss it. There were fifteen minutes before the next train so I indulged in an egg sandwich and coffee from a trackside cart. The heavy-set vendor, who wasn't much cleaner than me, looked genuinely surprised when I pulled out cash; he'd apparently assumed I'd be looking for a handout. The egg sandwich, clearly of the frozen variety, was far from fantastic but, as always, greatly appreciated. Frozen egg was still egg, and melted cheese was still cheese; neither was available on the Trail. I wondered if anyone had ever appreciated one of that man's sandwiches more than I.

I sat down on the train and became a structure—a seat with an out-of-order sign. Well-dressed citizens shuffled past glancing their displeasure at the hobo with his arms wrapped around his universe; their faces displayed a resigned lack of surprise that the government had failed to keep the seat operational for an honest, hard-working rear-end. The train stopped. The doors opened. And more people shoved aboard. To my eyes, the train was full leaving West Boelein, but somehow accommodated more and more suits as their owners mortared the cracks. I wondered if some great alien overlord crammed all the people on the Great Eastern Trail—including the crowds at Big Hill and Tawnamac—at any given time into one train car if it would get even half this crowded, or if any one of the small towns through which I'd passed had as many residents as this oversized soup can.

I located a map above the door, visible only when peoples' heads parted just right—after three or four brief glimpses, I ascertained what the kiosk lady had meant: all the rainbow spaghetti strands converged at Free Market Square. Its name was written larger and bolder than any other location. After half an hour I was even able to decipher Free Market Square being repeatedly slurred over the speaker. Just when I imagined the train's engine would start struggling with the weight, the speaker gargled Free Market Square; the train loosed its bowels, expelling me amongst a streaming portion of everything else it had consumed that morning. Once on the square, Billy's tower was easy enough to spot—it was the big one.

Pentland wore a different variety of wreak, one of car exhaust, musk, and industry, overpowering anything I may have carried in with me. Everything moved. A pressurized breeze gusted through the buildings. The people on the sidewalk stampeded in a bustling herd in a semi-synchronized, grinding lock step. I rode the wave around the square's perimeter to Billy's building, stopping at the intersections, turning where I needed to turn, doing my best to not ruin anybody's suit. Individuals split off from the herd along the way, never stopping or turning, simply using their accumulated momentum to slide out like a pitched baseball, hitting their intended door at an angle and disappearing. I judged my launch point, a crack in the sidewalk four or five steps before the glass doors, and timed my release.

It was close, but a touch too late—the herd's momentum carried me just past the revolving door. I had to creep back along the wall to the monstrous rotating doors.

The lighting in Billy's building was nothing short of amazing. The rich reds and whites of the high walls, marble floors, and vaulted ceilings glowed in a state of perpetual sunset. Despite the bustle of Free Market Square, once inside there was an epic tranquility, a sense that everything inside this glorious structure was going precisely according to plan.

I followed the marble side trail to the front desk and smiled at a young man in a dark suit. He glanced up from his screen, taking a surprised moment to look me over. He pressed his headset and whispered before addressing me.

"Sir may I help you?"

"Yes I am here to meet with Billy Jenkins."

"Do you know his floor?"

"I do not. He's with the law firm."

"We have eight law firms in this building, sir."

"The one near the top. Ma-something. Maggie Gravel."

"*Mahoney, Graves and Leatherstitch.*"

"That's the one. Billy Jenkins."

"Okay . . . is he expecting you?"

"I called ahead. I'm his father."

"I don't see a Billy Jenkins in here. Is it possible he goes by —"

"William. It will be under William Jenkins."

"Okay I'll see if he's in. Please wait here."

"Tell William his father is in from the woods, standing in the lobby, boasting to people about his dear child of the law, Billy Jenkins, the third. The country boy that made good in the big city."

I stepped aside to marvel at the room. The ceilings were at least four stories high meaning that it was at least four stories before this beautiful and exorbitantly expensive structure went to work. Sculpted arches met at the dead center of the room, from which point an intricate glass chandelier hung down to just above the young man's desk. I wondered if this is what people meant when they said *atrium*. The young man beckoned me back to the desk.

"Mr. Jenkins will see you now." He pointed me to the third of three golden doored elevators. "Seventy-second floor . . . of eighty-eight. His assistant will be waiting."

I thanked him and entered the elevator with another young suit with slicked back hair, doing just about everything in his power not to acknowledge my presence—taking a keen interest in a spot just above the buttons. I entertained the notion of disturbing him, giving him a story for his buddies, as Music Man would, but was still hesitating when he got off on the eighteenth floor.

A bell-like bing announced each passing floor. A bout of light-headedness swept over me; it became impossible to hold a thought. A kick drum pounded in my chest.

Bing. Sixty-Eight.

Deep breaths, in through the nostrils out through the mouth.

Bing. Sixty-Nine.

How would he greet me? What would he say? What would I say? Was Claire right?

Bing. Seventy.

The drum broke rhythm, going manic. I considered stopping the elevator and taking the stairs down.

Bing. Seventy-One.

My mind went blank, thoughts clogged the causeway.

Bing.

The doors slid open on a prim speck of a middle-aged woman, rising only to my chest and skinny enough to be a hiker herself. She wore her hair in a tight bun; her talons ensnared a clipboard.

"Mr. Jenkins?"

"Gabe."

"Mr. Jenkins, William, cannot see you now. He is in a meeting."

"In a meeting?" I stared at her in disbelief.

"I assure you he feels terrible about this but it is a particularly important meeting. Many moving parts. A long time in the works. People have travelled very far."

"You know I've travelled pretty dern fa—"

"He has asked that I provide you with his apartment keys and put you in a car." She tilted her clipboard to prevent the elevator doors from closing.

"Is this some kind of joke?" I sized her up. *I could make it past her, she was much smaller than the bear, although I doubted she would flee from a Juicerrman.*

"I assure you it is not, sir. He will be there as early as his obligations permit."

"So this is what he's about now—turning away his own father."

"Mr. Jenkins requested that you make yourself at home, eat whatever you like, and do whatever it takes to get yourself clean."

"You couldn't have done this downstairs?"

"I apologize but we needed to remove you from the lobby."

***

Billy's apartment was much as I remembered, clean, angular—my son in a nutshell; each and every placement deliberated on the front end, precluding any need for future adjustment. Furniture, rugs, knife holders, all culminated in sharp, well-spaced points. If I were to cross grid the floor with vault lasers, the lasers would measure their precision against the coffee table. Moody pastel smears and obscured figures adorned the walls in place of pictures. *My son had stonewalled me. Too good for his own father.* I considered bailing on the whole endeavor, catching an outbound commuter train, and getting some miles in before supper—I was dissuaded by the long-term familial ramifications of such an act.

I showered, cleaning myself twice and the shower once, taking a moment for self-inspection in the trio of silver rimmed, full-length mirrors in the corner of Billy's bedroom, angled to provide a full view of the subject. I had been strained and polished down to my best bits. My thin legs rippled with muscle and sinew, implying a long dormant spryness. My torso was a lean configuration of skin, muscle, and bone; gone was the accumulated doughyness of thirty-five years of seated deliveries. My pepper beard covered my neck.

I shoved my clothes in the laundry and called Claire.

"William!"

"Gabe."

"Gabe . . . You found him! You actually went to him? You're with him!"

"Well I'm at his apartment. *Your* son wouldn't meet me, so *your* son sent me home from his office."

"You went to William's office?"

"Stop saying William. It's the only place I knew he'd be. And the trains run right to it."

"I don't suppose he loved that."

"You know a place where he would've been thrilled to see me?"

"He wouldn't even meet with you?"

"I only saw his assistant. She said he was in a meeting."

"Oh that's right the Penske file. They're closing today. That's a huge deal."

"So I'm told. Does this satisfy my visitation requirement?"

"Don't blame this on him Gabe. *You* should've called ahead. The world doesn't start and stop as *you* pop on and off that Trail. *You* still need to be supportive, patient, and loving."

"I can't promise there will be time for all three. She said he will be home from work when he can. Hopefully he takes me to dinner. Otherwise, it will definitely be a short reunion."

"Gabe, you need to be nice to him. You're in his home, disrupting his world. Get clean and accommodate, do what he asks, whatever he recommends, without argument or snide comment. William's not evil and he loves you. He will take care of you if you give him the chance."

"I'm already clean and showered and I *always* do as I'm told."

"Yea you do, maybe, but you chirp and groan as you do it. It's impossibly annoying."

"I was under the impression that was endearing."

"Let me assure you it is not."

41

Billy woke me from my slumber, grumbling as I sat up, rubber gloves covered raised hands.

"I moved your clothes to the dryer."

"Thanks. I must've fallen asleep." I blinked at the sun hanging high over the skyline.

"Must have. Would you like to get something to eat?"

"So will Mr. Jenkins see me now?"

"I'm very sorry about that. You really couldn't have picked a worse time."

"And I'm sorry to be such an inconvenience, William. I can leave. Maybe come back another time with an appointment."

He exhaled and thinned his lips. A spitting image of his mother. "Would you like to get something to eat?"

"I would. Hiking does build a hunger."

"I'm sure. I can't help but notice you need pants. And a shirt. I have some old ones which may suit you."

Billy's '*old ones*' were much less worn than anything I'd put on in some time—I did not do them justice. My son had always been more substantial than me, a gap that had only widened during my hike. The shirt's shoulders hung down almost to my elbows. The pant legs caught under my heels. I made fists in my pockets to inflate my girth.

The restaurant Billy selected was out of the way, several long blocks off the main street and halfway down an alley. The dim interior had intentions of elegance—that is, there was plenty of light being produced, but the decorator had gone well out of its way to block it. The seating area was a long, narrow rectangle, almost just a hallway connecting the alley to the kitchen, lined on either side with evenly spaced white clothed two-seater tables: *intimables*, Claire would've called them. Each intimable occupied its own recession in the brick wall illuminated by a half-lit oversized bulb; a series of heavy beige curtains separated each recess, further dampening the light and setting the mood.

A waiter guided us down the aisle to a booth by the restrooms. Billy took the wall seat and leaned back, ordering two cocktails with *z*'s in the name before handing me a menu.

"You'll like these. They are artisanally crafted to taste like root beer."

"So is root beer." My son rolled his eyes. I took in the room. "Is this where high-powered Pentland attorneys take their mistresses?"

"No."

"It's tucked away and very private. Even inside it's hard to see the other patrons."

"Do you think I'd bring you here if there was even the slightest chance we would run into one of my partners with their side piece?"

"Didn't know if y'all had a schedule or made appointments."

"How's mom?"

"Mom's good. Hiked with me from Qannasseh to Sacred Place."

"She told me. Somehow that's easier to believe than *you* being out there."

"I've been *out there* for a while now."

"You know what I mean."

The waiter brought our drinks in tinkly, angled glasses. Billy lifted his, after a sigh, I raised mine to meet it. The waiter took our orders; I made no attempt to restrain myself. I assumed Billy was paying and cared little for his bank account. The drink did resemble root beer on the palette.

"The Great Eastern Trail is a big move for a guy who once went three calendar years without leaving Bodette proper."

"Outside of our beach trips."

"Sorry, outside of our scripted beach trips. Tell me about it."

"What is there to say?"

"Quite a bit I'd imagine."

"Nothing that'd be of interest to a big time, big city attorney like you. Wouldn't even meet with his own dad."

"What am I doing ri—" He stopped, taking a second to straighten his fork. "What is this dad? What the hell is this? What have I done that's so inconceivably wrong that you've spited your first born and only son for years now?"

"If you have to ask."

"And do you have any idea what it's doing to mom? How much it hurts her to see us like this?"

"At least I'm actually there with her."

"Are you? Do you have any idea what *this*," he pointed at the table, "is doing to mom? She's terrified that at sixty's doorstep, at the first hint of freedom, you bolted for the woods. She's terrified that the mail route was the only thing keeping you in Bodette and that she just happened to be there. She's terrified that you made it two months into retirement before setting out on this. I mean, she says there's still cake in the freezer from the retirement party. What do you think about that?"

"She should probably throw that out."

Billy cracked his hand against the table, upsetting both root beers. His face shot red. "Don't do that!" He was yelling. Heads poked around linen dividers. "Goddam it do not do that. I know you're clever. Everyone knows your clever. That whole town has been charmed to death by your goddam wholesome wit. What I don't know is the answer to my question. What I don't know is why you seem insistent on hating me." My son glared at me across the table. I studied him, for the first time noticing the light wrinkles extending from his eyes, and the flecks of grey he inexplicably let persist above his ears. "What I don't know, what Mom and I ask each other each and every time she calls, is why you so casually walked out on your wife."

"I did not walk out on your mother."

"Yes you did. You quite literally did. And from what I can gather she would have preferred catching you in an affair because at least that can be tied to something, some physical need that she can quantify and address. But this, this great big amorphous *I'm gonna walk really fucking far because I'm full blown dissatisfied with my life.* That scares the shit out of her. She doesn't know what she did to cause that."

"*She* didn't do anything."

"Right it was me. It was always me. Everything's my fucking fault."

"It's because you left Bodette—"

"I didn't want to run a hardware store or be a mailman—"

"And I never did . . . ." We looked at each other over the spilled root beer.

"That's nothing. You could have if you wanted to."

I turned up my palms as the words poured out. "I never even considered it. Never even perceived it as an option. So after Dullamore Canyon, when you told us you weren't coming back. It just shattered me. It was like I had been content looking out a window and you kicked down the wall. Opening up a whole new world. Except for you it was a world of possibilities but for me it was just a long list of *could haves*. Things I was too old, too unqualified, or too timid to even attempt. All I saw was how many chances you had and how many chances I'd missed."

The waiter used a curvy pitcher to refill our waters, collected the upturned glasses, then returned with our appetizers. I continued before eating.

"I'm just—I'm jealous of you. All that you have done. All that you have accomplished. All that you will get to do. The way you seem to know everything and be useful in every situation. How big decisions seem to come so easily to you. Sometimes it feels like your life is specifically designed, schemed even, to highlight my shortcomings. It's humiliating."

"Is that really what you think? That I am actively structuring my life with the intention of belittling you."

"You are a cruel measuring stick."

"You have nothing to be jealous of dad. You have a great wife. You led a long and happy life. Look at you now, you've walked over a thousand miles on the Great Eastern Trail. And you put yourself in a situation in which that is an option. Not everyone earns that opportunity. In one fell swoop you've undone any dearth of adventure. Even if you went home today. That's amazing. You should look at your situation and be proud of yourself. I am so far from being able to do anything like that."

"I love your mother very much and very much intend on spending the rest of my days with her."

"Good, tell her that." We sat silence, calm after the outburst. Billy mouthed an apology as the waiter removed the glasses and dabbed the table dry.

"You know I fought a bear last night."

"Explain."

I recounted my daring rescue of the fat man in distress.

Billy set his wrists on the table, pointing at me with both hands. "You, Gabe Jenkins, husband of Claire and father to William, heard a bear attack and ran *towards* it?"

"What is that word . . . incredulous?"

"Yes, incredulous. Exactly. I mean, Mom always killed the spiders in the house."

"No she didn't."

"She did and she does."

"Only because I let her."

"Hopper, the guy, is he okay?"

"Physically fine. Although the bear did a number on his pride and sleeping bag."

"No kidding. After all those years of running from dogs, I'm trying to picture you facing down a wild bear with an expired protein bar. Where'd you even get the *Juicerrman*?"

"The internet."

"Well, I have to say that's pretty cool, dad."

"Oh thank you, son. I like to think so too."

He set down his drink. "I, I suppose I need to apologize for my behavior. I should not have said those things. I should not have called you a listless bureaucrat who had wasted his life transporting messages."

"I believe you mean lethargic nobody who had wasted his life ferrying messages."

"Be that as it may, I'm sorry. I have come to appreciate everything you've done for me. Mom, too."

"I don't recall you and your mother ever having a problem."

"Well mom never called me an ungrateful, snot-nosed social climber."

"That one you remembered."

The waiter took two trips to set down my food. I unraveled my silverware and placed the napkin in my lap.

"Anything else you want to say to me?"

"I'm sorry. Obviously. Obviously, I should not have said that to you or about you. Obviously, I should have supported you. But I mean even as dern teenager you had better taste in food, liquor, cigars, and clothes. Now you've even got the moral high ground. And . . . I mean do you want to know why I'm actually out here?"

"A myopic over-reaction to thirty years of self-induced routine?"

"No, it's your fault."

He leaned back and rubbed his neck. "I really thought we were getting somewhere."

"It's not bad. Mom and I were going through old video cartridges looking for her commercial that featured you digging in the yard with that red shovel. And we watched an old news segment on a young couple who was starting off on the Great Eastern Trail. At the end, I told your mom that I would like to hike that Trail—"

"And I called and she told me. Then I told Len—"

"He told his dad. He told that wife of his. And then it made the sign for the rec center."

"Son of a bitch."

"Yep." I shrugged.

"You are a very consistent character. You know that couple didn't make it?"

"They didn't? How do you know?"

"The girl, Meghan Adler, she was Danny Wilborn's cousin. She and her dude quit to get married. Len told me they are now twice divorced." He held up two fingers.

"There's probably a lesson in that."

"I'm sorry to be the reason you're out here."

"Apologize to your mother. I'm having a blast. Did I mention I fought a bear?" I took my first bite, and then several more. "Oh, man. This is really good. Do you come here often?"

"I do. They don't have food like this on the Trail?"

"They do not. It's mostly just rice. Although now it's rice with Dank Sauce and fresh picked mushrooms."

"You're eating wild mushrooms now?"

"Sure am. A young fella showed me how to find and pick them. Settler's Fowl he called them."

Billy perked up and leaned across the table, almost knocking over his fresh drink. "Settler's Fowl? Do you have any with you?"

"You've heard of Settler's Fowl?"

"Have you not? It's like *the* food right now. It's this generation's bacon. Every restaurant is clamoring for it. I've never even had it. Do you have any with you?"

"I picked a whole bag just yesterday."

"Would you be okay if I prepared some when we got home?"

"By all means. The Trail is well settled."

"Good let's get out of here."

Billy waved for the check and, after I made sure all the remaining food was properly boxed and accounted for, hurried me home where I presented the Settler's Fowl. I took a seat at his granite island as Billy rinsed and dried each settler then pulled out a cheese grater.

"Why do you need that?"

"Ideally you use a truffle shaver but there's no need to have a truffle shaver if you never have truffles."

"You keep saying truffle."

"Yes. That is what Settler's Fowl is—a truffle. Wholly different than a mushroom. I've waited a long time to do this. How do you usually prepare them?"

"I just sort of split them with a spork and dump them in a pot with rice. Or eat them whole."

"*That's* what you do with Settler's Fowl? This might actually be our falling out."

Billy grated two truffles into a cast iron skillet, evoking memories of Bear slicing them with his knife, and re-heated some orzo. When they were properly toasted he sprinkled the Settler's Fowl on top of the orzo and joined me on the other side of the island. I took my first bite.

"If you ever met the fella who introduced me to Settler's Fowl you'd find their trendiness very hard to believe."

"What do you think?"

"I guess I shouldn't be surprised you got it right on the first try."

"Well almost right." Billy disappeared around a corner, reappearing with a bottle of wine and two stemless glasses.

I took a sip and smiled.

"What?"

"It's just nice to drink your booze again."

"Let me assure you this did not come from under the floorboards." We both took bites. "This is pretty remarkable isn't it? I've waited a really long time to do this."

"It is. But can I be honest?" He nodded. "I think I like my Dank Sauce version better." "Do I want to know what Dank Sauce is?"

"It's a condiment for gas station fried chicken."

"Oh shit." He covered his mouth, vaguely gesturing at his laundry room.

"What?"

"I have some."

"What? Is that fashionable now too?"

Billy stood up and left room, reappearing with a *Delmar* shoe box; strips of tape dangled from where it had been packaged and shipped.

"This got delivered to the office about a week ago. They made me open it outside in case it was a bomb." He placed the box on the counter and lifted the top. What had been a journal page had been ripped out and crumpled to fit the space. "I read the note before I realized what was going on."

I lifted the note, uncovering a bed of golden Dank Sauce packets.

Mister Gabe,

I hope you are doing well. If you are reading this it means you stopped being a little bitch and went to see your son. As a reward, please find enclosed what should be more than enough Dank Sauce for someone to make it from Pentland to Daemon's Peak—even if that someone is as slow as you. I trust young Billy is treating you well or otherwise he would not have received you and given you this box. Which likely means that he is not as bad as you made him out to be. As such, please be nice in return. Beyond all that, once you have exchanged the requisite niceties it is imperative that you return to Trail and finish what you started.

Very truly yours,
Jezebel

P.S. I HOPE AT THIS POINT YOU DIDN'T NEED ME TO TELL YOU THESE THINGS.

Tears welled in my eyes as I put down the note. My face flushed. "I am really sorry Billy. I'm sorry that it came to all this. This . . . this is embarrassing."

"How many women do you have telling you that I'm not an asshole?"

"At least two."

"Is it starting to take?"

"It's getting harder to deny."

"Great. Now I guess I have to try this Dank Sauce?"

I nodded. "The more you eat the less I carry."

Billy pinched up a packet and held it to the light. "So this is your reward for coming to see me?"

"You'll understand after you try it."

Billy separated a portion of orzo with minimal Fowl, snipped the packet's corner, and applied a thin straight line of Dank. With one final look, he took a bite.

"Holy shit."

"Right?!"

He squeezed in the rest of the packet and mixed the entire batch together. "I really don't want to admit how much I like this."

I added a packet to my food and together we swarmed our plates clean, washing it down with several glasses of my son's wine.

After dinner, Billy removed a large, folded piece of paper from a kitchen drawer, unfolding it to reveal a map of the Great Eastern Trail. It was an old map with holes dotting the folded seams.

"I got this to follow your progress. Let's see, there's really not too much left now." He ran his finger along the portion between West Boelein and Daemon's Peak.

"Nope, just a couple small towns, the Copper Swamp, and the Kingstons. Three, maybe four weeks." The map's proportions did not permit my standard thumb and hand method of measuring distance. "Then back to your mother."

"She'll be excited to hear that."

"What are all those red dots South of here?"

"Those mark the addresses I found when I tracked down all the strange numbers that had been calling me."

42

Two days later, my son cut right angles through Pentland's skyscrapers towards the West Boelein highway and the Great Eastern Trail. Billy worked the previous day but had gotten off early enough for dinner and a baseball game—I averaged a hot dog per inning.

"What happens when you get to Daemon's Peak?"

"What do you mean? Your mother is going to meet me and take me back to Bodette."

"Yea, sure, but how? Do you run through red ribbon? Is there a ceremony? What is the big finish?"

"I can't say I've ever given that much thought. But I assume someone would've told me if something big happens. I think Daemon's is just another hard mountain."

"Is there even a parking lot there? How is she going to meet you?"

"We'll figure that out when the time comes."

"So for all you know you just end up at the top of a mountain? Do you just hike back down?"

"I, I don't know, like I said—I haven't given it much thought."

"Okay then, what happens when we get to the Trail today?"

"It's actually just a side trail but it's only a little ways to the actual Trail."

"But do I just pull up to the side of the road and let you wander off alone into the woods? Are you planning to meet up with anyone?"

"Nope. It is just me."

"And you're going to be okay?"

"I've made it this far. So if I'm not it won't be your fault."

I directed Billy through the sleeping town until we located the blue blaze. Billy pulled off on the shoulder; a button on the steering wheel popped the trunk. Billy stood up, leaning on his door as he examined the strip of blue paint.

"It really feels like I am abandoning you, sending you away. Like in those sad dog movies."

I laughed. "*Go on now go. . . GO, BOY I can't help you anymore.*"

"Exactly."

"Your mother didn't have a problem with it. Just pretend you're dropping me off at camp."

"Right. Old man wilderness camp." Billy joined me at the trunk, brushing my pack's dirt smear from the fabric. "This is kind of wild, dad."

"You're welcome to join. There are endless villages of Settler's Fowl to pillage. You could be the coolest guy in Pentland."

"That is the dream—but no, this is your thing. I don't think I'd last ten minutes out there. I do relish my comforts."

I adjusted the straps until my freshly weighted pack rested just so.

"It's not as bad as you think. You just sort of have to do it—if that makes any sense."

"You know it really doesn't, but I'm glad you came into town. Let me know if you need anything from here on out. I'd love to help." I initiated our embrace.

"Absolutely."

"And call me, um, where I actually am, and leave messages if you guess incorrectly."

"Of course. I love you, Billy."

"I love you too."

I stepped away from Billy's luxury sedan and towards the side trail. My son remained leaning against his car, watching me split the trees and return to the mountains. I did not hear the engine start.

I spent the day maneuvering over make-shift log bridges and fording streams. An unforeseen obstruction brought me to an evening halt—a colossal moose straddled the Trail, facing the setting sun; its front feet pillared the west and its back feet the east so that it formed a furry, tick-infested archway. Despite its healthy belly, I would've had to duck only slightly to pass through untouched. The brush and trees were too thick for me to pass on either side. For a long moment I stared at the moose's side, wondering how to proceed.

"Excuse me, moose. I would like to pass through . . . ." The moose submitted no response.

"Ma'am."

"Sir."

"Now I don't mean any harm, but if it comes to it . . ." I removed a pack strap, tilting my pack to unsheathe the mighty *Juicerrman*—then chose against it. Instead I set my legs shoulder width apart and lifted my arms out wide, making myself as big as possible.

"HEY MOOSE!" The moose turned its head ever so slightly in acknowledgment. "My name is Mister Gabe and I want to go north. You are in my way."

The moose readjusted its body to face me, one knobby leg at time, tilting its head as it assessed me with immense brown eyes, checking me over as if I was applying for a loan. After several moments, it let out a bureaucratic sigh, and shuffled into the forest.

When the way was clear, I proceeded, turning back to verify the moose's rear-end stationed several yards off Trail.

"Dern right."

The following days were long and the Trail easy. My pack, unburdened by *Juicerrmen*, swung light and loose across my back; my feet glided beneath me. Dark, brown northern squirrels jetted across the Trail at intervals, pausing to inspect the two-legged intruder. I startled birds from the roosts, setting off a perpetual cresting wave of feathers. For the first time on my journey I was completely and utterly dependent on the orange blazes and my wits, having neither an informed friend nor my long gone, and ill-conceived, print-outs to guide me. I scouted out and uncovered several easy scores of Settler's Fowl.

I thought about Claire, realizing that in our excitement Billy and I had not called her to inform her of our reunion. She would be thrilled. I sat down and pulled out the family photo, considering where her mind must have been, how truly terrified she must have been to slip it into my pack. I had been so all consumed with how wild it was that I was hiking the Great Eastern Trail that I had never once given any thought to how it would affect my wife. What it told her about our relationship. I wilted, breaking into tears on the side of the Trail. *How could I have been so selfish?* I resolved to call Claire as soon as possible and tell her I was coming home.

I started early each morning, hiking long into twilight. When I walked in to Louden several excruciating days later, I located a gas station, paid off the clerk, and called my wife—Claire picked up on the first ring.

"Claire, it's me. I'm sorry."

"Gabe? Why are you sorry? Billy said y'all had a great time."

"It's not that. We got along famously. Dinners, baseball game. I had a wonderful time. But I'm the turdball that started all this .

. . so I'm apologizing for what I've put you through. I should've talked this through with you and, you know, invited you. It was great having you out here."

"You were a pretty big turdball for a while there."

"I'm coming home. Now. I haven't figured out the details yet. But I want to get back to you."

"Gabe, no."

"No?"

"I've been thinking too. This is important. And I don't want to turn into that woman who picked us up, Gladys. I don't want to shrivel into some timid old raisin who locks her doors at sunset. And I certainly don't want you to turn into that."

"I may have been pretty far down that path."

"I know. But you spent a long time accruing good behavior credits by being a decent, steady husband and a great father. So you finish what you're doing out here and come home accomplished. Just maybe next time you get the itch to do something like this, maybe we could do it together."

"That sounds nice. I'll even let you pick where. I love you Claire."

"I love you too, Gabe."

Billy was in a meeting so I asked Diane to tell him where I was and that I was okay. I had no patience for town food, foregoing a stay to make good time before dark.

43

Several days later a dissolving metal sign welcomed me to *Somebody's Copper Swamp*—the name of whatever entity had previously claimed the area had, with the aid of several generations of shotgun blasts, long since rusted through. The Great Eastern Trail followed an old logging road, now just a wide dirt path, which had been constructed with no regard for the natural topography, bisecting the stagnant ponds and motionless streams. The Great Eastern Trail's instructions were clear—don't turn, don't quit, don't drown, don't die, finish and get the heck off me.

For three, maybe four days, the Swamp sent up no landmarks. My body attuned itself to the earth: the sun rose and I began walking—my stomach growled and I ate. I tried camping the first night but rustling and heavy wet splashing filled the darkness, sometimes drawing near, always evading my headlamp. The next night I walked, pacing straight down the middle of the Trail as far from the spectral waters as I could without breaking equilibrium.

On the third night, well after dark, a light appeared on the horizon, glinting just at the edge of my sight. I chased its corona for hours without it growing until, at last, it seemed to catch on my screen and increase with each step.

A figure came into view, scruffy and rail thin, capped and smothered by a mat of sloped black hair, sitting in the light of a silver campfire. He had his back to me.

"Do you mean harm?"

"Me? No. Do you?"

"No." He gestured at the ground near him. "Are you alone?"

"I am." I said, sitting. "Have been since Pentland." He tapped a maroon ballpoint pen against the notebook in his lap, paused to scribble something, then ripped the page and threw it into the fire. I recognized the paper. "Mongrel?"

"You found me."

"I've been reading your poems since Grambling's Pass." Mongrel arched his eyebrows without looking all the way up. His disintegrating grey long sleeve t-shirt provided more holes than coverage.

"I've never thought of them as poems." He plucked a white growth out of a jar and ate it whole. "Just musings, really." He started tapping on his new page.

His pristine flame bowed out into the darkness, twirling and curling together at the top like an alabaster rose. The brilliance prevented a proper examination of the base, but I could not determine any sticks or fuel.

"You might not remember, and I didn't know it at the time, but I met you in Qannasseh. You also spoke with some younger gentleman, teenagers."

"Qannasseh."

"Bear, Speck, and Cass, the boy with the torn up hand. You were asleep on a city bench."

"I remember. I just like the name. *Can-I-See*." A swamp insect buzzed over the water. "How have you found your hike?"

"It's been good. Very good. Although now that I've met with Billy, my son, I'm ready for it to end. I just want to go home, see my wife, be done with it. Seems a shame to end it that way but I don't see much point in pressing on." Mongrel looked down, tapping his pen against the page. "Sorry."

He looked up and shrugged.

I set up my tent and rejoined Mongrel by the fire, boiling my rice, and squeezing in two packets of Dank Sauce. The viscous ooze was still searching for the pot's wall as I shaved the first truffle of Settler's Fowl. Mongrel stopped tapping to watch with interest.

"Jezebel was still using bottled ketchup when I found her. Glass bottled ketchup. I was directed to Bear when he resorted to throwing rocks at squirrels."

"Excuse me?"

"You didn't just walk into a gas station and pocket their sauce did you? Or have a mind to start picking wild mushrooms?"

"Truffles—you actually spent time with Jezebel and Bear?!"

"If people remain on the Great Eastern Trail long enough, our paths tend to cross." He wrote on his fresh page then ripped it as well, discarding it into the fire.

"Is that like a law of averages thing?"

"It is just the way things seem to work out here."

"What does that mean? You show up at a certain point in people's hikes and help them bring it all home?"

"I'd ask that you not put me in situations in which I have to respond with something . . . vague and pretentious."

"Do you seek out worthy hikers who have proven themselves and guide them to the promised land?"

"What did I just say?"

I searched for a question which prompted a straight answer as Mongrel used the lip of a tin pot to gently separate some glowing coals from the rest of the fire. When they were a safe distance, he set the pot upside down on the coals and placed several of his white lumps on the new top, using a stick to roll them, toasting each side.

"Would you like some Dank Sauce?"

He nodded and I tossed him a packet.

"Thank you."

A squirrel scurried out of the darkness, stopping at Mongrel's side to haunch and stare at the seated man. Mongrel shifted his gaze to the squirrel. My eyes darted from man to rodent, rodent to man, as the two exchanged some silent communique. At last Mongrel nodded and the squirrel disappeared past him. Mongrel looked to me.

"You've seen the movies Gabe?"

I checked behind me for additional squirrels. "I mean not all of them."

"The war movies?"

"Sure."

"The heroic, action-hungry protagonist, undone by some injury, finds himself recuperating in a hospital far from the front lines." He paused to tend his food. "Our young hero grows restless, threatens to leave before he is fully healed until an older, more tenured patient takes him under his wing and convinces him to stay so he can eventually return stronger, wiser."

"I think I've seen that one, yea."

"This Trail is a hospital. A port in a storm. The hikers are both patients and nurses. If you have indeed been healed Mister Gabe, the question now becomes *what are you going to do with it*."

He removed the pot from the coals and placed a single drop of Dank Sauce on each lump.

"What'd the squirrel say?"

"First you need to understand that you are making a choice to stay out here. This is not just accumulated momentum carrying you through."

"Right . . . reckon I can get my mind around that."

"And Daemon's Peak is not the end——it is only part of the beginning." He perked up, quickly setting to work writing then separated the page from the notebook, creased it, and set it on the ground. "Good night, my friend. I trust you will enjoy the rest of your hike."

Mongrel stood up and stepped into the night, leaving me to tend his flame. I picked up the note.

> MONGREL COME, MONGREL GO
> SHOW YOUR BEST, BEAR THE LOAD

44

In the morning, a faint scorch mark was the only sign of Mongrel. The Copper Swamp continued for two more days; I reached the road to Whitton wanting for both food and water. A road sign indicated that Whitton proper was six miles west, well beyond my range—I would have to hitchhike. I went through Speck's routine as best as I could recall: feet spread, arm straight, thumb high, smile broad. The cars motored by, some shifting to the center lane when I came into view. I rotated arms, switched back, and repeated. The sun drifted west.

It was almost evening when the cloudless sky emitted a soft thunder, growing louder until the grumbling tightened into something approaching rhythm, laced with lingering strains of a gentle guitar. Loose gravel shook down the embankments as an old yellow 4x4 skidded around the granite corner, grinding to a slanted stop several yards past me. A layer of orange mud provided an extra coat of paint.

I waved at the driver, loaded my gear, and climbed in the backseat.

"Thanks for stopping."

"Of course, man. Let's take a ride."

Whitton had been left off the train route and thus sentenced to die a long slow death—besides a scattering of late model pick-ups, the town was deserted, growing silent upon the 4x4's departure. A light mist floated over Main Street, collecting on surfaces, darkening odd portions of the road. The restaurants were no doubt closed.

I turned left on a side street, towards the outskirts in hopes of an open gas station—the fishbowl thump of someone pounding on thick glass turned me round. Music Man's bearded face grinned through the nearest store front. He waved me towards the door and pushed it open.

"Allons my good friend. Welcome to Whitton." He spread his arms wide, almost dropping his bottle. Monroe greeted me with an affectionate punch me in the groin.

"Dern is it nice to see you. I was worried I would be alone for the duration. What is this place?"

"Don't rightly know. It's verifiably abandoned though. Figure I've been here about forty-eight hours. Unchecked and undisturbed."

Music Man led me back to a nook where he reclined on an unfinished wooden bench with his whiskey. The storefront wreaked of dust and booze.

"What are you doing here?"

"Squatting. Rocking out. Rock bottoming. Bottoming out. Select your rhetoric." He took a pull and offered the bottle. I declined. "How's your boy?"

"Good. Better than expected actually." I gave Monroe a series of soft slaps on either side of the head while he snapped at the air behind my hand. "Turns out I'm the asshole."

"Not exactly a big reveal."

I looked out through the dusty plate glass window. "Have you found a place to eat yet? Or have you just been swillin' whiskey and spoonin' beans?"

"Whiskey and beans, mostly. But I've seen a nice place if that's more your fancy. We've got to go out the back though. Don't want the town folk observing us frequent the front door."

Music Man shut a pitiful Monroe in the main room and led me through the back alley, bracing himself against the brick wall. From there we took several turns to arrive at a deli somehow clinging to business. A gloveless, hairy-armed behemoth manhandled the bread, meat, and cheese into formation, handing the cratered sandwiches over the counter with a grunt. We returned to Music Man's storefront.

"So what brings you into Whitton?" He asked through a mouthful of roast beef. "It can't be the lively night life."

"Habit and need—this is where Claire sent my next box of *Juicerrmen*. Although I must admit I haven't been able to eat them since the bear."

"No, *Juicerrmen*, no son-sourced indignation—what will fuel the travellin' mailman through his final act?" A small sip.

"I've sorta been wondering that myself."

"You're welcome to stay here while you figure it out. I am in possession of whiskey and a great many beans. I also know a place with gigantic pizzas."

"Pizza sounds good. Alright, I'll just ask it . . . Where's Hopper?"

Big sip. "Hop's off. Took a train into the city the same morning as you. I imagine his fat ass has been reunited with his grooved couch, watching his stories and plotting his world domination. Are you just now noticing?"

"It was all so pleasant. I didn't want to conjure him. Was it the bear?"

"The bear gave him a good excuse, an anecdote to fascinate his fellow drones. But Hop was done either way. It was only a matter of time after he figured out I was not going to make him money."

"Stubbornness took him a good ways."

"Not far enough." A small sip. "I honestly believed that I could him get to enjoy it, to clear out the bullshit that had fueled his miserable life, and make him embrace this simplicity, to see that the sacrifices were liberating and important."

"If it's any comfort, I think you were doomed from the start. I'm just glad you failed relatively early."

"Now we're just two old men, squatting in an empty store."

Night found us seated on the dusty floor, our backs against bare posts, separated by a stack of extra-large pizzas and every variety of cheap beer. Music Man, drunk to numbness, doused the entire pie in pepper flakes—both our noses ran freely. At some point, Music Man uncovered a discarded rubber ball which he tossed at the wall so that it bounced back around our pizza tower in the direction of my groin. I returned it and the game progressed. His radio played a slow bluegrass ballad.

"What kind of mailman were you, Gabe? Were you the grouchy, break toys, shove bent envelopes in the wrong mailboxes kind, or were you the smiling pet the dog kind?"

"It's actually very explicit postal service policy that we don't pet dogs. Not even the friendly ones."

"Not even the wee little ones?"

"The wee little ones are the worst. They'll tear your hand to shreds and put you off your route for a month. The big ones, for the most part, just want to bark at you. The little ones have something to prove. In any event, it only takes one grouchy, scared, surprised, mean, or over excited dog to clean out an insurance policy."

"Fuggin' attorneys." Monroe's head tracked the ball as it hit the wall and returned to me.

"But, to answer your question, I was the smiling and waving kind. Always figured it was part of my job to be a friendly face in the community. Considered it an honor actually."

"My mailman was an ass."

"Maybe he was nice once, the world got the better of him."

"Maybe I was the ass. I liked to leave dog shit in the mailbox and put the flag up."

"Yep. Maybe someone just kept filling his mailboxes with poop."

"You know he was our mailman for my entire childhood? Never once confronted me, or told my parents."

"Then what made him ass?" Temptation overcame Monroe—he pounced on the ball and trotted it off to a distant corner.

"Exactly that. I must have done it to him fifty times and the son of a bitch never gave me my satisfaction."

"A true icon of the trade. What was it like to have a job that didn't place you at the mercy of the weather, dogs, and bored urban children? You know, build a career, get great at something, work towards paydays, promotions, and negotiate deals?"

"Stressful. Overrated. Those bored urban children become bored urban adults who grow insatiable when they realize you can help them. Each and every day you feel like the world is ending, like everything can be taken from you."

"Even towards the end?"

"Especially towards end. The more you've earned from yourself, the more you've taken from others, you've somehow lost more and still have more to lose and, *and*, the more people that want to take it from you."

"Good lord. How'd you manage all that?"

"Poorly. Wives. Paralegals. Booze. And hush money."

"Was it worth it?"

"It was not without its moments. Have you ever purchased something because it's expensive? And don't say yes because I know you haven't. I'm not talking about a new lawnmower or even a convertible. I am talking about something exorbitantly expensive, something that is precisely as expensive as it is unnecessary."

"You mean like a second ultra-luxury sedan?"

"Not even close. At least that potentially can drive you somewhere. I mean a yacht that never even gets wet. I mean a yacht you essentially have to buy its own climate controlled condo to keep dry docked in the most expensive city in the world. It's fucking incredible. A surge of power and self-worth the likes of which you can't imagine."

"You have a yacht that's never gotten wet?"

"I get sea sick. What got you through the mailman days, driving in circles, putting slips of paper in metal boxes?"

"I liked it, loved it actually. The routine, the predictability of it. Every day I could hang my hat on starting at 8am and ending at 3:30. And if I didn't then I'd have something to whine about when I got home. Claire's business, especially at the beginning, was up and down, to put it lightly, so it was very satisfying to be that rock. And get us on that government insurance."

"There's something to be said for steadiness."

"I watched a whole neighborhood grow up and old. Kids become adults. Newlyweds become retirees. And I never missed a single of Billy's games. I never bought a yacht, but I was part of something. Now, that I'm watching Billy go through life, I can't help but regret never pursuing something, trying to move up."

"Regret plagues us all." Small sip.

"Are you gonna be okay without Hopper?"

"It'll be easier. Faster. That's for damn sure." The whiskey bottle missed his lips, leaving a trail to dribble through his beard.

"He was a . . . well . . . he was an asshole. And something of a moron."

"You're not wrong."

"And you say he was the head of a big company? I always thought you had to be smart or hardworking for something like that."

"Oh Gabe. That's just—" small sip, "the opposite of true. You know that trite bullshit where someone starts off by saying *there are two kinds of people in this world* and then finishes with some trite bullshit about one and the other? Well the whole thing's trite bullshit." An attempted sip. "There's only one type of person—

morons. We're all morons. Terminal. Fucking. Morons. Some may hide it better, some have the right last name, and some may have an idiocy better-suited to their time and place, but they still have it, and it always shows. Hopper was and is just such a moron. But because of his last name, and because he's so fucking loud, dumbly arrogant, it took people thirty years, and millions of dollars to catch on. But they did and now he is like some shit sitcom trying to retain peoples' attention by pulling in the stars of yesteryear."

"So what do you mean? We're all the same and it's just circumstance?"

"You can put your water in a tall glass, you can put it in a small glass, or you can spill it on the floor. Water has very little say in it."

"Well that's bleak."

"But it's the truth. And it's the shared moronic gene that gives everyone a chance. So I . . ." His head slumped; he was silent for a long moment. "I should sleep."

"Not a bad idea if we're going to hike tomorrow."

"Right. Hike tomorrow."

Music Man stood up, disappearing into the corner, far from where he'd arranged his bag, leaving a half full bottle of whiskey in his place.

45

The morning light prismed through an empty bottle.

I rolled the ball into the corners for Monroe as we waited for Music Man to pull himself together. If the fella was a hiker and a drinker, there was no arguing his experience at both; he labored himself to his feet, alternating sips of booze and water. It was still well after lunch before we made any northern progress.

The Great Eastern Trail cut a straight line through the northern half of the massive bowled valley surrounding the Copper Swamp. We passed the day in silence, stopping for frequent rests, snacks, sips, and bathroom breaks. Music Man was back in form by the time we made camp at *Bryson Shelter*, humming along to his tunes. Monroe chased squirrels into the woods.

> MONGREL COME, MONGREL GO
> WANT A PIZZA, KNEAD THE DOUGH

The next few days were more of the same: long stretches of indistinguishable trees and flat, extended drag strips of dirt. Each morning Music Man and I plugged the coordinates into our systems and switched on autopilot, putting in just enough thought to keep our feet moving, permitting the remainder of our conscious minds to stew without distraction. Sweating, always sweating.

Bowleg State Park rested at the northern end of Pentland's bowl at the base of Boyston Mountain, marking the end of the Great Eastern Trail's time in the lowlands, and the beginning of the long line of vaunted mountains comprising its grand finale. Boyston was of the Delmures which, Music Man explained, would eventually mature into the Kingstons, culminating in mighty Daemon's Peak.

Bowleg's proximity to Pentland and Cartee, another sizable city, made it yet another very popular and crowded strip of protected land. Music Man, for the first time I could remember, leashed a confused Monroe as the Great Eastern Trail became a shoulder-to-shoulder highway of clean and stable families, friends, and couples—all out to spend their allotted time getting in touch with nature. Faces, branded hats, shirts, soda cans, and logos assaulted my eyes. My ears rattled with the airport hum of mindless chatter. The sinners had infiltrated my cathedral. I tread stiffly amongst them, doing my best to touch no one, eyeing a little boy's chocolate bar and his father's sunflower seeds. The crowds had pounded the forest floor into brown cement and littered it with candy wrappers and empty chip bags. I finished a jerky stick and tucked the wrapper in my pocket, turning around to find Music Man holding up traffic, swearing as he stooped to pick up each bit of trash, shoving them in his already overflowing pockets.

"Don't you animals have any respect?" he growled at a passing family.

I bent over and plucked a ketchup packet, releasing the last of its entrails onto my fingertips. "No one seems to give a dern."

"I give a damn, goddammit."

The civilians began squeezing into single-file on the far edge of the Trail, giving a wide berth to the two old men tottering around with pockets, hands, and arms loaded with trash, dropping as much as they collected. The population and trash density increased as we approached the parking lot. Brown, waist-high signs counted down each tenth of a mile in case any of these tourists somehow got lost and were not sufficiently gifted to follow the mashed Trail and trashcrumbs back to their vehicles. An immaculate trash can at the three tenths of a mile marker allowed us to dump our loads and start anew. We were at capacity by the next sign.

The parking lot was its own ecological disaster heated by idling cars waiting for room to maneuver in or out of spots; people milled about, anxiously weaving in handheld lines around the vehicles to visit kiosks, utilize bathrooms, and consult maps. We shuffled between cars to get out of the crowd and onto a bordering berm, trying to locate where the Great Eastern Trail left the lot, praying that it was separate from the road. Music Man rubbed his hands against the dirt, inspecting and reinspecting for hints of garbage. Twice a car reversed into its parked neighbors, then made an aggressive exit, thrusting its auditory horn at potential witnesses. I counted four children screaming their separation from their parents.

"You reckon this the only time they let people in?"

"The downside of a nice day. Yuppy bums who call themselves hikers but only go out on nice easy trails during nice easy weather. Self-correcting problem though: all those shit birds come out and ruin it for each other."

"Or at least ruin it for us. They don't seem to mind."

Music Man poured some medicine on his hands and rubbed them together. "Here," he said offering the flask. "Disinfect."

The Trail stayed flat out of Bowleg State Park, maneuvering around the mountains to meet up with the Bowman River, clipping itself to the winding river as it alternated between pounding white rapids and vast still pools which reflected the blue sky and craggy granite cliffs of the opposite shore. A cool northern breeze gusted over the water. We ambled against the current, stopping frequently to marvel at the water thundering over and between rocks, and to let Monroe cool his paws in the shallows. We kept moving well into the summer twilight, ensuring that we out distanced any of the park's weekend warriors, making camp on a sandy beach tucked between the river and the Trail. The roar of the rapids insulated against the silence. Music Man fumbled with his mobile abode then missed the log he was trying to sit on, landing on the ground with a plop, and staying put. I constructed an easy Jezebelian fire out of the driftwood, then squeezed an extra packet of Dank Sauce into my rice to ward off the river's chill. I scraped my pot clean then laid down on my back by the fire, feeling the greasy glean on my forehead, rubbing my belly as the warmth pushed me towards sleep.

The Trail continued following the river the next day, permitting a leisurely pace. Music Man and I stopped on several occasions to soak our feet in the Bowman's cool waters. In the afternoon, after we'd worked up a full lather, we lounged in a quiet pool just downstream of a particularly fierce stretch of rapids. Music Man reclined against a rock, combing an old hand through his thin flip of hair and drooping mustache which, when soaked, hung limp, connecting his nose to his chin. His skin clung to his ribs, tufts of sparse gray hair dotted odd portions of his chest. It was hard to imagine him manning fancy conference rooms, boardrooms, and courtrooms. I looked across the river to where the sun was setting over the granite cliff, turning the frothing waters pink.

"What's waiting for you after all this? Are there any more Great Trails?"

"Just the five."

"So are you going to go home?"

"I don't have a home."

"What about all that money? What about the dry yacht?"

"Got rid of it. All of it. Although I'd have to double check on the yacht."

"Can't you stay with one of your kids?"

"It doesn't just work out for all of us Gabe. Some of us have actual family problems which can't be solved by a walk in the woods. I spent thirty years fucking things up. And, given my talent and obvious enthusiasm for cementing terms and relationships, now found myself in an unfixable situation."

"That just can't be true."

"Do you have any idea how good I was at structuring relationships? Laying the foundation for years of consistent ironclad trade and coexistence. And this family stuff is just my masterpiece. Air. Fucking. Tight." Sip.

"You still gotta try though right?"

"I have tried. Time and time again. At a certain point it just becomes selfish, interferes with their ability to move on."

"What are you going to do? You are literally running out of trail."

"Honor my contract, serve my sentence." Big sip.

We remained in the pool a long time, letting the cold water do its work, and again camped on the banks of the Bowman.

The Great Eastern Trail split from the Bowman River late the following morning, peeling off with an abrupt left turn up the valley wall; the flattened path, and soothing river, continued right.

We were still climbing long after the pounding rapids had faded out, reaching Sherwood Shelter just as the clear light of day waned into twilight's golden rays. In lieu of a picnic table, Sherwood Shelter sported a set of thick hardwood logs circling the fire ring. I kicked around for Settler's Fowl then tended fire while Music Man rested on a log. Monroe scratched his back against the brush.

When the fire was sustainably lit, I selected a log and sat down with an aging sigh.

Music Man set down his medicine and spoke. "By my reckoning we have two more days of easy living before the Kingston Mountains put our little hike to big the test."

"You think we're up for it?"

"They are what's in front of us. So we'll just have to get through the damn things." Small sip.

"Are you going to be able to drink like that through the Kingstons?"

"Only one way to find out."

"It'd be nice if we didn't have to."

I checked the shelter log and removed Mongrel's note, reading it aloud for Music Man.

> MONGREL COME, MONGREL GO
> HAPPY IN THE LOWLANDS, HIGHLANDS WOE

"That's less than encouraging."

For the next two days we snuck glimpses of the shadowy Kingstons peaks in between the trees.

46

Forty-eight hours later, we stood in front of Farragut General Store and Campground's log façade, the last patch of flat ground for at least a week. An athletic middle-aged woman took our payment, directing us back to the campground where we deposited our belongings and returned to the general store for our wares.

I located a Great Eastern Trail map hanging on the wall and lifted my hand to the top—less than one thumb to go. The woman cornered me as I measured my accomplishment in hands.

"You come up from the South?" I nodded. "Well, these aren't your southern mountains, all soft dirt and easy grades. These are proper northern mountains. Rock and stone. Boulders, some sharp as daggers, from here to Butonken. From my back porch to Mt. Atonement's northern slope." She pushed the words across her tongue; they oozed out as if blown through a squanky brass horn.

"Thank you, ma'am. But I know what I'm doing—"

"Peaks, one after the other, each one higher and crosser than the last. A series of sharp, jagged ridges, each one separated by a valley just as low as you are now. So don't go getting' to the top of Mt. Delaney tomorrow, if you make it, and think you've done the hard part." She pointed to a picture hanging on the wall, an aerial landscape featuring a series of high peaks, long strips of shattered granite looming over their surroundings; one in particular stood out, a man amongst boys, towering over its friends.

"Would you prefer I didn't g—" Music Man smirked behind her.

"And it's not just the terrain. When the steep and endless slopes of Mount Atonement have sapped your legs of their last gasp, that's when the storm blows in out of nowhere, turning blue skies black—that's when the Kingstons show their true colors." She ran her finger to a separate picture of a demon dark cloud spitting electric hellfire and, through some cruel miracle, striking four peaks at once. "The rain falls sideways. The winds been known to lift a man from his feet and deposit him in the valley. Every rock you step on is either wet, or gonna be."

Music Man and I paid for our goods and exited through the back door.

"You think she rehearses that."

"You should catch the matinee."

When we'd set up our mobile abodes, I coaxed a Bear fire in the campground's store-bought ring. "I mean people have to have made it through them before."

"Pay her no mind. That's just a townie running her mouth. Everyone's local mountains are the highest, hardest, most dangerous, most beautiful, most spiritually rewarding. She's spent a lifetime accumulating horror stories about the Kingstons and never travelled to any other mountains to hear theirs. So she assumes they don't have any. You've been to these other places; don't let her act like she knows more than you." Small sip.

"To be fair, these are the Kingston Mountains. It's not just the locals, it's everyone. Even you."

"And you saw the picture, it's gonna be a helluva hike, probably harder than most shit we've done. But my point is that there's no one better prepared for these unstable rock piles than you." Small sip. "It's seven days of rocks, storms, and steep climbs. Six days if we're good. Seven if we're lucky. Which we have been so far."

I declined when Music Man offered me his medicine as we cooked our dinners and settled in by the fire.

A young couple joined us at dusk, nestling down next to our fire as if we weren't there, paying no mind to the two old men on the other side. Monroe lifted his head from his paws to inspect the newcomers as they wrapped themselves in a quilted embrace, then set it back down, and returned to sleep.

The boy's beard was symmetrical and very well-manicured. I ran my fingers through my scraggly tree moss.

"Evenin'." Their heads lifted in unison at the sound of Music Man's voice. "How long you two youngins been out?"

"We just parked." The girl spoke.

"That long, huh. Where you headed?"

"All the way." Monroe lifted his head.

"To Daemon's?"

"Demons? No. To the last mountain. Atonement."

"Atonement is the last in the Kingstons yes. Daemon's Peak is the last mountain on the Trail." Small sip.

"Trail?"

"The Great Eastern Trail."

The girl looked at the boy. "We don't know what that is."

"A fool's errand for those who've abandoned their commitments."

"How long does it take?"

"We've been out here several months now and are just now at the end of it."

"That sounds like quite the commitment. Tony's just proposed."

"Well congratulations. Always happy to see the youth taking a shot at love." Small sip.

"I haven't answered yet. Melissa Tradewell says it's harmful and selfish for your partner to expect a spontaneous answer to such a cataclysmic question. She says you have to take time and consider it. She also says that if we can hike and camp together then we're a true match. So I won't answer until we've reached Atonement."

Music Man looked at me. "She writes about relationships in the *Daily Saga*. Claire has a friend who reads her."

"I see." Sip. He turned back to the young folk. "So you've taken the man's proposal under advisement. How long have you two been dating?"

"Three years. Four and a half if you count the courtship period."

"I do. So even with all that, you are of the opinion that what happens in this next week will determine whether you're right for each other."

"Ms. Tradewell says that dating is easy. You're always seeing someone at their best—clean, showered, prepared. It's important to see someone sweat, eat, get sick, and snore before you commit long term. She also wrote last year that it's important to have a mutual accomplishment on which to build your cooperative future."

"*Ms*. Tradewell. Fascinating."

"She says that it's absolutely crucial that each member of a relationship maintains their own distinct emotional identity."

"That is something to consider."

"I know. And she's, like, so funny."

"Have you two ever hiked before?"

"Of course. On Sundays we do the trails through Imogene Park, you know, in Pentland near the brunch district. And every other night we do the stairs in our apartment building—eight stories." The beard wagged in agreement.

"And when you decided to go hiking, were the Kingstons just the first place to pop up?"

"Everyone says they're the hardest. Melissa Tradewell says it's important to challenge yourself at the outset. That way there is less time to get discouraged."

"I hate to be the bearer of bad news. But I think Ms. Tradewell may be leading you two astray."

"Melissa Tradewell has been writing about relationships for twenty-five years. She's the reason my parents got divorced. She's amazing." My mouth opened but I decided to close it. "What could you possibly know about relationships?"

"Just let them be, Music Man. We don't know any bet—"

"I've endured enough to know where they go wrong."

"Excuse me, sir, but you don't know us. We're strong." The quilt deflated as she pulled her boy closer. "And Melissa Tradewell is a genius, and the reason we're still together. When Tony said he needed some time to focus on his career, I showed him Ms. Tradewell's article on overcoming adversity. When he said he needed some space, I showed him Ms. Tradewell's piece on sacrifice. So pardon me if we don't accept relationship advice from a vagrant."

"Be that as it may. I can tell you that the only values that matter in a relationship are the ones of the people in them. It's not fair for you to cram some third party's bullshit down this boy's throat." I put a hand on Music Man's shoulder.

"They're just trying to get their relationship started on the right foot."

"But it doesn't make any sense."

"Yea but we don't know any better."

The beard moved to speak but the girl cut him off. "Right that's why you're out here isn't it? Because you don't know anything about relationships."

"I have been married for thirty years."

"And you're either out here because it's grown stale and you're miserable with her. Or you've just abandoned her."

"I'm out here because I goddam want to be and I know dern well my marriage is strong enough. I've spent decades building trust and earning the right to be out here. And you'd be wise to learn a lesson before you dispense it." My voice echoed through the campground. I had not intended to project.

The girl harrumphed and whisked the beard off into the darkness.

Music Man gaped at me. "This is when you choose to speak?!"

He took a long pull of medicine—I accepted a calming snippet. The night passed in quiet apprehension of the days to come.

47

The young couple's tent was already gone when I strolled to the much appreciated campground facilities. The shopkeeper had also set out hot coffee for her patrons; I drank one, returning with another for a predictably groggy Music Man. I idled next to his tent while he assembled his mind, body, and things.

After a quick breakfast, the three of us whispered our goodbyes to Farragut and followed the Great Eastern Trail north out of the campground. Soon we were several thousand feet above Farragut and still climbing—Music Man sweating, cursing, and burping in between our frequent breaks. Monroe trotted around us claiming the mountain one raised leg at a time. We cleared the tree line onto our first of the famous Kingston vistas. Music Man sat down with a grunt as I marveled at the spectacle; we were only halfway up the mountain, but the view was immaculate—a rolling forest of dark greens, cratered with still lakes and piles of granite. The slope concealed the general store, but it was easy to see where the Great Eastern Trail rode the ridgeline back south, almost all the way to Grambling's Pass.

"Can you believe that? It's gorgeous."

Music Man closed his eyes, pressing his fingertips into his temple.

"I don't mean to go all broken preachy record, but you would do well to drink less."

"I will take that under advisement."

From there it was all rocks and boulders, thankfully in the shopkeeper's *'gonna be'* stage, which permitted for easier traversing. Big bowed steps carried me over crags, points, and edges to search out the next safe hold. Monroe coiled his legs and feet under him like half a tip-toeing spider, launching himself from boulder to boulder, turning around to gloat each time his process proved more efficient. Music Man failed to recover, growing slower and surlier as we climbed.

We caught the young couple soon after lunch. The boy lay on his back, panting, his shirt pulled up over his thin wet belly. The girl had removed her shoes and swore to herself as she rubbed her visibly bruised feet. Music Man straightened and calmed his breathing.

"Little taller than your apartment building eh?" The girl jolted from her task, collected herself, and gave us the finger. Monroe made a swiftly rebuked pass at licking the salt off the boy's belly.

Mount Delaney, the first peak of the Kingston Range was also the first one-off; after a long sit at the peak, during which the couple failed to make an appearance, we spent the rest of the afternoon winding down the mountain's northern slope to Balsam Grove Shelter. The mountain's girth blocked the latter portions of the sun's descent, prematurely ending the day; it was almost full dark when we settled in at the shelter. On the opposing ridgeline, a solitary fire floated in the darkness. I watched it flicker across the valley, picturing the wayward adventurer huddled up to its light.

"What do you reckon that poor sucker is up to?"

"Resting tired legs. No different than us." Music Man could barely open his eyes.

"Do you think it's another thru-hiker?"

"I'm privy to the same information as you, Gabe. Although . . . it could be another couple trying to prove their compatibility."

"Then kudos to them for surviving more than one day."

MONGREL COME, MONGREL GO
NOT IT ALL, JUST SOME MO'

The first day in the Kingstons took its toll; my legs were heavy by mid-morning. Music Man displayed more severe signs of slowing, hacking, wheezing, tumbling—frequently stopping altogether. I wondered to what extent this was driven by his fear of finishing. Although, the summer sun certainly did not help, hanging huge and close in the sky, ripping the moisture from our bodies.

After the dip, the climb was near vertical. It was early afternoon when we threw ourselves down at the campsite, using our packs as portable chair backs, gasping for several exasperated minutes before beginning lunch preparations. We were one with the blue sky, only matched in our height by the massive slope opposite us. To our right and left we could look out for endless miles at other mounds struggling to push their peaks above tree line. Shadowed birds of prey rode the thermals high above the tree-rimmed lakes.

"You know . . . with a good start . . . I think could jump off and make that near lake." Music Man kept his eyes closed, scooting so that his pack took the brunt of the sun. "What do you think . . . Worth the risk?"

He leaned over where I was pointing. "It'd be a helluva splash but I cannot make the jump. Toss me or leave me." He coughed, rubbed his temples, and laid back down.

Beyond the slanted fire pit, a rock spring was the sole suggestion of a campsite. After a considerable amount of water, a trail bath, and a refill, I felt adequately moisturized to start on a peanut butter tortilla. I filled Music Man's water bottle, pouring some in a bowled rock for Monroe. The fire ring appeared to have been used only sparsely, lacking the significant charring and accumulated ashes which filled most.

"This must be where that fellow stayed last night. But where do you think he slept?"

"Tired man can find rest just about anywhere."

"Yea but it's all vertical rock. Kind of sharp too."

I paced around the campsite in long, low steps, leaning to stretch weary thighs and hamstrings. Around a corner I found a cranny in the mountain, a flat space no bigger than my tent, big enough for a single body. There was something tucked under a rock in the far corner—a folded piece of smooth paper.

> MONGREL COME, MONGREL GO
> DON'T EAT MY FISH, YOU HIPPO

"It's Mongrel! It's Mongrel that was up here." I returned to Music Man, waving the note. "Holed himself up in a nice little crevice over yonder."

"How do you know that?"

"He left a note."

"Did he date it?"

"No."

"Then how do you know he was here last night?"

"The note's completely untarnished. And they say it storms just about every couple days. So it must be him. Don't you think?"

"I think you're making more assumptions that you realize."

For the next couple days the mountains peaked, ebbed, flowed, then peaked again. When above tree line, the Trail split the sky at a width of about fifteen yards; the rock tumbled down in steep slopes on either side. There were no orange blazes on the ridgelines as only birds and goats had the option to get lost.

We were on the ridge on the fourth, maybe the fifth, afternoon when I noticed the sun getting ready to set between two distant low-lying ridges which reached up to funnel it home. I decided to stop Music Man and enjoy the day's end.

"What do you say we stop and take in the sunset?"

"I'd rather keep moving. Get this damn thing over with."

"We're up here above tree line. The sky's crystal clear. I don't know if we will ever catch one like this again. It's like it was meant to be."

He shrugged and plopped down, pouring some water for the dog, cooling his fur with a wet hand, then laid back and closed his eyes. Medium sip. The giant *v* glowed like a pastel furnace as the sun nestled into the earth; the neighboring sky blossomed in layers of deepening red, orange, pink, and purple. Across the horizon the light softened, dimming the world's furthest edges, unveiling both night and day. Music Man snored as the sun slipped over the world's edge entirely, pulling with it the remaining light like a cloth slipping from a table.

I shook my companion awake—he started, then looked from the sky to me.

"And now we finish in the dark."

48

The next morning the Trail returned us to sea level—noon found us scaling a new foe. During one of our water breaks, Music Man put out his hand, opening and closing it as if massaging the air.

"Storm's coming."

I scanned the horizon for clouds—and birds. "How do you figure?"

"It's getting cooler, air's heavy too."

I inspected my own condition: the wet heat no longer draped itself over me; I was sweating significantly less than I should have been.

All too soon we were able to observe the storm's approach from the west, darkening the sky and casting its shadow across the landscape. We moved quickly, knowing full well there was no way we'd make it to the northern end any time before midday tomorrow. The lights dimmed to an eerie twilight. The wind throttled down to stillness.

"Do you have a preferred deity?"

"The main one, what with the white churches and bake sales."

"Then I'd suggest you pray. This is going to suck."

I muttered a prayer, promising to do right in the event of survival. A searing trident punctuated my *amen*.

There were no introductory droplets—the torrential sheets of rain simply burst into being as if a great god had paused a disaster movie, drawn us in, and clicked resume. Lightning struck the surrounding mountains at random. I bent at the waist, frequently checking behind me to make sure everyone was still present and upright.

The first fall was almost comical—I had just started up a rock scramble when my left foot slipped its hold; I pivoted my right foot under me and planted my left hand as a brace, ending up sprawled out like a cat on ice, when these measures gave I flattened out on my stomach with defeated thump. The next was sudden and worse—a full unabated transition from strong and upright to bruised and horizontal. Music Man helped me sit up.

"We're toast up here. We need to find some cover." I had to yell to be heard.

"The ridge goes on for miles. There is no cover." His face was inches from me—I could smell whisky through the rain. Monroe leaned against his master, cowering with each fresh belt of thunder.

"So what? We stay up here to drown at altitude?" Music Man shrugged his shoulders. I pointed to our left down the ridge's side. "What about down there? Ought to be a little better."

"We'll be lucky if we don't end up at the base, wet as it is." Lightning struck south on the ridge, illuminating our path. The wind whistled through our loose ends, blasting us with grit.

"Less luck than we'll need up here." I started down to my left.

Music Man tugged my jacket. "At least go this way." He pointed right. "Let the mountain take the brunt of it."

I put my bottom to the ground and scooted down the mountainside. Poor Monroe slithered paw by paw, rock to rock, plopping onto his chest with a brave yelp whenever his footing failed. The slope did somewhat diminish the rain and wind, but nowhere near enough for comfort. After a couple hundred yards we came to a small level patch, just big enough for Music Man's mobile abode. The rocks had torn my hands and bruised my tender bottom; I stopped and pointed at the ground.

Music Man dropped his pack.

I had to sit on the ground sheet as he staked it and wrapped myself to the central pole as he pulled everything tight; even then it flapped and popped around us. A barrage of lightning displaced the darkness. We were a soft-tissued barnacle on a great impenetrable hide, huddled and flinching as the wind sent tent-sized rocks tumbling like marbles down the slopes.

Music Man and I shared a few doses of his prescription before I turned to lay flat and pray. Music Man's bottle continued to tinkle through the night, barely audible over the atmospheric rumbling. Monroe could not have been closer to me if were a limb.

I thought of Claire and Billy.

The storm roared through the night, petering out shortly before down.

I emerged slowly. A few hesitant bands of sunlight slipped through the clouds. A steamy mist breathed up from the ground, clinging to the mountain like lather on a spent racehorse. The tumbling boulders had redesigned the slope. I took a knee to relieve myself lest I provoke the beast into another display of strength.

Music Man surfaced behind me.

"So much for that." He pushed against a boulder and, failing to move it, hurled rocks at the mountain.

We lugged ourselves back up to the crest as the morning sun burned off the mist, revealing an infinite world of sharpened greens. The still lakes mirrored the mountains in such detail that it was impossible to discern water from earth.

That night we camped under a starry sky. Music Man started a fire but lost interest, laying down before it got past embers leaving me to assume the mantle. The stars took their turn to dance on the lakes, connecting sky and water in a seamless spectrum of needle point lights. I laid down next to the fire. Monroe shifted to rest his warm head on my diminished belly.

"You know those lads I hiked with."

"I'm aware of them." Small sip.

"They were always smoking cigarettes. All the time either rolling or smoking, smoking and rolling. I never smoked with them. But sure wish I had one now. A cigar though. I don't think I could handle what they smoked."

"Cigar would do nicely." He sat up to hand me the bottle. "I was a cigar man myself."

"Not terribly surprised. You'd have to pick though. I've never trusted myself to pick a good cigar. Always ended up coughing behind a smoky tube of heat."

"I just picked the ones with the highest numbers. No real trick to it."

"Is that so?"

"Beware of the man who claims to know shit about selecting cigars." We were silent for a long time.

"Well look at that." I could hear Music Man motion down the ridgeline and turned to see a fire floating in the night sky. "Your buddy survived the storm."

"Bully for Mongrel." I propped up on my elbows and watched the flame flicker in the distance. "He seem closer to you?"

"Hard to say. But he's definitely not further away."

It drizzled all the next day—an acceptable compromise of the preceding extremes.

We dipped to Pullman's Gap then returned to altitude. That night we camped on the southern slopes of Long March Ridge, eating our dinners next to my fire. To the south a solitary campfire reflected across a lake, not four-hundred yards from where we'd lunched.

"Mongrel?"

"No telling. If it is then how, and why, did he get behind us?"

"I can tell you the why. Look at where he's camping, and look what he dealt with today compared to us. If it is Mongrel, the young man's got it figured it out."

49

Even with the head start, we spent most of the next day climbing, conquering several false peaks split by short, winding descents. It wasn't until mid-afternoon that we were able to appreciate level ground ahead of us.

"Well Music Man. Congratulations on your ascent of Mt. Kolb and welcome to Long March Ridge. May the other side find us in good spirits."

"May the other side find us an elevator."

It was a cold night on the ridge. Monroe mouthed his joints then put himself to bed early, stationing himself in the warmth of Music Man's mobile abode as his master emptied a jar. The wind thwarted my many efforts to start a fire. I ate quickly and was about to duck into my tent when Mongrel's fire sparked up again on the banks of a new lake far beneath us. The waters amplified his firelight into a halo of wavering orange. He had used the day to pull parallel.

Music Man noticed as well. "Little bastard. He's lazing around, living it up by the lakes while we're hauling ass over rocks and boulders. I bet it's warm down there, too." Small sip.

"Yea but we have each other."

"Another big mountain tomorrow, too. Mount George if I'm not mistaken."

"When's Atonement?"

"It's actually Mount Charles. Atonement's a colloquial, dramatic, appellation. In any event, unless we die—which I'm not wholly against." A small sip. "It should be the next day."

"And it's the biggun."

"Well unless you take the tram."

"The tram?"

"Yep. Highest point on the eastern seaboard and they built a goddam tram right up to the tippee top. Pentland folk take their families. Firm took us as a team building thing. There are hot dogs and ice cream; they even sell t-shirts that say *I GOT HIGH ON ATONEMENT*."

"Well that actually reminds me of another question—what happens when we get to the top of Daemon's Peak?"

"You climb back down."

"Really, that's it?"

"So I'm told. You climb right the hell back down the way you came. Then hike back a piece to the road. And *then* you have to hitch into to Butonken."

"Not really a big climactic finish."

"Would you expect the Great Eastern Trail to do you any different?"

***

The next day took us up and over Mount George to the base of Mount Charles. Mongrel's fire below marked that he had retaken the lead.

"You think that little bastard has a red and white checked blanket and a wicker basket, picks wildflowers and writes his notes with a feather pin; narrating them wistfully as he goes then dozes off in the shade of an apple tree."

I pictured my meeting with Mongrel, seated by his white rose in the Copper Swamp, tapping his maroon pen against the page.

The Great Eastern Trail saw fit to dip just before Charles's Atonement, further humbling us before the glory of the most royal Kingston. Music Man, Monroe and I stood at the mountain's base, just before the first risen step, craning our necks at the granite slopes.

"Didn't you say there was a tram?"

"I did and there is. I believe it's to our right, hidden by the slope."

"You reckon it would stop for us if we waved it down?"

"I do not suppose it would."

"What if we put our thumbs out?"

"Cash only my friend."

We climbed forever. My legs tightened. My hands tendered and bruised anew from sliding and scaling the rough granite. For all I could tell the slope scrolled beneath us, tucking under at the base to traverse a series of internal gears and reappear at the top —and be retread. I picked out distant rocks at the upper rim of my vision and set them as goals, only to lose track and start anew. I counted to a hundred, forwards and backwards, fighting the constant urge to turn around and check my progress. At last, we drifted out of the sun and into the clouds' cool mist.

"Well that's something."

"No it isn't. These clouds came down to meet us. And look how dark it is." I looked up from the rock—the peak was no longer visible; indeed a gloom had descended on the mountainside. "Just another fun alpine storm."

"Should we turn back?"

"Turn back to what? We might as well make a little progress before we perish. Say goodbye to Mt. Charles—it's Atonement from here on out."

The clouds contracted around us, darkening our world. The pitter-patter dampened the rocks, putting us on all fours to rove low over the uneven terrain. Monroe's tail sank between his legs; his ears pinned themselves against his neck.

We occupied the throat of the storm; it breathed and hissed around us. The wind, rendered inaudible by the thunder, asserted its physical presence, thrusting its momentum into us, trying to set us skyward. We were teed-up, the point of contact; before us was just preparation, after us only follow through. The air cracked and blazed with passing bolts.

We were crawling upward when a rigid spasm seized my body: my bones locked and constricted—for a few visceral moments my inner world snapped into focus as a new sensation percolated inwards from my hands and feet, up my arms and legs, converging at my spine. Then my mind blanked, rebooting in a frenzy. It was some time before I registered the preceding crash had been distinct, prolonged, and close, the accompanying flash hot and piercing. Monroe gave a pitiful whimper.

I wobbled to a knee, fell to a sit, and struggled to remember which muscles drew breath.

"Don't stop. We've been hit." I blinked at Music Man. "Fucking bolt just blasted the mountain." He had to get very close to me to be heard. His hands shook as he raised his flask. His face swayed in and out of clarity.

"What? What do we do?"

"Get up. We got to keep moving so I can get this piss ass dog out of the rain. There are structures at the top. We're liable to get blasted again but at least it won't be out on these rocks."

The electricity receded, leaving my body heavy and tired. I crept low, clinging to the granite with frozen talons, half expecting the glass mountain to shatter beneath me.

And so we reached the top of Atonement.

A small structure, no bigger than a shed, flicked in the lightning. A miniscule awning covered a sliver of cement, onto which we slithered. Music Man tugged at a locked door, punched it, then scanned across the mountain top for other structures.

I laid down, pressing my face against the cool, stable cement, vaguely wondering if it conducted electricity. Monroe wedged himself in between me and the wall, pressing his shivering body against mine. I heard Music Man slide down the corrugated steel siding, meeting the cement with a bruising thump.

"Be careful this is a restroom," he said, "this cement is probably a biohazard."

"So be it."

"We should keep moving. High places are the most likely to get struck."

"This was your idea."

"It was a shitty one."

"You're right. It was better out on the rocks."

A mechanical rattle cut through the rain, coming from over the precipice, growing steadily louder.

"What fresh hell is this?"

An angel's light crept over the edge, strengthening until it illuminated the suspended cables and gears. I propped up on an elbow as the beast emerged: a white snub-nosed vestibule peaked over the lip with a metallic squeal, exposing its vulnerable belly as it angled over and came down parallel to the ground, revealing 360 degree windows and a crowded interior. The gears stopped, leaving the vestibule to rock in the wind over its own large cement pad—a storm tossed halo.

"I can't believe they run that thing during storms."

"It was probably not their intention."

A young brown-headed boy, maybe seven, manned the window facing me. His head bobbed above the pane as he stared out wide-eyed, bruising his ears against the elbows of the adults around him. The vestibule was close enough that I could faintly detect the garbled drone of a pre-taped overhead narrator and observe the boy's face change into speculative acknowledgement of my presence. He leaned forward against the glass, head tilting slightly. We studied each other through the storm and curved glass. Then the boy leaned back, closed his eyes, and released his previous meal onto the window.

"Good god."

"That's something to consider."

The gears kicked to life, returning the blessed vestibule down the mountain.

50

The cement was warm on my cheek. I lifted my face, rubbing debris out of my flesh as I pushed myself back to lean against the siding. The morning sun extracted wavering tendrils of steam from the mountaintop. Monroe rose at movement, saying hello before claiming a strip of shade. His owner snored to my left; an open flask rested against his nose, lifting with each rough inhalation. When he awoke it was because I shook him—civilians were arriving by the tram full, with some expressing a desire to make use of the facilities.

"What? What's going on?" Music Man rubbed his eyes twice before opening them.

"It's morning and the park's open. We've got to move. People are starting to stare."

He blinked his eyes open and recoiled. "I liked it better in the storm."

I dragged Music Man to the side of the building where he continued to massage his temples and shield his closed eyes.

"Why are you like this? Why didn't you just go to sleep?"

"I was standing watch."

"Against the lightning?"

"And other such perils."

I laid claim to the first five hotdogs the concession stand sold that day; Music Man was on his feet after his second, but it took three spiked sodas to get him moving down the mountain. The ice cream stand didn't open until noon.

The steamed boulders made for poor walking. I stayed low, keeping one hand down as a brace at all times. The hot, wet air wafted into my nose and eyes, leaching moisture from my body by the droplet. Music Man was moving, but the humidity was no friend to a hangover— he thunked his heavy feet from rock to rock, frequently losing his balance and scampering desperately from rock to rock until he could use a crouched body and miniscule footsteps to skitter to a stop at a semi-suitable landing strip. Each such occasion was accompanied by a flurry of expletives and a nice, long sit. Monroe stayed closed to me, hopping over to check on his master each time he challenged gravity.

It was early afternoon when Music Man found no suitable landing, instead catching his toes against a rim of stone, setting off a small gravel avalanche, and catapulting an over-weighted torso over a ledge. Monroe and I scurried down the rocks after our friend—there was a pregnant moment in which I expected to observe him only as a speck on a distant boulder. Instead we found him lying on his back, torso supported by his pack, maybe two feet below us.

I knelt by his head, greatly relieved when his eyes raised to my face.

"Ow."

"Are you okay?"

He patted his chest and sides. "Are my legs all together?"

"Yes."

"Then I seem to be intact." He had to push Monroe away to get him to stop licking his face.

"Good. Intact is very good."

"Although if it's all the same to you I intend to remain here for a second. Catch my breath if you will."

"I think that's fair."

He tilted away from me and vomited. Two small metal cylinders rolled out from underneath him; I picked them, examining them before looking up at the tangle of thin brown ribbon bulging out of the music box's splintered base; the plastic edges of a cassette tape peaked through the retro carnage.

"It was a tape?" Music Man finished his business and turned back round to me, wiping his mouth. "It was all just a tape and batteries."

"Well sure. Available at any old drug store. What did you think it was?"

"I really don't know."

Music Man leaned back and closed his eyes, resting his head less than a foot away from his partially digested hotdogs.

Here lies a man who achieved greatness.

On the other side of him, to the north, a massive steep-sloped boulder broke the smooth horizon, lording over the plains. Daemon's Peak. It was not sharp or dramatic like the Kingstons; after the steep slopes, the top rounded off, extending horizontal for what appeared to be several miles like a great bald head. I shifted to a sit, studying my hike's conclusion over my fallen friend.

Music Man croaked between us, spitting up a ghastly soda-colored residue. "What are you looking at now?"

"Daemons."

He tilted his head. "Well fuck me. There it is. Is that all that's left?"

"That's all that's left."

Music Man shifted to his back. "I think I'll just die here."

"You said you were okay."

"Not okay: intact. There's a difference. My bits are all present and connected, sure, but they are still producing a great deal of pain."

The sun baked the mountainside. I wetted a towel and placed it on Music Man's face, then found a suitable rock to continue surveying the distant mountain. Monroe pressed against his master's side, panting in the sun.

"We should go soon. We don't want to be navigating these rocks after dark."

"What about my condition?"

"If it's not set to improve, then we need to get you off this mountain. Preferably in daylight."

"Fair point. You still have that *Juicerrman*?"

"What of it?"

"Figured this might be the time to uncork it. I could use the boost."

"But, but what if we meet a bear?"

"Then I'll breathe on it. Or let you run away. And we still have Monroe. They seem pretty chickenshit of him as well."

"It's just that . . . I was really hoping to finish with it."

"More than you were hoping to finish with me?"

I unsheathed the holy bar and tossed it to Music Man who flinched when it stuck against his ribs. He took two bites, choking them down with some effort. "Okay let's get moving."

"You sure?"

"Yep. Help me to my feet." I stood up, offered him a hand, dragging him upright like a groaning sack of grain, steadying him with my free hand. "Splash of medicine wouldn't hurt."

"Just the one."

I frowned as Music Man indulged in a full gulp, snatching the flask away from him when he lifted it for a second.

"If I'm tasked with carrying you, it's my rules."

Music Man gave me a long look as I slipped his straps off his arms and onto mine so that his pack hung over my stomach. "So be it. Slow and steady then." He slunk past me to maneuver the first boulder.

We crawled down the mountain—at various points Music Man's shoulder, back, and behind forced breaks. He fell once more, finding rest on a boulder before he could reach a terminal velocity, and finished the *Juicerrman* at intervals, putting down the final bites in the early evening, about two hundred yards before we achieved flat ground. At this point he could barely stand.

"Road should be close. You want me to get us a ride into town?"

"No. No more. There's no telling where the road is. No telling when or if someone will stop. I need a place to lay down and be still. Now if not sooner."

"We need to get you to a doctor. Or at least a bed."

"No. If I go to one of them filthy white coats they won't let me back out here."

"Then what do you say we cut left? Try out one of those lakes."

"You trying to find that mongoloid fellow?"

"Maybe I am. Maybe I just want a nice place to camp."

"I don't care Gabe. Just lay me down flat, soft, and soon—I'll be good."

"I had an eye on a nearby one as we were coming down. Shouldn't be too far."

"You know where you're going?"

"Sure. Like I said. I was paying attention, got me a vector."

I ducked under Music Man's arm, assuming his weight as we slipped through the trees. It wasn't long before Monroe bolted ahead, followed by the sounds of splashing. We emerged onto a sandy beach to find Monroe rolling in the shallows of a hidden lake.

I helped Music Man ease himself into the sand, where, after some water and medicine, he fell instantly asleep. I scanned the beach and the far shores for fires, then bathed in the shallows, splashing Monroe as he chased water bugs and fish. When I was clean I cooked my Dank Rice and built a fire, relishing that it was now my firelight shimmering across the surface.

51

I woke up early, chewing dry tortilla remnants as the sun rose over the water. Music Man lay exactly where I left him—his back straight, arms crossed over his chest, legs elevated slightly by the sand.

He woke with a start, frantic, raising halfway, and collapsing. "Ow."

"Good morning."

"How do you do?"

"Are you fit for moving?"

He tried to rise again. "No." He said settling back down. "I am unwell."

"I'm going to make a run into town. Anything I can get for you? Maybe some aspirin."

"Aspirin, aspirin sounds good."

"Well okay then. You just stay put. Monroe you keep an eye on him."

I returned to the Trail and headed north, finding the road about a mile later. Speck's routine brought the first car, a respectable silver sedan, to a gliding stop. The driver, the most nondescript gentlemen one could ever hope to meet, dropped me off directly in front of the Butonken grocer, pulling into an actual delineated spot and placing the car in park.

I found a payphone and called Billy.

"Son."

"Father?! Where are you?"

"Butonken . . . with even the smallest amount of luck this will be the last time I call you from the Great Eastern Trail."

"Holy hell. Really?"

"Really. I've almost dern done it."

"Hot damn. Congratulations. What then?"

"I come back here. It's really the only place to meet your mother."

"And then?"

"Bodette, obviously, for a spell. Then I don't know—I'm thinking maybe another adventure."

"That's what I like to hear; I was worried the, uh, amber would set again."

"No, no. Don't you worry about me. I'm done with standing still."

"Good to hear. Have you called Mom yet?"

"I have not."

"Then I'll let you get to it. Proud of you dad. Call me after you finish."

"You can count on it, Love you."

"Love you too."

I called Claire.

"Hello?"

"I call you now from the clean streets of Butonken. Where I await my bride."

"It's about time, Gabriel. How soon until I see you?"

"As fast as you can get up here. We pretty much yo-yo Daemon's tomorrow; I should be back in Butonken in the early afternoon."

"Who are you with?"

"It's just me and Music Man now. And the dog. We're camped up on a lake outside of town."

"What're y'all doing for your last night?"

"Music Man's pretty down, literally. He took a bad fall yesterday. I guess it wouldn't hurt to throw him a surprise party. A little boost to get him to Daemon's."

"And then get you back to Bodette."

"Reckon that'll be up to you. Remember I owe you a backlog of adventure and I'm itching to make it up to you."

"That's an idea Gabe. I'll give it some thought."

Butonken was a tourist town of some size and renown that had somehow retained its charm. Antique and craft shops lined each side of the street. It took several stops to complete my shopping list; I hired a taxi to return me to Trail. A rainbow of bulging plastic bags choked my fingers as I waltzed back onto the beach in time for a belated breakfast. Music Man was asleep, groaning when Monroe's ecstatic paws peppered him with grit.

"What have you got there?"

"Brunch. Lunch. Second Lunch. Dinner. Dessert. Midnight snacks. And plenty of fluids and party favors. I figured if we're going to stay here we can at least eat well. Make a picnic of it. How are you feeling?"

"Somewhere between better and worse. I don't think anything's broken, but everything hurts."

"That's something to be thankful for. What would you say to some eggs?"

"Eggs?"

"Yessir. Seeing as we're staying put and all—it gives us the chance to expand the menu."

"I like the sound of that. What all did you get?"

"You'll just have to wait and see what the day reveals."

I started on the food preparations, cracking the eggs directly into my pot, sprinkling in bacon bits, and mixing with my space spork. Once on the heat, I stirred them constantly, doing my best to keep the residue from sticking to the sides. When they were done I sporked some into Music Man's bowl and put some on a leaf for Monroe, retaining a healthy portion for myself.

"You know what we couldn't see last night when we got in?"

"What's that?"

"It's something that consumed a great deal of my morning. Prior to and between naps, of course." He gestured his utensil across the lake which extended for some time to the north, right up to the southern slopes of Daemon's Peak.

"Would you look at that . . . ." The bare rock soared above the trees like a bald giant.

"Mesmerizing, is it not."

"And we're to climb that?"

We spent the day alternating between sunning on the sand and soaking in the shallows—always in close proximity to the beer. The cold water spited the heat, soothing sore muscles and creaky joints. We lunched on store bought sandwiches, washing them down with root beers. Monroe pranced back and forth across sand, flaunting a new stick with each crossing. A meat and cheese tray by the fire ring kept us satisfied in between the formal meals. By the end of the day, Music Man could move between stations with something approaching a natural gait.

Around dusk I began collecting wood for a fire, finding ample supply in what was clearly a rarely settled spot—Monroe made it known that each stick I selected was crucial to his collection. I constructed my fire in the Jezebelian style, starting small, working my way up to a life size outhouse. When it was almost dark, I set the tender, giving life to the dried wood.

"And now for dinner." I removed two mammoth T-bones from the bags. "And something for you as well Monroe." I said, unveiling an additional filet.

"Well damn Gabe. How do you intend to cook those things?"

"Very carefully. If you'll allow me some salt and pepper, this should be pretty good."

When the fire was right I shuffled a bed of coals to the side and arranged a rock perimeter. I flipped my pot upside down, set it on the coals, and oiled the bottom, letting it take on a great deal of heat before placing the first steak on with a satisfying sizzle. I stayed on the steak, giving each bit its turn near the heat, before flipping and repeating. Monroe sat and stared at me throughout the entire process, eyes glistening with hungry moonlight.

"Is this another of Jezebel's little tricks?"

I stared at the offset bed of coals for a moment. "It is not. This I learned directly from the source."

"What do you mean?"

"Mongrel."

"You met Mongrel?"

"Sure did. In the Copper Swamp, only a couple of days before Whitton."

"What did he say? What was he like?"

"For starters, you said he probably writes his notes with a quill, he doesn't—he uses a maroon ball point pen. Just as ordinary as can be."

"Okay. Glad we cleared that up. What did he say?"

"Well I told him that I was thinking about quitting, or at least not pressing on. And he told me that the rest of the hike wouldn't be about me—that I would have a purpose."

"A purpose?"

"Something about being both a patient and a nurse. And that I would enjoy the rest of my hike."

"A purpose . . . I like the sound of that. You think he has a purpose for everyone?"

"I tried to get that out of him. He asked that I not ask him questions which would force him to be vague and pretentious."

"Okay, so what was he like?"

"Pretty vague and pretentious. But in an interesting way. Mentioned that he had met with Bear and Jezebel. And was even writing a note as we sat there. Then just sort of disappeared into the night."

"Well I'll be damned."

When I'd flipped the meat twice, I used my diminutive spork tongs to shave strips of Settlers Fowl onto the steak, and carefully set it on Music Man's pot.

"Well damn Gabe. You touch up your presentation and this'd be fit for a steakhouse."

"There's wine in the bag over yonder. I hope you like red."

Music Man poured wine into his coffee mug. I drank from the bottle.

We ate next to the water, the fire on our backs.

"So this is it?"

"This is it and there is no more. Although I do have one last surprise for you. If you don't mind being a touch premature." I removed two metal tubes from my pack.

"Did you have someone pick these out for you?"

"I used your method: all the cigars had little numbers next to them; these two's numbers were closest to one hundred."

"As good as any other method."

Music Man cut the ends; we lit from the fire. Our cigars embered in the wind, the tips glowing red as we studied the hulking black silhouette on the lake's far shore.

"You know that feeling, when you find yourself in what is supposed to be a conversation," I tapped the ash from my cigar, "and you're either knowledgeable on a subject or you've spent some time collecting your thoughts—and you've just started speaking when someone cuts you off to lump their own idea onto your half-finished one?"

"It's been awhile but sure."

"That's what my life felt like. Growing up, I always thought I was going to get to finish my own thought without interruption, everybody, the whole world, would just shut up, listen—let me say my piece. Then I got out in the world and Claire was speaking, jobs were speaking, rent was speaking, insurance was speaking. Then Billy came along and good lord that boy could talk. All of a sudden I was drowned out. At first I bucked a little, raised my voice, but, sooner than I'd care to admit, I just stopped speaking. This hike has been the first full sentence I've spoken in thirty years."

"Is that how you perceive your problem?"

"I reckon that's the most sense I can make of it."

"At least you had the good sense to listen. I was the asshole speaking over everyone. Look where that got me."

"Do you think there are men, people I guess, our age that look back at their lives and just say *yep, that'll do* and close the book?"

"You really want know what I think? I think I could've settled down with my second wife, treated her right, worked less, cared for the children, mowed the grass and built a home, and I still would've ended up out here."

"You don't think that was ever in the cards?"

"I don't think it was ever in our cards."

"Yea, neither do I." A squirrel ventured too close to the fire; Monroe launched himself into the darkness in pursuit.

***

The next morning I frontloaded Music Man's pack over my belly, wrapping my arms around it to stem the friction. Together we shuffled north, humming a tune recalled from his tape days. We crossed the Butonken road and continued towards Daemons.

"Take it easy. Anytime you need to stop, just let me know."

"No breaks today Gabe. The best way to do it is to get it done."

"Up, down, and back to Butonken."

"A strange way to end it, but not necessarily out of character."

"They should get one of those Atonement trams to take us from the peak to a Butonken bar. They can run it direct, and for hikers only, comes with a free pint."

"And a burger."

"A triple cheeseburger. One slice swiss, one slice provolone, two slices cheddar."

"And bacon."

"Yep six crispy strips of bacon. And a fried egg."

"I'll allow it."

"And mayonnaise, for the calories. And fries."

Despite the slow pace, we arrived at the base of Daemon's Peak well before noon. A plastic sign stapled to a sapling marked the mountain's southern ascent. I slipped out of both packs, setting them on the far side of a more robust tree, removing everything from mine except water and beef jerky, purchased at a trade shop during my shopping spree, making a point to include my spork in the trimmed down pack.

"What're you doing there?"

"No need for all this right? We're not camping up there and we're coming back this way."

"They've come all this way too—seems a shame to deny them the ending."

"Do you want to carry them?"

"I do not."

Daemon's Peak presented a fresh set of challenges—iron handles jutted out from sheer rock faces, narrow crevices separated obstacle formations. Music Man took them without complaint. Monroe displayed the craftiness of the determined canine, bouncing off adjacent rock faces, launching himself up four and five foot boulders, clawing the tops to find his balance.

"So Mongrel, you think he chose to make himself available to you?"

"That's one way to put it."

"You feel any different after you met him?"

"I don't know, maybe. It was nice to put a face to the handwriting. And I didn't think about quitting afterwards."

While it was a clear day at the base, when the Trail leveled off onto Daemons Peak's plateau, it did so under a veil of heavy fog permitting no view on either side. Music Man kept moving, now striding purposefully over the flat terrain.

A patinaed plaque set into the mountain stone marked the Great Eastern Trail's northern terminus. We stood over it, looking down at the bronze figure lugging his pack over a boulder.

"Right then." I knelt down and put my hand on it. The cloud's chill penetrated my thin summer garb. I stood up, breathing in the good air of a completed hike. I smiled at Music Man and he nodded in reply.

"Congratulations on your completed thru-hike."

"You as well my friend." He set his gaze southward. "You as well."

We lingered; our gazes alternating between each other, the plaque, and the beige abyss.

"Well look as this," Music Man leaned over and plucked a brown folded note from under the plaque. "One final lesson eh."

> MONGREL COME, MONGREL GO
> IS THIS THE END . . . I DUNNO

"What do we do now?"

"It's cold as shit up here. Let's take this party elsewhere."

Monroe claimed the plaque and we descended back into the clear heat. Music Man reassumed his pack at the base. When we made the Butonken road I set down my pack and started through Speck's routine. Music Man stood next to me, thumbs hooked in his straps, staring south across the road.

"You know this would work better if you hid in the woods. People will be less inclined to stop for two old men so it'd be better to introduce you once I have my foot in the door."

Music Man started across the road.

"Where are you going?"

"Mongrel."

"What?"

"I'm going south. I'm going to keep walking south until I find that damned Mongrel. You got to meet him. Sounds like others have as well—I do not care for being left out."

"You're kidding, you're going to go back over the Kingstons?"

"I won't have to—remember looking down at his fire on those lakes?"

"But—"

"No buts."

I considered my companions for a second. "No time for a drink?"

"No time for a drink. I may change my mind."

"Would that be so bad?"

"Yes. You've got a reconciled son and pretty wife coming to get you. Ain't shit for me. The only thing I've got to look forward to is that way." He pointed south into the trees. I stared at him; he planted his feet on the two yellow lines splitting the road. "I've got something in front of me, that will have to do for now."

"Okay then." I stepped forward and hugged him. "It was a real pleasure getting to know you Music Man."

"Same to you, Mister Gabe."

I knelt down and scratched Monroe's hear—he pressed his body against my leg. "Goodbye Monroe, you take good care of Music Man."

"Okay then. That's enough you big oaf. You go on and get your super cheeseburger. My best to you and your wife."

I watched them disappear south into the woods, then put my thumb out and caught a ride into Butonken.

I located a bench, shooed a squirrel, and sat down to wait for Claire.

Also By

Nothing . . . yet.

If you'd like more from Brian Livingston, please make sure to review *The Habits of Squirrels* on Amazon. Please also be sure to follow Brian on Instagram @brianlivingstonbooks, Twitter @Livingstonbooks, Facebook - Brian Livingston, or visit his website at brianlivingstonbooks.com.

Acknowledgements

The Habits of Squirrels would not have happened without the patience, love, and common sense of my friends and family many of whom were extremely gracious with their time and thoughts. *The Habits of Squirrels* would never have risen above cloying, self-indulgent drivel without the wisdom and generosity of Randall Klein who went well-beyond whatever could or should be expected from an editor. And, of course, endless thanks to my loving and patient wife Olivia, who sat through more diatribes about continuity, theme, and barcodes than any person should ever endure.

Finally, many thanks to the countless organizations, businesses, and volunteers whose hard work and commitment keep the world's long trails open to all.

About the Author

Brian "Mister Frodo" Livingston thru-hiked the Appalachian Trail in 2013. Now he supplements his hiking with reading, fishing, and copious live music. Mister Frodo currently resides in Charleston, South Carolina with his wife and black lab, Maddux. *The Habits of Squirrels* is his first novel.